THE
ASTRONOMER
WHO GAVE BACK A CROWN

Books by Joe Bergeron

The Endurian Universe

1: *The Astronomer Who Didn't Like Magic*

2: *The Vigil*

3: *Space Mariners*

4: *Space Mariners: Elves and Aliens*

5: *Space Mariners: Children of Rral*

6: *The Astronomer Who Hated a God*

7: *Acts of the Vigil*

8: *Behold the Vigil*

9: *The Astronomer Who Gave Back a Crown*

Other Books

The Way of an Eagle

Cosmic Cat

For someone who I've never met, who may not exist, and who may not possibly exist.

THE
ASTRONOMER
WHO GAVE BACK A CROWN

Book Nine of the Endurian Universe

JOE BERGERON

Endurian Press

Prologue

The witch Erraine stepped onto the porch of her rickety wooden penthouse and looked down the stairs onto the untidy rooftop of her Tower of the Mystic Arts. It was a fairly desolate scene. Not only was the sky gloomy and the wind cold, but the Tower itself was crumbling, its summit flagstones littered with leaves and other debris. A few puddles exhibited little shorelines of mud. She really must see about clearing out the drainage openings, before someone living below complained about leaks.

From this height she could look out over the uneven wall which in better days had turned the Tower's circular roof into a cozy courtyard and a place of much activity. All around the Tower loomed wild hills clad in dark firs and brandlevanes, with grey mists and clouds swirling among them. The Tower's location in the western foothills of the Mynd Bannock range had once enhanced its reputation for sombre glamour. Now, given Darteharn's sorry state, its setting only added to its isolation and abandonment.

Erraine adjusted her greying hair while her dusty green and purple skirts flapped in the wind. In the past she never would have ventured from her rooms without first perfecting every detail of her appearance. Now the chances of anyone seeing her were small. Oh, a few tenants remained. She heard old Vababar chanting in his apartments a few levels below. Once he had been a sorcerer of some promise, but his ambitions had waned over the years. Now, more than likely, he was merely trying to conjure a little warmth into his hearth, not summoning some potent spirit from beyond. Erraine also heard a muffled thudding. That would be Egreggio, who usually labored in silence over his crystals and books, pounding on the wall to quiet his neighbor's incessant incantations. As Vababar was nearly deaf, Egreggio's efforts must be in vain. She should offer him a quieter apartment, if she could find one which was still habitable, or if she could summon the energy and ambition to refurbish one.

Now she heard something else, something new: footsteps on the Tower's winding main staircase, light and quick, unlike those of any of her tenants.

Erraine drew herself up with her hand on her chest, a little flustered. What could this be? A break in her long, boring decline might not be unwelcome. Still…

A figure appeared from the stairwell: a smiling young woman with curling black hair, dusky skin, and friendly dark eyes. She wore a scarlet shawl over skirts of rust, deep blue, and green. Erraine, though surprised, maintained an air of composure as she descended to greet this newcomer.

The girl approached the foot of Erraine's private stair and stood waiting, still smiling, offering a little bow as Erraine halted before her.

"You are the Mistress Erraine? I am Natulakh, a student of magic. I am pleased to arrive here at last. I have heard many stories of your famous Tower, and am hopeful that you will rent or sell me a dwelling here, so that I may partake of the exchange of knowledge upon which your fame is based."

Erraine smiled back, charmed by this flattery. "My dear, I would be pleased to accept you, but as you may have surmised, the glory days of my Tower, and perhaps of Darteharnelandua itself, have passed. In all honesty, I can offer you little. It was bad enough when Namirnakh was thrown down so many turns ago, but with the god Ahriman also silent these past fifteen turns, and his Eye blinded, one might well think us all bereft."

Natulakh grew more serious, and nodded. "Yes. The rule of Darteharn has long been an uncertain thing. We no longer enjoy the favor of any god. It is indeed a sad time for the glory of Darteharn. But surely, those of us who remember it must make an effort to uphold and revive it, if we can."

Erraine, though wondering how much of that glory a woman so young could possibly remember, nevertheless admired her spirit.

"It is well now to recall and name those to whom we owe our diminishment. Let us remember the King of Eranior, whoever he may be; the sorcerer Imhotep, also called Sha Totek; and the Earthman, Leonard Ronar."

"Yes. Let us remember them," said Natulakh in a distant tone. Then she shook herself, renewed her bright smile, and said, "Together we may yet do much. To begin with, I bring an artifact which I think may bear some magical significance. Perhaps you can assist me in identifying it?"

"I shall try, daughter."

Natulakh produced a small box of dark, worn wood. Cushioned within it was a tiny replica of a sword, perhaps five inches long.

Erraine delicately removed it from the box, cautious of its sharp little blade.

"What an exquisite object," she said, peering at it closely. "The blade appears to be made of steel, and the guard and grip are very finely worked. I see glints of tiny stones: green, red, and white. It looks familiar, but I can't place it. I believe I see some very fine markings engraved upon the blade."

She straightened up, holding the tiny sword on the flat of her left palm. She held the thumb and forefinger of her right hand a short distance apart and said *"Oculo aerius, appareo!"*

A small sphere of refractive air appeared between her fingers. Erraine squeezed it to form a usable lens, then held it to her eye for use as a magnifier. Her peripheral vision revealed the pleasing sight of Natulakh beaming in delight.

"I can read the writing now, my dear. This is...oh my! This is a small version of the Sword of Bran itself. Yes, the very sword of that cruel and ancient king of Eranior who once drove our lord Namirnakh into exile. The sword which now, by all accounts, is under the command of that arrogant stargazer, Ronar, known as Greylock. What a very curious thing. I wonder what its purpose could be?"

Natulakh opened the box to replace the sword. As she did so, something rattled inside the box. Looking puzzled, she pried loose the padding and looked beneath it.

She lifted out a medium-sized faceted garnet, smoldering beneath the gloomy sky. As she handled it, it flared briefly, and gave out a spark.

The two witches looked at each other, bright-eyed.

Chapter One

The Cold Sword

How many kings has it been now? thought Leonard Ronar as he stood stiffly in his heavy woolen costume, watching the solemn progress of the coronation ceremony.

Conducted beneath a windy, cloudy sky, the ceremony was impressive in the typically melancholy Eranian way. The witnesses and participants stood arrayed on platforms, parapets, and terraces which ranged up and down the cliffside city of Myrddin, capital of Eranior, whose stone structures perched precariously over the turbulent grey waters of the Bay of Kiruna. The city's marble facades, its gold leaf, its balustrades and bridges, had all been cleaned and polished, while magical flames leapt up sourceless here and there, burning in every color but red. Yet the light filtering through the clouds was dim. Somehow the city looked like a freshly-dusted diorama which would soon return to disuse.

Ronar stood near and slightly above the scene of the actual coronation, where the greatest druids and witches of Eranior endlessly ministered to the newly chosen king. Ronar had been persuaded to be clad in native Eranian garb, though he felt ridiculous in his kilt with his bare legs. A checkered cloak was gathered around his shoulders. Standing with him were many foreign rulers and dignitaries, including a few blond chieftains of Tíuheimr, several petty kings of the city-states of Mersinea, and even a young prince of the house of Cotavion, looking haughty and uncomfortable to be caught outside the dream-boundaries of his land of Faerie. Still more surprising to many, there too stood none other than Sha Totek the Sorcerer, known here as the Gatekeeper, or simply Imhotep. He, of all those present, looked the most out of place with his colorfully exotic clothing and his glossy saddle-brown hide.

Ronar eyed the new king, who was not an especially young man, and resumed his mental tally of the sovereigns of Eranior he had known. First had been Sionyn, of course, however brief their acquaintance. Following his murder at the hands of Namirnakh, Sionyn's young Queen Ganifer had gained the royal torc. Though she'd proven surprisingly wily and enduring in the face of louts who were uncomfortable with a female ruler, she too had died young, under circumstances somewhat mysterious, to be succeeded by her nephew, who took the name Sionyn II. That boy, alas, had possessed neither the wit nor the strength of his namesake, and his rule soon collapsed, leading to a period of instability in which kings either weak, brutal, or foolish succeeded each other after periods of a few turns or even moonturns. Rule passed out of the hands of the clan of Aneirin for the first time in centuries. It was as if Eranior, no longer faced with an imminent threat from neighboring Darteharn, had lost all discipline and resolve.

Now the nobles of Eranior, fearing the gradual dissolution of their nation, had selected Lugaid, a military captain and peripheral member of the clan of Aneirin, to be their new king. He was reputed to be a stolid, sober man of great rectitude, though unproven in battle, inevitably so since Eranior had been at peace for...how long had it been now? Almost thirty turns. Sixty five years of Earth. By now Sionyn himself was almost a legendary figure, as few remained who could recall either his reign or the events which had ended it.

The coronation was being performed with Eranior's greatest relic, the sword of King Bran itself, held aloft with surprising ease by the ancient sorceress Morwenna. Ronar found it odd to see that sword in any hand but his own. It was a sight he must learn to get used to. He glanced at the garnet ring on his finger. This time the magic that connected the two had not brought forth the sword. Rather, it had simply been carried from the corner of the palace where it was usually displayed as it awaited Ronar's summons, which had become a rare event in the past five or ten turns. After today, according to Ronar's plan, it would no longer happen at all.

Morwenna lifted up her voice. In the Eranian tongue, the syllables of her speech flowed together like liquid.

"Lugaid, son of Glythvir and Nerys, son of Aneirin... Eranior calls you. This dominion founded by Bran the Blessed calls you to serve. All the gods, both above and below, await your answer. Do you, Lugaid, accept this summons? Will you wear the Royal Torc and strive to lead us with honor, mercy, strength, and justice?"

"I will."

Morwenna's expression assumed a still greater asperity. "I hope so. Too long have we been ruled by little men. I hope you will end that sad trend."

Looking nonplussed by this departure from the familiar rote, Lugaid said, "By Llyr, Lugh, and the Hunter, I swear to do what is right and just, no matter how long my reign may last."

"Then take these tokens of office, and bear them well."

Ronar saw little enthusiasm on the austere face of the sorceress as she conferred the emblems of royal authority upon Lugaid. With the torc of gold and steel around his neck and the sword of Bran swinging in a scabbard at his side, the new King Lugaid moved off to greet each of his high-ranking guests.

Reaching Sha Totek, he said, "Well, Gatekeeper, I'm surprised to see you here. I thought it took events more profound than yet another coronation to pry you from that tower of yours."

She Totek grinned and said, "In the past this was true, my friend. But Ronar here relieved me of my chief responsibility some turns ago, when he destroyed the last of the Bronze Portals, without consulting me, may I add. I half expected another Portal to arise somewhere else, but none did. Apparently I am a Gatekeeper with no gates to keep. Therefore I am free to travel as I will."

"I see," said Lugaid. "And you, Greylock, why did you destroy this link between the worlds?"

Ronar said, at the slow pace demanded by his infrequent use of Eranian Welsh, "At that time, Earth, the Other World, was suffering great turmoil, caused by enemies beyond the control of the powers there. These evil influences leaked through the Portal to endanger our world of Colibdis as well. I sundered the two worlds with regret. I have no way to learn whether Earth was saved. If not, Colibdis is now the last outpost of the human race in the universe."

Lugaid nodded, in such a way that Ronar doubted the king had fully understood his words. Ronar continued gamely, glancing at the grip and guard of the Sword of

Bran where it hung at the King's side, with its diamonds, emeralds and garnets. A single empty socket had once carried the garnet which now resided in Ronar's ring.

"I have a gift for you, King. That sword you carry is rightfully the property of the Kings of Eranior, as you know. Let it then be at your disposal at all times. You'll find it's much more convenient to summon the sword with the ring than to carry the weapon on your person." Ronar began to work the ring off his finger. The surprise on the King's broad, tawny-bearded face was comically apparent. Sha Totek's surprise was not visible to Ronar, yet he could not help but sense it.

But the ring was stubborn.

"The ring does not wish to be parted from you, Ronar," said the King.

"It's been on my finger for a long time. But don't worry, I'll have it off if I have to hack off my finger." And indeed he did draw it off, though it took some skin off his knuckle and left a smear of blood. He dropped the ring into the King's waiting hand, who stood staring at it dubiously.

"Thank you," said Lugaid simply, moving on to the prince of Faerie. "My Lord Prince, I hope your presence here means we may expect more intercourse with your people in the future."

The young Elf's words spun out like a silver thread. "That is unlikely, Majesty, but our Queen wishes you to understand that she bears your people no ill will."

Ronar thought it just as well for that perilous Queen and her people to confine themselves to the borders of their land. He had never yet been forced into conflict with Faerie, and he hoped for this trend to continue indefinitely.

"What are you playing at, Ronar?" whispered Sha Totek when the king had passed on down the line.

"What?"

"Giving away your ring!" hissed the sorcerer.

"Oh, that. I'm retiring."

"Retiring from what?"

"From everything. From the University, and especially from wars and adventures."

"But why? Yes, your hair now tends more toward silver than iron grey, but apart from that, you still look like you're ready for anything."

"And yet I'm one hundred and five years old. Earth years, of course. I've been Chairman of my department at the University since it was founded. Hal Holder is my obvious successor, but he's already an old man. He takes after his mother, and never had whatever it is that keeps me going. If I don't step aside now, he'll never get the chance he deserves."

"So what will you do instead?"

"I'll build a cabin on the rim of Blue Water Canyon in Thunderbird. It's a beautiful place, shady, with a nice spring that feeds into the stream below. There's a ledge where I can build an observatory. Just a small one, mainly for sightseeing, not a big, scientific one. Just a place where I can keep an eye on the stars and galaxies, as I've always done. There's an Indian village nearby, friends of mine, and I can trade with them for food, or hunt for it."

"Why don't you just stay in Two Suns and continue your research, even if not as Chairman?"

Ronar shook his head. "As long as I'm anywhere near the University, I'd dominate it. Hal would still be in second place, even if we acclaimed him King of the Stars. That's just the way it is. It's time for me to move on, like any mortal man. I don't seem to have the knack of doing it by dying, so I'll just place myself out of the way. Flora is dead, and no, I have no desire to seek a replacement for her. I've had enough, done enough, seen enough, to satisfy anyone. Time for me to take it easy. No more magic ring. No more battles."

"Er...but a remote cabin? Don't you think that much solitude might drive you a little crazy?"

Ronar cocked a little grin at his companion. "Has it you?"

"Well...yes, actually."

"All right, granted. But I'm not likely to last as long as you have. I'll be fine, don't worry. I like solitude."

Astil-Cotavion, the Prince of Faerie, suddenly leaned on the balustrade with a look of concern on his pale, delicate face.

Ronar, sensing something amiss, approached him and said "What's troubling you?"

The Elf turned to Ronar with a look of disdain before realizing who he was dealing with. Then, with greater courtesy, he said, "It is a sound, Greylock. A deep, booming sound. Do you not hear it?"

"Whoa there..." said Sha Totek.

The polished limestone blocks of the terrace trembled. A few faint cracks and pops could be heard.

A mutter of consternation arose from the crowd.

One of the chief druids threw up his hands and cried "Behold! The world itself takes heed of the great event which occurs here today!"

"Idiot," muttered Ronar.

"No," whispered Sha Totek. "He is wise. What he said is not true, but it is wise nevertheless."

Indeed the crowd grew noticeably more calm. The King's glance strayed to the Sorcerer, as though he wondered about the source of this tremor. Sha Totek offered him an innocent shrug.

"What is happening there? Out on the bay?" cried Astil-Cotavion.

Ronar squinted in that direction. At first he saw nothing unusual…merely the normal seething of Kiruna's cold waters, moving westward toward the open sea under the urging of the tide.

But then he remembered that the tide should be coming *in* by this time. Also, the water level at the island of Avalon was lower than he'd ever seen it, exposing buttresses of rock he had never suspected. And still the level was dropping, fast enough to see.

"Somehow, Kiruna is emptying," said Ronar, in English so that only Sha Totek would understand.

"How is that possible?"

"I don't know. You know the general shape of it well enough. It's a crater with only a single exit to a funnel-shaped outer bay, which concentrates the power of the tides and turns the Bay into a maelstrom."

"Yes. And I remember very well that it was once a placid lake, until Namirnakh breached the crater wall and created that opening to the sea."

No one else had understood that exchange, but everyone nearby had heard and recognized the name of Namirnakh. People turned toward the two of them with fear on their faces.

"Oops," said Sha Totek.

"I'm the chief idiot around here," spat Ronar. Hurrying to the edge of the platform, he bellowed, "All who can hear me! Abandon the city! You heralds, sound your horns! Everyone, climb, climb! Climb out and away!"

Confusion and dismay erupted among those who were within earshot. They milled about, looking at each other with round eyes.

"Climb!" cried Ronar again. He saw the King, now several levels below, trying to make his way back to Ronar though the suddenly disorganized crowd.

"Ronar, what are you doing?" asked Sha Totek with a strained smile, placing a hand on his arm.

"Yes, that is a good question," said Astil-Cotavion.

Ronar whirled on the sorcerer. "Have you any power over the waves? Over the earth itself?"

Sha Totek gaped at him for a moment, and said, "As I stand here now, right this second, I do not."

"That's too bad. I know no way for the Bay of Kiruna to be emptied without again being filled. And when it is filled, it is likely to be accompanied by great violence."

"And the city of Myrddin clings to the cliffs," said Sha Totek, his dark face somehow managing to appear pale.

"Exactly."

"Greylock! Ronar, what it happening here?" This was from the King, who had finally arrived, out of breath, with several retainers in tow.

"King, I believe this city is about to suffer terrible damage. You must order everyone to leave at once. Tell them to carry nothing, but to flee for their lives."

Lugaid turned to Sha Totek. "Gatekeeper? Do you agree with this?"

"I do. If we are wrong, the worst that will happen is that the people will be exercised, your celebration disrupted, and Ronar and I made to look foolish."

The King turned away and cried "Pass the word! Everyone flee the city! Climb beyond the rim, and assemble to the south!"

Now horns cried out, and figures began to rush up stairs and ramps all along the arc of the city. Lugaid and his men made to descend before the flow of refugees made that impossible.

"King, you're going the wrong way!" called Ronar.

"No, no, I must be among my people to organize the flight." And so he passed out of sight.

Ronar turned to Sha Totek, Astil-Cotavion, and the others who shared their platform. A growing rumble began to shake the blocks beneath their feet.

"Let's go," he said.

They ran up the side of the cliff, moving from one staircase to another, crossing platforms, at times dashing though small buildings and guard stations.

And then the pervasive rumble built to a roar, and the world tilted beneath their feet. Ronar and Astil-Cotavion were flung against a railing, hanging on to avoid being flung into the void. Sha Totek somehow managed to keep to his feet. Ronar, clinging to the heaving stone, looked out and beheld whole buildings crumbling and falling into the mud of the emptied Bay like a rain of sugar cubes. Human figures likewise tumbled to their doom. Great sheets of rock, most with structures still attached, broke free of the cliffs with hideous cracking sounds, then slid or tilted into the Bay, disintegrating as they went.

With a strangled curse, Ronar averted his eyes from this disaster and concentrated on what was going on near or below him, where he might yet accomplish something. The platform immediately beneath him was cut off from any escape, its stairway having shattered and fallen away. The high-ranking group beneath him, their finery torn and disarrayed, glanced at each other in consternation.

Ronar stripped off his cloak and leaned over the railing to dangle it toward that frantic crowd. A dozen hands clutched at it, threatening to yank it from his grasp.

"One at a time, damn you!" he cried. "Take heed of what you do now! This is your final chance to die with honor, if die you must."

A large fat man grabbed the shoulders of a slight young woman and said, "This one first!" He lifted her by the waist.

"Grab on to the cloak with both hands, and hold on tight!" yelled Ronar. When she had done so, she screamed as he twisted his torso and yanked her up to his level, where Sha Totek and Astil grabbed her and helped her over the railing. Ronar lowered the cloak again, although his back and shoulders felt like torn fabric after performing that feat even once. A larger woman was lifted into place. This time Ronar was obliged to haul her up in a slower, more gingerly manner.

In this way Ronar was able to evacuate nine people, while hundreds more perished beyond his reach. When the tenth grabbed on, the cloak suddenly ripped into pieces, stranding that unfortunate man, and many others.

"A rope!" he cried. "Who has a blasted rope?"

But no one answered. He leaned over the parapet, looking at those below.

"I'm sorry," said Ronar miserably.

"You did your best, Lord Greylock," replied the fat man.

"Ronar..." said Sha Totek, resting a hand on his shoulder.

A new sound was emerging from the west: a booming, continuous thunder unlike the erratic cracks and roars of the earthquake. Ronar peered into the west, toward the gap in the encircling crater wall which marked the Bay's exit to the sea. A grey wall was visible there, moving toward them with a deceptive slowness, so distant was it, and yet it moved, and a wind was rising before it. Huge sheets of rock split free and fell, further adding to the violence of the waters.

"Kiruna is returning!" he cried. "Run, climb!" He glanced down in regret at the crowds now sundered from any aid. Standing there among them was the King, who stared resolutely into Ronar's eyes, holding aloft some small thing which glittered red and gold. Ronar put out his hand, and the King tossed up the ring. Almost by itself, it seemed, it resumed its accustomed place on Ronar's finger. As Ronar studied it, some other object struck him which he caught without thinking and shoved into his belt. He was more concerned with the Sword of Bran, which the King now held like a spear, meaning to throw it as well. Catching the sword would be a tricky thing if he meant to keep all his fingers, yet Ronar meant to attempt it.

But the new King never got to make his throw. The platform upon which he and many others stood finally gave way, sending them all to their deaths.

Yet the ring was already on Ronar's finger. He could summon the sword and save it from the indignity of this fall, even if he could not save the King or anyone else. The ring crackled and smoldered red, then Ronar's vision went briefly black and his head was rocked back. After a few confused seconds he realized that a wild-eyed Sha Totek had punched him in the face.

"What are you doing?" screamed Ronar over the rising roar.

"You mustn't use that ring! Not now, not with the sword in motion! Look! We must flee!"

Indeed the colossal wave was nearly upon them, nearly as tall as the very rim of the crater. They turned and scrambled up the last few levels, reaching the rim at last, and fled as the mountainous wave collided with the cliff, exploding upward, sending down a deluge of cold salt water, drenching all the survivors, sweeping many off their feet, dragging a few back over the rim.

When the tumult had died and the screaming ceased, a dazed Ronar and his two companions crept as near as they dared to the crater's unstable, redefined rim.

The city of Myrddin had been erased. Only a few stumps of dressed stone still projected from new headlands which were the remains of the crater's original inner rampart. All else had toppled into the seething waters which still sloshed back and forth far below.

Ronar extended a trembling hand and stared at his ring. Sha Totek came to stand beside him. Astil collapsed onto the ground, staring over the Bay with a blank expression.

"What if the sword has been broken?" asked Ronar.

"Then it will lie broken in your hand," answered the sorcerer.

Ronar set his jaw and invoked the power of the ring. It flashed red, then white—there was a metallic note, and the Sword of Bran appeared in his hand, intact.

And yet...

"The sword is dry, but it is cold. It is as cold as these northern seas."

Chapter Two

The New King

A count was taken. Of the eight thousand or so residents of Myrddin, a few more than two thousand had escaped the destruction of the city. For a while bodies could be seen bobbing on the grey, foamy waves far below. Mercifully, the retreating tide soon bore them out of sight. Many dreaded the thought of their passage gladdening the garrison of the Darteharnian fortress of Larguc on their way to the open ocean.

Among those lost were a few petty kings of Mersinea, the chieftains of Tíuheimr, and of course the king of Eranior himself. The greatest magic-wielders of Eranior had been worse than decimated, taken so unawares that their powers had gone unused as their world shattered beneath their feet. So too had perished most of the land's military leaders.

Expeditions from the remaining cities of northern Eranior arrived to succor the refugees. Tents and canopies were erected to shelter them. Porridge bubbled constantly in cauldrons over open fires. The remaining military leaders rode pell-mell over the land, trying to organize an army in anticipation of an invasion from Darteharn. For few doubted the source of the disaster which had laid waste the capital and slain their king.

Sha Totek, thought Ronar, seemed more stunned than anyone. When not using his magic to assist the survivors, he often sat on the crater's edge, looking over the newly scoured cliffs at the inhospitable waters below.

Occasionally Ronar sat and joined him in his brooding. While brooding was one of his own specialties, such a protracted spell of it seemed out of character for the usually volatile Sorcerer.

Ronar was at a loss for a means to elicit something more from his friend. Now and then he opened his mouth to say something, but always he closed it again.

"Damn my clumsiness!" he snapped at last, barely aware he was speaking aloud.

"I'm not really Sha Totek, you know."

Ronar's head swiveled, his eyebrows high. "What?!"

"Well, I sort of am, but then again, sort of not."

"What are you babbling about?"

"Sha Totek dispersed himself through the Prism of Pandelume to create a duplicate, which he sent in his place to attend the coronation. I am that dispersion."

Ronar drew back. "What? Why would he do that?"

The duplicate shrugged fitfully. "He recognized the advisability of attending, but loathed the thought of stirring from his comfortable Tower to make the journey. He supposed he could avoid it through this ploy, with none being the wiser."

"Yes, and so he would have, if things had gone as planned. Why have you revealed yourself now?"

"He expects you to go off on some mad quest to take vengeance on Namirnakh for what has happened here. He wishes you to understand that I will be of limited use to you on such a venture."

"Why? I have seen you use your magic."

"You have seen only a few minor tricks. You know that Sha Totek's powers are much reduced when he is away from his Tower. I, as a mere image of him, am even more limited."

Ronar's thoughts spun in confusion. "And yet you are aware of his thoughts and wishes."

"He can see through my eyes and speak through my mouth."

"So are you Sha Totek, or not?"

"I am. After a fashion."

Ronar shook his head. "This is all very clear. What is less clear is why you imagine me to be responsible for cleaning up after this disaster."

"I never said you were responsible for it. I merely said you would do it. Who else could?"

Ronar waved his hand vaguely around him. "The entire nation of Eranior is here. They're the ones who've been outraged."

"They are leaderless."

"Only for the moment. When they recover from their shock, they'll select new leaders. Why should they look to me? Who am I? I'm just an old man, my adventurous days well behind me."

Sha Totek's black eyes twinkled with a mixture of pity and amusement. "You are Leonard Ronar, the Great Hero of our Age."

"Quiet," growled Ronar. "Yes, you're Sha Totek all right, for most practical purposes. Why have you been staring into the water so glumly?"

"Well, there are a couple of reasons. One is that two days ago, thousands of people fell to a cruel, needless death in those waters."

"Point taken."

"For another...I find it hard to believe that Morwenna could have succumbed to such a fate. Even I, a diminished creature, managed to avoid it, while she is one of the greatest and most venerable magicians in the world. Trained, I might add, largely by myself."

"And more than trained, or so I recall you mentioning."

"Yes." And once more Sha Totek, or at any rate this "dispersion" of him, grew distant and silent.

Three days later, Sha Totek was still sitting on the edge of that chill, turbid cauldron, staring and muttering. The plight of the refugees grew worse. They could not camp here much longer. Winter was approaching in the slow, ponderous way of Colibdian seasons. Already some survivors were becoming ill from exposure and inadequate food. The food stores that should have lasted the city through the winter were now in the Gulf. For the remaining cities of Eranior, finding a surplus for even two thousand people was proving difficult, especially with their leadership destroyed, and their people in fear of invasion.

Ronar wasn't sure why he remained here. He could accomplish little other than to provide moral support, consume scarce food, and try to straighten out whatever logistical errors became too absurd to tolerate. Yet something held him here. The camp possessed a strange feeling of timelessness, as though life had always been this way, and would continue thus in a grey, twilight existence, quiet and without any chance of joy or change.

Beyond that, as long as Sha Totek's double felt compelled to remain, so did Ronar.

"Somehow, new homes and new lives must be found for all these people," said Ronar as the dispersion sat in the mist. "Leadership must be restored. A new capital must be established some—"

Ronar almost jumped as he was interrupted by a high, clear voice.

"The Lord Greylock speaks wisely! I have remained here among you, in the name of Queen Seren-Cotavion of Faerie, who wishes me observe the plight of Eranior and to offer my assistance."

This of course was Astil-Cotavion, Prince of Faerie. Ronar turned to him and frowned. He couldn't recall seeing the Elf or anyone in his party rendering assistance to anyone since the disaster.

Astil resumed speaking, now that a curious crowd of Eranians had gathered around them.

"You are indeed bereft of leadership. Your efforts to deal with the catastrophe which has befallen you are worthy, but are unfocused and poorly organized. The fact is, your land requires a new king. None who remain among you has emerged as a logical successor. All who might reasonably have taken the throne now lie beneath cold waters. This is why I now offer up a candidate for kingship…myself."

Ronar wondered if his own expression reflected the surprise and puzzlement he saw on the faces around him. A number of questions occurred to him, but he was reluctant to intervene in an affair he perceived as not his own. He glanced behind him; Sha Totek still sat looking outward, seemingly oblivious to this turn of events.

Astil continued speaking. "I see uncertainty on many of your faces. You wonder what qualifies me to become your king. First, as a Prince of Faerie, obviously I am of royal blood. Second..."

With this, Astil fell silent and lowered his head, apparently reluctant to proceed.

"Lord Elf?" asked a bystander.

Astil remained silent.

"Well?" said Ronar, his irritation overcoming his reticence.

Astil gave him a veiled look and went on. "You may not be aware of this, but in the distant past, the ancestors of what would become the House of Cotavion came from Eranior. Therefore, in some sense, we are kin."

This was interesting. Ronar had never before heard an Elf acknowledge any human kinship, or make any reference to the mortal lands from which their forefathers had come. Of course they were essentially human, but they held themselves apart enough that this admission was not easily made.

The Eranians looked at each other, eyebrows raised, apparently wondering which of them would be the first to speak. None were eager to inform this foreign upstart that his services as King would not be required, or so Ronar judged.

Astil seemed to view the situation similarly. "You must of course gather your highest remaining men of authority, debate my offer—"

"Ah, at last," interrupted Sha Totek in a tone both quiet and penetrating.

"Eh?" Ronar turned and leaned forward, peering down to the Bay, which seemed to be the focus of Sha Totek's attention.

Something new had been added to the chaotic swirl of the waters. A circular eddy had appeared, hundreds of feet across, not a whirlpool, but rather something that appeared to be rising from the depths. A bulge broke the surface, then a coiled brown form glinting with blue and green came into view, an immense, serpentine fish. Opening the streaming grotto of its mouth, a golden light was revealed, backlighting a small figure which stood there with arms outstretched.

"You know, after spending a few turns in the relative sanity of Thunderbird, I tend to forget how things work elsewhere on this planet," remarked Ronar.

The great fish straightened its body and made its way to the shore with slow, majestic strokes of its vast tail. Reaching the crumbled debris at the rim, it paused while the figure stepped hesitantly from its mouth, climbing onto a pile of broken blocks barely out of reach of the waves.

With a few flips of its pectoral fins the fish backed away, and then dove back beneath the surface, vanishing from view.

An uproar went up among all the onlookers. Men assembled with hooks and ropes. Sha Totek rose to his feet, shaking, and conjured a great fire which burned off the mist for a hundred feet in every direction. "Bring her here!" he called to the men who were already descending the cliff. "Ronar, you are skilled at clambering about on deadly rock faces. Why don't you assist them?"

"They appear to be competent. I'll let them handle their own affairs. Who is that down there?"

"Morwenna, of course."

"Morwenna? I thought she…"

"We shall see."

And indeed they did see, soon enough. With considerable difficulty, the men of Eranior drew her up the cliff in slings and on their own backs, and then conducted her to the place where Ronar and Sha Totek awaited her. With their charge delivered, the men shrank back with stricken faces.

Ronar and Sha Totek beheld a grey, pale creature, her flesh swollen, her murky eyes darting about in confusion. She was still wrapped in the sodden remains of the costume she had worn at the coronation. Her hair was loose, plastered to her face and shoulders by moisture.

Her gaze fixed upon Sha Totek as she stood swaying dangerously. She opened her mouth to speak and water bubbled out of it. She drew air into her lungs with a gurgling wheeze and rasped, "Why have you done this to me?"

"Sha Totek, she's still—" began Ronar.

"Yes," interrupted Sha Totek in a voice both tired and pained. "She's still dead. I'd hoped...I believed..."

"You hoped to return me to life?" she demanded in that horrid wet wheeze. "Not even Sha Totek at his Tower could do that, let alone you, you partial thing, you trick of the light. Why have you done this to me?" she repeated.

"I thought...I'd hoped...Eranior...the land needs a leader."

"Then why not bring back the King? No, you hoped to revive me for reasons more personal. And it was an ill-done deed."

Sha Totek hung his head. Ronar observed this scene with distaste and discomfort. He was astonished when the sorcerer turned and fled sobbing toward the tent they shared.

"Oh, for pity's sake," muttered Morwenna, biting her puffy grey lip. She began to shamble after him. Ronar watched for a moment, bemused by the spectacle of the zombie sorceress lurching after his friend, then ran to catch up with her.

"Morwenna."

She paused and turned to him. "Eh?"

"Morwenna, I think we both agree that your existence in this form is—unfortunate. Might I suggest you turn and fling yourself back into the Bay?"

Morwenna gave a bubbling chuckle. "Blunt as always. Fear not, I will not prolong this unpleasant state beyond need. But as long as that self-indulgent fool has animated me, I will take a few moments to set right such things as I can."

"Why do you speak of him with such contempt? I was under the impression that he was once dear to you."

"Do not be fooled, Lord Ronar. This is not Sha Totek, or at least not more than a shadow of him. The real Sorcerer would never have attempted to summon me, and indeed, with his true power at hand I might never have fallen in the first place. No, this image was never intended to do more than stand and lend gravity to our coronation ceremony. Still, I shall comfort him if I may."

"Astil-Cotavion has presented himself as a candidate for the kingship."

Morwenna's fishy gaze speared toward the Elf, who stood a distance off, feigning a benign interest in the proceedings.

"He says his people came—"

"Originally from Eranior. Yes, this is well known to us. Well, I shall deal with him presently." She resumed her course toward Sha Totek's tent. Ronar followed at a distance, along with a crowd of ashen-faced Eranians. He did not approach the tent closely enough to hear what was said within, but stood off, muttering vague answers to the questions addressed to him by the wan, weary people around him. Many of them appeared dazed, as though uncertain what was dream and what was real.

Astil came drifting up, looking as though he were debating whether to make some new announcement.

"If I were you," said Ronar quietly, "I would wait a little before further pressing my claim."

The Elf glanced at him in surprise, then nodded acquiescence.

After a time Morwenna emerged, followed by a chastened Sha Totek. The gaze of the sorceress was locked on Ronar. Her face held a peculiar restrained intensity. In her hand was a loop of braided gold and steel wire.

"Lord Ronar, what is this?" she asked, holding up the object.

"Oh, that's the King's torc. He tossed it to me as he was falling into the waves."

Morwenna's jaw clenched. Her dead eyes shifted back and forth. "He—tossed it to you."

A murmur arose around them, rising in intensity. Ronar looked around, puzzled. "Yes, that's right. I've barely thought about it since. I would have eventually returned it, I assure you."

"That is not the issue. This is not merely the 'King's torc', as you put it. It is, more fully, the Royal Torc of Eranior. No one may possess it but the sovereign ruler of Eranior."

"I see. In that case, I'm glad you have discovered it, and may now confer it upon whoever is chosen to replace Lugaid."

"The new King has already been chosen."

From the corner of his eye, Ronar noted how Astil straightened and brightened.

"Oh? Very well then. I was unaware of that," said Ronar. "Shall it be the Elf, then?"

The hubbub around them had subsided into a frozen tableau of expectation. Ronar glanced around in growing irritation. The trinket had been returned; what more was required of him?

Sha Totek, inexplicably, bore a small smile, although his eyes were still downcast.

"Lord Ronar, the new King is yourself," said Morwenna.

Ronar rounded on her and snapped "What?"

"Lugaid conferred the Torc upon you in his final moments. You also possess and command the Sword of Bran. You are our King."

Now a ragged, desperate cheer shot up, rippling outward as the word was passed. Ronar flung out his arms to try to stop it, but was obliged to shout to make himself heard.

Astil appeared flabbergasted.

"Nonsense. Nonsense! I am no king. I am not your king."

Only then did the noise die down.

"Why not?" asked someone in a painfully plaintive tone.

"In the first place, I am not Eranian. In the second, I don't even follow your religion."

"Ronar—the Lord Ronar speaks the truth!" sputtered Astil. "He is merely...he is not even..."

An uncanny glance from Morwenna silenced the Elf. She spoke again. "I seem to recall King Sionyn declaring you his brother a number of turns ago. Surely the brother of a King can be considered an Eranian, whether blood is shared or no. As for the issue of your religious suitability, that is a matter for our Witches and Druids to decide. In life I was the highest priestess of the Lady and the Horned God. I raise no objection to your ascension, and I doubt any of the others will either. The gods themselves are silent on this matter, and I take that as their assent."

"Then consider this! I have never heard that the kingship of Eranior is a matter to be decided by the previous King. It is not hereditary, nor a matter left to the discretion of the ruler, but must be decided by a council of your greatest leaders, and their choice acclaimed by the people."

Now a thunderous uproar shook Ronar where he stood. Morwenna smiled.

"Great Hero of Our Age," muttered Sha Totek. Somehow Ronar was able to hear him.

Ronar raised his hands again. "I..."

He had been about to declare that he did not wish to be their king, that he would not be their king. And he would have done so, if not for the expressions of desperate hope on the faces around him. Sha Totek and Morwenna studied him with a more guarded expectation. Astil looked at him as if to say, "Well? Refuse this, and make way for someone more fitting to take your place."

Ronar scowled. "I warn you," he resumed. "I warn you all. If I become your king, I will tell you all what to do, and I will damn well expect you to do it."

"We would expect no less," said Morwenna calmly.

Ronar lowered his hands, prevented from flinging them out in exasperation only by an effort of will.

"Then I shall be your king, if you can think of none better. But only temporarily will I serve. I will do my best to see you through this crisis. Then you must find another."

Morwenna approached him, holding out the torc to place it around his neck. Ronar snatched it away from her and slipped it around his own neck.

"Morwenna, I mean you no offense, but I will not be crowned by an animated corpse. Here is my first command as King. I order you, Morwenna, to release your grip on this unnatural existence. Do so here, so that we may give your body the honorable burial you so richly deserve."

Morwenna smiled, lowered her eyes, and bowed. "As you wish, Lord King." With that she collapsed and moved no more.

Ronar issued orders for her body to be taken up and properly laid in a barrow. When that was done, he gave out a great number of orders for the more efficient ordering of the camp. Then he retreated to what was now the royal tent to brood and to curse his ill fortune in privacy. He made it a point to pass near to Astil, so that by the look in his eyes the Elf would know better than to raise any further objections to what had taken place.

Chapter Three

Matters of State

King Ronar emerged suddenly into the morning light, startling his heralds, who gave forth an uncoordinated blast on their horns until Ronar silenced them with an annoyed wave.

The overcast had partially broken up. Ronar took a moment to squint at the disposition of the newly-risen suns. The small white sun Photos was nearly centered before the ruddy aureole of the cooler sun Kudu. This configuration was held to augur good fortune, as it was the opposite of the Gloaming, when the red sun obscured the white. Ronar nodded. It was just as well, given what he was about to propose.

Various Eranians came striding up, the undistinguished remnant of the nation's former power structure. Ronar remembered few of their names, and yet he must choose from among them if he wished to delegate the powers needed for the daily operation of the kingdom.

Sha Totek, or the nearest available semblance of him, also appeared, still looking wan and subdued.

Ronar studied the faces of the men surrounding him, looking for any sign of unusual insight, fortitude, or indeed any useful quality. He settled upon one man of ordinary appearance who wore a cloak patterned in dingy rusts and browns, yet whose eyes held an atypical degree of clarity, or so it seemed to him.

"You. What is your name?"

"I am Gahareet, Lord King."

"Gahareet, I would name you, er, Steward of Eranior, to arrange internal matters under my authority."

At this, isolated laughter broke out here and there, quickly smothered. Gahareet himself staggered back, dismayed.

"Well, what is it?" snapped Ronar.

"My Lord King, I—I don't know what to say. I am not fit to hold such a high office. I wear no torc. In truth, I have come to—well, I am here to—straighten out your tent and empty the chamber pots, if need be."

Laughter resumed and became more general. Gahareet appeared mortified. Ronar bit his lip and lowered his gaze. He was tempted to join the laughter at his own gaffe. At the same time he was tempted to remove the Royal Torc, place it around Gahareet's neck, and stride very far away from all these people.

But these responses would not serve the purposes he had agreed to make his own.

Instead he reared up and cried "Be silent!", startling everyone. In the subsequent quiet he looked around imperiously before continuing.

"Under my rule, Gahareet, tasks and offices will be assigned according to whatever merits I perceive in a man. In this difficult time, when so many able men and women have perished, we must all stand up and do what we can, without regard to prior status, or nothing will be done. I myself am proof of that. So now are you, Steward. You wear no torc? You shall wear a torc, if one is needed, even if I must twist the wire with my own hands."

Gahareet still looked uncertain, while all around them mutterings began to arise.

"Unless, Gahareet," roared Ronar in a manner most uncharacteristic, "you hold yourself too witless to perform these tasks. In that case I will seek out a man who is both more capable and less servile."

As Ronar had hoped, at these words Gahareet stiffened a little, regarding him more directly. "No, my Lord King, there will be no need of that. I have seen enough of the ways and methods of the high-born to imitate them, if I must."

A red-faced man pushed himself through the crowd, brows knotted, his cloak damp and smoking with vapor. "What is this nonsense?" he demanded. "Lord Ronar, I am Llwyd of South Brinn. I know this man Gahareet. He bears no rank, no distinction. He does not belong in any royal court, save in the low station into which he was born."

A number of men murmured approval of this statement.

Ronar glanced at Sha Totek, hoping for support, but the lesser sorcerer merely stood gaping at the proceedings.

Ronar surveyed the crowd, working to conceal the disgust that strained to express itself on his face.

His hands moved toward the torc, preparing to remove it and fling it into the mud at Llwyd's feet.

Seeing this, Gahareet spoke up. "Llwyd! Do you acknowledge the Lord Ronar as King of Eranior?"

Ronar hesitated.

Llwyd's mouth worked for a few moments as he considered his reply. "I do. I must. I heard the words of Morwenna. Yet not even a king has the right to overturn our way of life."

"Our way of life has already been overturned. The entire city of Myrddin has been overturned. All you people! Do you acknowledge the kingship of Ronar?"

"Yes."

"I do!"

"He is our king!"

These sporadic replies gradually swelled into a general affirmation, which Gahareet quelled by raising his hands.

"In that case, must you not also acknowledge the King's right to appoint whoever he chooses to his court? Must you not acknowledge me as Steward? And I say to you, Llwyd, you would do well to accept this new state of affairs with all the grace you can muster."

Llwyd lowered his gaze and was silent, though his expression still clearly showed his dissatisfaction.

Ronar nodded slowly.

"Very well then. Gahareet, thank you. I wish you to choose officers and officials to administer the needs of the kingdom. Select whomever you deem fit, regardless of their former rank. As for you, Llwyd..."

"My Lord King," interrupted Gahareet, "I wish to inform you that it was Llwyd who sent me, as his former servant, to look after your needs. Without this gesture on his part, you would have selected some other person to be your Steward."

Ronar blinked. "I see I have chosen well, Gahareet. Please go about your duties. Llwyd, go in peace. Sha Totek, please accompany me to my tent. We have matters to discuss."

The sorcerer gave a slightly ironic bow and fell in beside Ronar as he stalked his way to the royal tent.

"Well, Your Majesty, for a moment I thought yours was going to be the shortest reign in the history of Eranior. You might as well have chosen your Steward by throwing darts into the crowd until one stuck in someone's eye. Yet once again you exhibit the famous Ronar skill for finding success through reckless, foolhardy actions which inexplicably resolve in your favor. How the gods must adore you."

A dozen possible replies swirled through Ronar's brain. In the end, he chose to express himself in the most basic possible manner.

"I don't want to be King."

"No, no, of course you don't. I remember your motto: you neither follow nor lead, and all that. So I must say, it's good of you to forego your usual disdain for working with the multitudes to help these people. Now that you've succeeded at shrugging off the especially insipid task of actually running the country on a daily basis, may I assume you will take a more strategic view of the situation as a whole?"

"Yes. I have already decided on my course of action."

They entered the tent. Ronar closed the flap, darkening the interior. In a brazier burned clumps of dried peat, releasing a little warmth and a still smaller quantity of light into the clammy space.

"You have?" said Sha Totek. "And what might that be?"

Ronar explained.

Outside, those guarding the tent were surprised to hear the sorcerer's voice raised in incredulity.

Chapter Four

Three for the West

Ronar emerged an hour later, followed by Sha Totek, who was still muttering and shaking his head. Ronar summoned Gahareet, who had already made a number of appointments. He arrived followed by a disparate group of men and women who for the most part appeared somewhat dazed by their new responsibilities. Ronar also called for whatever military leaders were present. When he was satisfied that enough people had gathered so that whatever he said would be transmitted widely, he commanded their attention and spoke.

"I will be brief. We all wonder what Namirnakh will do next, now that he has destroyed the capital. There is still no word from your scouts. No signal from the stations on the frontier. No sign of any disturbance to the west. Yet surely another stroke must fall. We must know the intentions of Darteharn. I will discover them by entering that land, and then, if need be, by confronting Namirnakh himself, in whatever new form he has contrived for himself."

They all looked at him blankly, puzzled, as though convinced he could not have said what he seemed to have said.

Finally Gahareet cleared his throat and said, "Lord King, forgive me for saying so, but your command of our language, though excellent for...for one not born among us, is nevertheless at times imperfect. Perhaps you did not mean to say that you, you yourself, the King, intend to go into Darteharnlandua."

"That is exactly what I intended to say, and to do."

"Alone?"

"No, not alone."

At this, a military man whose name Ronar did not remember, the leader of a small company based along the southwestern frontier of the Mynd Bannock range, spoke up. He had but recently arrived, not having been important enough to be invited to the investiture of the new king. "Lord King, we have no reliable way of knowing what is taking place in Darteharn. If they mean to invade us, surely we could mobilize every man in Eranior, yet still have too few to brave the passes of the Mynd Bannock and survive, even with you at our head."

"True, but leading an army is not my intention. I will not go carrying banners and blowing horns. I'll go in quietly, inconspicuously, determine the threat, and then return, having done whatever I can to abate it."

Gahareet looked most dubious. "Even if that includes confronting Namirnakh? Can you hope to do that inconspicuously? Why must you personally undertake such a mission? We have scouts. We have men who have skulked in those mountains for many turns, watching the passes. Why not send some of them?"

Ronar scowled. "That's just not my way of doing things, Gahareet. I have spent many turns indeed exploring the roads and pathways of this world. I am most qualified to go. If you had appointed some other King, and he had wisely asked me to go, I would have gone. Now I appoint myself."

"And who...who will accompany you?"

"I will bring Sha Totek, here."

"Oh, of course," said the sorcerer, throwing his hands in the air and walking in quick circles. "I must go, by all means. After all, I am expendable. I am nothing but a dispersion. In fact you might as well chop my head off right now."

Ronar glared at him. "Control yourself, whatever you are."

"And who else will you bring?" asked Gahareet, pointedly trying to ignore Sha Totek's antics. "Surely not you two alone."

"No, perhaps not. Tell me, what has become of Astil-Cotavion?"

"The last I heard, that princeling was packing his belongings, preparing to return to his homeland with his entourage."

"Send someone to him at once. Ask him to come here."

"Yes, Lord King."

Astil appeared a few minutes later. It looked as if they'd barely caught him before his departure, as he was dressed in a riding costume consisting of a grey cloak over garments of soft black chamois leather, He sat astride his horse, a mare of a liquid silvery appearance quite as exotic as his own.

Looking down his nose, Astil dismounted with visible reluctance, approached and addressed himself to Ronar.

"How may I serve you, Lord Ronar?"

"That is well put," said Ronar. He outlined his plan as Astil listened with little nods and steadily rising astonishment.

"That is a bold plan indeed, Lord Ronar. How may I assist you in advancing it? Do you wish me perhaps to remain here, as regent, while you undertake this task?"

"No, I wish you to accompany us into Darteharn."

Astil staggered back, somehow managing to become even more pale. "Lord Ronar, I..."

Ronar interrupted. "You recently expressed your desire to be of service to Eranior. Here is your opportunity."

"But I, what can I—"

"I'm sure you will be a valuable member of our little group. You Elves are creatures of magic, aren't you? Sha Totek here is diminished. Your powers would no doubt be invaluable to our mission."

"But I...the truth is, Lord Ronar, I know very little magic." This admission emerged from Astil with obvious reluctance. Ronar doubted he ever would have said this if he were not so desperate to avoid this summons.

Ronar acted to spare the Elf any further public humiliation.

"Come, Astil. We will discuss this in my tent. Come, Sha Totek."

Within the tent's dim confines, Ronar turned to the troubled Elf and said, "Now then Astil, what is this? I admit I have had few dealings with your people over the turns, but from what I understand, they are infused with magic. How then can it be that you command so little?"

Astil fretted, sinking onto a stool and wrapping his cloak around himself so that only his face shone out, like a patch of moonlight.

"These are matters we prefer not to discuss with outsiders."

"Naturally. Your people are famously secretive. Yet I ask you to share this information with me."

The Elf sighed. "It is simple enough. Being filled with magic, even being re-made by magic, is not the same as commanding it. We are indeed magical creatures, but to make use of that magic requires years of difficult study, just as it does for you mortal men. Most members of our royal family choose not to devote themselves to this labor. Why, even my aunt, Seren herself—but no matter. The fact is that I am no student of wizardry and sorcery."

"I see. But surely your magical nature gives you some advantages. Some skills or traits which might be of use to us on our journey. Some basis for that famous Faerie superiority."

Astil looked at him with bright round eyes that seemed to glow.

"Perhaps."

Ronar restrained a smile. "I'm sure you will prove to be a valuable companion."

Astil again looked dismayed, as though he believed he had just somehow been tricked. "But Ronar—Lord Ronar —it's out of the question. I was sent here to lend dignity to the Eranian coronation ceremony, that is all. Now I have duties to perform at home. I have no permission from my Queen, no mandate, to do as you ask."

Sha Totek spoke up in a wry tone. "And yet you did not hesitate to offer yourself up as King. Surely you had no mandate or permission to do such a thing either?"

"I—of course not. But the fact remains. I cannot undertake this task without the permission of my Queen, which you have no means of obtaining." Astil sat back, his arms crossed, looking obstinate.

"Don't be so sure of that," said Sha Totek softly.

Astil made a dismissive gesture. "It is difficult for any magic to cross the boundaries of Faerie. It is like entering another world."

Sha Totek now bent forward, his lean face catching a red glow from the brazier beside him. "You are speaking to Sha Totek the Sorcerer, to Imhotep of the Two Lands. More or less, anyway. But even I, poor limited creature that I am, am not utterly devoid of resources. Ronar, if I may command your minions for a few moments, I think I can produce the means to communicate with the Queen of Faerie."

"By all means."

Sha Totek rose, bowed, and swept out of the tent, leaving a faint scent of sandalwood as the breeze from his swirling robes subsided.

Ronar turned in his seat to face Astil. He rested his left forearm across his knees, where the light of the brazier was caught by the garnet ring on his finger.

"I think, Astil, that in the end you will find yourself accompanying us into Darteharn. It would be better if you were to accept this."

Astil said nothing, but the silvery glow of his eyes was steady.

Sha Totek returned after twenty minutes, carrying a wooden frame, perhaps three feet by four, which had been crudely pounded together from scraps.

"What is this?" asked Astil.

"You'll see." Sha Totek stood the frame on a small table, leaning it against the tent wall, which placed it at about eye level. He rummaged through his bags until he produced a cylindrical hat which he planted atop his head.

Then he stood before the frame, snapped his fingers, and looked around. He grabbed a large wooden spoon from Ronar's dining table and returned to the frame, standing still before it, holding the spoon in his left hand like a scepter.

"Not an exact match by any means, but it will do," he muttered.

For long minutes he stood there, doing nothing but making slight adjustments to his posture now and then, leaving Ronar to wonder what in the world he was doing. Astil's impatience was more obvious, signified by a tapping of his foot.

At last a faint, diffuse light emerged from the frame, dimly illuminating Sha Totek's features. "Ah!" he said. Still without abandoning his pose, he called out, "Hey! Someone out there, pay attention! Sha Totek and the King of Eranior wish to speak to you!"

A puzzled guard stuck his head through the flap of the tent; Ronar waved him away. With his curiosity no longer to be denied, Ronar stepped behind the sorcerer, so as to see what he saw. Astil followed his example.

The wooden frame had become a window into another place. It was a large chamber with high ceilings and stone walls, lit only by a few windows of dusty stained glass. Scattered about were tables littered with curious artifacts and books. Everything looked neglected. The room radiated a hush which could be felt even through the frame.

"I—know that place," said Astil in astonishment. "It's in the palace. It used to be the workshop and study used by —by—"

"By Cal-Cotavion," said Sha Totek. "I know. Hey!" he said more loudly. "Would someone please wake up in there? Damn lazy fairies."

Ronar thought he detected a flicker of motion behind a cabinet. "What's that? I thought I saw a shadow move over there."

"Where? Oh yes. You there! Behind that cabinet. Come out! Sha Totek compels you."

A tiny, indistinct figure slowly emerged into view. It crept closer, into a broader light, revealing itself as an Elven child, her hair a shimmering silver curtain over a delicate face with enormous silver eyes. She wore loose-fitting clothing of blue and silver with a short white cloak.

"Sneaking about in the forbidden laboratory, are you?" said Sha Totek sternly.

Her voice rang out like a sequence of tiny bells. "I— when your picture began to move, and then to speak, I thought I had done something wrong."

"No, child, you had no part in this. Go find your queen and tell her you were passing by in the corridor when you heard a strange, outlandish voice coming from inside. And don't worry that I'll give you away. It's good to see one of your folk taking a real interest in magic again. Go on now."

The girl smiled, turned, and scampered out of sight, employing a scamper far more elegant and fluid than any mortal scamperer could have managed, or so it seemed to Ronar.

"Who was that?" he asked.

"That was Kortraine-Cotavion, my sister, the Queen's niece," whispered Astil. "I always thought there was something unusual about the feyness of that child. Our mother is Amshardion, Seren's estranged sister."

Fascinated, Ronar and Astil stood flanking Sha Totek as several minutes passed.

Without any warning a much larger figure moved into view, startling them. This was a tall woman whose hooded black cloak obscured much of her face save for a fine nose, a lustrous full-lipped mouth, and a small pointed chin. She carried a staff, a spike of black iron ornamented with tiers of iron thorns.

Her cloak was closed before her, concealing her body and her left hand and arm.

Ronar, feeling faintly feverish, stared at this apparition, enthralled. He had heard much of the Queen of Faerie, a whispered legend about whom men seldom joked. He had always hoped, and perhaps feared, that he would someday behold her.

Slowly she raised her head, bringing into view the shadowed glimmer of her ice-blue eyes. Gravely she regarded Sha Totek.

"Well, Sorcerer. I have always disliked this portrait of yours. I never understood why my cousin kept it. I should have gotten rid of it long ago."

Sha Totek chuckled. "Well, Seren, my dear, you may find that it has its uses, even if it doesn't suit your tastes. Today, for example, it may spare us all a fair amount of trouble."

Seren peered more closely. "Who is that I see in the shadows behind you? My nephew Astil? And that other… none other than Greylock, I believe?"

"That is correct," said Ronar, surprised and oddly flattered to be recognized.

"And what is that around your neck? Is that…the Royal Torc of Eranior?" Seren's expression grew much more intense at these words.

"That's exactly right," said Sha Totek. "You appear to be surprised?"

Seren was speechless for a few moments, then said, "Of course I am surprised. I was led to believe that the next king of Eranior was to be Lugaid."

"Then you've heard nothing of the disaster which has befallen this kingdom?"

"I have not."

Sha Totek spun out the tale, concluding, "Your nephew was then kind enough to offer himself as a replacement king."

"Oh, he 'offered' himself, did he?" she snapped in irritation.

Astil retreated half a step and blanched.

Ronar noticed a small figure who had quietly reappeared in the background.

Sha Totek went on to describe Ronar's plan for the investigation of Darteharn.

Seren nodded, appearing calmer. "That strikes me as a sound idea, under the circumstances."

It does? thought Ronar. *Then you're the only one, beside myself, to hold that view.* But instead he said, "I wish for Astil to accompany us."

Here Astil broke in. "I have explained, my Queen, that my duties at home prevent me from undertaking this journey."

"Duties? What duties?" Seren glanced at him, then back at Ronar. "By all means, take him."

Astil gasped. Sha Totek said, "Are you quite sure, Seren?"

"Oh yes, quite. Astil has no duties here which cannot be performed by others. You may command him for as long as you find it convenient."

Astil gasped again.

"Very well then," said Sha Totek. "Thank you. We will do our best to keep him safe."

Seren inclined her head in such a way as to suggest this was not a matter of major concern to her. Her left hand emerged from her cloak, bearing on a slender finger a ring with a fierce red stone. With that hand she drew back her hood, revealing a disconcerting orange stone bound to her forehead by a golden band. She then opened her cloak, uncovering black garments, but more significantly, a great smooth yellow gem at her throat, from which emanated woe, and worst of all, a dangling pendant, a faceted black teardrop, at the sight of which Ronar's heart sank.

Astil shuddered.

Ronar had seen the brighter counterparts of these Stones many years ago on Earth. Viewing them through Sha Totek's magic portrait did much, he suspected, to mitigate the impact they would otherwise have.

Apparently realizing this, Seren again withdrew into her cloak, hiding the Stones, and also the dizzying perfection of her face and form.

"I wish you good fortune on your quest, Sorcerer," she said. "Your portrait will continue to hang here, in case we should need to communicate again. Also...a guard will be posted, to alert me to your presence, and to prevent any further mischief from occurring in this chamber."

"Very well, Seren. As always, it has been a pleasure to speak with you."

Seren removed herself from view. The scene in the frame grew silent and still.

Nevertheless, Sha Totek did not move, nor did the other two.

After a few moments, the small form again crept forward.

"Sha Totek…is that really you?"

"Yes, Kortraine, it is I. And I advise you to be cautious. If your aunt really intends to guard that old laboratory, you might be obliged to find another place in which to…play."

The Elf-girl nodded and smiled. "There are many possibilities. I wish you luck, Sha Totek, and you too, King Ronar. As for you, Astil…" She stuck out her tongue and hurried out of view.

Chuckling, Sha Totek turned around. "Cute kid," he said, in English.

The scene within the frame had vanished.

Ronar studied the stricken Elf with some sympathy.

"It's all right, Astil. Come with us. You'll accomplish something, see the world, and when you get back home, you'll have gained in stature and experience. You'll be ready to stand up for yourself and command more respect."

Astil looked at him with an unreadable expression, saying nothing.

Chapter Five

Out of Eranior

The next morning dawned clear, with the two suns still superimposed, but with white Photos now offset from the center of red Kudu. A cold breeze flowed from the west, flapping the cloaks and streaming the misted breath of those who had gathered to see Ronar's little party on its way.

Grooms tended and loaded the horses to be ridden by Ronar and Sha Totek, the same animals they'd brought up from Thunderbird far to the south. Astil, when he appeared a few minutes later, cantered up on his uncanny Elvish steed, with its trappings of silver and blue. He himself was clad in snowy finery that shone like a field of stars next to the stained, earthy colors of the Eranian costumes around him. As the Elf dismounted, Ronar, who wore a humble traveling costume of dusty green and brown, approached him and said quietly, "Astil, you must leave your horse behind, and these clothes as well. Both are far too conspicuous for what we intend. We don't want to shout that a prince of Faerie is on the way."

Astil looked fretful, clearly laboring to hold in a bitter retort.

Three other Elves rode up, arraying themselves behind Astil, their expressions compounded of wariness and disdain.

"Where do you three think you're going?" asked Ronar.

"We are friends and servants of Astil-Cotavion, Lord Ronar, and so of course we follow him."

Ronar shook his head. "No, you don't. This is not some Faerie picnic excursion. This is a serious scouting expedition into a hostile land. We do not go with bells tinkling and silver horns blowing."

The leader of this group compressed his lips and said, "Lord Ronar, if you feel that one of our people must join you in this danger, I beg you to take me, Phanerol-Rantavion, and spare our Prince."

Ronar regarded him steadily as he considered this.

"That is a worthy offer, but I think you will find, Phanerol, that when your Prince returns, he will be better for it, and a better leader for your people. Even if he is not, that too should be knowledge worth having. If you wish to serve him now, find him plainer clothing, and a more ordinary mount as well. And weapons." He turned. "Astil, have you any weapons?"

"I have—only a small ceremonial dagger. I did not come here expecting to go to war," he said sullenly.

"It may not come to that," said Ronar. "But then, it might. Phanerol, please provide whatever weapons are appropriate for Astil, or if you have none, locate them among my people, in my name."

The three departed to do his bidding.

Astil wound up atop a shaggy grey pony, with a rust-colored woolen cloak covering his shoulders. His Faerie nature was still unmistakable, but at least it would not be seen from a distance. A light bronze sword had been found for him, as well as archery gear. As Astil eyed them, Ronar suspected he had little if any idea of how to use either.

"Don't look so glum, Astil," said Sha Totek. "I have ridden with Ronar on several of his adventures. You will find that they are invariably stirring, exciting, grueling, uncomfortable, painful, and unpleasant. On second thought, let's both look glum."

"Let's get started," said Ronar.

By now a large crowd had assembled to watch the three ride out. They lined the path, standing silently, looking at them with sad dismay.

Ronar was uncomfortable beneath their scrutiny. What were they thinking? Perhaps they were wondering how it had come to this: to see their greatest city crumble, their greatest people drowned, and now to see their new outsider King ride off toward oblivion with only two dubious companions in tow.

Well, if that's not what they're thinking, they just aren't paying attention, he thought.

"The sword. Show them the sword," whispered Sha Totek.

Ronar grimaced, never one to understand why a flamboyant act of bravado might be preferable to simple dignity. Nevertheless, he held out his ring hand and concentrated on it. For a moment it sputtered strangely, then it flared red, and flashed white. With a ringing crash, the Sword of Bran appeared in Ronar's hand. He held it aloft as they rode along, bringing forth cheers from the onlookers, mostly weak and uncertain, but better than silent dejection.

All Ronar could think about was the coldness of the grip as he held the sword on high. The chill seeped into his hand and threatened to numb it. He kept the sword in his possession well after they'd left the crowd behind, reluctant to return it to the dark waters of the Bay.

Ronar and his two companions continued westward during the next few days. Kiruna curved away to the north, leaving them in a rolling landscape of moors and pastures. The weather remained clear, keeping the slow endless tumble of the two disparate suns in view, but the air was cool.

Astil expected to stop in each town and village along the way, demanding treatment commensurate with his status. Ronar felt otherwise, avoiding settlements and attention in general, forcing them to camp in fields and on hillsides, sometimes in the midst of sheep or cattle.

Three days into their journey, with the jagged line of the Mynd Bannock visible in the west, Ronar took note of the way Astil handled his weapons as he unloaded his horse at the night's camp. The Elf dropped them on the ground as though they were bits of firewood.

Ronar winced and said, "Astil, let's see what you can do with that bow, which you treat so casually."

Astil frowned at him. "Must we? Riding that lumpen nag all day has already drained me enough. The prospect of spending the night on this barren hillside further depletes me."

Sha Totek laughed. "The virtue of traveling with Astil is that his complaints relieve me of the need to voice my own."

Ronar ignored the sorcerer and said, "Yes, Astil, your skills may someday keep us all alive. Let's see them."

Grumbling, Astil unwrapped his bow and struggled to string it. Ronar watched this clumsy display for a while, and then reluctantly asked, "Astil, have you ever handled a bow before?"

"Yes, when I was very young."

"But you never strung one, did you?"

"No, I had servants for that."

Ronar rolled his eyes. "Keep trying. Brace it with your leg while you bend it."

At last the Elf succeeded, holding up the strung bow as though it were some kind of war trophy.

"All right, let's see you hit that tree over there. Try for the spot where those two large limbs join the trunk," said Ronar.

"From here?"

"Yes, from here."

Ronar watched as Astil clumsily nocked an arrow, drew using very poor form, and aimed.

"You'll never hit it that way. The arrow will not travel to its target in a straight line. You must raise it a bit to compensate for the distance."

Astil elevated the arrow and released. The string struck his forearm, causing the arrow to fly off wildly. Astil cursed, dropped the bow, and drew up his sleeve, where the string had raised a welt on his arm.

"Perhaps the King of Eranior would be good enough to refresh my skills."

Ronar didn't bother to mention that in addition to being king of Eranior, he had long ago won a bronze medal for archery in Earth's Olympic Games. With the suns already below the horizon, he instructed the Elf in how to stand, how to draw, and how to hold his arm to avoid fouling the string. This was as close as he had ever been to anyone from Faerie, and the first time he had ever touched such a person. Comparing himself to Astil's physical perfection, he could not help feeling gross, hairy, and crude. Despite their travels, the Elf gave off a faint undefinable scent which was like how starlight would smell if it had a smell, Ronar supposed. He tried not to dwell on what the Faerie women must be like at close range.

After half an hour, Ronar had given Astil a reasonable start at basic form, but his marksmanship was still poor.

"Well, Astil, it's getting dark. You can continue this some other time."

"There's plenty of light." Astil continued to shoot at the tree.

Ronar shrugged and went off to join Sha Totek, where they prepared some food.

"Maybe you should test our friend's swordsmanship as well," whispered Sha Totek.

"Yes, but I'm not sure how to do it. My sword would snap his bronze weapon at the first blow. Anyway, I don't want to give him an excuse to attack me. Tell me, are all Elves as—callow as this one?"

"Oh no, not at all. They are as diverse as any other people. But whatever any given Elf happens to be, he or she is that thing to a very great degree."

A little later the three sat around their tiny fire eating the very simple fare which was their usual diet. Sha Totek made a great show of relishing his gruel (though Ronar was fully aware that he did not), while Astil glumly picked at his. When their meal was concluded, Astil again picked up his bow, even though it was now full night. Ronar supposed they'd have to hunt for stray arrows before they could leave in the morning. To his surprise, he soon began to hear the *thunk thunk thunk* of arrows actually hitting the tree.

Sha Totek set up his favorite magical tent, while Ronar unrolled his sleeping bag near the embers of the fire. He fell asleep to the unnerving sound of the sorcerer weeping in his tent, then awoke hours later to the steady sound of *thunk thunk thunk thunk thunk*. Hauling himself upright, he made his way to the shadowy figure of the Elf, who turned to regard him.

"Astil, that's enough. Get some sleep."

"Sleep? Apparently you haven't noticed that we do not sleep."

"You don't? Then what have you been doing every night?"

"Thinking, missing my home, and when the sky is clear, looking at the stars and the frothy sky beyond them."

Ronar's ears pricked up at this phrase. "The frothy sky?"

"Yes, the vaguely net-like pattern that covers the night sky, made of innumerable little flecks of soft light, like bits of sea foam. You are said to be a stargazer. Surely you must know it."

"I know it. But you're saying you can see this with your eyes alone?"

"Of course. Are you saying you cannot?"

For the first time he could remember, Ronar found himself keenly envying the gifts which magic could convey.

"I cannot see this cosmic background of *galaxies* unaided. I, and all mortal men, see only a dark sky sprinkled with stars."

"I did not realize you were all so blind in the dark. But what is a *galaxy*?"

"It is an assemblage of a vast number of stars. The Whirlpool is a galaxy, and among its stars is the sun of my home world of Earth. All the others you see are similar, but much farther away. I can see a few of them myself, faintly. But nothing like what you can apparently see."

"Very interesting. Now, if you wish to resume your sleep, I shall continue with my archery practice. I find it oddly satisfying."

In the morning, Astil announced, "I think you will now be satisfied with my archery skills."

Ronar glanced over at the tree. The target area was now a ragged pit three inches deep in the wood. He looked at Astil's quiver. The arrows were fewer, and in poor condition. Ronar nodded.

"Very good. Too bad about that poor tree though."

Astil shrugged. "It is merely a tree."

They rode on, with the Mynd Bannock rising further above the horizon with every mile. In the afternoon they sighted what was likely to be the final village they'd encounter before entering the mountains. Ronar halted his grey mare and sat looking at it, considering. Finally he said, "I'm reluctant to call attention to ourselves, but I believe we should enter that village. We might get news, and besides, we should restock our supplies, and try to find new arrows for Astil."

The other two readily agreed to this.

"I'm especially reluctant to reveal that we travel with an Elf. That is news unusual enough to spread far and wide. Sha Totek, do you have any magic which would disguise his nature?"

The sorcerer eyed Astil from atop his black stallion and said, "I believe I do. Astil, if you would kindly dismount?"

Astil did so, waiting with visible trepidation while Sha Totek also dismounted and then approached him. The sorcerer raised his hands and placed them on Astil's shoulders. He then grasped the hood of Astil's cloak and pulled it forward, shading his face.

"Behold! Now only the closest scrutiny would reveal his Faerie nature. Astil, please also refrain from speaking in front of others. Your voice is distinctive."

"You are easily amused," said Ronar.

"It is a necessity for one of my span."

Ronar wondered if he were speaking as the ancient Sha Totek or as his short-lived dispersion.

With Sha Totek still chuckling, they rode into the village, a cheerless place populated by people who viewed them with suspicion. They reached a marketplace in the center of the village, dismounted, and tied up their horses.

An old woman wearing grey rags and bedecked with charms hanging from bits of string walked up to Sha Totek and squinted into his face.

"Dark of skin ye be, stranger," she said, speaking a dialect archaic even for Eranior. "What far-off suns burned ye so black?"

Sha Totek smiled. "I am Sekani, a wandering sorcerer out of distant, exotic Ammon, lady. Would you like to see some magic?"

"Bah, I am myself a witch, and in no need of any petty spell of thine." She glanced at Ronar, then turned her attention to Astil. "And what of ye? So pale are ye, 'tis like ye are soaked with milk, or raised among mushrooms."

Astil frowned, making ready to reply.

"So, I am too dark, while our companion is too light," said Sha Totek quickly. "It would seem, lady, that only a narrow range of skin tones meets with your approval. Your own mottled tones would be difficult to imitate."

The old woman hissed and fumbled at her collection of trinkets. Sha Totek cut her off by crying out something in ancient Greek that sounded like an invocation of the goddesses Hebe, Glorith, and Projectra, whoever those latter two were.

At once the old woman dwindled slightly, her wrinkles blurred, and her flesh firmed. She stood before them as a nine-year-old girl, gaping at her pink-skinned hands. She stared at Sha Totek for a moment, then ran away, shrieking with laughter as she cast off her oversized rags.

"That was a considerable spell," said Ronar, impressed. seemed to diffuse"I never saw any version of you do anything like that before."

"Nor have you now, as a matter of fact. Her new semblance is only an illusion. It will fade the first time she does anything which only an adult should do. In the meantime she will enjoy herself and annoy us no more. She really should have left her clothes on, though."

"I take it you could have done something similar for Astil."

Sha Totek shrugged. "Maybe, though possibly my magic might work differently on one of the Fay. In any case, why exert myself needlessly?"

Ronar shook his head and led them into the marketplace. Their shopping was a mixed success. They were able to obtain adequate food—adequate only, even in Ronar's eyes; sorely lacking to the other two—but weapons were scarce. The only available arrows were crude, with flint tips. Nevertheless, Ronar bought a bundle of them, just in case. "We'll have to try to repair some of your old arrows, Astil," he said.

The merchant at whose stall they bought these things was eager for news. "You come from the east? Is it true, as we've heard, that Myrddin has been destroyed?"

"Yes, it is true."

"And the new king was killed? Have we another new king?"

Ronar was silent.

"Yes, you have a new king," said Sha Totek. "A fine new king, if I may say so."

"What have you heard?" asked Ronar. "Any sign of trouble in the mountains?"

"Well, the scouts and soldiers who watch the passes and man the watchtowers sometimes visit our village, when they can do no better. They say the mountains are quiet. If Darteharn intends some mischief, there is as yet no sign of it along the usual routes of invasion."

"Have any of these scouts ventured far enough to get a sense of what's happening within Darteharn itself?"

"Not that I've heard! That would demand a man brave to the point of foolishness."

Sha Totek snickered. "Yes, wouldn't it?"

Ronar looked up from the merchant and his ill-stocked booth, beyond the huts of the village, to the Mynd Bannock. He did not especially like the look of that range, but there he must go.

"And what of you, sir, if I may ask? What brings such an imposing trio to this bleak frontier of Eranior?" said the merchant.

Ronar said, "We are traveling entertainers. My Ammonite friend here is a magician. Our silent, hooded companion is a mime. I am a comedian."

"Well, sir, if you don't want to say, you need merely say so."

Ronar paid for their goods. The three returned to their horses. Ronar noticed a shabby little inn nearby. No doubt it was a wretched, verminous place, yet when the alternative was sleeping on the ground in this semi-abandoned land with its cold airs sliding down from the west, he was tempted to spend the night there.

He abruptly realized what a lapse of rigor and discipline this was, shook himself in disgust, mounted his horse and led the way out of the village.

He started out for the south, not wishing to make it obvious that he and his companions were headed toward Darteharn, but then they veered back toward the west.

The mountains rose ever higher. They intercepted a faint track which led toward one of the more obvious passes in the range.

Now Ronar was faced with a difficult choice.

"My friends, here we must decide how to proceed. We can enter Darteharn using one of the passes, but then we must surely be accosted by the watchmen of Eranior, to say nothing of whatever guardians Darteharn might station farther in. I do not wish to reveal myself as the king, nor would it be easy to concoct a reason why three innocent vagabonds would wish to enter Darteharn. The alternative is to strike out on our own, seek our own path over the high mountains, and so hope to avoid detection."

Sha Totek groaned. "I think I can predict what your choice will be."

"Ronar, are you actually aware of any such paths over the mountains?" asked Astil in a doubtful tone.

"No, we'd have to make our own."

"It seems unlikely we'd find a path suitable for our horses."

"That is true. I was planning to turn them loose."

Astil pulled back his hood and stared at Ronar with his disconcerting silvery eyes. "That seems a very doubtful plan. Poor as they are, these horses are better than walking. It seems to me that, rather than just blundering about on our own, with little notion of where we are to go, we would do better with a knowledgeable guide."

"I think our friend has a point," said Sha Totek. "If it were you alone on this expedition, I would encourage and expect you to forge your way over any number of unknown, merciless icy peaks, if only to avoid feeling dependent on any other person. However, for once you did not arrange things that way, for some odd reason. You have as your companions one rather effete and not even fully competent sorcerer, and one Faery Prince who also does not seem to have made a great study of wilderness survival. These are factors which you must not ignore."

"So what would you both suggest? That we simply stroll over the nearest pass until we encounter the gatekeepers of Darteharn, and then ask their permission to enter?" As soon he said this Ronar regretted it, knowing it to be both foolish and churlish.

Astil appeared affronted. Sha Totek smiled at Ronar with gentle pity and said, "No, my friend. I propose that we proceed into the pass until we encounter the watchmen of Eranior, explain who we are, and then require one or more of them to guide us further."

Ronar turned away to mull this over. He knew they were right, and that he had not thought this through. For that matter, he had barely thought anything through since Myrddin fell. Before that event, he'd been executing personal plans which he'd pieced together in his mind over a period of months. He was not one to be easily turned aside from his plans. Perhaps his mind was less flexible than it once had been. Since all the woes of Eranior had been thrust upon him, he had made huge decisions with little consideration, pursuing his current plan without even really knowing what he hoped to accomplish.

It was time to step back a little.

He turned to his companions. "Yours is perhaps a better plan." A small, wry smile shaped his lips.

Sha Totek laughed but also looked like he was about to burst into tears. "It is a wise king who heeds the words of his advisors. Lead on, Your Majesty, lead on."

Ronar urged his horse toward the pass. From behind he heard, "Since you are being so reasonable, my friend, I wonder if you would answer me this."

Ronar rolled his eyes, which the other two, being slightly behind him, couldn't see. *Well, here it comes,* he thought.

"You say you are intent on confronting Namirnakh himself, if need be. I wonder how you think you can get away with that. The last time you encountered him, as I recall, you were completely at his mercy. Oh yes, you stung him, but otherwise, he handled you like a child. Without substantial outside assistance, including some from my better self, you would now be but a fond memory. What's to stop Namirnakh from killing, slaying, mauling, maiming, dismembering, or squashing you now? Or all of us, for that matter?"

"I'm not the same man I was back then," insisted Ronar stubbornly.

"No, as you've pointed out, you're sixty five years older than you were then. Er, that's roughly thirty turns for your sake, Astil. But I'm sure that's not what you meant, Ronar."

"No, it wasn't. It's a matter of experience. In the course of those twenty eight turns, I have destroyed the City of Wraiths on the slopes of Ashelak and also ended the foul city of Nartar. I have stalked my own black-hearted *doppelgånger* through the deserts and alleyways of Ammon. I escaped my servitude to a dark Sorceress on the other side of the world—you remember her, don't you? I have married and then mourned a princess of Varma...that spoiled brat, may all her gods embrace her. I later married and then mourned my housekeeper. And not least, in spite of the opposition of Varanu himself, I pulled the very God of Evil out of the heavens once and for all. Having done all that, and more, I will not be intimidated by Namirnakh and whatever new form he has managed to crawl into."

"That's a very impressive list of accomplishments," said Sha Totek. "I would remind you once again that you did have assistance in some of those cases."

"I haven't forgotten you, or Albianor, or Perturbare, or Adam himself, for that matter. I certainly haven't forgotten Asterope. Now I'll ask you a question. You and I, or I should say Sha Totek and I, have shared several journeys and expeditions over the years. How many times was it actually him, and how many times one of you dispersions?"

"Well, er, you have traveled with dispersions two or three times before. This is the first time I have come to regret that choice. But maybe I'm being hasty. Namirnakh stood no chance against me when he faced me before my Tower. Sha Totek might find himself equally disadvantaged in Namirnakh's domain. At least this way, he is safe."

"Who knows what we'll find in Namirnakh's domain?"

Chapter Six

Amulree

A few hours later they entered the gorge which led up into the mountains. The track was still faintly visible, though obviously it was little used. They rode beside a river which bubbled over rocks and through beds of brown reeds. Native birds of some sort stood among them, reaching their delicate forelimbs into the mud, peering at whatever they withdrew with bright inquisitive eyes.

Although it flowed out of Darteharn, the river appeared perfectly ordinary, wholesome, even pleasant. Likewise the mountains, though they were bleak at this time of year and had a low tree line, gave no indication of marking the boundary of a land of notorious evil.

Still, signs of conflict and warfare in times past were visible. Ronar spied worn arrowheads and spear points on the riverbanks. Occasionally they crossed the remnants of ancient stone walls which had once crossed the valley. Although he looked up and down the sides of the gorge, Ronar saw no recent fortifications, nor any sign of watchmen. He found all this peace and quiet increasingly strange. Even in ordinary times, this range marked the boundary between two hostile nations. Something should be happening here.

As they climbed, the walls grew lower on either side. The gorge became a small valley, and then was nothing more than a slope. The river diminished to a stream, and then a trickle, and then to nothing. The air grew colder.

They left the last trees behind, leaving no hiding places save for occasional outcroppings of rock. The summit of the pass was visible not far ahead. The suns moved in and out of the clouds overhead.

They reached the summit without incident and looked out over a broad, hazy valley which ran north and south for as far as they could see. On its far side was another mountain range which looked higher and more formidable than the one they had just crossed. On the valley floor, a settlement lay along both banks of another river.

Ronar reached into his clothing and produced a small white device which he raised to his eyes.

"I didn't know you still had that thing," remarked Sha Totek.

"Oh yes. But I'm cautious with it, and try not to risk it. I won't be getting another."

Astil rode closer. "What is it?"

"It's a viewer. A small *electro-optical binocular*," said Ronar absently. "Er, it makes distant objects appear closer," he added.

"Is it magical?"

"No, it's..." Of course neither the Eranian tongue nor its Faerie variant had a word for "science", any more than it did for "electro-optical viewer".

"Its workings rely on the way things function in the natural world. It's something like a bow and arrow in that respect, but much more complicated. That's a poor explanation, but it's not an easy matter to communicate to you. It's from Earth."

"Very interesting. And what do you see?"

"It's a village of course, and much like the last one, if somewhat larger. I think this explains why our passage has been so easy so far. We haven't even crossed the border yet. That next range must be the true border." Ronar lowered the viewer and gave a short laugh of relief.

They set off down the hill. Astil urged his mount to canter a few hundred feet ahead.

"Ya know, pardner, I noticed somethin' right funny a few miles back…"

Ronar winced whenever Sha Totek lapsed into his ridiculous faux-cowboy accent. "And what was that?"

Still speaking English, the sorcerer continued, "You remember when I mentioned how our old friend Namirnakh might easily kill us all? And then how I sorta emphasized the idea? Well, I was watchin' our new friend up there out of the corner of my eye, and I noticed he didn't look too scared. Not even worried."

"Hmm. Maybe Elves can't be killed?" said Ronar, now also in English.

"Oh yeah, they can be. They live a long time, sure, but they can die. They can especially die when they're away from home. That ain't the answer."

"No, I suppose not. Tell me, have his people ever shown any inclination to make mischief in foreign lands?"

"Nope. All they've ever wanted is to live in their little play-land and be left alone by ordinary mortals. Any man or woman who was ever unlucky enough to stumble over their border will tell you that, if he's able."

"Just the same, we'll keep an eye on him."

The faint sound of a tolling bell reached them from the village, which was still far off. It did not cease. Astil brought his horse to a halt. The other two caught up with him and also halted. The three sat there looking ahead.

Ronar again raised the viewer. He saw human figures scurrying about, assembling on the near side of the village, facing them in a line.

"Now what do you suppose all that's about?" said Sha Totek.

"The people look afraid," said Ronar. "They may think we are riders from Darteharn."

"Coming from the east?"

Ronar shrugged. "We will approach slowly, and halt out of bowshot. Sha Totek, if you can manage any spells that may defend us if they should attack, prepare them. But I see no serious weapons among them. These people are not prepared for battle."

They continued at a deliberate pace, stopping when the line of villagers began to yell and wave their clubs, scythes, and other improvised weapons. "Go back! Go back!" they cried.

"We are of Eranior!" bellowed Ronar, startling the other two. "Do not be afraid!"

"That is why we are afraid, invaders! Go back!"

Ronar cursed and lowered his head, feeling an utter fool. What, after all, had he expected a village of Darteharn to look like? A cluster of ominous black towers with demons hanging from their parapets?

"It would appear you have miscalculated, O King," said Astil.

For some reason that remark made Ronar want to backhand Astil's smooth-skinned face. However, he could not ignore the justice of it.

"Indeed it does. Sha Totek, do you have any suggestions?"

"Turn around and go home?"

Ronar grimaced. He sat studying the body language of the people confronting him, and then called out, "We mean you no harm! We wish to enter your village and speak with you. Please put down your weapons."

"Good, good," said Sha Totek. "I have long desired an opportunity to hobnob with citizens of Darteharn."

Those citizens did not move or change their attitude.

"Proceed slowly," said Ronar. "Make no hostile move. Do not identify yourselves. Make no mention of who I am. Astil, put up your hood."

With all caution they moved forward, watching for any sign of bows, slings, or other distance weapons. Presently they were close enough for Ronar to make out the faces of the villagers. They were a dirty, poor-looking lot, but apparently no different from any group of similarly marginal Eranians.

One old man stood astride the pathway, a little ahead of the others. He was short, and plainly quite aged, though his long unkempt hair was as black as Sha Totek's.

"For many turns now have we awaited your invasion! Come forward now and tell us your terms, if you would conquer us."

Ronar was puzzled. With a gesture he halted his little party. "I think you have matters reversed. We have no desire to conquer you. We have come to discover why Darteharn has attacked Eranior yet again."

"Attacked? What are you talking about?"

Well, Ronar reflected, it would not be surprising if this poor frontier village was unaware of the machinations of its distant leader.

"A great upheaval somewhere north of here resulted in a cataclysm in the Bay of Kiruna. In ancient times, your master Namirnakh overthrew great masses of rock and earth to change Kiruna from a placid lake into the turbulent tide-tossed bay it is today. Naturally we attribute any further such deeds to him."

The spokesman gave a bitter laugh. "That is all very well. In fact we also felt a tremor a week or so ago. But we would be surprised indeed if Namirnakh were responsible for your plight. He was thrown down nearly thirty turns ago, as I'm sure you know. If he has arisen again, he has not yet made himself known to us. Believe it or not, at one time our village of Amulree was prosperous. We had a garrison of soldiers, and the fortifications in the pass through which you must have come were manned and well maintained. But since the loss of Namirnakh, our land has been adrift, and in decline. All we had left was the comfort of our great god Ahriman—at least until he too was destroyed, it is said by the Earthman Ronar, the same hated outsider who, together with the Egyptian Sorcerer and the king of Eranior, brought down our ruler.

"Now at last you come to gather the spoils. How long until your armies pour over the pass, using the excuse of this supposed attack against you? What more will you take from us? What, if anything, will you leave?"

Ronar lowered his gaze. When he looked up again, he said, "Eranior wishes nothing from you save to be left in peace. That is all it has ever wanted."

The little pot-bellied spokesman laughed again. "We are poor, but we are not ignorant of history. We have heard how Bran, the First King of Eranior, drove into the wilderness Namirnakh, who had an equal part in founding that country, and who was its co-ruler at the time."

"One slight correction," said Sha Totek with a smile which was blatantly false. "It was not Bran who drove out Namirnakh, but his successor. It would have been difficult for Bran to do it, as Namirnakh had already murdered him, and placed his skull on the throne beside his own."

The spokesman glowered at him. "So you say. It would be difficult for anyone who was not present to say for certain."

"I—"

"I say again, we mean you no harm," interrupted Ronar. "Our business is not with you. The people of Darteharnlandua and Eranior are kindred. Perhaps the day has come at last when your differences may be put aside. But we must venture further, to discover the truth. For now, may we enter your village in peace?"

"What will you do if we deny you?"

"We will ride around you, traveling up or down your river until we find a place to ford it."

The spokesman stared at Ronar for some moments, plainly conflicted.

Finally, he said, "We should kill you if we can. Yet you seem like a fair-spoken man. I never thought to see such a day, but you may enter."

The three closed the distance to the crowd of villagers and dismounted. The villagers gathered around, looking at the trio with expressions of wonder and a strange hope.

Their spokesman stepped up as they dismounted and said in some embarrassment, "Forgive me, but we will not reveal our true names, lest you turn out to be the sort of magicians who take advantage of such knowledge. You may call me Caradoc. I have put myself forward to speak for Amulree, but in truth I am nothing but a farmer who happens to be in town for the day. We have no formal leader, except for the witch Emogen, who is away gathering materials for her craft."

Ronar hoped his relief wasn't too obvious. Now he need not lie to these people, moments after being called fair-spoken.

"We then shall do likewise. You may call me Raintree. Refer to my fellow travelers as Sekani the Ammonite, and this other will be called, er, Fauntleroy."

Leading their horses, the three followed Caradoc into the village. The other villagers followed in fascination. Some of the younger men stared at them with more hostility than curiosity, which prompted Caradoc to say, "You boys, go about your business. For the moment, these men are our guests, and I'll not have you glowering at them."

"Yes, War Chief." Still sullen, they slunk away.

Ronar looked at the wild little figure of Caradoc.

"Yes, yes, I was once a leader of warriors, but that was long ago. Come."

He led them into the village's central square, which was lined with shabby little wattle houses and shops. Its finest structure was of black-painted timber, a chapel devoted to Ahriman. In front stood cold braziers in which red flames would once have danced. Ronar suppressed a shudder at the sight of them.

Caradoc indicated some benches. "Let us be seated. Permit us to offer you something to eat."

Ronar obeyed, wishing he had something worth offering in return. Sha Totek and Astil sat on either side of him. Small children swarmed over Sha Totek. A little girl sat astride his leg, rocking back and forth. With a smile plastered on his face, he resorted to English once more. "Oh, excellent. I have become a plaything for the shameless brats of Darteharn. Now my life feels complete."

Women brought leather mugs of ale, loaves of bread, butter, and three brown apples. Again Ronar felt ashamed to accept this hospitality. As he ate, he attempted to make polite conversation.

"Caradoc, were you present at the Battle of the Bronze Portal?"

"No. You would have been no more than a child during that struggle, or you'd know that none from Darteharnlandua returned from that field. I was involved, but only peripherally. I was part of a garrison left at the mouth of Aegeos to prevent the Mersineans from contesting our fleet's return passage through the strait. Afterwards I tried for many turns to hold our armies together, but after the demise of Ahriman that became impossible. Thus I returned here to my ancestral lands to work my fields."

Actually, Ronar was fully aware of the fate of Namirnakh's army. He had witnessed it, and it seemed to him far more merciful than they had deserved.

A murmur rose up from the far side of the crowd. It parted to allow a breathless boy to pass through, running. He halted before Caradoc and panted, "War Chief, Emogen is back, and she is coming!"

Caradoc rose to his feet. Ronar followed his example, as did Astil and Sha Totek, who sent children tumbling as he stood.

A minute later a peculiar figure approached them. Like Caradoc she was short, and her hair equally long and wild, albeit colored bright copper red instead of black. She was very pale, her eyes burned bright green, and her costume consisted of a motley assemblage of rags and scraps in bleached earthy colors. She carried a basket overflowing with various leaves, twigs, fungi, and small aquatic animals.

Her voice as she spoke was low and thoughtful. "I had a feeling something odd was going on back here. Now tell me, what business have a man, an Elf, and a blackamoor here in Amulree?"

"An Elf?" said Caradoc, looking nonplussed.

Emogen waved her free hand toward Astil. "Of course, are you blind?"

Astil lowered his hood. "It seems my disguise is of no further use."

"Let's see. We have here a looming, grey-haired man wearing a garnet ring, accompanied by a sly-looking Ammonite who reeks of sorcery," continued Emogen. "Could it be...?"

"Uh oh," said Sha Totek.

Emogen's eyes rolled back in her head, a disconcerting sight. She extended a trembling hand.

"Caradoc, do you know who you have admitted into our midst? This is none other than Ronar, the Earthman, foe of Namirnakh and destroyer of Ahriman! This other is a sending of the sorcerer Imhotep, the ancient foe of Darteharn and nemesis of Namirnakh! And finally, here is a princeling of the Faerie House of Cotavion!"

This announcement sent most of the crowd scrambling back with many cries and wails. Caradoc stayed put, though he looked confused.

"We mean well, though," said Sha Totek.

Emogen's sightless gaze was locked on Ronar. "And you—you are a king!"

"It's only temporary," growled Ronar.

"Temporary? No, you have always been a king. Your ancestors have always been kings, going back many thousands of turns. But not on Colibdis. No, not on Colibdis."

"Very insightful," said Sha Totek appreciatively.

"What are either of you talking about? My father was a forest ranger in Colorado. He was no king."

"So," said Caradoc slowly. "We have welcomed the two greatest enemies of our land, our lord, and our god. But what then...?" He glanced at Astil.

Emogen's eyes rolled back to their proper position. "Yes."

"Archers!" bellowed Caradoc.

From behind every nearby building appeared villagers bearing bows, with arrows pulled back to their ears.

Ronar cursed and invoked the ring. The cold sword appeared in his hand with its customary flash and clamor. All around him, people screamed and fell back. If arrows flew, Caradoc and Emogen would fall first, on that point Ronar was intent.

"They mean us no harm," said Emogen quietly.

"Harm," repeated Caradoc. "Harm! What more harm can they do us? They have already, between them, smashed down our ruler, cast our armies into oblivion, and silenced our god! Only if the king of Eranior himself also stood before us could any group be more infamous! Now they are at our mercy. We must kill them. No one in Eranior or elsewhere will ever know their fate."

"Actually, that's not true," said Sha Totek. All eyes turned his way. "As Emogen said, I am but a sending of the true Sorcerer, a partial thing, not overly to be feared. But the true Imhotep sees through my eyes. He knows what I know. He can even speak through my lips, and he chooses to do so now."

As they all looked on, the dispersion straightened. He seemed to grow taller, and most certainly he took on an aura of greatly enhanced formidability.

"Heed the words of Imhotep of the Two Lands, of Sha Totek of the Black Tower! Kill or harm these three, and I will come myself to Eranior, in all my power. Indeed, I will move the Tower itself to your border, and there it will become a spike of menace, poised to pierce your land. Eranior has suffered a sore blow, but it still can field armies. From me they will know of the weakness of Darteharn. Nothing stands between them and this valley of yours. They will gladly overrun it, and you will be crushed. Do not harm these three. I have spoken."

Sha Totek again diminished, a foolish grin on his face. The bows of Darteharn wavered. Even Caradoc looked dismayed.

"What do you want here?" asked Emogen.

"Eranior has suffered an attack which was probably magical in origin," said Ronar. "We assumed the source was Darteharn, and we came here to determine the truth of the matter. In fact, I am beginning to doubt that assumption. We have seen here neither the will nor the capability to launch any further assaults. But we must go on, to learn if Namirnakh is resurgent, or if some other leader seeks to resume Namirnakh's conquests."

"And what will you do if you do find Namirnakh?"

Ronar lowered his sword by a degree, but kept it in his hands.

"We will ask him, with all due courtesy, whether the destruction of our capital was his doing."

"And if he takes credit for this deed? You will try to kill him?"

"Yes."

"And what if you find him and he disclaims any responsibility?" asked Caradoc.

"Then we will counsel him to restrict himself to the borders of Darteharn, and never again seek a wider realm. We will inform him also that the last Bronze Portal is fallen, and that his wish to invade Earth is no longer possible."

Ronar and Caradoc stared at each other for long moments. Caradoc, Ronar had already discerned, was a worldly man, and no fool. Nevertheless, it was he who first averted his eyes.

"Archers, put down your weapons," he said. "For the safety of our lands and families, we will not molest these three." He looked once more at Ronar. "That sword. It is the actual sword of King Bran?"

"It is."

"May I examine it?"

Ronar handed him the weapon with only a moment's hesitation, knowing that if Caradoc should try to flee with it or use it against him, he could easily summon it back to his hand.

"It is cold."

"Yes. It now spends most of its time in the Bay of Kiruna."

Caradoc studied the grip and guard, turning it in his hand. "It is the most superb weapon I have ever seen, with the greatest amount of steel I have ever beheld. Too bad two of the gems on the grip are missing."

"Only one gem is missing. It's the one in my ring."

"No, two. See?" Caradoc handed back the sword.

The socket that had once held the garnet on Ronar's finger was empty as usual. He turned the grip in his hand. The corresponding socket on the opposite side was also empty.

Ronar felt as if he'd been robbed, the sword desecrated. He almost shoved the handle into Sha Totek's face. "Look here! What could have happened to it?"

"The stone could have been dislodged when the sword fell into the bay. Or someone could have pried it loose while it was on display at the palace."

"Yes. It could have happened years ago without my noticing. I manifest the sword so rarely these days."

Then he noticed something else that struck him as though he'd found one of his own fingers missing. At the base of the blade of the immutable sword was a small patch of rust.

He felt frozen, stunned, as though the suns had failed to rise. But this was not something he wished to announce before the people of Amulree.

Emogen looked at him strangely.

"War Chief, what is this?" This surly cry came from a large young man who strode up armed with a bronze sword and a large copper-bossed shield covered with leather. "We cannot allow these enemies to go unharmed. You, Ronar, will you fight me?"

"If you attack me, I will defend myself," said Ronar, wishing he also had a magic ring that would summon up a shield.

"Conall, put down your weapons," said Caradoc. "I know you wish to impress Sabrina, but this is not the way."

Conall shot Caradoc a look of disdain and charged Ronar.

Ronar raised his sword to a defensive position, trying to remember the last time he'd been in a sword fight. *This could be it,* he thought as he watched Conall approaching in what appeared to be slow motion. *This could be the time when I lose an arm, or my head, or get skewered though the chest.*

Conall raised a war cry and lifted his sword for a blow as he came on. Ronar stepped back as though he were dodging a bull, swinging at the same time. The flat of his blade caught Conall on the back, sending him sprawling. With a roar of fury Conall leapt to his feet and wheeled.

Ronar was displeased. He had hoped this quick shock and humiliation would knock the fight out of his opponent. Conall pressed in, attempting to slam Ronar with his shield, too canny to swing his bronze weapon against Ronar's steel. Ronar gave way before the impact, staying on his feet, alert for a sweep of the sword beneath the shield.

Ronar thrust his own sword past the shield. As he'd hoped, Conall could not resist trying to knock it out of his hand with a swing of his shield. At the last instant Ronar permitted the sword to vanish from his hand, causing Conall's swing to go wild, and Conall to lurch. Ronar flung himself at the exposed warrior, knocking him down, pinning his arms to the paving stones. Conall was every bit his equal in strength, but Ronar was just enough bigger to maintain his advantage. He stared into the hate-filled Darteharnian face just inches from his own.

"You cannot toy with him forever," said Caradoc. "Either you must kill him, or he must kill you."

"I do not wish to kill this feckless oaf!" snarled Ronar.

"Kill me, or release me and regain your weapon!" demanded Conall.

Ronar spat a curse. He released Conall's empty hand, but before the lout could react, Ronar broke his jaw with a blow of his fist. Conall continued to struggle, trying to claw Ronar's eyes with his free hand, so Ronar smashed his nose.

Conall's eyes fluttered and closed. Ronar checked his carotid pulse, then heaved himself to his feet.

"There. By the time this fool recovers, if he does, we'll be long gone from here. If he still insists on fighting, he can follow me, and I will kill him then."

A great tension filled the air. Ronar was not entirely certain that Caradoc and the others would not attack them, but then all were distracted by the sound of Sha Totek's weeping.

Ronar stood panting and staring at the dispersion, wondering at his odd emotional instability.

Sha Totek looked at him with his face working with distress. "Ronar, thank you for not killing that boy. I don't know if I could have borne it. There has been far too much violence and death already."

These words seemed to defuse the situation. Ronar sank trembling onto a bench. Emogen moved to tend to Conall.

Sha Totek sat beside Ronar, asking through watery eyes, "Are you all right? You look upset."

"Of course I'm upset! Who enjoys having some maniac hurl himself at him with a sword?" He took a moment to compose himself, then addressed himself to Caradoc and

Emogen, who stood nearby, along with Astil. "I am forty five turns old. I am a student of the stars by nature, not a warrior. Yes, I have killed many men, far too many. But I do not seek it. I do not enjoy it."

Caradoc stepped forward. "I'm not sure Conall will be grateful for your mercy, but I can see it was well intended. As far as I'm concerned, you are free to continue into Darteharn, though I do not have much hope for your survival. If not for your trickery, I'm not sure Conall wouldn't have beaten you. It seems very strange, that a man of your reputation could be at all challenged by an untried fighter like Conall."

Ronar laughed. "I have never been a great swordsman. Very often I survive through trickery, or through the properties of my magical weapon, or through superior strength and reach. It is a lack I keep meaning to make up, but somehow other priorities always intervene."

Caradoc gaped at this candidness, then said, "When will you leave?"

"At once, I think. I think it best that we camp somewhere away from your village, lest other hotheads take exception to our presence."

"So soon?" said Emogen. "Wait a few moments while I pack some things."

"What?" said Ronar and Caradoc simultaneously.

"I'm going with them, at least for a while."

"But why?" said Caradoc.

"Hmm," said Ronar.

"Because I have lived my entire life within a few miles of this village. I wish to see more of Darteharnlandua."

"Can you guide us?" asked Ronar.

"Not really. As I said, I am not widely traveled. But I may be able to help keep you out of trouble."

"Emogen, you are the most adept magic user in Amulree. We all look up to you. The village will suffer without you," said Caradoc.

Emogen smiled. "They can look up to you instead, if anyone needs to be looked up to."

"But I am no healer."

Emogen's face fell. "True. But who knows what I'll be able to do when I come back? Maybe I'll find the Tower of the Mystic Arts itself and return with more craft than I now possess."

"If you come back."

"I promise to come back. This is my home."

Ronar stood blinking at this new development. Was he really about to accept a witch of Darteharn as a traveling companion? It seemed he was.

"Emogen, please prepare to leave. You will also need a horse."

At that she bit her lip. "I have no horse. What few horses we have are used as draft animals."

"She can use my pony," said Astil carelessly.

"What about you?" asked Ronar.

Astil shrugged. He raised his hand with fingers spread and stood poised for a few moments.

A faint sound of tinkling bells rose in the east, rapidly growing louder. Hoofbeats rang like deeper bells. An ethereal silver mare galloped into view, passing through the crowd as easily as a breeze, halting before Astil with her head lowered.

Sha Totek laughed. "You've had her following us all this time."

"I didn't have to. Moonmist was wise enough to follow me on her own. And you can stop scowling, Ronar. Moonmist can avoid attracting attention whenever she wants to."

A few minutes later, Emogen returned from her dwelling carrying a few small bundles which she tied to Astil's former mount. "What is this pony's name?" she asked.

"I didn't bother to ask," said Astil.

"I will get to know him and then decide what to call him. I'm ready to go."

"Farewell, Caradoc. I appreciate your courtesy. Maybe we'll meet again," said Ronar.

After a few more parting words, Ronar and his little band rode westward, crossing the river on a stone bridge, finally leaving Amulree and its people, to Ronar's relief.

Chapter Seven

The Watchmen

By now the day was well advanced. They rode a few miles, bypassing a swampy area with Emogen's help, then camped on a slight prominence which offered good forage for the animals and ample fuel. Ronar made a fire, then cooked a simple stew made from grain and some fresh vegetables he'd purchased in Amulree. Emogen watched in fascination as he prepared it, then gingerly ate it, keeping her eyes on him at all times. Ronar was about to ask her to stop staring when a doleful-looking Sha Totek spoke up.

"Ronar, Leonard, I know you have been puzzled by some of my recent behavior, and I wish to apologize for it."

Glad of the distraction, Ronar said, "You mean your crying episodes?"

"Yes. I cannot help them. It is the nature of my place on the emotional spectrum."

"What?"

"The Prism of Pandelume creates seven copies of the original. They are not identical. Each exemplifies one of the seven primary human emotions. My primary trait is sentimentality. Sha Totek selected me to represent him at the coronation knowing I would be moved by the ceremony."

"The ways of sorcery are strange," said Emogen.

"What about the other six copies?" asked Ronar.

"They could be recombined, or even dispelled with no loss to Sha Totek. Another result of this process is this: I am only one seventh as effective a wielder of magic as Sha Totek himself would be, if he were here. And as you know, even he is greatly reduced when away from the Tower. I explain it in these terms because I know you are fond of defining things as numbers."

"I don't understand that. You must know all the spells Sha Totek knows. Why can't you use them as effectively?"

The dispersion shrugged. "That's just the way the magic works. The stature of the magician also plays a role. I am used to encountering such seemingly arbitrary limitations."

Ronar turned suddenly to Emogen, who was watching him so intently that she jumped. "And what about you? What are you good for?"

"Oh, I'm a healer, as you've heard already. And you saw my other specialty. I'm good at seeing the truth behind people, who they really are. Besides that, there's the usual fertility spells, love charms, some weather influence, everything you'd expect from a village witch. I'd be surprised if I'm as powerful as even one seventh part of Imhotep, even a part who is overly emotional."

Somewhere in the darkness howled a wolf. One of the horses nickered uneasily.

"Emogen, are there any local animals we should fear? Or any monsters?" asked Ronar.

"Only the wolves, as far as I know, but they know and respect me. Monsters? Why should there be monsters here?"

"The army Namirnakh sent against the Bronze Portal was largely composed of monsters."

"Really?" she said incredulously. "What kind of monsters?"

"All kinds. Werewolves, vampires, devils, and others less easily defined."

"I find that hard to believe. I have never seen or heard of such things."

"It's true, child," said Sha Totek. "Have you ever heard of the land of Wauk?"

"No."

"It lies far to the west, between Darteharn and the sea, and is now only a narrow strip running up and down the coast. Before Darteharn was founded, it was inhabited by men whose ancestors were woodland natives of one of the continents of Earth. When Namirnakh and his followers were pushed over the Mynd Bannock, he found these people already occupying what is now Darteharn, and he crushed them, pushing them steadily westward, until they were left with only that coastal strip. Finally Namirnakh wiped them out entirely. It was the first time any of the cultures which migrated from Earth was ever wholly exterminated. Namirnakh then used the Waukwood as a breeding ground for monsters of all kinds. It is one of the worst places in the world, or was. Hard to say what's going on there now."

Emogen's mouth hung open in amazement. "That was all before my time. People like Caradoc have told me how things were while Namirnakh still ruled. He speaks only of how united we all were, how purposeful and proud."

"No offense to Caradoc, my dear, but older people sometimes remember only what was good about the world of their youth, not what was bad. I'm immune to this tendency myself, of course," said Sha Totek.

Emogen did not reply. Ronar looked at her and found her staring skyward. Following her gaze, he saw the small reddish moonlet formerly called the Eye of Ahriman, passing across the sky as an inconspicuous star.

Emogen resumed speaking in a small, breathless voice. "I was only a small girl when Ahriman fell silent and his Eye went dark."

"I didn't think you were even that old," muttered Ronar.

"I remember hearing his voice in my mind, feeling wanted and secure. I always imagined what wonders must exist up there in the heavens, on his Eye. I loved him then. I cried every night for a turn after he was gone, because my head was so quiet and lonely."

Ronar sat very still, his teeth clenched, making a stern effort not to order this polluted woman out from his presence.

"The Eye is dimmer than it used to be," said Astil.

"It's farther away now," said Ronar in a dangerous monotone. "It was never much more than a great airless rock."

"How would you know that?" asked Emogen, affronted.

"I have been there."

"What?"

"I have been there! Your precious god once swept me up there, where it made me its prisoner and tried to devour my mind." He was trembling, on the verge of fury.

"What did you do to make him so angry?"

Ronar whirled on her, his eyes ablaze. "I defied it! The first thing I experienced when I set foot on this world was that devil looking down on me, prying into my mind, trying to make me its own. After that I destroyed its followers wherever I found them, because they were usually in the process of corrupting or capturing innocents for their cause."

"You—you would have killed me too!" said Emogen, shaken.

"Yes. If I had found you still an active worshipper of Ahriman, I might well have killed you. But probably Ahriman would have pitted you against me first."

Ronar paused to see how this would affect her, but she only sat there gaping at him, her eyes huge and round. Ronar continued.

"Eventually I did my best to ignore the damned thing, but it would not permit it. It directed its lust against— against someone who I loved very much. It dirtied her, ruined her, and would have destroyed her, if not for her sublime strength of will. I could not then cease until I had seen that thing consigned to oblivion!"

Ronar's hands were clenched and working. The garnet ring sparked and smoldered. His breathing was fast; his heart pounded. The years seemed to fall away, until he was back in a place he did not care to visit again.

Emogen stared at him in horror and astonishment. "This woman you mention…she was not killed?"

"Her body died. But she made herself a goddess!"

At this, both Emogen and Astil sat back with round eyes.

"Which one?" asked Emogen.

"The one the Mersineans call Athene."

A great owl wafted over their heads, silent, its pale underside catching the firelight for a moment.

Emogen gasped. "I call her Brighid," she whispered. "I have prayed to her before, and she has answered."

"So have I," said Ronar.

"She was once human? And you knew her?"

"Yes. I was her teacher. I did not know her as well as I might have, or should have, but I knew her, as well as anyone did, or better."

I was a very young girl.

This quiet voice came from the air around them.

They eyed each other in silence, not daring to speak.

Emogen looked around in all directions, smiling, her eyes glistening.

The tension palpably decreased. From the corner of his eye, Ronar saw Sha Totek sag back with a look of exaggerated relief on his face.

They arranged themselves for sleep: Sha Totek in his colorful little pavilion, Ronar on the ground near the fire, and Astil prowling through the darkness beyond its light.

Emogen also spread her blankets near the fire, a little closer to Ronar than he would have preferred.

Ronar awoke to find the scarlet dome of Kudu climbing into a violet sky. The white knot of Photos did not follow; they had entered the Gloaming, the three-day period in which the larger sun concealed the smaller.

Emogen sat near the fire, brewing some sort of tea in a little copper pot. No one else was yet in evidence.

Emogen glanced at him and said, "If you have a mug, you may have some of this."

Ronar leaned over from his sleeping bag and fished in one of his bags for his camp cup, which he had carefully preserved for many years. Emogen took it and examined it.

"This metal is strange. Very light."

"It's called *aluminum*. It is not used on Colibdis."

Emogen nearly dropped the cup and her pot alike. "You mean this cup is from Earth?"

"Yes, it is."

"You are a very surprising man. Where is Earth?"

Ronar thought about the disposition of the constellations for a moment, then pointed into the sky. "Out there. Very far off. It's in the Whirlpool."

"Why have I never seen it? It must be very small."

"It is considerably larger than Colibdis. There the air is thicker, objects are heavier, and there is only one sun in the sky. You have no basis for understanding how far away it really is. From here it is less than a bug on a distant mountainside." He accepted the tea. "Thank you." He sipped it, finding it had a smoky, green flavor.

Sha Totek poked his head out of his tent. "Not drinking that witch's brew, are you, Ronar? I heard her muttering something about newts or flipperpricks last night."

Ronar compressed his lips, resisting the urge to spray the drink into the fire. Instead he swallowed and said, "It's only tea."

Emogen turned to scowl at Sha Totek, who was laughing.

"That's right, it's tea, so you just keep quiet. What's a newt?"

"It's a small, slimy Earth animal which never found its way to Colibdis. Witches there used to enjoy turning their victims into them, or so I've heard."

"I don't turn anyone into anything, though if such a spell were to present itself, I would be tempted to learn it."

They ate, packed, and were on their way before Kudu was well clear of the horizon. The Gloaming brought chill, and the chill often brought clouds, but so far the sky remained clear, which lent more glamour to the landscape than gloom. As they rode along, Ronar could not help noticing how the warm light glowed in Emogen's hair and on her pale skin.

The next range of the Mynd Bannock which confronted them was indeed more formidable than the last. Their path climbed steadily toward a notch which might more correctly be called a chasm, narrow and steep-walled. When they entered it, the hoofbeats of their horses could he heard echoing from the walls, except those of Moonmist, who flowed along in an eerie silence. The walls blocked the sun, leaving only the purple light of the sky to bounce its way down from one side to the next.

They rode beside what had once must been the bed of a swift and turbulent stream, but which now carried only a trickle. When they halted for a midday meal, Ronar examined this water, detecting a musty scent that seemed familiar, but which he could not place. He also found traces of recent passages through this ravine: rocks which had been overturned, and torn vegetation.

The sound of falling rocks echoed from around the next curve in the ravine.

"Be watchful, everyone," muttered Ronar. "I think we may not be—"

A flurry of unpleasant sounds interrupted: the hiss and *thunk* of an arrow; a shriek from Emogen; a gurgle from Sha Totek. From close at hand came the vibrating *spang* of a released bowstring: Astil had released an arrow. A body fell from the dim heights far above, crashing into the rill beside Astil. Ronar ran over to it, recognizing the raiment of a warrior of Eranior. He looked up and spied another archer, who was just about to send an arrow at Astil. The oblivious Elf was staring at the body of his victim.

Ronar yelled and flung out his right hand, trying to shield Astil. He succeeded; the arrow pierced his hand and dropped to the ground after bouncing harmlessly off Astil's chest, its energy exhausted. The Elf looked at Ronar in amazement.

"You up there!" roared Ronar. "Stop firing! We are not your enemies!"

Awaiting either an answer or a further attack, Ronar looked around and saw Sha Totek clawing at the arrow which pierced his throat. Blood sprayed from his mouth as he tried to breathe. His eyes bulged out in terror. Emogen ran to him and eased him to the ground.

"Who are you then? Speak!" This challenge came from around the bend.

"I am Leonard Ronar, the king of Eranior!"

That provoked laughter. "Indeed? And I am—well, I am also the King of Eranior. Do not move, any of you. We have other archers on these cliffs. We will see who you are."

Five men bearing spears and bronze swords emerged from the dimness, halting a few paces away. Their leader surveyed the scene, noted his fallen comrade with a pained look, looked at Ronar, and said, "You are the one who claims to be King?"

"I am."

"The last I heard, Greylock and the King of Eranior were two separate people."

"Until recently, they were. But things have changed. Now we are the same."

"If you are Greylock, show me the sword."

Ronar raised his left hand and invoked the sword, its light and clamor shocking the brooding quiet of the gorge.

"The Sword of Bran," said Ronar. His other hand was beginning to feel as though it were dipped in fire.

The soldiers goggled at it. "Very well. How will you prove you are also King?"

"He is the king," said Astil.

Ronar reached into his jacket with his bleeding hand and hooked out the Royal Torc. He flipped it at the leader, causing blood to spin from it as it flew.

"Do you recognize that?"

The leader nodded, wide-eyed and confused. His men were equally astonished.

"Who then are these others? My lord? And what—"

Ronar let the sword lapse. "That can wait. First I will see to this man you have shot, who is the sorcerer Imhotep, whom you call the Gatekeeper." He went and knelt beside Emogen, who had the dispersion's head cradled on her lap. She had already cut the arrow and drawn out the ends, leaving Sha Totek with two profusely bleeding wounds. Ronar looked into the dispersion's clammy face. He was mute. The sound of his breath was a horrible wet sucking. The look in his eyes was more than enough to convey his pain and fear.

"I don't think he can help himself if he cannot speak," said Ronar.

"You are *king* of *Eranior*?" hissed Emogen.

"Yes, I thought you already knew that. Can you help him?"

She glanced at his hand. "I can help you both. But him first."

Ronar nodded and stood, approaching the soldiers. "What is your name?" he asked of the leader.

"I am Bari, captain of the watchers of this pass."

"What are you doing so far into Darteharn?"

"This is our accustomed station in recent times. The valley to the east offers no threat, so we ignore it. We bypass Amulree and the other villages there, and they know nothing of us, being nothing but farmers and herdsmen."

"I see. Have you heard nothing of what has happened in Eranior?"

"No, Lord Greylock, we have not."

Ronar briefly described the circumstances which had led to his kingship and their presence here. "This is Astil-Cotavion, a prince of Faerie. The woman is Emogen."

"My lord, if you insist on venturing further into Darteharn, it is our duty to accompany you, especially given the trouble we have already caused you."

"There's no way you could have expected to find us here. You are not at fault. How much do you and your men know of what lies further to the west?"

"Very little, I'm afraid. This is our station, and we rarely go beyond it."

"What have you seen here?"

"Nothing of any consequence, for as long as any of us have been here, except for you and your party. Well, sometimes great birds wheel overhead."

Ronar clutched his injured hand to his chest. "I will speak with you again later."

He staggered over to Emogen and Sha Totek. Sha Totek presented a terrible sight. His pallid face was streaked with tears, while his neck and much of his upper body was covered with blood. His eyes locked onto Ronar's, full of fear and pleading.

Emogen had sliced a small brown apple in two, and had placed a half over each wound on Sha Totek's throat.

"This is how I would heal a minor injury," she whispered, "but these are not minor, and it will not be enough. Ronar. Please bring me four white candles from my green bag."

Ronar fumbled though the bag with his good hand. He discovered a variety of candles, selected four plain white ones, and carried them to Emogen, feeling somewhat lightheaded as he did so.

"Now arrange them around us, at the cardinal points."

Ronar set them up around the witch and the sorcerer.

"Good. Now light the one on the east."

Lacking time and manual dexterity, he lit it using the crimson glare from his magic ring, stopping short of letting the sword actually materialize.

Emogen began an incantation.

Candle glow, cast your light,
to the confines of the dawn.
Undo harm, make things right,
pain and injury begone.

She waved toward the candle on the south, which Ronar lit.

Candle shine, bright as moon,
where the suns ride high at noon.
Withdraw pain, quiet fear,
health and wellness reappear.

Ronar lit the western candle.

Candle bright, cast your glow,
where the suns go down below.
Bring back strength, restore vigor,
spare this man from death's cold rigor.

Finally Ronar lit the northern candle.

Candle flare, shed your light
on the dark things of the night.
Cast out death, mend flesh and bone,
Leave life and happiness alone.

A white light began to flow from Emogen onto Sha Totek.

Four candles light arise!
Flame up high, flame up bright.
All pain and injury excise!
Darkness, death, and weakness smite.

She repeated this verse a number of times. Each time the light from both the candles and her own body grew brighter. Astil drew nearer, taking in the glow.

But Emogen was distressed, and Sha Totek shuddered but did not improve.

"It is not good to attempt this spell during the Gloaming," said Emogen, panting. "Not does it help that this is far from an ordinary man. He is like glass; the magic shines right through him. Ronar. The goddess Brighid. When you knew her as a mortal girl, what was her name?"

Ronar swallowed, and pronounced the name with reluctance.

"Asterope."

The word was like a spell in its own right. It brought a moment of silence, a brief uncanny stillness.

Emogen nodded.

Brighid, Athene, Asterope pale,
We call upon you, do not fail.
Stave off death and heal wounds,
Grant us please this godly boon.

The light grew still brighter, and clarified, until it was in no way dazzling, but illuminating, showing everything in perfect detail, a radiance divine in every sense.

The wounds on Sha Totek's throat closed. Ronar gasped and looked at his own hand. The hole that pierced it wove itself closed as he watched.

The light faded. All within the chasm was as before. Somewhere nearby a small bird sang its song.

There was a roll of thunder. The ground shook, and rocks bounced down from the canyon walls.

"I believe that was her way of telling us not to call upon her again," said Ronar when the tumult had subsided.

Sha Totek coughed and buried his face in Emogen's breast, sobbing. "Thank you, thank you. You are a very fine witch. Thank you."

Emogen looked up at Ronar in embarrassment.

"You are a very fine witch," said Ronar, rather more calmly. "Rest."

"Will we take these soldiers with us from here?"

"I don't think so. I think we will soon encounter situations where ordinary men, however brave they may be, can do little except die. Rest now."

Ronar returned to Bari and his men, who stood in a compact group, shaking and wide-eyed.

"That was a mighty magic, Lord King," said Bari, his voice quavering.

Ronar nodded. "Bari, send two of your men back to Eranior to report our progress. A man called Gahareet is my Steward. Tell your men to go carefully, for the men of Amulree may not be as unwary as you think."

"Yes, Lord Greylock. And are the rest of us to accompany you?"

"No, I want you to remain here on station."

Bari looked uncomfortable and said, "Lord Ronar, you may think us useless because we are only men, not wizards, fairies, or heroes such as yourselves. Let us not mention the fact that we shot you. But we are not wholly to be despised. We have remained on duty here for many moonturns on end, steadfast. Eranior has lost two kings in recent days, and we would not wish to lose a third because we were left behind."

Bari's speech made Ronar ashamed of his dismissal of him and his men. "Captain, your willingness to go still deeper into Darteharn with us shows your courage plainly. But remain here, and be prepared. It may well be that whatever we find will drive us back this way. If so, you must be ready to defend our lives."

Bari bowed his head. "Very well, my lord."

Chapter Eight

Ronaryana

Emogen threw the remnants of her candles into the little stream, then offered prayers and blessings for the fallen soldier. Two of Bari's men used a litter to carry the body away to the east, where they could bury it in soft earth and not in this rocky gorge, before continuing on their mission to Eranior.

Bari and his remaining men led Ronar and his party a little farther west to an inconspicuous trail that wound precipitously up the north side of the canyon. The three mortal horses were reluctant to attempt this highly exposed path, until Astil whispered something to Moonmist, who in turn communicated something to the other horses, which persuaded them to follow. After a climb of a few hundred feet they reached a shelf where the Eranians maintained their primary camp and vantage point.

There they ate, cooking over a fire pit which was ingeniously baffled to prevent its light from being seen from below, or from shining on the walls of the canyon. They shared their humble rations with the soldiers, whose even more meager fare was an embarrassment to Ronar. He somehow felt responsible for their poor living conditions, though he had not been their king for very long.

As if to make up for his weak performance earlier, Sha Totek passed around some of his favored delicacies, which he'd purchased at a Thunderbird bakery on his way north, and since carefully hoarded.

Night fell, and the sorcerer retreated to his pavilion, which occupied almost half of the platform. Most of the soldiers retired to their hut, leaving a few to keep watch from other stations. That left Ronar and Emogen alone at the fire, at least until Astil crept up and crouched beside Ronar, to his surprise.

"I wish to thank you, Lord Ronar, for your sacrifice earlier in saving me. I had never killed anyone before, so I admit my vigilance was lax as I pondered what I had done. Without your action, that arrow would have found its way into my heart. I thank you."

"That's all right, Astil. I didn't bring you here to get you killed. I also know how it feels to kill, especially that first time."

Astil bowed his head and vanished into the night.

Ronar and Emogen sat in silence for a while. Ronar brooded as he poked at the fire with a stick, still shaken by the near-death of Sha Totek. He knew this was not the real Sha Totek, and was indeed a relatively weak and foolish thing. The true Sorcerer was safe in his Tower far away. Still, the sight of the life draining from his dispersion had seemed to Ronar uniquely terrible. To Ronar, Sha Totek practically *was* Colibdis. He was one of the very first men ever to reach it, and he'd watched over it ever since. If a planet could have a soul, it was Sha Totek. It was hard to imagine one without the other.

So intent was he upon this thought that he was startled when Emogen spoke.

"Ronar. Please tell me."

"Tell you what?"

"Tell me why the goddess, who was your friend and your love, would not want you to call upon her now."

Ronar was almost glad of the distraction, even for this reason.

"We—had a falling out. A quarrel. More than one, actually."

"Tell me."

Ronar looked at her. Her eyes were round and open, and bore no trace of darkness or ill intent.

"It started not long after her transfiguration. I learned that something of value to me, a ship I'd been given, had been stolen by the dwellers of the city of Ashelak, which lies on the slopes of a great volcano, very far to the southeast of here. These creatures had been followers of your god Ahriman, and wished to revenge themselves upon me for destroying him. I resolved to recover this ship, and set out from Thunderbird, first on horseback and then on foot when I tired of the beast. I crossed first a wilderness, and then the land of Assuria, and then entered the land of Varma, just over halfway to my goal.

"In Varma I came upon a band of *Rakshasa* demons attacking a group of travelers in a mountain pass. You probably haven't heard of the *Rakshasa*. These creatures are manlike, fanged and clawed, very strong, and skilled at magic and deception. Luckily, they know nothing of tactics, and tend to attack their foes in ones and twos. If they acted in concert they would be truly dangerous. Using my usual sword tricks I was able to surprise the demons and kill most of them. One or two escaped. I also carried an exotic Earth weapon at that time, against which they had no real defense. Still, the only person to survive their attack was a young woman, a princess of one of the many small states of Varma. Her name was Taralalita.

"Instead of thanking me, she brazenly demanded that I escort her home to the kingdom of her father, a fair distance out of my way, seeing as I had failed to save the rest of her party. For some perverse reason I gave in to her nagging, though ultimately it would have been better for me, and maybe even for her, if I had left her to the demons. We descended the mountains into the jungles and fields of Varma's lowlands.

"During the journey she delighted in tormenting me. She mocked me at every opportunity, making many unreasonable demands, and was in general extremely annoying. She was the opposite of Asterope in every way: vain; spoiled; petulant; materialistic; and silly. We encountered various dangers, and I fought off further attempts on Taralalita, which led me to observe that someone was intent on capturing her, not killing her. Athene sometimes appeared to offer advice and minor assistance, and to chide me for my interest in Taralalita. Of course she could have snapped her fingers and resolved the situation at once, but she knew better than to compromise my self-determination that way.

"The confrontations between Athene and Taralalita were sometimes amusing, but Tarala was badly outmatched, despite all her airs and bluster."

"Why were you interested in this girl Taralalita?"

Ronar shrugged uncomfortably. "She was exotic, and strange to me, and challenging, and very beautiful. I suppose I was interested in her because I was a man. Anyway, the wizard-king who had sent the demons eventually succeeded in taking her from beneath my nose. I was able with some difficulty to retrieve her from that king's palace. It was a splendid place, all marble walls, lacy filigree, and lavender domes shining like pearls, similar to the Mughul architecture of Earth, though of course that means nothing to you.

"Again I did not receive the gratitude I expected. She laughed at me. She told me I could no longer hope to claim her virginity, because the king and his demons had seen to that. Of course I'd had no intention of claiming it in the first place. We resumed our journey, still pursued and harried. Her taunts became more cruel. She began to insult my manhood, claiming the reason for my forbearance toward her was that I was unable to take her as a man."

"And why did you resist her allure?"

Ronar paused, wondering at his willingness to disclose so much to this witch of Darteharn. He had never before spoken so much of this to anyone, but he did not wish to delve into the introspection needed to answer her question. Still, he said, "Asterope, or Athene, was watching. Asterope, whom I had never touched. I did not wish her to see me indulging my baser desires with this lesser woman." He plunged on.

"Eventually I reached the end of my endurance and committed a most shameful act. I attacked Tarala. I assaulted her. I raped her.

"Athene then appeared to me in wrath, for if she held Taralalita in contempt, she hated my crime against her still more. I could offer no defense. Athene departed in a cold fury."

Ronar found that he was no longer able to look Emogen in the eye.

"My deed left me mortified. I vowed that from then on I would treat Tarala with much greater care and circumspection, regardless of what provocations she might offer."

"That's certainly the least you could do," said Emogen.

Ronar's face burned.

"As for Taralalita herself, if I expected her to treat me with even greater disdain after that, I was quite wrong. In fact, she grew quiet and submissive, and clung to me. I eventually decided she was the sort of woman who must test every man. Any man who treated her with deference she held in contempt. She probed and abused until she provoked a response. Then she was satisfied. She wished to be dominated and overcome. Anything less she interpreted as weakness."

Emogen cocked an eyebrow but did not object to this interpretation.

"We finally won our way to her home. At first her father wanted to execute me, but when Tarala revealed she was pregnant, he instead insisted I marry her, and take the soiled creature away, so he could forget her and the shame she had brought him.

"I did marry her."

Emogen was startled. "What happened to her?"

Ronar looked into a black well of grief, still yawning wide despite the passage of so many years.

"She died in childbirth. With her final breath she called me Rama, and I called her Sita. These are names of great import in her culture. The child—which I made sure she never saw—did not survive for very long. I should have known better. I did know better. I had actually hoped her child was not mine, but belonged instead to that wizard-king, or even to a *Rakshasa*, but it was mine. My seed was tainted long ago. This I will not discuss any further."

Emogen was silent for some time, staring into the fire. Finally she looked up and spoke again.

"Did you ever recover your ship?"

"I did, for whatever that was worth. The price I paid for it was very high. For some time after that I was scarcely human. I became most grim, a killing machine, merciless to anything that got in my way. I fought and killed recklessly, with little regard for my own life as well."

"What happened then?"

"I took my time in returning to Thunderbird. First I spent some time on an uninhabited island in the southern ocean, trying to reconstruct myself. When I believed I was once again fit for human company I went back to Thunderbird, where I found once again that its hopeful, loyal people had not given me up for dead.

"Eventually I married Flora, the woman who looked after my house. She too was unlike Asterope, albeit in different ways. She was gentle, kind, patient, and not especially intelligent. Athene also scorned her. I made sure Flora bore no child of mine. I am happy to say that Flora died peacefully in her sleep, and that while she lived she was somehow content."

"Did you love her?"

Ronar hesitated. "I felt a great affection for her. At times I still miss her quiet voice and her smile. I honor her memory. But no, I felt no great passion for her. I have always hoped she gained more than she lost in marrying me."

"I wonder why the goddess seemed so opposed to your happiness."

"Asterope was a Mersinean girl, and Athene a Mersinean goddess. Neither was a typical example of her breed, but both were Mersinean at heart. Therefore they could be perverse, and proud, and prone to jealousy."

Somewhere nearby an owl cried out in anger.

"And also prone to eavesdropping."

"Are you likely to rape me, Ronar?"

Ronar felt that question like a blow, but he knew it was justified.

"I am nearly forty six turns old."

"Yes, I've already heard that mentioned, I think. You don't look a day over thirty. But that doesn't answer my question. I will answer it myself. You have the look of a cruel, hard man, with your cold grey eyes and fierce brow. Hard you may be, but not cruel. I do not believe you will rape me."

"Thank you."

Well, that's something, thought Ronar. *The witch of Darteharn deems me a trustworthy companion.*

Chapter Nine

The Wall

Ronar roused his party at first light, no easy matter in Sha Totek's case. They took their leave of Bari and his men, descended from the ledge, and continued eastward through the gorge.

They rode though the dimness of the Gloaming without incident for several hours. The gorge gradually straightened, permitting them to see farther along its length. As the day advanced, their distant view became blocked by a great cliff or precipice of some kind. Either the chasm turned sharply to run along this wall, or it was a serious barrier to their further progress.

Ronar's viewer revealed a nearly sheer rock face pocked with dark openings or caves which seemed to conform to distinct levels or strata in the stone.

Dusk caught them before they could get close enough to make out anything more. For some reason Ronar did not want to camp in view of that wall, and no one argued with him. They selected a site behind a spur of rock and set up their camp while maintaining a cautious silence through unspoken agreement.

At full darkness Ronar and Astil stepped out from behind their concealment to study the wall. It was visible only as a black silhouette before a starry sky.

Suddenly a point of yellow light appeared on the featureless blackness. It moved slowly toward the right, and then vanished after traversing a short distance.

"What the hell?" muttered Ronar.

A few minutes later, a second light appeared, this one lower down, and moving to the left.

The next time he saw one, Ronar raised his viewer. In the few seconds it was visible, he made out that it was a flame.

No more lights appeared for several minutes. When one did, Ronar quickly aimed the viewer and turned on its image amplification feature. Now he saw a man carrying a torch, walking past one of the openings or niches in the face of the wall. He was pulling something like a child's toy wagon, in which was an object that looked like a large leather sack. Ronar could not help smiling in satisfaction at the capabilities of his viewer.

"What do you suppose is in those sacks those people are towing?" whispered Astil.

"I don't know," said Ronar, slightly crestfallen. "I think they might be miners of some kind."

They watched the torches pass back and forth for a while longer, and then retreated to their camp. It was too dark to explore further without using a light, and no one thought revealing themselves was a good idea.

Ronar slept fitfully, uncomfortably aware of the proximity of something he did not understand.

Morning brought the third and final day of the Gloaming. Ronar crept up and cautiously observed the wall for a while. Even with his viewer, he did not see anyone passing through the openings. That emboldened him enough to explore a bit more closely, leaving the others behind. He soon found that the ravine did not terminate at the wall, but instead gave onto another valley running north and south, with the wall acting as its western boundary.

This valley was narrow and rocky, and extended as far as he could see. They could not travel it in either direction without being in full view of the wall, even at night. The wall was uniformly tall, sheer, and unbroken except for those high windows or galleries.

Ronar used the viewer to examine the nearer base of the wall. He found a large closed gate. Not far from it was an opening from which emerged the waters feeding the little trickle in the chasm.

Ronar returned to the camp and addressed his companions. "From here our path becomes uncertain. That wall is a serious obstacle, and there's no way of knowing how far it extends. I've never seen anything like it. It appears to contain tunnels and passages which are inhabited by men. I saw a gate and a low opening for water. If I were alone here, I would scale the wall to one of the higher windows, and then enter and look for a way through to the west. It would be a difficult climb, which I'm not sure we're all up to attempting."

"The horses certainly aren't," said Astil.

"Yes, the horses. We won't be able to bring them in there with us, however we may enter. I think it's time we sent them back."

The other three emitted various moans of disappointment.

"Just a moment," said Astil. "Horses or no horses, you propose we enter an unknown system of passageways or caves, which we know to be inhabited, hoping we can sneak through to continue our journey on the other side?"

"Yes."

"I have a better idea. Why not attract their attention, and ask them if we may pass though?"

"What?"

"You've already said it seems to be a mine, and nothing of a martial nature. We've observed that Darteharn no longer appears to be organized for war, at least not the parts we've seen. Who can say that this gate you saw is not maintained to permit travelers to pass the barrier? If we try to skulk our way through, we will almost certainly be discovered and treated as enemies. If we instead ask permission, what then? Even if they issue forth to kill us, we will at least have a head start and a chance to escape on our horses."

"The boy makes some good points," said Sha Totek.

"It is a good analysis," said Ronar. He had, he admitted to himself, been thinking as though he were alone, when he could expect to simply sneak or fight his way past any obstacle.

"I'll go talk to them," said Emogen. "I'm of Darteharn, and probably don't look very threatening."

"No," said Ronar. "If anyone is to go, it will be me. I won't expose you to whatever danger may exist."

"Will you go now?"

"I will wait. No one is visible there now, and I want them to see my approach, so I may gauge their intentions."

They spent an uneasy day waiting for dusk. Then Ronar emerged from hiding carrying a torch. As he crossed the half mile of broken ground between himself and the gate, another torch appeared at one of the lower windows, and then two more. They vanished abruptly when he had only a few hundred yards yet to cross. Then a loud cracking sound echoed though the valley. Ronar looked around for the source of the danger, then was relieved to see dust puffing out from around the joints of the stone gate, which slowly opened with a creak and a rumble. A torch appeared there, and a voice emerged, stern and frightened at the same time.

"You out there! Who are you, and what do you wish?"

"I have come from easternmost Darteharn. I seek passage for myself and my friends."

"Come closer, and quickly! I have no time to waste."

Ronar covered the remaining ground, halting before a man who stood at the base of stairs which led through the gate and into darkness. He was scrawny and sallow, his hair filthy and matted, and he was naked except for a few rags. He gave off the same vaguely familiar musky odor which Ronar remembered from the water.

"It has been many turns since anyone sought to pass through here." He looked Ronar up and down. His eyebrows shot up. "You are the one they call Greylock, are you not?"

Ronar fell back and began to summon the sword. At the sight of the ring's scarlet light the man cried hoarsely "No! No! We mean you no harm."

Ronar aborted the sword's appearance. "How do you know who I am?"

"Even here we have heard stories, and how many like you can there be in the world? You wish to pass through this place? We will gladly permit it." He appeared oddly excited, even eager, though fretful, always glancing over his shoulder. "With whom do you travel?"

Ronar stared at this man for a few moments, and then answered. "The sorcerer Imhotep, an Elf, and a young witch of Darteharn."

The man's eyes grew even wider. "Indeed? Indeed. A small party, yet formidable. Yes, we will gladly let you pass."

"Also four horses."

"Horses? No, no horses." The man gave a brittle, uneasy laugh, and looked again over his shoulder. "Unless you have horses who can climb stairs and fit through narrow passageways. No horses. Now I must return to my employer. I have no more time. Come back with your friends at dawn, and I will arrange for the gate to be opened. Goodbye!" He dashed back into the shadows, where Ronar had a glimpse of him turning a huge crank which slowly closed the gate.

Ronar blinked, frowned, and returned to the camp.

"Well?" said Astil.

"They will allow us passage."

"Excellent."

"They know who we are. Or they know who I and Sha Totek are, at any rate."

"That is less excellent, I would say, is it not?" said Sha Totek.

"How did that happen?" asked Emogen.

"The man I spoke to said he recognized me from stories."

Emogen giggled. "I also heard such stories when I was a girl. More than once, my mother threatened to feed me to Greylock if I didn't behave."

"He also said the passage is impractical for horses."

Three faces fell at those words.

"Oh well," said Emogen. "My pony is a dear beast, but my fanny will be happier for not riding him. Too bad I never thought of a name for him."

By firelight they sorted through their baggage, choosing what was most essential and arranging it into packs small enough to carry. Ronar wound up packing three times as much as anyone else, followed by, he was annoyed to note, Emogen. Astil and Sha Totek burdened themselves only lightly.

Ronar awoke at first light to find Astil again whispering to Moonmist. The Elf horse then led the other three back down the canyon, carrying that part of the baggage which their riders could not manage. Moonmist and Emogen's mount cast mournful glances over their shoulders before disappearing into the dim distance.

"I hope this is a good idea," said Astil.

"So do I," said Ronar.

They roused the other two, ate quickly, and assembled their packs. When they were all in place they stood around looking at each other uneasily for a few moments, except for Emogen, who appeared blithely unconcerned.

"Are you not at all nervous, my dear?" asked Sha Totek.

"No. Why should I be? It's just a mine. Maybe it will be interesting."

"Well, let's go," said Ronar.

They trudged out into the rapidly rising light, proof enough that Photos had emerged from behind Kudu during the night. Soon the gate loomed before them, looking not very inviting. They mounted the stairs. The gate creaked open slightly as they approached. A torch-bearing figure shuffled out, as decrepit as the one Ronar had met the day before, or even perhaps the same one.

"Come in, come in quickly. Are we all here? Good, good."

They filed into the dark antechamber just beyond the gate. The man placed his torch into a bracket. "I am

Mylor." He looked at Ronar. "Please, my friend, help me close the gate."

Ronar grabbed the levers of the capstan that controlled the gate and wound it shut with little difficulty. The stench which Ronar associated with the place now had no competition from the outside air.

"You are strong, very good," said Mylor. "Now, you wish to pass through. Follow me, but you must all do everything I say. First, you must be quiet at all times. Second, you must be prepared to freeze in place at a moment's notice, making no noise at all. Whatever you see, you must remain silent. Follow me."

"Mylor, what is going on in here?"

"Oh, I can relate that as we go along, but we must not dally. Come now." He made his way to a steep, narrow tunnel carved into the stone, starting up it on bare feet so calloused and worn they looked barely human. Ronar also noticed a number of puncture wounds running up his arms and his back, some not healed.

Ronar felt Emogen's hand on his arm as the others started up the tunnel. He hung back a bit, looked into her face, and lowered his head so she could whisper to him.

"Ronar. That man is a slave."

Ronar nodded and muttered "Come."

The tunnel floor was slippery and no easy climb. Eventually they emerged into a long, straight corridor which was illuminated at intervals by daylight streaming in from outside.

"We'll follow this outside corridor for a while," said Mylor. "Not much traffic here at this time of day."

Indeed it appeared deserted. They passed many cross corridors leading further into the mountain, and also several of the windows they had noted from the outside. As they passed these they looked longingly at the clean, bright world outside. Debris was scattered in the niches of these windows, including fragments of what looked like giant eggshells.

Ronar eased up to the front of Mylor's line of followers. "Mylor, are you the same man I met yesterday?" he asked.

"No, no, that was Ramagen. I regret to say he is being punished by his employer for being away too long."

"And what of your employer, Mylor?"

The old man's face looked ghastly in the mixture of cold skylight leaking in from outside and the red flickers of his torch.

"I—I—I have killed him! Yes, I have killed him. It was the only way I could get away long enough to guide you. No doubt they will find me soon, and then that will be the end of me. No doubt others are being made to suffer terribly, even now. Yet we cannot waste this opportunity."

"What opportunity?"

"For you to free us."

"Free you from who?"

"You shall see, soon enough. Come, we must now take this path. I regret to say you will not see daylight again for some time."

"Wait a minute. Nobody said anything about freeing you. We have a mission of our own."

Mylor halted and looked into Ronar's eyes. "When you understand the depth of our misery, I think you will free us, if half the stories about you are true."

Ronar looked back at his companions, who returned various looks of trepidation. Nevertheless, they followed

Mylor into a narrow, stinking tunnel hewn into rock, away from the sunlit world outside.

They passed many cross corridors and slanted tunnels leading up or down to other levels. The stonework grew more crude the deeper they penetrated into the mountain, until the floors were no longer properly flat and the ceilings were only irregular slabs set at odd angles. Liquids puddled in depressions on the floor. No one cared to determine what they were.

A trundling sound emerged from a cross corridor a short distance ahead. Mylor poked his head around the corner, then scuttled back with a look of terror. "You must all stand here in this niche until they pass!" he hissed. "Make no sound. Do not move. Our lives depend on this."

He pushed them into a widened area of the corridor, slid in with them, and froze.

A woman, carrying the usual torch, appeared from the cross corridor. She was perhaps younger than Mylor, but was as poorly clad and groomed, and just as dejected. She glanced at them as she turned into their corridor, but then averted her eyes. She was pulling a wooden wagon similar to the one Ronar and Astil had already glimpsed. In it lay…

Suddenly Ronar remembered where he had experienced this stench before. The thing in that little wagon was no leather sack, though it resembled one superficially. It was a fat brown worm with a covering of leathery plates, perhaps four feet in length. A pair of blunt-tipped tentacles lay curled against its body. Its body pulsed and throbbed.

Yes, Ronar had seen these things before. He knew it as a Dusk Rider.

The woman drew abreast of them and began to pass. Her wagon was now about two feet from their knees. The worm stank.

Emogen emitted a tiny quaver of fear and revulsion.

The thing reacted by raising one of its tentacles. An inch-long black claw protruded from its end. The worm drove it into the lower back of its slave. She dropped the handle of the wagon and arched her back, throwing back her head. She stood trembling, her mouth open and working, her hands raised, making futile gestures.

"N—no, no, I see no one. No one is here. There is no one. There is no one. Oh, gods help me. Yes, yes, there are strangers. Yes, and Mylor as well."

The other tentacle lifted up, questing.

That was enough for Ronar. The ring flashed and rang, and the Cold Sword appeared in his grip. His first swing severed the tentacle that was attached to the woman, the second the other tentacle, while the third blow cut the worm into two wet sections which jerked and spasmed, shattering the wagon as it died.

Emogen leaned forward with a cry and yanked the claw out of the slave woman's back.

Mylor gave a mad, wild laugh. "Oh, may the gods grant I should see such a sight a thousand times over!"

The woman flung herself at Ronar, fell to her knees, and clung to his legs, weeping while blood ran down her naked back. Emogen knelt beside her and took her in her arms.

The two segments of the worm continued to writhe. Sha Totek leaned out into the corridor and vomited into the ruins of the wagon.

Ronar kept the sword in his hands. "Mylor. We will not leave this spot until you explain what this place is. Sha Totek, get a grip on yourself."

"Yes, yes," said Mylor, "though I don't know how long we'll have before their retribution begins. Here is our tale. That thing you slew came from the depths of the world, where for long ages their kind has preyed upon other dwellers of the deep hollows, feeding upon them and mastering their bodies. When the Lord Namirnakh learned of their existence, he conceived of a use for them. He made them allies of a sort, employing their ability to usurp the bodies of the creatures of the upper world, as well as the lower. They could even enslave the greatest Birds of the air, the Teratorns. Being easily burned by sunlight, they were called..."

"Dusk Riders," said Ronar. "Yes, some of us have encountered them before."

"Indeed? Well, Namirnakh sent men to hew out this warren of tunnels to assist the worms. We wrangled their bird-hosts, fed them, saw to their breeding, and did any number of things which they themselves could not readily do. The open niches on the outside wall were once nesting places for Teratorns, as well as ventilators for the mountain. The work was never pleasant for us, but we were rewarded adequately, and if we worked well we would eventually be released to return to more pleasant surroundings.

"All was well until shortly before Namirnakh's downfall. At that time a lone Teratorn fell upon us, a devil-bird if ever there was one. With savage beak and talon that War-Bird attacked those of its own kind that were ridden and controlled by worms, tearing at the Riders, ripping them loose, casting them down. Only a few Birds survived this violent separation, but those that did added to the rebellion. Before we could properly react, all the Teratorns were either dead or freed, and that was the end of the Dusk Riders.

"The worms, however, did not wish to give up their easy lives, and so they enslaved us. Without Namirnakh to free us, so it has been in all the turns since. They are unable to fully master our bodies, thank goodness, and we are in any case too weak to carry them on our backs for any length of time. But they can put us to many other uses, and they do."

"How could they enslave you all?" asked Astil. "We have just seen that they are not difficult to kill, though it seems to take a while for the fact of their deaths to sink into their repulsive brains."

"They too can kill, if given warning," answered Mylor. "When they decided to enslave us, they first gathered together a large number of our wives, children, and the weaker men. Somewhere down below they are still confined, guarded, and kept as hostages. The worms already know one of their number has been murdered. I do not know exactly how they will react. Perhaps the hostages are already dead. But a few of us decided we could not ignore the coming of you four heroes, sent by whatever gods remain to free us from our bondage."

"They cannot see?" asked Ronar, ignoring the issue of whether they had in fact been sent to free anyone.

"No, unless they are attached to and commanding some beast, they cannot see. They are parasites, designed to take advantage of the faculties of other creatures. But they can hear, and understand our speech. They can also sense any slight tremor in the ground. And they can communicate with us as you saw, by driving in that claw, which somehow inserts their thoughts into our minds, if not their will."

"What does that other tube do?"

Mylor shuddered. "That—is for feeding."

"All right, Mylor. If we're to help you, here's how it's going to be. First, you must escort us to a secure western exit via the most direct and safest path available. We'll fight our way there if need be, but there we must go. There we will leave Emogen. She is no warrior, and I will not risk harm to her."

Mylor appeared nonplussed. "But—if I do that, what is to prevent you from abandoning us?"

"The fact that I tell you we will not," thundered Ronar. "And if you again question my word, you risk a wrath worse than anything these slugs can offer."

Mylor raised his hands. "So be it, Lord Greylock. I see the stories about you do not exaggerate. Let us go."

"Wait," said Emogen, who still knelt beside the dead worm's ex-slave. "I have healing to do here, and then this woman shall come with us, to the outside. What is your name, dear?"

"Corey."

Ronar nodded. "While you work at that, I'm going to carry the remains of this thing back to one of those windows and pitch it out. No sense letting the other worms know what has happened here. The rest of you wait here."

He released the sword. The worm-slime which had coated it splattered to the floor. He set down his pack, then managed to scoop up the remains of the cart and both halves of the worm into his arms, a heavy and awkward burden.

Despite the gross and stinking thing he carried, he was almost relieved to be away from the others for a few minutes. For a while he could pretend he had no responsibilities to anyone else, no duties to perform, no mission to achieve.

The return trip to the outer corridor was a matter of a few thousand feet. Having no light, he caused the gem in his ring to sputter out a red glare, a trick he often employed in such situations. He attained the corridor and looked left and right. The nearest opening was about three hundred feet to the right. Ronar marched over to it, feeling the ache in his biceps. Once, long ago, he had been among the strongest men on this planet by virtue of his upbringing on the larger planet Earth. Now, thirty five years after last setting foot there, he had declined. He was still strong, but only because of his size. His advantage had dwindled away.

Reaching the window, Ronar sent the worm and the cart crashing down the outside face of the precipice. He took a moment to catch his breath and savor the sweet air that entered through the opening. The barren valley outside was like a glimpse of Eden compared to this dark, stifling warren.

He turned to retrace his steps. As he did so he came to a terrible realization. He had passed quite a few cross tunnels on his way to the window. He had barely noticed them, had not counted them, and now he wasn't sure which one he had come from.

Cursing himself for a fool, he walked back, making the best estimate he could of how far he had come. That still left him with three possible tunnels. He examined each one carefully, searching for footprints or other signs of recent passage, but finding none. Nor did he see any trace of light in any of the tunnels.

But now he was hearing things. Distant sounds, echoing so that it was impossible to guess their origin. Cries, thuds, the clatter of worm-carts, and other sounds less easy to define.

Well then, surely he must try them all. He entered the first of his candidate tunnels, running, his way illuminated by the fitful glare of his ring. At about a thousand feet in he encountered a stone cistern which was fed by a trickle of water running down the wall. He didn't remember it, so he scooped up a handful of water, drank it, and started back. Passing a cross tunnel, it occurred to him to cut across to the next candidate tunnel. A good time saver, if the tunnel layout was so straightforward as that. He decided to risk it. He soon reached another long radial tunnel, presumably the second of his candidates. Turning left, it seemed that the noises were getting louder and clearer, and perhaps he also detected a glimmer of light. He ran in this direction, and was soon satisfied he had made the correct choice. In the distance he saw shifting pools of torchlight, struggling figures, and a number of those accursed little wagons. He all but flew into this melee, encountering first a prone figure, apparently dead, with an overturned wagon nearby. A worm was hunching its way toward the main battle. Sensing Ronar's approach, it turned and reared up, both tentacles raised, a posture which revealed the degenerate little legs on its underside, good for little more than clinging to feathers or fur.

Ronar unleashed the ring, brought forth the sword, and with a single sweep lopped off both tentacles. He then tried to swing it over his head to cleave the thing in two, but in his eagerness he forgot the low stone ceiling. The sword struck it and was knocked from his hand. It fell on his head, stunning him and cutting his scalp. Ronar fell on his back; the sword vanished.

The scene before him was total confusion. The worm continued to approach, with what intention he did not know, since the severed ends of its tentacles only squirted out vile juices. Ronar kicked at it, a sensation like kicking a bag full of rotting vegetables, wiped the blood from his eyes, and leaped to his feet with a roar. He brought back the sword, and now it became a stabbing weapon, spitting the thing like a wad of meat on a stick. He yanked it free and leaped over the spasming worm, looking for his next victim. He beheld another worm, this one with one tentacle wrapped around the arm of a woman, preparing to strike with the other. Ronar flung himself at it and split it down the middle with a single blow. The woman screamed.

The struggle was taking place at the intersection of two tunnels, so there was a bit more room for action here than elsewhere. Without thought or consideration, Ronar attacked every worm in view, hacking away at them, distracting them before they could bring down any more of their rebellious slaves.

And then all the worms were dead. Ronar stood panting, glaring around in search of more enemies.

He belatedly realized that he recognized none of these people. His friends were not among them. These slaves knew nothing more than that a huge, bloody savage had erupted out of nowhere to chop their tormentors into pieces. He gave a loud laugh, which caused them all to back off in uncertainty and dismay.

"Where are the others?" he demanded.

"What others? Which others?"

"The other strangers. Never mind. I'll find them. Get away from this place, your servitude is over!"

He released the sword, snatched up one of their torches and ran down the nearest transverse tunnel, hoping he wasn't merely running deeper into a maze whose layout he did not understand.

A few moments later, thinking he heard a call, Ronar stopped to listen.

"Ronar! Ronar!" It was faint but definite, and sounded like Sha Totek. Ronar ran on, made another left-hand turn, and soon enough came upon his group, standing around as though nothing had happened. They stared at him in astonishment.

"By the bristling breasts of Bast, what happened to you?" asked Sha Totek.

"I encountered a group of worms who were attacking their slaves. I slew them."

"You're scalp is bleeding!" bleated Emogen.

Ronar snatched up his pack. "Self-inflicted, due to my own stupidity. No time for that now. Let's be off."

Gaping in awe and terror at the stormy power he had unleashed in his dismal yet formerly predictable world, Mylor led them deeper into the mountain, then upward via a series of ramps. At last they came to a sort of hatch in the ceiling, a massive construction again controlled by an immense crank and crude gearing. Ronar, Astil, and Sha Totek applied themselves to it eagerly, keen for a ray of sunslight and a breath of clean air. The hatchway opened grudgingly, and they all crawled up the ladder into the light, blinking.

They had emerged onto a plateau which tilted down gradually toward the west, where a rolling, hazy country could be dimly seen.

Ronar turned and stared down into the blackness, knowing he must immediately plunge back into it, lest his resolve should falter.

"Ronar, your hair is matted with blood," said Emogen. "Come sit on this rock and let me tend to it."

Ronar obeyed, settling on the rock more heavily than he had intended.

"Your scalp has been opened. This may take a few minutes."

"The rest of you make ready to return below. Except you of course, Coral, or whatever your name is."

"It is Corey, Lord Greylock."

"I am not your lord."

Astil appeared in Ronar's field of view.

"Ronar, I think I shall not go back down there."

"Why not?" growled Ronar.

"Because that is not our mission. It is a distraction, and quite possibly a fatal one. I look forward to a long life, and I do not wish it truncated for such as these. I do not like the suffering which has befallen these wretched creatures, but consider. They collaborated with those monsters in inflicting evil upon the Teratorns. If they now suffer from that same evil, this is a form of justice, is it not?"

"Yes, it is. If anyone deserves to be victimized by those worms, it's these people. It is indeed justice. But what would justice be for any of us? How blameless are you? Are you so eager to achieve justice for yourself? I know I'm not. I have committed many crimes, and I'm as happy as the next man to avoid paying for them. But I won't compel you to go. I do, however, insist on this. Stay here and protect these women. That woman Corey, she is too young to have taken part in any oppression of the Teratorns. I expect to find many others like her, down below."

"Most Elves do poorly when they try to make moral distinctions," said Sha Totek. "They are like colorblind men who try to distinguish red from green."

Astil nodded and withdrew, looking troubled and uncertain.

"Lord Greylock, perhaps I too should remain. Two men could better protect—" began Mylor.

He was interrupted by Ronar's bitter laugh. "No, Mylor. If you don't go back, none of us will. I will not compel you either. I may cut off your arm, but I won't compel you to go."

Emogen leaned down and kissed him on the forehead. "I am finished."

Ronar hadn't even noticed what she was doing, so intent was he on Astil and Mylor. He stood up. "Thank you, Emogen. Come on then, Sha Totek. You're coming at least, aren't you?"

"I am certainly coming."

"And I can count on you for assistance?"

The sorcerer answered in a dreamy voice as he stared into the suns. "Oh yes. I have a few surprises in mind."

The two of them dropped their packs, carrying only their weapons and torches. With Mylor in the lead, they descended into the tunnels, leaving the hatch open behind them.

They had not gone far, always penetrating deeper into the mountain, when they heard a clamor coming from the tunnel ahead. Ronar waved his companions to a halt and waited. A few moments later a group of people hurried into view, coming their way.

The man in the lead saw them, stopped, and pointed. "There he is! The crazed giant who slaughtered all those Riders! And look, there is Mylor with him!"

"This is Greylock! Yes, Ronar himself!" cried Mylor in answer to their shrieks. "And if that is not enough for you, this other is the Sorcerer Imhotep!"

"Hello," said Sha Totek amiably, waving.

"Save us from the devils of history!" wailed an old man. "Are we all to die, then?"

"Not by our hands, fool," snapped Ronar. "We are going to free your hostages. You just keep on your way, and you'll soon be out of here, unless any of you would care to help us rescue your people."

They all goggled at him in silence.

"I thought not. Go."

They filed past, some casting haunted looks back over their shoulders.

"Well," said Mylor. "I at least am beginning to feel quite the hero, even though I am guided in my path by the promise of death or dismemberment, should I shirk."

"That's a better reason for heroism than many," said Sha Totek. "Lead on then."

Deeper they burrowed into the hill, far below the levels they had already plumbed. The air grew ever more dank with the stench of the worms. They passed many chambers, the nature and purpose of which Ronar did not care to know. The stonework grew rougher and more crude, until it seemed they were traveling natural passages rather than dressed tunnels, crossing into the natural domain of the worms from the higher regions delved by their human allies. Therefore they must go more cautiously, watching their footing, which was often slippery with water seeping down the walls and tricking over blocks and ledges on the floor.

"I have ventured so deep only once before" whispered Mylor. "My master once had business here, and I was forced to carry its repulsive form in my arms, because the carts are impractical here. We men are not normally allowed to approach so closely the chamber where the hostages are kept. I believe only the turmoil you have caused above explains the lack of Rider guards here. Still, we must be careful. They will hear us coming and detect our footsteps. They can hide in crevices and strike as you pass."

"How exactly do they kill?" asked Ronar.

"They inject a poison through their feeding tube."

The passage grew ever steeper until it terminated in a grotto which had a small black opening in its floor. A terrible stench of filth wafted up from this, enough to nauseate Ronar.

"This is one of the ceiling entrances to the hostage chamber," whispered Mylor.

"You mean we must descend through *that*?" hissed Sha Totek.

"I'm afraid so. The lower level entrances will surely be guarded."

"How long is this shaft?" asked Ronar.

"I don't really know. I have seen worms plop down through them, but have never entered one myself."

"Very well," said Ronar, though he thought this situation was anything but well. "I will go first, followed by Mylor. If I can fit through, you others surely will. We won't be able to carry lit torches. I can get a little light from my ring. Sha Totek?"

"Magicians are good sources of illumination. I can manage."

Ronar smothered his torch beneath his boot heel, sat on the edge of the narrow pit, and slithered in, feet first. The walls of the shaft were rough and irregular. The odor was stunning. Ronar longed to hold his breath, but he knew that couldn't last long at this level of exertion. He eased himself down as carefully as he could, feeling for footholds in the darkness. The shaft was so narrow he could not use his ring without risk of burning himself. He heard Mylor enter above him, followed by Sha Totek, whose presence was indicated by a weak, shifting green glow that worked its way down, slightly easing Ronar's situation, yet also revealing the rock wall, never more than a few inches from his face.

The shaft was far from straight, with kinks and bends which might be easy for a three or four foot worm to negotiate, but far less so for a bony two meter human.

At last his feet encountered a choke point he wasn't certain he could pass at all. He halted, stretched his left hand down as far as it would go, and summoned a little scarlet light from the ring, revealing a narrow, roughly oval constriction in the rock. It could not be much more than twelve inches wide, and less than that in height.

Mylor's bare, horny foot whacked Ronar in the head as he descended.

"Hold there!" hissed Ronar in annoyance. "I'm not sure I can go any farther."

"What? What then shall we do?" quavered the old man.

"Be silent while I think."

In truth there was not much thinking to be done. Ronar could either attempt to pass, or they could all withdraw and seek another path.

The latter option was by far the more appealing. Ronar had to admit that the prospect of getting stuck in this dark, confined throat of the earth had him sweating with terror.

He stuck his legs through the hole, and quickly forced himself in to his hips. The space beyond wasn't much wider, meaning he could barely move his legs. Pushing himself in still deeper, he promptly found himself jammed into place. His feet found no purchase to push himself out again, nor could he reach an adequate handhold for pulling. Short of assistance from his companions, he was trapped.

As he lingered there without moving, faint sounds reached him from below. They were something like what a small child might imagine to be the sounds of a graveyard on Halloween night: a mixture of moans, weeping, and things being dragged over rough ground.

These sounds awakened Ronar's wrath.

"What's going on down there?" came Sha Totek's whisper.

"I fear there is some dire presence in the tunnel just below me!" cried Mylor.

"Yes, there is. What do you hear?"

"A terrible sound...a low growl from the throat of some great beast!"

"Ah, that is good news."

"Ayyyeeeiii! Something has flung itself against my legs!"

"Fear not, it's probably Ronar."

"And now a burning red glare! And a flash of white!"

K-tang!

"Ronar has freed himself, and is chopping at the walls of the tunnel with his blade! Sparks are flying! No weapon can withstand such treatment. He has broken it!"

K-tang!

"And now it is whole again!"

"Splendid."

K-tang!

"And again! Those terrible noises! Many worms will be drawn into the chamber below."

"So much the worse for them. Mylor, my friend, soon you will see things worth relating to your grandchildren, if you should ever have any."

Panting, Ronar surveyed the result of his excavations by the dim light filtering down from Sha Totek. He had done the job. He could now slither through the enlarged opening, and did so.

Curiously, he heard no change in the lamentation coming from below. At least that probably meant the hostages were not yet under attack, or so he hoped.

The remaining length of the shaft was much greater than he had expected, but it presented no more serious obstacles. At last a glimmer of reddish light appeared from below. He reached the end, and now he must be careful to avoid slipping down and falling into the space below. He twisted to place his head at the opening, looking down into a large chamber lit only by a few weak lamps mounted on the walls.

There he beheld perhaps the worst scene of human degradation and torment he had ever seen. Naked people, mostly women and children, sprawled everywhere. Nearly every one of them had the feeding tube of at least one worm attached to their bodies. They writhed helplessly or lay motionless, some with their emaciated hands wrapped around the pulsating tubes that entered their breasts or bellies. Ronar watched as one woman gathered up her parasite in her arms, then staggered over to a pit in the ground, where she squatted, defecating.

Guards were arrayed around the perimeter. These were worms mounted on subterranean creatures of some sort, pale and eyeless, standing on multiple slender legs, with additional limbs armed with chitinous spikes and blades. Their whiplike antennae were eight feet long or more, ceaselessly waving to test the air.

If Ronar had felt himself roused to wrath before, the emotion that thundered through him now made that seem like serenity.

A child, his head lolling as his worm sucked blood from his body, happened to notice Ronar as he peered from the hole.

"A demon!" he moaned weakly. "A demon looks down upon us! O Demon, please, come down and kill us all."

The woman at the toilet pit also looked up, saw him, grimaced, and dropped her worm into the cesspool, its feeding tube tearing from her as it fell. She shrieked, clamping her hand over her bleeding wound.

That was enough for Ronar. He twisted and dropped, manifesting the Cold Sword before his feet struck the ground. He swung it, his goal being to sever as many of the feeding tubes as possible before the worms could gather their wits and begin to kill the hostages. To cut the tubes without slashing the worm's victims required both speed and precision. Each man or woman seemed to think he was attacking them, only to goggle up at him in astonishment when their worm writhed helplessly beside them, their tentacles detached. A few of the stronger or more willful people tore the stubs of the tubes from their bodies and fell to kicking or beating the worms.

Behind him, Mylor came flopping down with a cry, apparently pushed, quickly followed by Sha Totek, who gave forth a disconcerting laugh as he alighted.

Now the guards moved in on their pony-sized insectoid mounts, their feet making rustling noises as they advanced. Ronar flung his sword at the nearest of them, causing its head to detach quite neatly, which did little to hamper it as it was under the control of the Rider on its back. Ronar summoned back the sword and threw it again, this time skewering both the Rider and the abdomen of its mount. Both collapsed to the ground in a twitching heap of legs. With the sword once more in hand, Ronar held it cocked against the charge of two more guards. With a two-handed swing he cut the legs out from under both at once, then hacked their bodies and the worms that rode them apart with further blows.

He was knocked flat by an impact from behind. The sword skittered away and vanished. He felt a searing pain in his middle. *Another scar,* he thought, as he violently twisted onto his back. He found himself straddled by one of the guards, surrounded by its legs, with its bladed forelimbs poised to strike at him again. With no time to do anything else, he grabbed those limbs, engaging in a contest of strength to avoid being stabbed again.

His arms were gradually forced back. Once, he knew, he would have readily overpowered this spindly Colibdian creature. Now, his waning physique might mean the end of his long life at the claws of a gigantic subterranean bug.

Well, his body might be in decline, but not his will. He'd always had the ability to overcome the limitations of his body at times of great need. With a terrific flare of resolve he increased his grip, cracking the limbs like crab legs. He brought up his knees, then threw the thing off him with a thrust of his legs. He regained his feet, called back the sword, and stood ready for further battle, although he was aware of a deep pain in his side.

He was also aware of being able to see better than he could just moments before. The entire chamber was being lit with a white-gold light whose color seemed strangely familiar to Ronar, and powerfully evocative. It took him several moments to realize he was seeing, after an absence of many years, the color of the Sun of Earth, which was only approximated by the blended red and white lights of the suns of Colibdis.

The sight of it here, in this benighted pit of Colibdis, affected him unexpectedly, bringing about a yearning for that lost world of soft blue skies and sumptuous air. A lump thickened in his throat as the light waxed, along with radiant heat, until every surface in the cave seemed ablaze.

Shading his eyes, Ronar turned, finding, as he'd expected, the light emanating from the incandescent figure of Sha Totek. All the people cowered away from him, while the mounted worms fled, the nearest actually smoking from the heat. Ronar also retreated into the partial shade of a projection from the rock wall. He dared not look directly at Sha Totek, so powerful was his light.

"Morgna antiregulus!" cried the sorcerer. *"Zaxton aureus, adaugeo vis vires!"*

Ronar considered Sha Totek's Latin a little shaky, but in this case it seemed to be the thought that counted.

The sorcerer raised his hands. From them speared bolts of radiance, too intense for Ronar to face at all. They blasted into the remaining Riders and their mounts, burning them, or even causing them to pop open with disgusting spurts of fluid. The smell of burning flesh added to the general miasma.

The doors around the periphery of the chamber trundled open, admitting more mounted guards. Sha Totek's beams sought them out, but they were many. Ronar was preparing to leap back into combat when a new pain burned his leg.

He looked down and found a smallish worm also concealed in the shadow of this little spur of rock. It had pierced him with its claw, and its feeding tube was wavering. Ronar grabbed the feeding tube, then spun the sword in his free hand, about to pin the thing to the floor.

But then a peculiar feeling radiated from the thorn in his thigh, and strange words entered his mind.

Why do you kill us, O man?

Ronar's face worked in revulsion and astonishment. How could it ask such a question? The obvious answer was "I kill you because you prey upon my people, you enslave and feed upon them, you foul, vile wad of filth."

It entered Ronar's mind to descend into the deepest caverns of this world, to root out and destroy every vestige of these creatures and whatever weird lightless ecosystem in which they dwelt. Yet that would conflict with the more vital mission. Ronar also suspected that these worms, natural parasites whose world view must perceive their use of other creatures as natural and just, would not understand his indignation.

Therefore he said: "I kill you for making yourselves known on the surface of this world. The surface is the domain of Men and Birds. Retreat to your ancient caverns, remain there, and you'll have nothing more to fear from me."

It was one of you who first urged us to venture to your upper world, promising us both mounts and food. We were content with the Birds, and used them to do the bidding of that one, but then the Birds were taken away.

"Things have changed. That one has been cast down. His words now mean nothing."

We must have food.

"You will find no more food here. You will find only death. Go back to your underworld, or I will slaughter you all."

We go.

The claw withdrew. Ronar released the feeding tube. The worm humped its way toward one of the doors, along with those of its fellows who remained alive.

"Sha Totek, stand down," shouted Ronar. The sorcerer complied at once, fading to red, then darkening, and slumping in exhaustion. His clothing incinerated, he stood as naked as the hostages themselves, though he was notably better fed.

"The rest of you, stop fighting. The worms have surrendered. They are leaving. You are free. Gather yourselves and we will lead you to the surface. Mylor, where are you?"

"Over here, Lord Ronar. Just pitching the last of these things into the muck."

Ronar spied the old man, who was tipping another worm into the cesspool.

"You're sure that worm is dead?"

"And what difference would that make?"

"Because they have *surrendered*, I told them they would be *safe*, and I will not be made a liar by *you*!" he roared, which caused still more pain in his side.

Mylor blanched and straightened up. "As you wish."

"Come on, all of you. Mylor, lead us to the surface. Ignore the worms if they offer no threat."

Ronar and Sha Totek followed Mylor out of the chamber. Behind them came the surviving hostages. Many of them had been killed by the worms, while the remainder moved slowly, both through weakness and a lingering terror. Ronar caused scarlet light to sputter from his ring, until he came upon some torches which he passed around.

In the passages were many worms, humping along toward deeper levels, moving aside at their approach, their tentacles carefully coiled beneath them. Some were mounted, and these creatures also made themselves low and compact as they passed. A murmur of wonderment rose up from the growing crowd of refugees, many of whom cried out gladly as they recognized freed hostages whom they had never hoped to see again.

"Who has saved us?" they called out.

"Who has saved you?" answered Mylor. "Truly the world has turned upside down. Mylor the Miserable has saved you, with the help of Greylock the God-Killer, and none other than the Sorcerer Imhotep."

Ronar decided to let it go at that. He was beginning to feel light-headed. "If we don't get out of here soon, I may never get out," he whispered to Sha Totek.

"I feel much the same."

"That was an impressive spell you cast."

"It would have been impressive for the true Sha Totek. For me, it was an astonishing exertion. It's enough to make me weep."

Without fear of detection, Mylor was able to lead them by a more direct route than previously. It was a long climb. Ronar had to exert the greater part of his will to keep his stride steady and firm.

They accumulated hundreds of refugees by the time the gleam of daylight appeared above and before them. Led by their three saviors, they climbed through the hatch and stumbled into the light of the suns, squinting and shielding their eyes against the almost forgotten glare. They were a sorry-looking group, emaciated and filthy, with skins dead white, or burned red if they'd been exposed to Sha Totek's solar outpouring. Most had open feeding wounds, while all had multiple small wounds and scars from the communication claws.

Ronar looked around for his party. The ex-slaves who had already emerged sat huddled together. Emogen and Astil stood near the horses, watching wide-eyed as the exodus from the underworld continued.

Emogen's face went white as she came forward. Ronar thought she would pass him by to tend to the newcomers, but she stopped before him, effortlessly pushing him to the ground with her hands on his shoulders, as if he were a child.

"All those other people are starving and wounded," he muttered.

"Hush. They can wait. You cannot. You are bleeding to death. Sleep."

And Ronar slept.

Chapter Ten

Pond Life

Ronar awoke to firelight and the gleam of the moon Sinanna. Huddled near him were Astil, Sha Totek, and Emogen, who slept. Astil's bow was strung and he stood alert. Sha Totek sat, his tired eyes glowering out into the night while the occasional tear rolled down his cheek. At least he had found some clothing.

Ronar examined his side. His wound had closed, the pain reduced to a dull ache. Still, he felt somewhat weak.

The watchful attitude of his comrades disturbed him. "What's going on here?" he asked quietly.

Astil indicated the large fires in the near distance, around which clustered or slept many naked or poorly clad figures. Without removing his gaze from them, he spoke. "Those people have created some difficulty. Emogen cared for them to the point of exhaustion, and when she collapsed, those still untreated reacted with resentment. Nor have we any means of feeding so many. They asked for the horses so that they could eat them; I refused. They have been eyeing them ever since."

"Ungrateful wretches," said Ronar. An incongruity came to his attention. "The horses. The horses?" He twisted his neck about and saw all four horses standing nearby in the moonlight.

"Before we sent them away, I asked Moonmist to find a way over the wall and to bring the others. He did very well. They arrived just before you emerged from the caves."

"That was well done, Astil."

Still without looking at him, Astil said, "It is well that one thing I did today was of use."

Today? To Ronar it seemed incredible that less than a day had elapsed since they first ventured into those hellish pits.

"Can't those people go back down long enough to bring out some of whatever fungus or other filth they ate down there?" asked Ronar.

"They refuse to go."

Their speech awakened Emogen, who sat up and looked at him with sleepy eyes.

"Emogen. Thank you for curing me."

"You are not cured, you are merely no longer dying. You need rest, and you need to eat a lot, especially meat."

"We must continue our journey in the morning."

"You must rest. A day or two will not make any difference to your mission. As for the journey...I don't think I can go on with you any more." She looked miserable as she said this.

"Why not?"

"It's all these people. My people, for better or worse. They are all weak and many are still injured. They are naked, aimless and homeless. They need guidance. I intend to lead them back to my valley, to try to ease them into normal lives, free of the wicked evil they have done."

"I—somehow I had imagined you going on with us to the end of this adventure."

"So had I. But I cannot leave these people to languish in the open, or to turn into a mob of brigands, preying on whatever people may live nearby."

Ronar was surprised by the depth of his disappointment at this news. He hadn't realized how much he'd come to value the witch's presence in such a short time.

Naturally, being who he was, he did not express this sentiment, but moved on to support her decision.

"I'm glad you recognize the depravity of these people. They willingly aided the worms in the enslavement of the Teratorns for many turns. When they themselves became slaves, no injustice was done. They are steeped in evil. You should not trust them, not until all memory of the culture they created and endured in those passageways has been erased."

She nodded, looking over at those who lurked in the firelight with worried eyes.

"I will speak to them now," said Ronar. He slowly raised himself to his feet, impressed by the difficulty of this simple maneuver. Once upright, he stood very still for a while as his head spun.

The former slaves, noticing his great form looming in the darkness, grew more hushed as they regarded him.

When he felt he could proceed without betraying his weakness, Ronar gathered himself and called out, "Listen to me now! You have been drawn out of darkness by people whom you have always deemed your enemies. And yet you might readily have freed yourselves at any time. The worms were not so formidable that you could not have risen up against them. You have not distinguished yourselves. Now you must decide what to make of yourselves in the future. This fine witch. Emogen. has offered to bring you to the valley where her village, and others like it, stands. It is a fair valley where people who are prepared to work hard may establish themselves and live as well as people live anywhere in this world. I advise you to accept this offer with all the grace you can muster."

A figure shuffled to the fore of the refugees. Ronar recognized Mylor.

"Are we to be farmers and herdsmen then?"

"It would seem so."

"We realize this is not your area of expertise, but there is little call for worm-lackeys in rural Darteharn," piped up Sha Totek from his position on the ground.

Mylor scowled at him, then said to Ronar: "We shall consider your offer."

Ronar promptly returned to sleep.

He awoke at dawn to find Sha Totek snoring on one side while Emogen emitted a gentle trill close by on the other.

He sat up and looked around. All the ex-slaves were gone, as was Astil and his horse Moonmist. The three mortal horses were also not in view.

"I don't like the looks of this," muttered Ronar.

Sha Totek blinked and sat up. "Nor do I."

Emogen yawned, rubbed her eyes, and sat up, frowning.

Just then they heard a call. "Lord Ronar! Good day to you!" It was Mylor, emerging from the nearby hatch to the underworld, holding a rag before him to ward off the rays of the newly-risen suns.

Ronar and his friends stood up. "What were you doing down there? Where is Astil and our horses?"

"Your Elf friend? I do not know. As for us, we have decided to return to the catacombs below and dwell there."

"Why?"

"We are not suited to life above. The suns would sear us. We know nothing of agriculture. Down below, we have shelter and we know our way about. Our sources of food are meager and coarse, but adequate. We will of course block off the tunnels to the deeper levels so that the worms may not return."

Ronar fretted for a few moments, loath as always to impress his will on others, yet feeling a certain responsibility toward these wretches.

"I do not advise this."

"No?"

"No. Men were not made to dwell underground, separated from the light. If you remain there, you will gradually adapt to this existence, and someday your descendants will not be considered wholesome by those who live above."

Mylor had the grace to at least appear troubled by this, and said "We shall be mindful of your warning."

"One other warning. Do not ever seek out the worms again. If I, or anyone who follows me, learns that you have made any alliance with them, or attacked them, it will go ill for you."

Mylor nodded gravely. "As you say." He bowed, turned, and returned into the ground.

Ronar stared after him for a while.

"They are fools. They will degenerate and be lost."

"I kept waiting for you to inform him that it was you who freed that rebellious Teratorn he hates so much," said Sha Totek. "You who brought about the end of their tidy little arrangement with the Dusk Riders."

Ronar shrugged. "I saw no need to rile them up on that account. If they had asked, I would have told them."

The sorcerer chuckled. "Well, at least now there's no reason for Emogen to leave us."

And yet Emogen looked as troubled as ever, if not more so. "I don't know," she said. "I think I should still go to them. They are weak, and surely I can—"

"No," said Ronar firmly. "That I will not permit. I will not suffer you to sacrifice yourself to those dank caves for the sake of those wretches. There are limits to what I will endure. If I must bind you and gag you and return you kicking to Amulree, I will do so, rather than see you descend that ladder with that despairing look on your face."

Emogen brightened.

"Well, child, it looks like your fate is sealed," said Sha Totek. "Ronar can be quite merciless when dealing with errant females."

"Yes, so I've heard."

Ronar and Emogen smiled at each other.

"A smile from Leonard Ronar, and it does not chill my marrow? Surely these are the end of days," said Sha Totek.

Ronar's smile proved ephemeral. "Yet perhaps you should return home, Emogen."

"Why?"

"You have seen that men are different here, even this short distance from your country. I doubt they will improve as we travel further. There is no telling what dangers we will find as we go westward."

Emogen's smile lit up again. "What can happen to me with three such mighty men to protect me?"

"Two, at the moment," said Ronar.

"Three," said Emogen, pointing.

Astil approached, leading Moonmist, who bore on his back a slain deer. The other horses followed, stopping to resume their grazing when Astil halted.

"When the slaves withdrew into their crypts, I thought it safe to go off to hunt some food for you. I heard what Emogen said about your need for meat."

Ronar looked into the Elf's unfathomable silver eyes, wondering anew what lay behind them. "Thank you, Astil. That too was well done."

"It was a strange thing. I did not have to stalk this deer. It came up to me, and stood looking at me, presenting its side, as though waiting for me to do something. When I did nothing, it lowered its head, snorted, and pawed the ground, as though it meant to charge me, then again stood watchfully. I drew my bow and released the arrow, which pierced its heart, and it fell dead at once."

"Perhaps it was making a sacrifice of itself," said Emogen softly.

"I ask only that we move away from the opening to those pits. The stench from them assails me, nor do I appreciate the memories it brings."

"I agree," said Ronar.

They travelled a few miles to the west, where they discovered a pond fed by a small stream. Around it stood tall willows, leafless at this season, which managed to coexist with a peculiar Colibdian plant consisting of several stalks wrapped around each other in helical fashion and then expanding into a stiff brush of foliage. Here they made a camp more elaborate than usual, as they intended to stay for a day or two. Emogen dragged off the deer to dress it. Ronar insisted on building a fire pit and makeshift rotisserie out of rocks and branches. He soon encountered the limits of his strength while doing this and was obliged to rest frequently; nevertheless, he would not stop. When it was completed, they spitted the deer and roasted it for hours. Emogen cast a spell over the meat, claiming it would render it more healthful and sustaining. She and Astil then collected greens and a few edible roots from the vicinity. When all was ready late in the afternoon, they gorged themselves, except for Astil, who kept to his usual abstemious diet.

The deer's flesh seemed to radiate strength and vitality throughout Ronar's body, clear out to the ends of his remaining toenails (he had lost a few toes to frostbite many years before). Sha Totek caught his eye; the two shared a startled look of satisfaction. Emogen, who ate much more daintily, smiled at them both.

As they sat quietly around the fire with the suns wheeling toward the horizon, Ronar was aware of the incongruity of his sense of well-being. He was well into Darteharn, bound to go farther still, in the company of one of its witches, and near a concentration of some of its more morally dubious inhabitants.

And yet this deserted tableland had a quiet beauty. As he looked around at his companions he found himself content.

Then a matter occurred to him with which he was less pleased.

"Don't be startled, everyone. I'm about to bring forth the sword." He did so, the clash of it startling the horses and echoing over the landscape. He examined the chilly blade, on which the rust had spread, though so far it was still superficial. He offered it to Sha Totek. "Take a look at this."

The sorcerer held the weapon in his lap and studied it with a bleak expression. "This is a sad thing, though not unexpected. The nature of Gromer's spell is that the sword comes to you in whatever form it has when in its normal, resting condition. For many turns it was carefully stored, protected, and maintained, either by myself or the Eranians. Now it lies on the bottom of the Bay of Kiruna. As long as it remains there, it will continue to deteriorate, and someday it will rust away entirely. Yes, very sad."

"It seems to me," said Ronar, unnecessarily loudly, "that some god or spirit who was kindly disposed could fish the sword out of the Bay and so preserve it."

Sha Totek smiled. "Yes. If only you exercised that kind of influence over any of them these days."

As dusk fell, Sha Totek retired to his little magical pavilion, leaving Ronar and Emogen to converse while Astil lurked in the starlight somewhere nearby.

They were soon interrupted by the appearance of two pale, silent figures in the east. Ronar and Emogen, noticing them simultaneously, froze and grew silent. Ronar was mindful of the ring on his finger but did not call out the sword.

The moonlit figures drew nearer. As they did so, their stature became more apparent. They appeared to be children, or possibly hideous little gnomes of some kind, a possibility which anyone on Colibdis would be foolish to overlook.

But they were only children, a fact revealed as they entered the firelight. Two dark-haired waifs they were, a girl of about five turns of age and a boy of two, both naked except for rags tied around their waists.

They fell to their knees and bowed their heads. The girl said, "Great lords, I am Aithne and this is my brother Tadc. Our parents are dead. We have fled from the pits and corridors of the worms. We cannot bear it there any longer. We know nothing of the outer world, but we beg you to protect us. We will serve you in whatever way you wish."

Ronar scowled at them. "We are on an important and dangerous mission. We cannot be burdened with children."

"Of course we can!" flared up Emogen. "We will take them to the first town or village we encounter, and there find someone to care for them. Surely you don't mind if two people among all those wretches are saved!"

Ronar rolled his eyes but could make no real objection to this.

"Thank you, Lady!" cried Aithne.

"I am only Emogen, and no great lady. Come closer. I will find you both something to wear and give you something to eat. It's clear from looking at you that you've never had a decent meal in your lives."

The girl, at least, had provided meals for the worms, as Ronar saw from the feeding wound on her stomach.

Emogen produced her two spare blouses, which were as good as a dress to the girl, and as a tent to the boy. She gave them strips of venison which had been drying on sticks over the fire. The children grew wide-eyed as they held these in their hands. They nibbled at them tentatively, and then crammed them into their mouths, followed by more, as many as Emogen could hand them, until their bellies literally grew round. Then exhaustion overtook them. Emogen wrapped them in a blanket and arranged them near the fire.

Moments before he fell asleep, Tadc turned an apprehensive glance toward Ronar and whispered, "Lady Emogen, is that the one they call Greylock?"

"He is indeed."

"They say he is the worst man in the world."

Emogen laughed. "Yes, he may be that. But if anything comes to bother us in the night, you will find he is good to have nearby."

Ronar sniffed the air. "You will clean them up in the morning?" he muttered.

"Yes, I certainly shall. Oh, don't look so disgruntled. I know this isn't what you had in mind for tonight, but sometimes our desires must be put off for the good of others." She smiled at him with a mischievous gleam in her eyes.

"I don't know what you mean," said Ronar stiffly.

"*Shhh.* You mustn't convince me that's true, if you can avoid it."

Ronar awoke in the morning to find Emogen fulfilling her pledge, splashing with the children in the nearby pond. He watched them for a while, reflecting that he would be reluctant to join them. Who could say what might live at the bottom of some remote Darteharnian pond? And how cold must it be? Then he realized with a start that the three bathers were naked and he looked away in embarrassment.

Sha Totek had not yet emerged from his tent. Astil and Moonmist were not in evidence, though the other horses grazed nearby. Ronar busied himself by redistributing the contents of their heavy packs among the horses. He intended to set out again today. He felt fine; indeed he felt better than he had for a long time. He was eying the venison and wondering how best to pack it when Emogen and the freshly-scrubbed children came marching up, mercifully now all clothed.

"We've warmed up the pond water for you. Now it's your turn," said Emogen.

"What?"

"Fair is fair. Elves never seem to get dirty, and who knows what the sorcerer does in that flamboyant tent of his? You have no such advantages. You stink. Into the pond with you."

The children giggled.

Ronar cast it a dubious glance.

"Don't worry, there's nothing in that water that will get you, as long as you keep moving."

"Very well. But I expect you all to keep your backs turned."

"Have no fear. None of us has any desire to see your hairy man-parts."

With further annoying giggles, the three of them moved away.

The pond proved to be cold indeed, but Ronar bore it manfully enough. He concluded the effort was worthwhile, considering the amount of filth and dried blood that dissolved off his body. It was the first time he'd seen his own body in many days. If he wasn't mistaken, he was now in better condition than he had been when he departed Thunderbird all those weeks ago. That was something, anyway.

As he was pulling his clothes back on, he observed Astil approaching atop Moonmist. The Elf, spying him, halted and gestured for him to come closer. Ronar glanced at the camp. Sha Totek was entertaining Emogen and the children with magic tricks—not real magic, but common sleight-of-hand. Ronar angled away from them to meet Astil.

"Please follow me," said the Elf in a subdued tone. "It is not far."

Ronar did so. A hundred yards away lay a dead, naked man, his body pierced with many arrow wounds. He was a fell-looking character, his face harsh, his body lean and angular.

"I was bringing this corpse into the camp, but when I noticed those children I decided it would be best not to."

"Did you kill him?" asked Ronar.

"Yes. He was moving to attack the camp, but he was then in the form of a great wolf."

Ronar took a step back and looked more carefully at Astil. His clothing was torn, his flesh scratched and bitten.

"Astil…"

"Don't worry, I'm in no danger of transforming. I am of Faerie. Sometimes one form of magic trumps another."

"Still, let's get back to the camp. We'll leave this here for the scavengers."

They all gawked at Astil as he and Ronar returned, especially the children, who had never before seen a Faery. Emogen leaped up and approached him. Astil raised his hand. "No need, good witch. Your spells would be wasted. I will heal in good time."

"What was it?" she gasped.

"A werewolf," said Ronar.

"What?"

"Namirnakh used to breed them in the forests of Wauk, to the west," said Sha Totek, who had joined them. "It's no great surprise to find one here."

No great surprise, thought Ronar, to someone who had his wits about him, and did not heedlessly sleep on the fields of Darteharn without precaution. If not for Astil, quite possibly they would now all be dead, or dreading the coming of the night.

"Werewolves!" breathed Emogen, white-faced. "Such things were only tales in my valley."

"Well, my dear, we've been trying to hint all along that the reign of Namirnakh wasn't entirely nice," said Sha Totek gently.

"Come on, let's break camp," said Ronar. "We're leaving."

They were subdued as they prepared to leave. Ronar eyed his fire pit, uncertain whether to leave it standing for the benefit of future travelers or to conceal any sign of their presence. When he noticed the others were ready to depart, he decided to leave it.

The children clung to each other behind Emogen on her shaggy pony, round-eyed at the novelty of their situation. Broken clouds moved in from the west, and with them a rising breeze.

Chapter Eleven

The Tower of the Mystic Arts

The tableland tilted down somewhat as they rode along, a trend halted by a final range of rugged hills, chill with streamers of mist, and dark with conifers and tall blade-shaped plants Emogen called brandlevanes. They forded a cold river to cross from one domain to the other.

The faint trail climbed through the dark forest to emerge into a clearing atop a saddle between two peaks before descending again. Halting there to survey the bleak wilderness before them, Astil said, "What is that spike on the horizon?"

Ronar followed the Elf's pointing finger and barely made out a tall, slender structure rising somewhere among the further reaches of these hills.

Emogen said, "That may be the Tower of the Mystic Arts. I have heard rumors of that in my village."

"I too have some knowledge of this," said Sha Totek. "It is a communal dwelling for magicians, operated by a witch called Erraine. I had no idea it was so huge. That looks taller than my own Tower."

Ronar raised his viewer to study it more closely. The haze of distance wiped out most detail, but its outline was clear enough: that of a sharp, menacing steeple.

He looked over at Emogen, who peered ahead with her open, trusting face, and behind her at the children, who stared back as though they expected him to eat them.

He reached a decision.

"I don't like where this is going," he announced. "We are going into terrible danger, of that I have no doubt. Emogen, I will not risk you to it. I have seen too many women suffer through having the misfortune to be involved with me and my exploits. I believe you will be next if you continue on with us. I won't have it. We three men must go on. But you must take those children and return to your village. Now."

"Er, Ronar," began Sha Totek, "may I remind you, without Emogen both you and I would be dead at least once by now."

Ronar waved aside this irrelevancy.

Emogen opened and closed her mouth a few times, then finally said, "But I do not wish to—"

"I don't care what you wish. You are going back. If you refuse, then none of us goes forward. We will all go back, and if the world falls on account of that, then so be it. If you insist on seeing what lies beyond this point, return on your own someday. But I will not be the agent of your death. I will not."

They looked at each other in silence for a few moments.

Astil said, "Ronar, it's four days travel back to her village. Who is to say she will survive that journey? At the very least, other bands of worm refugees are likely to be wandering about."

"True. There is some danger, but it is much less than what she faces with us."

"He's right. I'll invoke the protection of Brighid. She will grant it. I'll go," said Emogen.

Ronar tried to maintain his stern expression and not show his surprise and relief.

"But Ronar, if I didn't have these children to worry about, I'd go on even if I had to change myself into a mouse and hide in your baggage."

"You can do that?" blurted Ronar.

She gave a merry laugh, though to Ronar it sounded a little strained. "No, not literally. But before we go, I must extract from you a promise. If you can, when this is over you must return to Amulree."

"I will do so, if I possibly can."

"All right then." Already her face was beginning to twist toward tears. "There's no sense in drawing this out. Goodbye, all of you."

"Your pony will know a way around the Worm Wall without entering its passages," said Astil.

"Wait, Emogen," said Ronar. "I will give you a message for the watchmen of Eranior."

He reached into his jacket and pulled out a notebook and the stub of an Earthly pencil. He wrote on a leaf, then pressed his ring onto it, scorching an image of the gem and the surrounding carved gold. He rode closer to Emogen and handed her the scrap.

"I'm not sure those men are able to read. It says that the valley of Amulree is to be considered under the protection of Eranior. Furthermore, your valley may opt to become part of Eranior, if it pleases you to do so."

Emogen said nothing, but carefully folded the slip and placed it into her bodice. She flashed him one last poignant glance, then wheeled her pony and galloped away. The children looked back at him with their haunted eyes.

Ronar watched her go until she disappeared into the trees.

Sha Totek sighed and said, "I can see from your face that we have seen the last of the kinder, gentler Ronar for a while. As for me…well, what do you expect?" He wept.

Ronar said nothing. He had done the right thing, and feelings be damned.

They rode on into those cold, wild hills, sometimes getting glimpses of the tower, which loomed ever higher. No one spoke for hours, until Sha Totek cleared his throat and said, "Leonard, my friend, I think I can guess what your plan will be when we reach the tower. You will stride through its gate with your head held high. You will announce yourself in thunderous tones of righteousness. Lights will flash, and you will hold your mighty sword before you. You will seek to smash and rend anything or anyone who offends you, or who places himself in your path. Is this not correct?"

Ronar nodded with a savage jerk of his head. "More or less. What of it?"

"Oh nothing, it's a noble plan, a worthy plan, one I wouldn't mind seeing unfold myself. I think, though, that an alternative plan might preserve our lives long enough for your outburst of wrath, when it finally comes, to be more effectively placed."

"And what is this plan?"

"I propose that we conceal our identities for a time, as we have before. I will pose again as Sekani, a middling sorcerer who seeks to study at the famed Tower of the Mystic Arts. You will be Raintree, my silent and threatening bodyguard and manservant. Astil here, er, will be…"

"I will pose as an outcast of Faerie, an unwanted pariah, which is close enough to the truth," said Astil.

Ronar looked at Sha Totek. "Do you expect to find Namirnakh at this tower?"

"Hmm? No. I do not. Even if he is again incarnate and active, his traditional centers of power lie far from here. But like you, I sense something awaiting us in that spike, something we must not bypass or ignore."

Horizons were deceptively nearby on the smallish world of Colibdis. Thus the tower grew in their sight with surprising speed, until all too soon their path left the forest and merged into a great clearing surrounding its massive base.

It was a quiet scene, lacking in guards or armies. The tower was of grey stone, and was apparently incomplete, as some of its lower spires ended in blunt tips. A few stacks of dressed stones stood here and there, yet there were no workmen, and no scaffolding.

Then one of the piles of blocks gently lifted into the air. The individual stones flowed into place to complete one of the side spires, without so much as a puff of dust to indicate any fuss.

They looked at each other, impressed.

"Hello!" A high, clear voice called out from the base of the tower.

Ronar and his friends jumped in their saddles, then urged their mounts to approach the tower at a walk. As they drew nearer they spied a female figure on a balcony overlooking the main gate. For a startled moment Ronar thought it was Emogen, but this woman was darker. She wore robes of grey, violet, and silver and smiled at them as they drew near.

"Welcome to the Tower of the Mystic Arts. I am the witch Natulakh, its mistress. Who are you, and how may I serve you?"

Sha Totek appeared nonplussed. "I was told that the mistress of this tower was the witch Erraine."

"She has retired. I think it might be polite for you to introduce yourselves before plying me with questions."

"Yes...yes, of course. I am the sorcerer Sekani of Ammon. I have heard much of this tower and its reputation, and I hope to increase my skill and knowledge by dwelling here for a time. This is my servant Raintree, a man of Tíuheimr. Finally we have the Elf-paladin Glomar-Vandelion, who accompanies me out of a perverse desire to see the world."

Natulakh nodded. "My tower exists to further the pursuit of magic. We rarely see anyone from Ammon here. I will be pleased to have you."

Sha Totek looked about with an expression of open wonder. "I had not heard that your establishment was quite so grand."

She laughed. "I have been making some additions lately, as you just observed. Please enter. We will speak further within." She withdrew.

With some trepidation they dismounted. Ronar and Sha Totek moved to tether their horses, but Astil assured them that Moonmist would look after them. Together they climbed the steps and passed through the tall bronze gate, which closed behind them.

They entered an enormous hall, dimly lit, with tiers of balconies on all sides. These were occupied by neat ranks of huge, motionless iron warriors carrying iron spears. Ronar had seen similar figures before, on the ice fields of

Hyperborea. Only now did he fully realize he had indeed come into Darteharn.

Natulakh stood one level up at the far end of the hall, smiling, bathed in a white light which emanated from some hidden source. When they reached the center of the room, she said "And now, my friends—"

"Lady Natulakh, hear me," interrupted Astil. "These men are not who they claim to be; nor am I. I am Astil-Cotavion, a prince of Faerie. This Ammonite is in fact the sorcerer Imhotep, ancient foe of your land, or at least a shadow of him. And this is Leonard Ronar, Greylock, who is also King of Eranior, and therefore two of your most bitter enemies in one person. They have come hoping to destroy your lord Namirnakh, if he lives."

Ronar wheeled to stare at Astil. The Elf's face was strained and unnaturally pale.

A clear laughter, yet wild in a way that reminded him of the wailing of coyotes, distracted Ronar. It came not from Natulakh, but from another figure, cloaked and hooded in grey and bearing an iron staff, who appeared from behind her.

"Very good, Astil. You may yet make something of yourself."

Ronar could not see that shadowed face, but he recognized the voice.

"Seren-Cotavion. Queen of Faerie."

"Greylock. King of Eranior." Her tone was acid with contempt.

Sha Totek raised his arms. With bulging eyes he began to chant in ancient Egyptian, a language whose spoken form even Ronar barely knew.

"Sha Totek, no. Stop!"

But the sorcerer ignored him.

Natulakh merely pointed. Moving as one, fifty iron warriors raised their spears and cast them, piercing Sha Totek and laying him low.

Ronar sprang to his side, fell down, and clutched him. Blood flowed from a dozen terrible wounds. Three spears still protruded from his body.

The sorcerer stared at him with fear-filled eyes. His mouth worked, he coughed, and managed to speak. "Sha Totek has withdrawn himself from me! He cannot bear to die, even in absentia, so to speak. I am left to die alone, my poor partial self. At least now I finally have something to cry about." And so he did.

Gathering himself again, he choked, "Ronar, have I been a good companion to you, poor as I am?"

"Yes. You have been brave and true. You are a better man than most of those who are born from women, and not from magical prisms."

"Thank you. Before he abandoned my failing form, Sha Totek left me with two messages. They are very brief. For you, Come. For those — women — Fear."

The dispersion stopped moving. It then dissolved into a pinkish-purple light, leaving behind nothing but its torn clothing.

Moving slowly, Ronar stood up and faced the witch and the Elf Queen. Astil moved away from him. Suddenly alone and friendless, Ronar looked up and said "You have just angered the sorcerer Sha Totek, and myself as well."

He could just make out Seren's unmoved expression in the shadows of her hood.

Natulakh nodded and said, "Yes. I could have contained his weak magic, but we could not afford to let him live. We could not permit the real Imhotep to view us through his eyes. You we can also contain. I will not assault you with magic, for you have a famous knack of somehow shrugging off its effects, despite your ignorance of the subject. Yet as a mere man, restraints of metal and stone will do as well, if they are stout enough."

More iron soldiers marched in through archways around the periphery of the hall. Ronar raised his fist; the garnet ring began to smolder.

"I have a magic gem as well!" cried Natulakh. Indeed, from a pendant around her neck came the familiar flare of scarlet, followed by the flash of white, and then the Sword of Bran appeared...in the hand of Natulakh.

The weight was too much for her slender arm. The point dropped and clanged on the floor at her feet.

Ronar was taken aback. His ring was inert. He was at a loss. He did not resist as the giants closed around him and laid their black-gauntleted hands on his shoulders.

"Ah, that sweet red light," mused Natulakh. "The last remnant of the Fire of Ahriman in all the world."

"What are you talking about?" flared Ronar. "It is no such thing!"

She laughed. "We'll discuss that some other time. For now, we'll conduct you to your new abode, before you lash out in some manly act of defiance which will get you killed."

"You are a fool if you do not kill me now."

"Yes, probably. Letting you live does represent a change of plans. Yet you are so interesting. And once you find out what we intend to do, you may not be so anxious either to kill us or to die."

A ring of silent iron giants grabbed him with their cold metal claws and bore him off, followed by Natulakh and Seren, and more distantly, Astil. To Ronar's surprise, rather than taking him to the expected buried dungeon they pushed and carried him up many flights of stairs, until they reached a low-ceilinged level with many cells. These were built into the outer wall, and were lit by large, cage-like structures of massive bronze bars which bulged out into the open air. Into one of these cells they tossed Ronar, slamming the door.

A small, scaly six-legged creature scuttled across the floor. Ronar stomped it flat with his boot, then kicked it through the bars at his captors, where it struck Seren-Cotavion in the face. Astil gasped.

She threw back her hood and glared at him in fury. The vermillion stone bound onto her brow flickered with a dizzying light. "You dare provoke me so? You have gained mercy from us. You dare smirk at me?"

"I don't want your mercy. Have I outraged you? Then take your revenge. Face me without all these others. I am unarmed. You have your Stones and your staff. Are you afraid?"

Seren loomed up in wrath and dark splendor. Ronar stood facing her with his hard smile intact.

Suddenly she turned and stormed away, her staff clanging on the stone floor with each quick stride.

Natulakh approached his cell with a small smile of appreciation. She extended her hand. "Your ring, please."

"You don't need my ring. You have already demonstrated that the stone in your medallion also controls the sword. How did you obtain it, if I may ask?"

She shook her head. "The ring. I do not intend to remain mindful of the sword at all times and thus keep it out of your hands. The ring, or we must enter and remove it by force."

Without removing his cold stare from Natulakh's face, he drew off the ring and dropped it into her palm.

"Thank you. We'll leave you in peace for now."

They all withdrew. The prison grew quiet.

Ronar examined his cell. The interior bars were three inches in diameter and closely spaced. The massive steel lock contained multiple latches and deadbolts. The cage that covered the outside opening was wrought of heavy bronze. It admitted cold air into the cell, which lacked any furnishings, even a hole in the floor. Evidently he was expected to hang his posterior out into the cage and befoul whatever lay below.

He leaned out and looked down and all around. The opening faced east, giving an excellent view back the way he had come. He could even see the sharp cutoff on the horizon that marked the Worm Wall.

He then collapsed on the floor and sat, shaking. He could not escape the mental image of the dying Sha Totek. True, he had not been fully or truly the Sorcerer, but he was very much like him, and was a part of him, certainly a person in his own right. Ronar had not expected the death of the dispersion to affect him so strongly. It was all too much like the real death of the real Sorcerer. Ronar had witnessed many deaths. For Sha Totek to die, a person who had existed for some five thousand years, seemed like more than a death, but more like the destruction of a world, a thing unnatural and catastrophic. It was something he would strive never to witness again.

A thin, querulous voice called from somewhere around the curve of the corridor. "Who is there? Who has that bitch locked up now?"

"I am Leonard Ronar. Who are you?"

"Leonard Ronar? Indeed, indeed. And I am the Lord Namirnakh." She gave a dry chuckle.

Ronar said nothing. He was in no mood to banter with this fool, whoever she was.

After a while, he heard, "Are you really Ronar?"

"Yes."

"What are you doing here?"

"At the moment, I'm languishing in a cell. Who are you?"

"I am Erraine. I was formerly the mistress of this tower, or at least of the more modest tower which stood here before this abomination was erected."

"I have heard your name. How did you come to be a prisoner?"

"It was the doing of that ungrateful upstart Natulakh, of course. She came to me, an ignorant novice witch bearing only a few minor artifacts. But she learned quickly, all too quickly. I sometimes think her ignorance was feigned, and that she flattered me only to gain my confidence and lower my suspicions. When she had learned whatever it pleased her to learn, she declared herself Mistress. When I complained, she locked me up. Also poor Vababar, and poor Egreggio, now enslaved to her evil purposes, no doubt."

"Who are they?"

"Magicians who once dwelt here with me in peace. I ask again, why are you here? Your reputation would lead me to expect more of you, you most infamous man."

"I came to discover who in Darteharn had attacked Eranior and destroyed its capital."

"Oh, that would be Natulakh, no doubt." Erraine said this as though accusing Natulakh of drinking the last of the milk.

"What do you know of her?"

"Little more than I've said. She rarely speaks of her past. She bears a kind smile and a pretty face, though rather a dusky one. But within her is a serpent. Oh dear, I've said too much."

Ronar heard a helpless cry that brought him to his feet and to the bars.

"Erraine, what has happened? Are you all right?"

The only answer was a quiet whimpering, followed by metallic footsteps.

An iron soldier came into view, carrying a pike. It halted before Ronar's cell, looking in at him.

Ronar stared into the featureless blackness of the thing's visor.

"Why don't you try poking that tin toothpick in here, you coward?"

The armored form moved on. Erraine spoke to him no more.

Ronar settled down to await the visitor he was expecting.

He came soon enough, carrying an armload of Ronar's possessions, mainly clothing and his sleeping bag.

"Hello, Astil. So, you saved both our lives, I take it?"

Astil looked at him in surprise as he stuffed Ronar's things through the bars. "Yes! I didn't expect you to realize that. From what I'd heard of you, I expected a more...a more..."

"A harsher response to your apparent treachery?"

"Yes."

"Even I have managed to learn a thing or two about life and people in my many turns."

Astil leaned on the bars with both hands. "If we had continued to represent ourselves with those false identities, they would have killed us all at once. If only Sha Totek hadn't tried to resist, I might have saved him as well."

"And now you're back on your aunt's good side."

"Provisionally, yes."

"You knew that Myrddin would be destroyed, didn't you? Seren tasked you with making yourself King after the disaster. When you failed at that, she wrote you off as useless and exiled you to travel with us."

"You knew all that? Why then did you ask me to come on this journey?"

"I saw that you were vain, and arrogant, and inexperienced, but I did not see that you were evil. I hoped that by treating you with respect I could bring you around to rejecting your aunt's schemes. Even though you're a prince of Faerie, you've known little respect, haven't you? Those beneath you in the social hierarchy of your land plot against you, or lick your pixie boots. Those above you treat you with contempt and try to hold you down."

"Yes. That is our way, especially in the House of Cotavion. But a small correction. I knew Myrddin would somehow be brought low, but I did not know it would be utterly destroyed. Is there nothing about this whole affair which has surprised you?"

"Yes, one thing. I knew the plot against Eranior must be the brainchild of either Seren or of some new or resurgent power here in Darteharn. What I didn't expect was that it would be both. Faerie has always held itself apart from the affairs of mortals. For its Queen to ally herself with a mortal nation is unprecedented. This is about something more than the overthrow of Eranior. Do you know what Seren hopes to gain?"

"No. She has never confided so much to me. I must say, I was astonished to see how you abused her. I have never seen or heard of anyone who dared so much, not since she came into possession of the Stones and won the throne."

"I do not fear her."

"But how can you not? She carries Stones controlling Illusion, Despair, Death, and Darkness. These Stones are terrible. I have seen how they tear at the minds of whoever perceives them."

Ronar shrugged. "Not mine."

"I'd like to see proof of that, someday."

"Maybe you will."

"I—I have not come to free you."

"I understand that. You don't wish to betray your family, even though your aunt holds you in disdain and was prepared to see you die, or to kill you herself. Your loyalty is twisted, yet admirable. But don't give up on me yet. Seren and Natulakh have made a serious mistake, the same stupid mistake made by everyone who has ever captured me. They haven't killed me. Thank you for bringing me my things. You'd best go now. You don't want to give the impression of being my friend."

Astil looked conflicted, but finally nodded and left.

Ronar fancied he'd given the Elf enough to think about for now.

He spread his sleeping bag on the stone floor and sat down on it.

Over the next days and weeks he was largely ignored. Occasionally a frightened mouse-like servitor brought him a little to eat and drink, usually a boiled potato or some other tuber and a bowl of water. Sometimes a bit of gristly meat would be added. Ronar suspected it was horse, likely the very animal he'd ridden in on. He knew he couldn't maintain his strength on such a diet, so he took to pouncing on any small creature that came within his reach, including birds that landed on the bars of the window-cage, if he was fast enough. These he perforce ate raw. Colibdian animals were not fully nutritious to Earth creatures, but at least they were generally not toxic.

The viewer was still tucked away in his jacket. He put it to good use, studying the landscape by day and the stars by night. By leaning fully into the cage, he obtained a restricted view to the north and south. Sometimes wet mists rose up from the northern horizon. Ronar suspected these marked the violent Strait of Kiruna which connected the Bay to the ocean.

He heard no more from Erraine, other than an occasional moan or hissed curse. He was surprised not to receive Natulakh as a visitor. He had expected her to come to gloat, or to pry, or to torture, or to explain her plans, but no such thing occurred. Nor did Astil return.

He did have a visitation most unexpected. One evening, as he sat watching the twilight descend on the outside world, he became aware of a pale glimmer coming from the cell behind him. He turned to behold the goddess Athene, tall in her armor, carrying her weapons, looking at him with a remote expression on her face, which so resembled that of Asterope.

"Hello there, Asterope. Have you come to free me?"

The goddess said nothing.

"No? That's the trouble with you gods. You could get me out of here with a blink of your eye, and probably stop whatever those two women are planning with two more blinks. Yet you won't. You weren't always like this. When you were first transfigured, it seemed like you were everywhere, righting wrongs, protecting the helpless, all those good things. It was a display of divine justice such as this world had never seen. But as time passed, you grew more distant, more passive, until now you just stand there looking at me."

She spoke. "When you are able to see as I now see, the wisdom of meddling in these affairs becomes much less apparent. One person oppresses another. Usually the victim is not less wicked than the oppressor, but merely less aggressive, weaker, or less successful. I give them the opportunity to turn the tables, and often they show themselves the more vicious. And you, Leonard Ronar. Would you have me relieve you of the need to strive and fight for what you believe? What would you be if I did that?"

"Would you do me at least one favor then? Appear to me as Asterope. In this form, the clatter of your armor might attract attention, and you're in danger of bumping your head on the ceiling."

With a small smile she complied, dwindling to a slight young woman with curls of dark blonde hair and light grey eyes. She sat down beside him, looking out the window at the dusk. Ronar also returned his attention there, not trusting himself to look at her for too long.

"Did Emogen return safely home?" he asked.

"She did."

"That's good to know. I like her. Do you?"

He felt her gaze return to him. "She is rather naive. She is somewhat simple of heart. But she is wise, kind and honest. Yes, I like her."

"Have I ever told you how much I loved you?" blurted Ronar. "No, of course I haven't. I didn't know how to say such things, back when they might have mattered."

"You seem able to say many things these days."

"Yes. I suppose it's something about old age. You begin to sense you don't have much time left, so anything that needs to be said must come out soon. But yes, I loved you. You were difficult, consciously superior, quick to judgment, and emotionally remote. But you understood your own heart better than I did mine. We were too much alike to function well together, I suppose. Any relationship can stand only one such person, if that many. But I did love you."

Her voice was now more gentle. "I believe I was always aware of that. As I recall, you put yourself through Tartarus, and assaulted the Great Gods themselves, to try to save me. It would be difficult to mistake that for indifference."

He turned to look at her. Her large eyes were like expanses of a winter sky at twilight. He heard a fluttering at the bars of the window grating, and saw perched there a little owl. When he looked back, Asterope was gone, and so was the owl.

He felt both more and less alone than he had before. He wiped away the tears his enemies were never able to evoke from him. He did not despair of emerging from this situation victorious.

From then on, he often awoke to find dead birds, mainly Earthly imports such as passenger pigeons and other doves, lying on the floor of his cell. Their wounds indicated death by the talons of a bird of prey.

With a better (though still unpleasant) diet, Ronar began to exercise, trying to stave off or even reverse the effects of his imprisonment. The bars of the window grating were good for pull-ups. He could brace his feet beneath the lower bars for sit-ups. It was a good way to pass the time and feel that he was accomplishing something.

As yet he had no idea what was happening in the outside word, no real notion of the full extent of the schemes of Natulakh and Seren. Yet in his heart he felt that time was becoming precious, and that he could not linger here much longer. He might have to see about escaping at a less than ideal moment.

One night, more than two moonturns into his imprisonment, he noticed a dim red glow in the east. In the morning he saw smoke rising from the vicinity of the Worm Wall. The viewer disclosed the occasional glint of sunlight on metal. That evening many fires were visible in the forest, not far off.

Ronar lowered the viewer with a strange mixture of emotions. He felt pride and gratitude at what he was witnessing, and also fear for what the result might be.

Hunting through his possessions in the last light, he found the Royal Torc of Eranior and placed it around his neck. He turned, hearing approaching footsteps and seeing a flicker of torchlight. He made sure he was standing as tall and straight as he could when a small party appeared. It was composed of a few iron soldiers, a few human servants, and Natulakh.

She halted just out of his reach and gave him a gentle smile.

"Well, Your Majesty. It seems your subjects in Eranior have somehow learned of your plight and sent an army to collect you. They will fail, but still, we can no longer afford to keep you as a pet."

Ronar eyed her. She was not, he noticed, wearing the pendant which contained the magical garnet.

"Where is your Faery friend?" he asked.

"Who? Oh, you mean Seren? She is no one's friend. She has returned to Faerie for now, along with her dubious nephew Astil. She has a great deal of work to do there. I must say, you are looking well, for a prisoner."

"Thank you…Namirnakh."

Natulakh was taken aback. She looked puzzled for a few moments, and then laughed loudly. "Namirnakh? Oh, I see. Because our names are similar, and I've gotten the best of you, and I look like I might be foreign to Darteharn, you think I must be the latest incarnation of Namirnakh. I must disappoint you. Namirnakh has taken many forms in the past, but they have all been male, without exception. It would not occur to him to do otherwise. Do you wish to know his doings? He has indeed taken a new form. It has been manifest for many turns now. He dwells in Kharnarnithon, where he does nothing. He does not organize the armies. He does not plot revenge. He reads, he thinks, he studies. He neither supports nor opposes my actions. I am his daughter, and a mortal woman, so far."

Ronar kept his expression neutral. That had been a shot in the dark, an attempt to goad her into revealing something, and it had been successful. Now on to the next step.

Her face fell. "Now it's my sad duty to do away with you, a most intriguing figure. I'm sorry I didn't take the opportunity to speak with you earlier, but I've been very busy, and I hoped there'd be time later."

She gestured. The warriors raised their spears.

This was not the situation Ronar had hoped for, but there was no help for it.

They threw the spears. A few glanced off the bars and were deflected. Ronar flung himself low, permitting the others to pass overhead. He managed to catch one, whose angular shaft sliced his right hand as he stopped its flight. He reversed it and flung it out at Natulakh, who nimbly dodged it.

She smiled at him with wide eyes. "Very good! I'm glad I was privileged to see that exhibition of prowess before your death."

"Without their spears, it looks like your toy soldiers will have to come in after me."

"Yes, not that it will do you any good. You should have kept that weapon in your hand instead of wasting it on me."

The soldiers drew their dark iron swords, opened the cell door, and filed in, facing him in a line.

"Oh, one last thing," said Natulakh. "You might as well have this back."

Into the cell she flipped something that glittered red and gold. Ronar caught it, looking at the light caught in its garnet stone.

"I have dissolved the spell that bound it to the Sword of Bran. It was surprisingly easy to do."

Ronar idly tossed the ring to one of Natulakh's servants. "A worthless trinket," he said. He reached into his jacket and produced an identical ring, which he slipped onto his finger. "This one, on the other hand…"

Ronar grinned at the shocked look on Natulakh's face as the ring flared and the great Cold Sword appeared in his hand.

He did not stand gloating for any length of time. He had seconds to even the odds before his enemies overcame their surprise. He gripped the sword in two hands and made a great swinging sweep that put his full weight behind it. The blade knocked back a few of the warriors and scored their armor, but did not bite in deeply. Ronar took an instant to glance at the blade. Having now spent over a month submerged in Kiruna, the entire blade bore a patina of rust. Its once magnificent edge was now dulled.

Ronar's return swing buffeted his foes again. While they were off balance, he took the opportunity to charge past them into the outer corridor, slamming the cell door shut behind him.

"Still satisfied with my exhibition?" he asked Natulakh as the iron warriors reached through the bars or tried to uproot them.

"I'm a bit overwhelmed by it, actually. Am I to gather you were in possession of the real ring all along?"

"Yes. I substituted the replica while I was being led to my cell. I learned long ago not to make it too easy for my enemies to deprive me of my main weapon."

"And yet the brightness of your famous sword is dimmed. Its end is near."

"It is still keen enough to deal harshly with human flesh, I assure you."

Ronar was satisfied to see uncertainty, and perhaps fear, appear on Natulakh's face.

"And now, before the army of Eranior arrives to throw down your tower, will you reveal your plan, and pledge to abandon it? Why did you destroy Myrddin?"

More uncertainty flickered across her face.

"You don't intend to kill me?"

"I'd rather not. Answer my questions."

Natulakh stared at him for a few moments. She then gestured with one hand. "No, Egreggio. I wish to speak with this man for a while."

But it was too late for her to intervene. Egreggio had already cast a spell that dissolved the lock on Ronar's cell. The iron warriors surged forth, grabbing Ronar roughly by the arms and neck, causing the sword to drop from his hand and vanish. Ronar was about to summon it back, hoping to startle his way to freedom, when the characteristic light and sound flared from some corner he couldn't see. Apparently one of Natulakh's lackeys carried the amulet, and had had the presence of mind to use it.

"Oh dear," said Natulakh. "How quickly the tables have turned."

At that moment a tumult arose from outside. Horns blared, drums beat, and voices raised up in a terrible massed battle cry that made even Ronar's hair stand on end. The rhythmic pounding of weapons on shields added itself to the din.

"The Eranians attack at night?" muttered someone.

Great flaring lights, white and green and blue, shone through the window gratings of the cells, illuminating everything.

"It seems they have dug up a magician or two," said Natulakh.

"Answer—my—questions!" choked Ronar past the iron gauntlet that was throttling him.

Natulakh gazed at him in wonder. "Truly you are a singular man. Completely at my mercy, yet still you demand answers, as does a king. Very well. I destroyed Myrddin to decapitate Eranior, to cast it into confusion, and eliminate its capacity to interfere with me. Clearly I was not entirely successful at that. We tried to place the feckless Astil-Cotavion on the throne, but with you on hand, why would they settle for that ageless stripling? The mechanics of the deed were interesting. We erected a magical dam between the highest walls of the Strait as the tide was coming in. When the waters were piled to the brim, we dissolved the dam, sending an incredible cascade of water into your Bay. Our own fortress of Larguc was also destroyed, but it was a worthwhile trade. We don't expect to need it again.

"It was a very great feat of wizardry. By itself, it would have been a master stroke against Eranior. But ultimately, it will not be Darteharnlandua that conquers the world. It will be Faerie. That land has never had a ruler like Seren-Cotavion." Natulakh sounded almost regretful.

"Why?"

Boom! The stones of the tower trembled. Natulakh looked around as dust filtered down around them. "Egreggio, lead the others to repel our attackers. I will join you in a few moments, after I've finished with Greylock."

Natulakh's human underlings scurried away, leaving only the iron warriors.

Natulakh looked at Ronar sadly. "I'm afraid your subjects are hastening events beyond what I would have wished. Your final question must go unanswered. Your gaze has grown distant. I fear you no longer hear me anyway. Goodbye."

"You—leave me—no choice."

Ronar had indeed been listening to her, but he had also been doing more.

He had been looking at his surroundings, forcing himself to see them for what they really were. Forcing himself to regard his body as what it really was.

Suddenly the iron warriors lost their ability to maintain their grip on him. He slipped through their hands as though they were made of smoke. He looked at them, and they did not move again. He looked at Natulakh, seeing her in that same dispassionate, analytical way, but he did not move against her.

She faltered, staggering away from something she saw in his eyes.

"You earlier accused me of being ignorant of magic," he said quietly. "You are partially correct. I have not studied the spells or mastered the incantations. But I understand magic in a way you never shall. I can say *quantum field*, and to you it is a meaningless phrase. To me it is the key to the underlying layer of reality that makes magic possible. You are like someone who has memorized a song. I know how notes and rhythms and words fit together to turn the locks in men's minds that make them weep."

"You are terrible," she said in a husky voice. "I had no idea."

He raised a hand to quiet her. "Don't be afraid. We will go down together and put a halt to the senseless battle which is about to erupt."

"No!" This high, thin voice came from somewhere in the darkness behind him. "She shall not escape! By fire and decay, by the rot of your own treachery, fall!"

Natulakh sucked in a breath and stiffened. Fissures opened in her flesh. Ronar looked away, crying out in dismay. The laughter of Erraine assaulted his ears. When he looked back, Natulakh had been reduced to a skeleton surrounded by loose chunks of meat. Ronar staggered away, collapsed against a wall, and closed his eyes.

"She is slain! Ronar, you so weakened her that she had no defense against my spell. I have beaten the backstabbing virago!"

"Silence!" roared Ronar in desperation.

There was silence. Ronar's eyes remained closed. He knew it would be days before he again felt as if he walked and existed in a real world. Until then it would all be less than a dream. Whenever he did what he had just done, forcing himself to see past magic and the gross properties of matter itself, he had thereafter to struggle to keep his mind from dissolving into the hissing sea of randomness that was the world. And why should he not? What did any of it mean? What was he? It was all illusion, all false. He wrapped his arms around his knees, buried his head, and rocked back and forth while oblivion glared at him from every direction and from past, present, and future.

"Let me out. Please let me out."

That small croaking voice eventually roused him from whatever stupor he had fallen into. He got unsteadily to his feet and staggered to Erraine's cell. The lights from outside had fallen dark, but Ronar summoned a red sputter from his ring (Fire of Ahriman? Would he ever learn what Natulakh had meant by that?). Erraine cowered away.

She was a shrunken, pitiful thing, dressed in rags which once no doubt had been colorful finery. To Ronar she seemed harmless, a middling witch better known as a landlord than as a magician.

"Erraine, you should not have killed her. I know your grievance against her, but it was less than mine, and I wished to save her. She might have answered many questions and undone much harm."

The witch lowered her head. "I am sorry, Lord Ronar."

The sword came at Ronar's bidding. He used it to pry open Erraine's cell, which was of much weaker construction than his had been.

"Go now. Do harm to none. That is part of your creed, isn't it?"

"It is now. My blessing upon you, Lord Ronar." She scuttled away, looking around uncertainly, unsure of her surroundings. She ignored the remains of Natulakh as though they were a pile of sticks.

Ronar, on the other hand, averted his eyes. Not long before, Natulakh had stood proud and haughty before him, speaking of her plans to conquer the world. Now she was obliterated. Where were her bold words now? When she woke up this morning, did she imagine she would not survive to sleep again?

Ronar stood still, sighed, and listened. Evidently, the death of Natulakh had not been enough to halt the battle. He returned to his cell, leaned out, and looked down. Iron warriors moved among the Eranian forces, attacking. Streams of fire and bolts of magic rained down from the tower. The attacking army, which seemed to number about two thousand, was hard pressed. It was a pointless attack.

This tower was no longer a threat to the world. That threat had moved elsewhere.

"Stop! Retreat!" cried Ronar, but from this height no one could hear him. He sighed again. He must go down and do what he could to stop this.

Then the tower trembled again. Then it was jolted. The battlefield below was covered with torches like red jewels sewn into a tapestry; now its fabric rippled. Fighters on both sides milled about, disengaging. They fled from an acre of ground only a few hundred feet from the base of the tower. Dim blue lights flickered and darted there. Magic? No, thought Ronar, it looked more like triboluminescence resulting from crystals cracking in the heaving soil.

The earth erupted. Molten rock spewed upward in arcs. With a hideous din, something bulged up from beneath the shattered surface, pushing skyward. Up and up it rose, a great black shape, wreathed in smoke and dust. A massed cry of terror and dismay rose from every throat capable of such utterances. It loomed there, now silent, an ominous new presence, wholly unexpected. To Ronar, in his present mood, it seemed a terrible thing, a new instance of madness of the sort which should not be seen in any decent world.

And yet he had seen this before. Here now stood the Tower of Sha Totek, a glassy black cylinder less than half the height of the Tower of the Mystic Arts, yet giving up nothing in formidability.

Ronar turned away and hurried down the stair, finding the tower abandoned as he went. He passed through the great hall without resistance, and thence through the gate into the outside air.

The battle was over. The iron warriors had toppled, inert. Natulakh's human underlings stood about with fearful faces. Scarcely less fearful were the forces of Eranior, whose gazes passed between one tower and the other, perplexed.

To call attention to himself, Ronar ignited his ring and brought forth the Cold Sword with its usual blinding clash. Seeing him standing there before the gate, the Eranians sent forth a huge cry of gladness, knowing that their mission to rescue their King was not in vain. Ronar raised the sword and his open hand until he obtained silence.

"Men of Eranior! You have done very well. This battle is now over. Behind you stands the tower of the sorcerer Imhotep, who has come in all his power to put an end to the fighting. Now I command you to take possession of this tower of Darteharn. Send in a captain, a few hundred men, and whatever wizards you have among you. Go floor by floor, searching everywhere. Do not despoil anything. If any surrender to you, imprison them, but do not molest them. There are prison cells on the twenty third level. Go."

He descended the stairs, maintaining the sword as he passed through the cheering ranks, approaching Sha Totek's Tower. Ronar ignored all greetings, intent only on gaining the Tower.

He found the Sorcerer awaiting him at its base. Ronar was struck by the difference between this man and the dispersion he had lately known, to the extent that he wondered how he ever could have been fooled. This man looked tired, squinting with fatigue, yet he possessed a vitality, a commanding presence, and a sharpness in his black eyes which the dispersion could never have matched.

"So, we've gone to all this trouble to rescue you, and you had already freed yourself? A typical lack of consideration on your part." Sha Totek looked at him more closely and winced. "You've been practicing some of that strange magic of yours, haven't you?"

"Yes. I couldn't avoid it."

"That's too bad. It's not good for you. You should stick to solving problems by bashing them with your sword." He glanced at the blade. "Oh dear. I do hate to see it in that condition."

Ronar let the sword pass away. "So do I. So. I must say, this is one of your more dramatic entrances."

Sha Totek gave a flamboyant shrug. "Ah, well. With the Bronze Portal destroyed, there was no real reason for me to remain there on the Red Plain, and I was getting tired of that view anyway. Plus mebbe I'll shed that gol-durn cowpoke accent you hate so much."

"So instead, you'll set up shop in Darteharn, of all places?"

"For a while at least, why not? There never was a Portal here, you know. This scenery is new to me. Namirnakh should prove an interesting neighbor. But for now, if there's nothing more urgent that needs to be done, I suggest you bunk in here for the night. You look like you can use some rest, and so can I. We'll talk things over in the morning."

Ronar slept poorly, plagued by feverish dreams in which the boundaries between reality and fantasy were uncomfortably blurred. He was relieved to see the suns rise, permitting him to put aside such doubts while the bright images of the daylight world pervaded his mind.

Chapter Thirteen

Scattered Forces

After he had eaten (and eaten well, along with everyone else, thanks to the apparently inexhaustible larder which Sha Totek somehow maintained), Ronar and Sha Totek met with the leaders of the Eranian forces in one of the lower levels of the Tower. This chamber took up the whole of that level, and was as luxurious as any other part of it, but while most levels of the Tower were dark with occasional islands of vivid light and color, this chamber was bright, and cool, and restful, which was a peculiar trick, as it lacked both windows and any visible source of light.

Gahareet, the Steward of Eranior, was present, looking determined but also uncomfortable. With him were the main military captains, mostly young men who had been raised to these positions only recently. Also present were a few young witches and wizards who looked around in undisguised wonder to find themselves not only in Darteharn but inside the very Tower of Sha Totek, in the company of some of the world's most legendary figures.

Finally there was a short but sturdy figure still wearing the black armor of Darteharn, Caradoc of Amulree, and beside him the bright-eyed witch Emogen, who had spent the night treating the wounded.

They sat on a ring-shaped divan which surrounded a pit containing a cool, sweet-smelling fountain of many colors.

Sha Totek stood up, gestured, and proclaimed, "Greetings, friends, and welcome. We come together today to confront monstrous evil, to devise a plan against yet another wicked overlord, and so forth and so on, blah blah blah. I give you King Ronar, whose natural gravitas makes him much more suited to affairs of this sort than I am. Carry on, Your Majesty."

Ronar blinked as Sha Totek sat down to drain a goblet. Without rising, Ronar said, "Gahareet, please tell me how you and your army came to be here."

"It was the doing of this witch, Emogen, Lord," said Gahareet, gesturing toward the witch in question. "According to her, she returned to her village as you instructed, but then she set out for the east after awaiting you for a few days. She made contact with our border watchmen, and convinced them of the urgency of her errand. Together they hurried to our encampment by the Bay, where she told me where you were and what you intended. Naturally I was not inclined to believe a Darteharnian witch, but she carried your note, and her words are fair. She told me there was nothing to oppose us between Eranior and that other tower. She said Caradoc and her entire village and valley were prepared to make an alliance with us. So I gathered the best force I could and set out."

"You did well." Ronar turned to Emogen. "So, Emogen, it did not take you long to discover what lay to the west of that pond after all."

Emogen smiled at him.

"How did you pass the Worm Wall, Gahareet?"

Gahareet answered in a somber tone. "We found a route through a crack in the face several miles to the south of where you entered the wall, with evidence that horses had recently used it. But it was narrow and difficult. It would have taken our full force too long to negotiate it. So most of us did not pass over that wall. We passed through it. We returned to the entrance and demanded passage of the creatures who inhabit it. They were reluctant, but we insisted. There was something they did not wish us to see, but we lacked the time and the inclination to investigate. We sent the horsemen over the wall via that crack, while the foot soldiers entered the passageways. Our chariots we were forced to leave in the valley."

Ronar nodded. "Has anyone seen any sign of Seren-Cotavion, Astil-Cotavion, or any other Elf?"

Heads were shaken. "No, Lord," said Gahareet. "Astil's retainers departed for Faerie when you set out, and that's the last I know of any Elf."

"I see. What I say now has been known only to Sha Totek and myself. We had naturally thought the threat to Eranior came from Namirnakh. Evidently it does not. Our true foes are Natulakh, the daughter of Namirnakh, and Seren-Cotavion, Queen of Faerie. Natulakh is now slain. Seren lives. I believe Natulakh's part in this conspiracy was largely complete, but Seren remains a grave threat to us all."

"What sort of a threat?" asked Gahareet. "I'm sure the Elves are terrible within their own domain, but I'm not sure how fearsome they would be outside of it."

"We don't yet know."

"It is puzzling," admitted Sha Totek. "The people of Faerie have never presented much threat to other lands before. Oh, if you happen to cross their border uninvited, watch out! Otherwise, they much prefer to remain within their own peculiar land, and disdain the outside world. Of course, Faerie has had only a few rulers in its centuries of existence. By that measure, Seren has not been long on the throne. Who knows how perverse she might have become? No other ruler of Faerie ever possessed those strange Stones of hers."

"And why was Natulakh involved in this scheme, whatever it is?" continued Ronar. "What advantage to her, or to Darteharn, could there be in Faerie taking over? We must know these things. And there is another matter which must be dealt with: Namirnakh."

"Why?" asked one of the captains. "You said he is not involved with any of this."

"True, but consider this. An Eranian army has invaded his land. The Tower of Sha Totek, his ancient enemy, now stands within his borders. His daughter has been killed. How would you expect him to react to all these provocations? We did not kill Natulakh, but why would he believe that? How are we to explain it to him?"

"Leave him a note?" asked Sha Totek innocently.

Ronar ignored this. "Even if he was somnolent before, there's no telling what he might do now. He must not become a factor in all this. Here is what I propose to do. Gahareet, take the bulk of your force, say twelve hundred men, back to Eranior. Station them, plus whatever others you can muster, in northeastern Eranior to be alert for any incursions from Faerie. Send messengers to Tíuheimr to alert them as well. Station another eight hundred men in the vicinity of Amulree to watch for any attack from the west. Establish a supply line with Eranior proper so that these men will not eat the valley folk out of house and home. Caradoc, try to raise additional troops from the men of your valley if you truly desire to become part of Eranior. Finally, two hundred men will occupy the Tower of the Mystic Arts.

They will occupy it, but not claim it for Eranior. If any substantial force of Darteharn arrives to contest it, they will yield and retreat to Amulree. In the meantime, they will examine it closely, question our prisoners, and maintain watchfulness."

"And what will you do?" asked Emogen.

"Sha Totek and I will ride from here with fifty men. It will be a force large enough to discourage any lone monsters or bands of brigands, but small enough not to pose a grave threat. We will ride openly, but not belligerently. This time we will go with banners flying and horns blowing. We will pay for our food and molest no one who offers us no injury. We will ride to Kharnarnithon, the capital of Darteharn, and there speak with Namirnakh, explaining to him the new realities of the world and asking his intentions."

"That is a bold plan!" exclaimed Caradoc.

"Ronar, if we confront Namirnakh in the very center of his power, I may not be able to match him," said Sha Totek.

"I hope there will be no confrontation. How far is Kharnarnithon from here, would you say?"

"We can consult my maps later, but it lies about two hundred miles to the southwest."

"About a single moonturn's ride, coming and going, if all goes well. We will return here as fast as possible, and then return to Eranior. Is everything clear?"

"Lord Ronar, do you value the advice of your Steward?" asked Gahareet.

In fact, Ronar did not care to listen to his predictable objections, but he could not cut the man's legs out from under him by admitting this before the others. "I am listening."

"You have said the threat lies to the east, in Faerie. You have said that Namirnakh appears to be uninvolved. It seems to me that this excursion of yours is a dangerous, unnecessary delay. No king of Eranior has ever ventured so far into Darteharn, let alone approached their primary seat of power. If you feel we must inform Namirnakh of our innocence in his daughter's death, let us send messengers, who may hope for the courtesy due them. How do you know you can afford a moonturn's delay in acting against Seren?"

Sha Totek and the others looked at Ronar, awaiting his reply with great interest.

"Your points are well taken," he said reluctantly. "Nevertheless, I am going."

"Well, I'm sorry to hear that," said Sha Totek, rising to his feet. "Because I am *not* going, not under these circumstances. I was willing to risk a dispersion on this errand, but not my own precious self, especially since we already know Namirnakh is not at fault. Ronar, you have chosen a Steward who is wise and prudent. Wiser than you, it appears. I however am not the servant of any king, not even if he is you. If you're going to convince me, you must offer a better explanation than any we've heard so far."

"Very well. I think we might make an ally of Namirnakh."

At this the Eranians goggled in astonishment. Even Emogen and Caradoc were amazed.

As for Sha Totek, he laughed. It was not an ordinary laugh, but the sort of booming, boisterous "Ho ho ho!" laugh he had learned from the less refined inhabitants of Thunderbird. It involved some knee-slapping as well.

"Leonard, my friend, I'm sorry to assault your massive dignity this way, but are you crazy? Half a dozen times has Namirnakh expended all the strength of Darteharn in attacking Eranior, me, or the entire world. You saw only his most recent attempt, and therefore in your heart you imagine it was a singular event. But if was not. True, he has done nothing since. Our good friends from Amulree here didn't even know he was still alive. But this is nothing new. It takes him many turns to rebuild his strength after each defeat. By the way, did you know that until a hundred turns or so ago, the valley of Amulree was the western frontier of Eranior? No, none of you did, it seems. Namirnakh has always been defeated, but never without some loss. What has changed?"

"The world has changed. Is changing. The last time I saw Earth, it was on the verge of destruction by forces I could not understand or identify. Either it has now been ruined or changed beyond recognition, of that I have no doubt. This world is the last bastion of humanity in existence. That it exists at all is due to powers none of us understands. Some strange agency made magic possible on Colibdis. They placed the Bronze Portals, each carefully timed and located to promote the survival of many of Earth's most seminal and vigorous cultures. I have reason to believe they even arranged the very suns themselves, and placed Colibdis where it now lies. You, Sha Totek, have worked for thousands of turns to preserve all this. I am only an upstart compared to you. But where you see the patterns of history and expect them to be repeated indefinitely, I see imminent change, or at least the possibility of change. I must convince Namirnakh of all this. I must convince him to put aside his vanity, his lust for power and revenge, and seek peace. Darteharn and Eranior are two halves of the same land, with much the same culture, populated by the same people. I never fully realized that until my journey here.

"If I cannot convince you, Sha Totek, of all I say, I hold out less hope for my ability to succeed with Namirnakh. Still, I feel obliged to try."

Sha Totek sat down again, looking at Ronar most thoughtfully.

"Ronar the Conciliator, eh?"

"If I can."

"That was a very fine speech. Still, it represents only hope, and contains little of fact. I will not go. I am sorry."

Ronar lowered his gaze and compressed his lips, bitterly disappointed. He maintained silence for several moments before trusting himself to speak again.

"Very well. I ask that you consider moving your Tower into Eranior. It may soon need your protection."

"I may do that."

Ronar looked at Gahareet. "May I expect the cooperation of Eranior in my mad plan?"

Gahareet stared at him in wonder. "Lord King, I think we can find fifty men with enough faith in your vision to give their lives for it, if need be."

"Thank you. There is one more matter before we disperse. Has anyone seen a wizard named Egreggio?"

"What does this man look like, Lord King?" asked one of the captains.

"I don't know. I never got a look at him." Ronar sighed. "He was one of Natulakh's assistants. I believe he holds a garnet gem which came from the Sword of Bran. Like the one in my ring, it is magically linked to the sword, and can summon it as I do. If he uses it, I cannot access the sword."

"Is that right?" said Sha Totek. "That is very interesting. How did they obtain this gem?"

"I don't know, but I suspect some spy removed it from the sword while it was still on display in Myrddin, possibly several turns ago. Egreggio was formerly an associate of Erraine, the witch who once owned the Tower of the Mystic Arts. Who has seen her?"

That same captain said, "Erraine? A scraggly old woman? We found her prowling about that tower and imprisoned her with the help of one of our own wizards. Did we do wrong?"

Ronar winced. "Yes. I promised her freedom. Release her."

"I go at once." The captain practically fled the room.

Ronar stood. "Our business here is done. Let the men be mustered and may we ride by noon."

Ronar left the Tower, distracted, barely noticing the others, though Emogen and Sha Totek walked nearby. He approached the other tower, vaguely intending to recover his belongings from his old cell. As he neared the stairs, Erraine burst from the gate, saw him, and shambled angrily toward him. Ronar halted, expecting to be scolded.

Instead, she hesitated, and her face showed confusion. "Egreggio?" she asked.

Ronar and his companions looked around.

"Where?" said Sha Totek.

"You!" she answered, approaching him with keen eyes. "But no. You are younger than he. Otherwise, you are exactly the same, whoever you are."

The sorcerer bowed. "I am called Imhotep, or more lately Sha Totek, madame."

Erraine jumped back a pace. "Indeed?"

"What can you tell us of this Egreggio, Erraine?" asked Ronar.

"He came to me from Kharnarnithon, quite a few turns ago, seeking to study at my tower. He was a fair sorcerer, and he always paid his rent on time. But he was treacherous, easily taking up with that hussy Natulakh." She looked again at Sha Totek. "He was so much like you, down to that hawkish nose. He could easily be your father."

"My father never set foot on this world." The Sorcerer turned to Ronar, regarding him with narrowed, glittering eyes. "My friend, I have changed my mind. I think I shall go with you to see what our friend Namirnakh is up to in his city."

Chapter Fourteen

Namirnakh

The two towers had dwindled to a grey spike and a shorter black post on the horizon behind them. Ronar's procession of fifty two rode on. It consisted of fifty volunteer warriors, led by the dashing young Captain Conall (Conall being quite a common name in those parts), and all very well armed, courtesy of Sha Totek's considerable store of weapons (though he insisted on getting them all back). Ronar wore a lordly costume of scarlet, dark green, and grey, bowing to everyone's insistence that if he were going to represent himself as a king, he should look like one. On his left side rode Sha Totek in a splendidly barbarous outfit of purple, gold, and green.

Emogen had also wished to go, arguing that having an actual child of Darteharn in Ronar's party could only help. Ronar's counter-argument was that Namirnakh could well consider her a traitor. Emogen had argued and pleaded, but Ronar would not be moved. He'd charged Caradoc and the army with escorting her back to Amulree, and keeping her there this time. He brooded on this as he rode along.

"So, how are the children?" asked Sha Totek suddenly.

"Eh?" For several moments Ronar could not think what children the sorcerer could possibly mean. "Oh yes, those children. The Worm Wall foundlings. To tell you the truth, I never thought to ask."

"Oh, that will impress Emogen with your paternal instincts."

Ronar looked aside at his friend. "And why should I wish to impress her?"

"Ha, I've seen you eying her. She seems like a likely Next Mrs. Leonard Ronar to me."

"Nonsense. There will be no further Mrs. Ronars. I'm too old for such foolishness."

"If you say so. For your information, I did think to ask her about those brats."

"What? Then why did you ask me—oh, never mind."

"She said their skins have grown brown beneath the suns. She said it's difficult to get them to go indoors."

"That's good, I suppose. Given your interest in them, perhaps you should adopt them. They could be a couple of apprentice sorcerers, to keep your Tower swept out."

Conall, a handsome young man who wore his war gear with panache, was riding a short distance behind them. He cantered up beside them.

"Pardon my eavesdropping, my lords, but I must ask you this. Do you commonly speak to each other in this manner?"

Sha Totek laughed.

Ronar said, "Yes, boy, we do. We've known each other a long time."

"It seems that way even to me," said the Sorcerer.

"Thank you, lords. It's good to know that legends can be human, also." Conall rode back to his station.

"Just the same," muttered Sha Totek, "perhaps we should converse in English from now on. There's no sense in totally dispelling our legendary stature."

"Speaking of your legendary stature," said Ronar, indeed in English, "there's something I've been meaning to ask. That name your double used...Sekani. I didn't have the impression he chose it at random. What does it mean?"

"Hmm. Come to think of it, it's my real name."

"So you are not, after all, the famous architect and healer Imhotep?"

"No, not if you want to get technical about it."

"This sounds like it could be an entertaining story."

Sha Totek shrugged. "In old Kemet I was Sekani, a nobody, a wandering magician, therefore a charlatan, and occasionally a thief. One day I was pursued into the desert by a group of men who I had offended with my poor magic, or through some other misdeed which I do not recall. I encountered the first Bronze Portal and naturally fled into it. On the other side I found an extremely frightened and disoriented troop of soldiers who had been ordered into it to investigate. They were like me, common men who had never seen the Pharaoh or any member of his court, let alone the fabulous Imhotep. Therefore I identified myself as Imhotep, a lie which, along with my now functional magic, made it much easier to take charge of the situation. As time passed the name just sort of clung to me, enhancing my reputation. Thus have I diligently kept the great man's name alive."

Ronar laughed. "Your secret is safe with me, Sekani. I have seen relics of Imhotep in museums on Earth. I never saw your face in any of them."

They passed farmsteads as they proceeded, and then villages, and then towns. Whenever they approached an inhabited place they let their trumpets call out before them. People lined their path, gazing at them in amazement. Some asked Ronar if he were their new king. He said no, as far as he knew they already had a king. They denied it and said their land was without a leader. Witches fled before them. Wizards and druids emerged to challenge them, but upon seeing the subtle manner in which Sha Totek moved his hands, they too melted away.

Once a haphazard band of armed men appeared in their path to contest their way. Ronar advanced on them alone, spoke with them firmly yet courteously, and left them disarmed, in the sense that they no longer wished to fight.

Wherever they halted, the laughing Conall and his men bounced the local children on their knees, while Sha Totek blew soap bubbles, which was the same as magic to such as these. Ronar met with the leaders of these towns, offering friendship, treating them with respect. It got to the point where local people would ride out ahead of them, and then cheering crowds would greet them in the next village.

No one heralded them as they approached the capital city of Kharnarnithon on a grey day. This was a sprawling place, with great dark walls, and a somber, angular architecture made mostly from a dark bluish-grey stone. At the main gate, which was open, they were met by a man of average height with dusky skin and ringlets of glossy black hair. He bowed at their approach.

"Greetings, travelers. The Lord Namirnakh knows of your coming, and has sent me to conduct you to him. Please follow."

Ronar nodded. The procession passed along the streets of this solemn city, attracting many silent onlookers, though the city seemed underpopulated to Ronar. Its structures grew taller and more imposing as they proceeded, until they reminded Ronar of buildings in some of the older cities of eastern Europe, sober and humorless, but not, at least on the outside, dreadful. It looked nothing like any part of Eranior, and indeed was nothing like any other Colibdian city Ronar had seen. Some of the largest and most uniform buildings, three and four stories tall, appeared to be apartment buildings, another first for Colibdis as far as Ronar knew.

Finally they entered a plaza which surrounded a very large domed structure, clearly a temple. Their guide asked that their armed escort wait outside, and then led Ronar and Sha Totek into the cool, incense-scented interior of the temple, through a few antechambers, and then into the great open space beneath the main dome.

Sitting there upon a great throne of black granite was an immense figure of polished dark metal. If it stood up it would have been at least a hundred feet tall. Its lean face was calm and impassive. Its lambent gaze, which came from eyes like gigantic rubies, was fixed upon them as they stood there before it.

In a whispered aside to Ronar, Sha Totek said, "Ah... you don't suppose..."

Their guide interrupted him with a laugh. "No, that is not Namirnakh. It is an image of Ahriman, though as you both well know, he had no true physical form. And yet his worshippers needed something to look upon. His Fire used to burn in those eyes, and that was an impressive sight in its day. No, indeed, I am Namirnakh."

They turned to study him in surprise. A man of average stature and appearance, with a roundish face, he was dressed in a simple tunic and trousers of purplish grey. He spread his arms in self-deprecation.

"I know, I am not terribly impressive. This body is fully human, and close to my original Persian form. I am returning to the basics. No more antlers or horns for me. I am tired of all that Druidic imagery. I have not announced my return to the world because I don't wish to be bothered. Let me say, I now wake up every day not knowing what to expect from life. I try to be surprised by nothing. But to find myself receiving as guests Leonard Ronar and Imhotep, well..."

He laughed. "I would ask 'What next?' but after this, any other surprises must come as a disappointment."

"Do you know why we have come?" asked Ronar.

"I have heard something of my daughter's plans. I know that she is dead. I know you are not to blame, and that you, Ronar, actually hoped to save her, despite the harm she caused to Eranior. I assure you, I am innocent in this. I do not know the full extent of her plotting, but I made it clear to her that I was not interested in assisting her with it. Daughters. They can be so very troublesome."

Sha Totek showed his most sardonic grin. "And why were you so unwilling to assist her, my old comrade? Got some better trick up your sleeve, have you?"

"Some trick of conquest? No, no. Such things are behind me, I believe."

"I repeat my question."

Namirnakh shrugged. "The world is changing."

Ronar and Sha Totek looked at each other.

"The Bronze Portals are no more. The road to Earth is closed to me. By the way, do you realize we three are the last men on Colibdis who remember the single sun and the soft blue skies of Earth? It is fitting that we should be here together. Anyway, Ahriman, the god who I worked so long to build up, is destroyed, and I have no desire to start over with a new one. And gentlemen, I have not forgotten that these reverses are primarily due to your own efforts. At the same time, I am aware that the most powerful god remaining on Colibdis is your patron, Ronar."

Ronar elected not to correct Namirnakh on this matter.

Namirnakh continued. "Finally, the hated house of Aneirin, which ruled Eranior for so many turns, has failed at last. This alone is enough to quiet my lust to conquer that land."

Namirnakh walked over to the base of the statue's throne and sat down on a ledge. His voice echoed as he continued. "So what am I to do? To tell you the truth, I'm getting tired of Darteharn. The weather tends to be chilly and wet, and there's so little color around here. I'm thinking about leaving, moving to Ammon or Assuria, someplace warmer, where people are more like myself. Ronar, you're widely traveled, you'd know this. Is there any remnant of the civilization of ancient Persia on Colibdis? Oh, I should be asking you, Imhotep. You would have been the one to usher them in, after all."

Sha Totek shook his head. "There is no such land."

"No?" Namirnakh seemed saddened by this. He turned back to Ronar, looking more animated. "What has become of Persia in your time? Is it still a great empire?"

"The last I knew, it was a middle-sized country, influential in its region, and of some importance elsewhere because of its stores of, er, stone oil. But it has been many centuries since Persia possessed an empire. I don't know the present situation. For all I know, Earth has been destroyed."

"Destroyed? Maybe you both should have let me conquer it. It sounds like it could hardly have been worse off for it."

Ronar said carefully, "When last I saw Earth, it was threatened by forces that make your reign seem like a desirable alternative, I admit. However, I don't know what the outcome was. I do know that Earth was defended by beings powerful enough to daunt even you and Sha Totek. I still chose not to risk the safety of Colibdis by betting on their success."

Sha Totek spoke up then. "Namirnakh, this little chat has been very pleasant, and at least as surprising to me as it has been to you. But I feel obliged to ask a question or two. You seem to know a bit about what has happened to Natulakh. How did you discover this?"

Namirnakh gave a sly grin. "Oh, Egreggio told me."

"Egreggio? He is here? Rumor has it he is something of a duplicate of myself."

"Yes, he is that. I made him, using a sample of your substance which I obtained on a previous occasion. Ronar, I believe you once encountered a similar double of yourself in Ammon, eh?"

"And why did you make this creature?" demanded Sha Totek before Ronar could reply. "To trick someone? To try to substitute it for myself?"

"No, no, it was far more innocent than that. I created him as a companion, nothing more. But he is not very satisfactory. While much like you, he lacks the depth and spark that you possess. He is perhaps like one of your dispersions, but more complete, with an independent existence. Perhaps given a thousand turns he might amount to something. I soon grew tired of him. He wished to learn magic, but I did not desire to teach him. Thus I was content to send him off to the Tower of the Mystic Arts. There he fell under the unfortunate influence of Natulakh. She was a much more interesting companion than Egreggio, I must say, yet she found me unsatisfactory. She was volatile and ambitious, and she complained bitterly about my recent lack of initiative. She was determined to avenge slights which no longer have the power to arouse me to wrath. And so she perished, at the hands of that silly witch Erraine. Egreggio fled back to me when you conquered his tower. He is around somewhere. You may kill him if you wish. Oh, that reminds me. He had something which belongs to you, Ronar."

From his tunic Namirnakh produced a gold pendant in which was mounted a garnet. He swung it on its chain and regarded it thoughtfully.

"I have used this to examine that fabulous sword of yours. As you know, I have unpleasant memories of that weapon from long ago. It was very strange to have it in my possession, to hold its cold hilt in my hand. I admit I destroyed it in numerous ways, just for fun. I shattered it, ground it to powder, melted it, dissolved it in cauldrons. Yet the spell is persistent, and it always came back the same as ever, except for that unsightly rust on the blade. In a few turns the sea will have eaten it, and then even that reminder of my past will no longer exist to trouble me. Even you, Ronar, will eventually be consumed. Despite your curious longevity, you are mortal, and will soon be only a legend of the past. In the meantime, you might as well continue to use the sword."

He flipped the pendant to Ronar, who caught it.

"Thank you," said Ronar, bemused, aware of the surreal nature of the situation. "I assume this Egreggio has also informed you of Seren-Cotavion's part in your daughter's schemes?"

"Eh?" For the first time during their interview, Namirnakh's brown eyes narrowed with anger. "What's this? The Dark Queen of Faerie?"

"Yes. As far as we can determine, she is the more dangerous of the two."

"No, Egreggio did not mention this, the fool. Of course I would have discovered it eventually. I don't like the sound of this. I have always excluded Faerie from my plans, because it stands apart from mortal lands and is not much susceptible to my magic. But if that young queen of theirs sees something she likes beyond her borders, it could be a problem unlike anything you two have ever faced."

"That's pretty much the way we see it too," said Sha Totek in a wry tone.

"Well, you gentlemen have proven adept at dealing with various crises in the past, as I know very well. Still, this meeting has been surprisingly agreeable to me. Yet I ask you now to excuse me, if we have no further business. I wish to have a word with Egreggio, if you do not."

"One last thing, if you will," said Ronar. "I have studied the history of Eranior, as it is taught there. I would like to hear your side of the story. I have heard how you and Bran came through your Portal from Britain. I have heard how you tamed the land, and founded the kingdom of Eranior. How Bran set you beside him as co-ruler. How you then betrayed him, murdered him, and ruled with first his head, and then his skull, resting on the throne beside yours, until the Aneirins rose up and drove you and your followers to the west. How would you portray these events?"

"Yes, this will be interesting to hear," said Sha Totek.

Namirnakh's expression grew sour. He lowered his head until the other two could not see his face in the shadows.

"You, Ronar, know Eranior only as it now exists, a high civilization. It was not always thus. Bran was a blue-painted savage who beheaded his enemies as a matter of course. He and his followers were not lofty heroes, but were outcasts driven through the Portal by more successful tribes. Once here, they quickly fragmented into tribal groups with no more ambition than to war on each other, as they always had on Earth. There was no Eranior. When I arrived, Bran was merely the leader of one makeshift clan among several. Only when I allied myself with him was he able to dominate the others. Only then was he able to consolidate the warring clans into a kingdom. Yes, he had grace enough and sense enough to set me beside him, but neither his goals nor his nature became more noble once he sat upon a throne. He was always looking for rivals, for real or imagined threats to his rule. He still wished to fight, but other realms of men were both distant and more established and powerful. His purges kept our land always on the verge of chaos, with cries for vengeance echoing from all corners. Then, when I urged him to adopt a more even-handed reign, he began to eye me as a potential traitor. So yes, I killed King Bran. Yes, I kept his head, as anyone there would have done. During my rule I tried to stop the interfamilial warfare and bring peace. This caused resentment. The Aneirins were able to use this to their advantage, aided by mistrust of my dark skin and foreign ways. They rose up against me and drove me and my followers out.

"Here in Darteharn I established my own kingdom and my own ways. In time it grew to surpass Eranior. I pressed it, did my best to conquer it. In response the Eranians were forced to unite, to stop murdering each other, to progress, all to defend themselves against me. So if you now find Eranior admirable, you have me to thank for it. I wonder though, how long will they stand together, once they no longer have you as king, Ronar, and without Darteharn as an imminent threat?"

"And without their capital city," added Sha Totek.

Namirnakh looked him in the eye. "Yes, there is that. It is a circumstance which can only indirectly be blamed on me."

Ronar said, "Namirnakh, we thank you for your courtesy and your candor. I believe you have related your story the way you truly see it. We will now depart in peace, to act against Faerie if need be. I am sorry for the loss of your daughter. Given time, I believe her heart too would have grown quieter, and she would have been a blessing to you. Goodbye."

Namirnakh gave Sha Totek a curious look. "One last thing. I have found that my return to my original form has produced a calming effect on me. The days seem to pass more slowly, and they carry with them a sort of gentle tranquility which infuses my being. You, Imhotep, might consider such a thing yourself."

Sha Totek laughed. "No, no, that's not for me. I wasn't as good looking as you are. I stood about five foot two, balding, with pocked skin and bad teeth. Although I rarely had enough to eat, somehow I had a pot belly. I am far better off as I am now."

Namirnakh nodded. "Peace be unto you both."

Ronar and Sha Totek turned and passed out of the temple of Ahriman. As they left they thought they heard a strangled cry, sounding much like Sha Totek might himself if he were being throttled.

Back in the daylight they approached Conall, who stood awaiting them with a worried expression.

"Is all well, my lords? You appear dazed."

"Yes, and well we might," said Ronar. "But all is well. Darteharn is no longer a threat to us. Muster the men. We return to the towers."

They rode in silence for quite some time before they looked at each other and said "Did that really just happen?" They laughed.

Ronar said, in English, "It seems to me that you should not fault yourself for not interfering in the struggle between Bran and Namirnakh. It seems it was a much less one-sided story than I was led to believe."

"Yes, perhaps you are right. But let's not romanticize Namirnakh too much. Darteharn is a wide land from east to west, and wider still from north to south. We have seen only a small part of it. There is still a great forest full of horrors somewhere to the west. There is still the Worm Wall. Namirnakh still created the god Ahriman, who caused you so much grief. And have you ever wondered what Namirnakh, a Persian, was doing in Britain in the first place? How he came to pass through the Portal? I bet it wasn't because he was so popular among his Persian neighbors. Still, I am forming a suspicion that it might be pleasant to play a few hands of poker with that man. I should send him a deck of cards and a rule book." He shook his head. "I must be going crazy at last."

Chapter Fifteen

Return to the Dark

They arrived at the two towers without incident, finding matters there unchanged, save that Erraine was trying to reassert her ownership of the Tower of the Mystic Arts, even though it had been tremendously enlarged and improved since her day. Ronar was inclined to leave a garrison to occupy it, but considering nothing of great import had been found within it, he decided not to create the provocation. He did speak to the small contingent of druids and wizards who had come with the army, finding one, who styled himself Glasohl, who was willing to take up residence in the tower under Erraine's tutelage, with the responsibility of reporting back to Eranior if anything of interest occurred.

That left Sha Totek's own Tower to deal with. The sorcerer agreed to move it to northeastern Eranior, not far from the refugee village which housed the remnant population of Myrddin.

"Sha Totek, is there any reason we can't all ride back to Eranior in your Tower? It would save several days or travel, plus spare us the necessity of visiting the Worm Wall again."

"Eh? I'm afraid any passengers would find it an unpleasant ride. You'd be surprised at what physical changes are necessary for the Tower and its contents to tunnel through the earth. Well, no, maybe you wouldn't. I'm used to it, but I'd hate to have a few hundred soldiers whining because they're melting or whatever. I'm afraid they'd be traumatized, and then they'd remember my bad reputation."

Ronar's curiosity almost led him to request a seat for this ride despite Sha Totek's reservations. The slightly mad light in Sha Totek's eyes told him the Sorcerer secretly wished the same.

"Maybe next time, then," said Ronar. "When will you leave?"

"As soon as you and your loyal followers pass out of sight into the forest."

That didn't take long to arrange. They camped there one night, and marched away at first light. As they entered the forest, Ronar kept glancing back for glimpses of Sha Totek's Tower. Finally he did that and found it gone. He fancied he could feel the ground tremble as the Tower passed beneath their feet. He wondered how Sha Totek navigated to avoid the caverns of the underworld, but then laughed at himself. There was no sense puzzling about the practical difficulties of a matter as ridiculous as Sha Totek's burrowing Tower.

They marched on, passing the willow-banked pond where Ronar had passed a pleasant day and evening not so long ago. Much less fondly remembered was the entrance to the Worm Wall, which lay only a few miles beyond. They reached it late in the evening after a hard day's travel. Ronar halted his horse and sat staring at the closed stone hatch in disdain.

Conall, who was riding beside him, said, "Lord, we need not enter the passageways if you don't wish it. Our numbers are not great. We can travel through the crack which lies to the south. Indeed we must, as we will not induce the horses to enter this place."

Ronar sighed in resignation and dismounted. "No. I feel an unwanted responsibility toward these people. Assign a few men to lead the horses through this alternate path. The rest of us will enter the Wall."

When the arrangements were made and the horses had been led away, Ronar addressed the remainder of his men.

"Do not allow yourselves to be separated. Every fifth man is to carry a lighted torch. Do not trust these people. Do not assume they mean you well."

Ronar strode over to the hatch and tried to open it. It did not budge. He was filled with an unreasonable anger. After all, why would he expect the dwellers to leave the door open to any beast or other intruder who might come along? He took a moment to master himself and then called over a dozen men, all as burly as anyone on Colibdis. Together they pried open the slab, working against the gearing that held it shut, and ultimately splintering a wooden pawl.

Below all was darkness and quiet. A waft of stinking air emerged. No one appeared, either to greet them or to ward them off.

Ronar raised a hand to his men. "Blow your horns. And then follow me. Do not speak unnecessarily. Tread softly, if you can."

They announced themselves with a braying of brass. Led by Ronar, they descended the ladder one by one and filed away into the smoky darkness. Ronar could only hope he remembered the route that led to the entrance he knew. They passed many side tunnels, descended through several levels, but saw no one. Ronar heard nothing except the sporadic murmuring of the men behind him, until he gradually began to discern an irregular thumping coming from somewhere ahead. Ronar raised his hand to signal a halt. The thumping grew fainter.

Conall sidled up to Ronar, whispering, "Whatever it is, it seems to be going, not coming."

Ronar nodded. "Let's go on."

They proceeded with enhanced caution. The thumping sound remained steady ahead of them.

Shouts and screams broke out somewhere ahead. Mixed with them was some kind of inhuman grunting. The cries of distress quickly faded, replaced by moans and whimpers.

Conall and some of the other men made to break off and run ahead.

"No!" cried Ronar. "We stay together. Whatever has happened up there, it won't be much worse if we arrive a minute later."

Soon enough they reached a group of women who sat around clutching at their wounds. When they noticed Ronar and the forefront of his party they shrieked, but then their eyes grew wide with hope. One of them staggered to her feet and advanced on Ronar. She wore tattered rags which she strove to hold together with one hand while she clutched at him with the other.

"Lord Greylock! You must save us."

"What do you need to be saved from now?" asked Ronar in distaste, drawing back. He frowned at this woman. There was something peculiar about her physique. Her abdomen seemed bulky for one of her build. Perhaps she was pregnant.

"It was a troll!" she blurted.

"A troll? Why didn't anyone mention trolls when I was here before?"

"We see them rarely, but they seem to be becoming more common. Save us!"

Ronar scowled. Trolls? "Did this creature kill any of you?"

"No, it slashed its way through us and continued on."

Ronar studied the other women. They looked back with their pale faces, careful to hold their clothes together to conceal their bodies.

"None of us are healers," said Ronar. "You must care for your own injuries. We will continue on, and if we catch this troll we shall deal with it."

"Oh yes, yes, you must move on, we would not wish to impede you by asking you to see to us," said the woman with sudden urgency.

Ronar gave her one last hard look and gestured for his men to proceed. The sound of the troll's footsteps had faded. Ronar continued at a deliberate pace, in no hurry to encounter it.

He almost collided with a peculiar torch-bearing figure who came shambling out of a side corridor. This person stared at Ronar with a mixture of astonishment and fear. It was Mylor, though it took Ronar a moment to recognize him. He had not remembered the man as being quite that ugly.

"Lord Ronar!" he gasped.

"Mylor. My men and I are passing through your realm, on our way back to Eranior. Guide us and you'll be rid of us the quicker. We'll kill your troll for you if we meet it."

"Troll? There's another troll? Very well, I'll see you out. Let us hurry. I was heading for the exit myself." He scuttled away, his gait somewhat erratic.

Ronar's frown persisted. Something was very wrong here. Mylor's form had become somehow irregular, bulkier, not in the same manner as that woman, but throughout his body, and his features had grown more coarse. Even the sound of his breathing had taken on a wheezing quality.

They passed another group of women in a widening of the corridor, some of them also nursing fresh wounds. Apparently the troll was also trying to escape. These women were also hasty in gathering up their clothing to conceal themselves.

With a sudden sickening conviction, Ronar halted and commanded, pointing, "Conall, strip that woman."

"If you insist, my lord," said the captain with a lack of enthusiasm. He stepped up to one of the women and ripped the rags from her body. Then he shouted an obscenity and leaped back.

Clustered on the woman's abdomen were a number of small worms, five or six inches long, pulsating as they fed, their tentacles sunk into her pasty flesh.

Without thinking, Ronar laid Mylor low with a single backhanded buffet. He loomed over the fallen figure, his ring sparking red.

"Explain yourself, Mylor."

Mylor fairly snarled his answer. "We cut eggs from some of the dead worms. We hatched them; we feed them. When they are old enough we shall enslave them. We will make them draw our carts, and if we please, we will pierce them and feed upon their juices." He was drooling as he said this, his mouth working. His teeth were irregular yellow spikes.

"He is changing," muttered one of Ronar's soldiers.

And so he was. Now Ronar witnessed what he considered the worst kind of magic, the kind that left reality fluid and rendered the very form of one's body and mind mutable and uncertain. Mylor's flesh shifted and swelled until he became a ghastly fiend, a thing with skin the texture of wet cheese, with huge red eyes and grotesque tufts of hair sprouting from its body.

Ronar called out the Cold Sword, meaning to plunge it into this creature, but it was too fast. It leaped to its feet, knocking Ronar aside. Doing this, it came into contact with Ronar's steel blade, howled, and sped away down the corridor.

Still in possession of the sword, Ronar turned on the worm-ridden women, ready to cut them down. But they, wailing, plucked the worms from their bodies and stomped them flat. Ronar glared into their terrified, degenerate faces, disgusted to the point of nausea, then turned away.

"Let's get out of here! I have had enough of this place. Kill anyone or anything that threatens us."

He set a faster pace, determined to brook no further delays in escaping. He called over his shoulder, "Why the hell did he change like that? Does anyone know what that thing even was?"

"A troll, as they said?"

"A ghoul, perhaps."

"It might have been a *dullahan*, if its head had come off."

"Lord, I don't think any of us knows," said Conall. "We rarely see such things in Eranior, I'm happy to say."

They reached the exit without further incident, emerging into full darkness, glad of the open sky and the clean-smelling air. Ronar brought out his viewer and scanned about in night vision mode. He spied a white shape loping out of sight at the far side of the valley.

Presently the remainder of their group appeared, leading the horses. Ronar questioned the lead man.

"Did you have any problems?"

"No, Lord King. Happily, as a lad I mastered a charm of light which enabled us to traverse that difficult path despite the darkness," said this man, rather pointedly.

"Very well."

I must give more thought to the details of leadership, and to the limitations of ordinary men, thought Ronar.

They resumed their marching order and rode a short distance into the valley before making camp. Ronar looked back at the Wall. Torches moved to and fro in the openings, just as they had when he first sighted it.

"Those filthy people are lucky I don't have another nuclear weapon," he muttered.

"What kind of a weapon, Lord?" asked Captain Conall. "Whatever it is, it can scarcely be too terrible for people such as those."

Chapter Sixteen

The Boundaries of Faerie

Night by night, day by day, Ronar watched the moon Sinanna spin through its full cycle of phases as he and his army made their way to the new site of the Tower of Sha Totek. That army now numbered in the thousands, including a few dozen who had joined them from the valley of Amulree. They'd also picked up another tagalong from that village: Emogen. The young witch had this time rejected Ronar's warnings of danger, arguing that if she were not safe in Ronar's own kingdom, then certainly Amulree could offer no protection. She'd left the foundlings behind, as they had come under the communal care of the entire village, and could get along without her for a while.

Ronar's progress had been without incident. No further monsters were sighted, though Bari, still on guard in the pass of the Mynd Bannock, had reported the passage of several, some of which had been brought down by his men's arrows. Ronar later passed through the Myrddin refugee camp, which was now notably better organized, if still a sparse and cheerless place.

The Tower stood five day's journey east of the site of Myrddin, in a region of nondescript hills, scrubby flats with meandering little rivers, and stunted woods. To their northeast lay the fractious land of Tíuheimr with its dark forests, tortuous inland seas and many lakes. To the south lay uninhabited land for many miles, empty since the original Roman immigrants abandoned it for their disastrous relocation northwest to Nartar.

Somewhere to the east and southeast lay Faerie.

A military camp already sprawled around the base of the Tower. Though it had not come under any attack, it appeared to be very much in disarray. A frantic Gahareet ran up to meet Ronar as he and Emogen rode in at mid-morning at the head of their column of soldiers.

"Lord King, I thank Lugh that you have arrived at last. I was not made for decisions such as these."

Ronar looked around. Everywhere warriors were running about, aimless and panicky. Many were tearing down their tents and pavilions, preparing to flee.

He stabbed Gahareet with an accusatory gaze.

"I am sorry, Lord, I could not prevent it. In truth, I can barely stand to remain here myself. The men of Eranior will confront any enemy, if need be, either natural or otherwise. But what we face here cannot be defeated by spears and axes."

"What is happening? I see no threat."

"Come with me, Lord, and you shall see."

Ronar first turned to Conall and his other captains. "You men stand fast. Remain here until I return to issue orders. Gahareet, lead on."

They rounded the Tower, then climbed a slight rise just to its east. It was a grey, cloudy day, but away near the horizon they saw a soft line of blueness which glimmered oddly.

"My king, there you see the boundary of Faerie."

"Yes, what of that?" asked Ronar.

"Until recently, that boundary lay two hundred miles farther to the east and south."

"Are you saying Faerie is…moving?"

"It is expanding. It is now well into the no-man's land which has always separated it from mortal lands. It is advancing at a rate which can be measured in miles per day."

"And what the devil does that mean?"

"I cannot say with any certainty. Nor could the Sorcerer. Three days ago he rode forth with a few brave men, pledging to discover the meaning of these events, and to turn it back if possible. He has not returned."

Now Ronar knew fear. He turned to Emogen. "Emogen, you're a magician. What can you tell me about what this all means?"

"Very little. My people have few dealings with Faerie, and we do not tell what few stories we know, except when both suns shine brightly. But maybe it will be enough. By all accounts, the people of Faerie act with cold courtesy on those rare occasions when they emerge from their country to deal with mortals. I think we saw as much with Astil. But when mortals venture into their land, matters are different. Then the Elves are capricious, and cruel, and take what they will from any visitors, even if that is their lives. I would not wish to live in Faerie. I would not go any closer. If Faerie is coming to us, then I too wish to flee." She shuddered, her haunted eyes fixed on the eastern horizon.

She looked so forlorn that Ronar held her shoulders. He turned his head to study the shimmering blue line of Faerie, which already looked slightly closer and more substantial.

"It seems to me that our best chance of meeting this threat is Sha Totek," he said.

"Perhaps."

"Therefore, if he has been detained within Faerie, I must go there and bring him out." He drew a breath, preparing to issue orders.

"One moment," whispered Emogen, placing a hand on his chest. "I feel that once you cross that boundary, nothing will ever be the same. Before you go, I must speak my heart. I have lived a simple life up until now. I never dreamed I would someday travel in the company of...of the Great Hero of our Age, as Sha Totek puts it. Although you are stern, I know you are also tender of heart. Someday I will tell my children that I knew you. They will ask how you compared to your legend, and I will tell them that I loved you, and that is all they need to know. Goodbye."

She jumped up, landing a quick kiss, then turned and hurried away with tears starting down her cheeks.

Heavy of heart, Ronar had to check himself from running after her, either to take her into his arms or to assure her he was less than she supposed...he wasn't sure which. Then he reflected that her chief magical talent was to judge the nature and character of others, so that to argue with her assessment of him would be an insult.

In the end, he merely stood and watched her depart until he came back to himself and addressed Gahareet, who stood waiting patiently.

"You said a few brave men accompanied Sha Totek into Faerie. If a few more are to be found, they may accompany me, if they will."

With a white face and bloodless lips, Gahareet said, "I will go with you myself, Lord King."

"No, you won't. Eranior needs someone to lead it. It may be that you are better suited to ordering Eranior, while I am better suited to investigating Faerie. Here are my commands. Keep the army in place here, if you can. If Faerie encroaches too closely on this position, you are to withdraw. Continue doing so until you reach the cities of Yethon and Tantuul. These you must defend, for you cannot allow the people of Eranior to be driven on forever.

"As for Emogen, she is to be escorted wherever she wills, and left to do as she wishes."

Gahareet bowed. "So it shall be. I am sorry, my lord, that your men are in such disarray. They never expected to be attacked by Faerie, and they are unnerved."

Ronar wasn't sure what Gahareet wanted him to say. Maybe he hoped for some exoneration of the army's lack of will, or for his own inability to impose discipline. Or maybe Ronar himself would be equally unnerved if he better understood what he was getting into.

Ronar's mind was too fixed on what he was about to do to give this matter much heed.

"Just get me a few men, if you can."

Gahareet merely stared at him in a mortified silence.

"I see," said Ronar gently. "Well then, have my horse brought. That is, if you think a horse can endure the journey any better than men. No? In that case, please provide me with some armor and other weapons. No, never mind. I'll get them myself."

He turned aside from Gahareet and strode toward the Tower, feeling less like a king and more like an idiot. To his relief, the Tower's portal opened to admit him. Ronar silently thanked Sha Totek for this foresight and courtesy. He could not command the magic that would levitate him up the shaft, so he was obliged to resort to the spiral staircase. The Sorcerer devoted entire levels of his Tower to collections of arms and armor. Ronar merely peeked into each level, not caring to know what was stored in the levels devoted to the more arcane items.

He discovered a museum of armor used by every culture on Colibdis. Much of it was highly ornamented and meant for show, but Ronar had no difficulty selecting a few practical items, including a byrnie made of precious steel rings with a padded undercoat, a pair of Roman vambraces, and a set of Mersinean greaves. He considered taking a shield, but as he often wielded the sword with two hands, that seemed impractical. He could not locate a helmet that fit, or that he could stand to wear.

He descended the stair. As he was about to leave the Tower, he hesitated, then removed the Royal Torc of Eranior and left it hanging on a hook in the vestibule. He had had enough of posing as a king. Soon either the Eranians would have no need of a king, or they could choose another. A king who couldn't even find a few subjects willing to follow him into danger wasn't much of a king anyway. Whatever Ronar did from this point on he would do as Leonard Ronar only.

He left the tower and headed east without looking back.

His long legs swung in a gait which had gone unused for too long. His spirits lifted. He felt liberated. No longer must he take into account the needs of a mob of followers. No longer must he reduce his rigor to account for their deficiencies. He was free and alone, on foot, Leonard Ronar on a mission, the way he did it best. The weight of armor and gear he carried would strengthen his body, if given time enough.

He made a cold camp on a rocky patch of grassland that night, perhaps halfway to the shimmering blue edge of Faerie. It stood ever nearer and higher as he watched, flickering with a faint light. He could choose to sit here and await its coming, but he preferred a more aggressive approach. He would stop it, if possible, before it sent the Eranians into full flight.

The sky had cleared. The golden stars of Colibdis shone bright and unusually numerous.

Ronar dreamed of the cabin he had hoped to build at Blue Water Canyon in Thunderbird. Standing in its doorway, smiling, was Emogen. Together they descended the path that led into the canyon, down to Blue Water Creek, the stream that had carved it. It was not really blue, but usually green, though it could flow red when heavy rains brought down sediment from the sandstone heights above. But there was a shallow stretch where the flow ran over a bed of the copper mineral azurite, and there the stream was indeed blue, as blue as anything could be.

Ronar awoke suddenly to the sound of cries, footfalls, and chinking mail. He leapt to his feet, calling out the Cold Sword and facing the oncoming men with bleary-eyed defiance.

But these men were coming from the west, not the east. Ronar lowered the weapon. The first light of the suns reddened the bronze armor of Captain Conall and three other warriors. The four ran up to him and collapsed onto their knees, panting and gasping.

When he could speak, Conall said, "Lord King, we awaited your commands for hours, until we heard at last that you had set out alone to face what approaches. We made to follow, all of us who fought with you in Darteharn, yet Gahareet bid us stay. I think he considers you as good as dead already. But I was ashamed and could not stay behind. I could not wait or flee while you marched off to your doom. Anyway, I've learned that a man who likes a fight does well to stay close to you. So I broke away, and with me came these warriors, Melor, Pembroke, and Tuathal. We would all have marched with you if you had come for us, all of us who were with you in Darteharn. Which is better, I asked: to die fighting alongside a King who has faced down Namirnakh all but alone, or cowering while that man dies in our name?"

Ronar found himself moved and grateful. He helped the four men to their feet. "First, I must say, I am no longer your king. I have laid the torc aside."

Conall snorted. "Well, torc or no, you're the closest thing to a king we've got, that's for certain. I don't think Gahareet's up to it, if you'll forgive me for saying so."

"Second, I prefer not to look at this as going to my doom. I hope to recover the Gatekeeper, persuade Seren to reason, and end this peacefully."

Conall gaped at him, open-mouthed.

Pembroke said, "That is surely a noble ambition, my King. Yet it's hard to look upon…that…and see anything but a weird doom ahead." He gestured toward the east.

Ronar turned on his heel and drew in his breath. The diffuse frontier of Faerie had moved quite close during the night, and was now only a few miles off. The suns were visible through it, but they had changed. They had drawn close together, which was very wrong, because in their normal orbits they were far from any apparent conjunction.

Worse still, the suns themselves had changed. They were now more like each other. White Photos had bloated and grown golden, while red Kudu had contracted and grown hotter.

No physical process could produce such changes over the course of one night. Ronar had no explanation, save that reality was somehow blurring around him.

"Men, if what we see here is real, then there is indeed no escape for any of us. If the suns collide, that will mark the world's end. Yet I do not think Faerie means to wipe itself out along with all of us. I must assume that what we see is somehow less than it appears. I will go on. You brave men have exhausted yourselves in your pursuit of me. I bid you to stay and rest. Wait for Faerie to come. If you can endure whatever changes it brings, then follow me."

The men looked stricken at this, as though he had kicked them.

"My lord," began Conall, flushing, "we have come far to accompany you, not to..."

Ronar raised his hand to silence him. "Captain, peace. You honor me with your presence, and with your faith in me. I'm ashamed that I left the camp without first calling on the loyalty of you and your men. I'm sure I'll see you again, when your strength has returned. For now, I'll scout ahead."

The warriors said nothing more as Ronar gathered his possessions and set off. Now more than ever, he felt only he was fit to challenge whatever was overtaking the world, but the willingness of those other men to follow him had given him new heart.

The transition to Faerie was not a line, but a zone. Ronar could not say exactly when he passed from one realm to the other. He watched as the suns approached each other, growing more similar, until finally they merged, without any fuss or disruption, becoming a single golden star much like the sun of Earth, lighting a bright blue sky unlike the thin indigo that prevailed over the rest of the planet.

With shaking hands Ronar drew out his viewer. He keyed it to its solar mode, raised it to his eyes, and studied the new sun.

This was a false sun, lacking every detail he'd expect to see on a sun-like star, including prominences and sunspots. This was a simple glowing sphere. Evidently the Elves were not astronomers, or did not care to mar their illusory single sun with any imperfections.

He stared at this apparition in awe, then lowered the viewer to take in the landscape of Faerie with his naked eyes. The contours of the land seemed the same as before, but everything in it seemed more vivid, brighter, and sharper. Greens glowed like burning copper. Flowers were like stars shining through petalled gems. Every edge, every detail, was preternaturally sharp. He looked back. He could see the men still waiting at their camp. He could see the worried expressions on their faces, even though they were miles away.

Had he become an Elf? He felt no different, yet he found it hard to otherwise explain this expansion of his vision. His hearing too seemed enhanced, as though he'd pulled wads of cotton out of his ears.

He continued on, at less than his usual pace, for he was constantly looking all around, taking in the changed aspect of the world. He was in Faerie...or at least the closest thing to Faerie that the peculiar nature of Colibdis and the minds of men could produce. Here anything must be possible, even more so than on the rest of the planet.

Often his peripheral vision revealed flashes of motion which vanished when he turned his head. The sighing of the breeze sometimes resolved into laughter and furtive speech when he was not listening for it. Ronar walked with his head held high, showing no signs of fear.

The end of the day arrived with dreamlike speed. A dusk of transparent prismatic colors softened into a night suffused with blue luminosity. The stars came forth in a profusion he had never seen on this world, yet still arranged as were the stars of Colibdis. And they were sharp, so very sharp in his eyes, like needles of light.

He did not feel weary, so he walked on, not daring to sleep in this whispering land in any case. Yet he must stop and examine the stars with his viewer. He aimed it at the star Tarized and thumbed the contact that increased magnification. Faint stars slid out of the field of view as he zoomed in. The appearance of Tarized itself did not change. It remained a perfect golden point of light.

Ronar lowered the viewer. At that power, and with the small optical aperture of the viewer, any bright star should reveal a spurious disk and faint surrounding diffraction rings, caused by light waves interfering with each other.

If they no longer did…

It could only mean that in this place light no longer possessed its wave nature. It had changed into some simpler thing that behaved according to the simpler laws of geometrical optics.

Ronar stood breathing heavily, more shaken by this than he had been by any witch or monster. In a daze, he randomly scanned the sky. Masses of stars and galaxies passed across his field of vision while the first stirrings of the implications for astronomy passed across his thoughts. Why, this could mean…

The faint sound of hoofbeats interrupted him. He jerked down the viewer and looked around wildly, suddenly plunged back into what passed for reality.

A liquid silvery blur appeared in the distance, approaching with unnatural speed. In moments it stood before him, looking him in the eye. It was the Elf-horse, Moonmist, riderless.

The horse told Ronar that its master, Astil-Cotavion, had sent him to serve Ronar's needs.

The horse did not speak, but somehow Ronar was aware of its intentions. Similarly, Ronar found that he need only form his meaning in his mind for the horse to become aware of it as well.

So this, mused Ronar, was what being an Elf was like.

Numbly he mounted the horse, which quivered beneath him. It hurtled into the night, now possessed of its full power, moving far faster than any creature of mere flesh and bone could manage. The air raged past him, obliging him to squint against it.

Then he discovered he could not guide the steed. As an Elf-horse it had no reins, and neither body nor mind could influence its course one bit. He dared not leap from the beast at this speed. His only alternative was to trust Moonmist to indeed serve his needs, and not to deliver him to his enemies.

The moon rose, full and huge, before them. This also made no sense, as a full moon rises only at sunset. It did appear to be Sinanna, the Greater Moon of Colibdis, but it was indeed huge, many times its natural size, unless it merely appeared that way because it was so crisply detailed, with its smallest craters visible as rings and points of light. Despite its great light, which illuminated the blue twilight through which they sped, the stars remained as numerous as ever.

When the moon stood high, Ronar made out something approaching, a low cloud of whirling silvery points, like a windblown mass of stars or snowflakes. It enveloped them, and resolved into a company of Elvish horsemen. Moonmist halted, prancing nervously. The Elves wore armor that shone like frost, and carried long spears like thin beams of light. Their cloaks flowed from their shoulders as snowdrifts lie blue in the moonlight.

The foremost of them rode out a few paces from the rest. He was immensely tall, a narrow, refined figure with an austere pale face in the shade of a high silver helm.

"Well, what is this?" called this person, his voice calm and controlled, yet with an edge of cold menace beneath it. "A mortal man, astride an Elvish steed? That is a rare sight, and not an especially agreeable one."

Ronar said nothing, unwilling to engage in any pointless banter. He merely stared at his inquisitor, forcing him to speak once again.

"Your mien is dark, and I deem it haughty. Who are you, and what do you in Faerie?"

Ronar's voice rang out, carrying a note that caused many of the encircling Elves to flinch or shy away.

"I am Leonard Ronar. I have entered your land to meet your Queen and ask the meaning of her causing the limits of Faerie to intrude into mortal lands. Who are you?"

"I am Aelvish Cres Leghe, earl of the West Quarter of Faerie, a domain which is indeed expanding as you suggest. We have heard of you, of course. We've also heard that you have already met our Queen, on which occasion you kicked a verminous animal into her face. Is this true?"

"Yes, it is true. I often react in such a manner whenever a tyrant casts me into prison."

"A bold reply."

Bows appeared in the hands of the encircling Elves. They drew as one. The points of their arrows shone like cold stars.

Aelvish ordered them down with a gesture. "This shot is mine. This man cast filth into the face of our Queen. In return I cast something into his, something better than what he deserves."

The Elf released his arrow. Ronar managed to get his right forearm up in time to block it, but the point easily pierced the bronze vambrace, stopping at the bone. The cold agony of it caused Ronar to try to flick the shaft out of his arm. A second arrow was already on its way, screaming in like an eagle. The icy point pierced his cheek, passed through his mouth and emerged just inside of the angle of his jaw. Moonmist screamed. Ronar roared in pain and anger. He called out the Cold Sword with a blast of thunder and tried to urge Moonmist to charge this murderous Elf, but the horse would not move. Ronar looked at the feathered end of the shaft hanging in front of his face. His cheek and neck felt wet. A numbing cold spread from that side of his head. The sword fell from his hand and disappeared. His vision dissolved into a hissing whiteness.

As he fell from the horse he heard himself saying *Asterope*.

Chapter Seventeen

Flight from Faerie

Ronar awoke in a dimly-lighted space to terrible agony. A quiet voice said "Hold him." Many strong hands pinned him down. He felt his head being torn apart, and his consciousness again fled.

When next he awoke he was able to determine that he lay on a hard bed in an austere, windowless room with walls of dressed pale stone. A figure sat slumped in a chair nearby, her head lolling forward, her tumbled hair obscuring her face. By that hair and her style of dress, he knew Emogen.

"Emogen," he rasped, the act of speaking bringing new pain.

She snapped awake, her hair flying clear of her face, which was wan, exhausted, and dejected.

"Ronar!"

"So—they got you too."

Emogen stood up to hover over him. "Do not speak. You may worsen the damage. I was not captured, I was delivered here. It was your goddess who brought me. I was riding east, seeking Conall and the other warriors who had followed you. Suddenly I heard a voice call my name. There stood your goddess, looking at me with those huge grey eyes of hers. Then her eyes grew even more huge, while around them her body blurred and expanded, until she stood before me as a gigantic earless owl, equal to any Teratorn I've ever heard of. My horse threw me and bolted. The owl wafted into the air, wrapped her great talons around my shoulders, and flew off, deep into Faerie. Finally she released me in the courtyard of this castle and stood beside me as Athene, very tall and stern, as a horde of Elves poured out to surround us. She said 'This woman is a healer,' and her spear point blazed with a light that caused all the Elves to wilt. Then with one final glance at me she vanished. I was brought inside, and here to you, where I found you pierced by two enchanted Elvish arrows, and near death. I have labored over you ever since, more than two days. The Elves left me to wrestle you out of your armor. They brought me water and such herbs and other items as I asked for.

"Before you ask, your arm is fine and should heal fully. Your head is a different matter. That arrow cut open your cheek, knocked out a tooth, broke your jaw, sliced some muscles, damaged some nerves, and caused serious bleeding. That would have been enough to kill you, but the magic on the arrow somehow froze you, not literally as a block of ice, but as though you were a statue. Thus you survived until I arrived, but I cannot promise that your poor face will ever be the same." A tear fell from her eye onto his chest.

Ronar tried to raise his right hand, but that arm felt like lead, so he cautiously brought up his left hand instead. He did not feel his own touch on his cheek, which was numb. He felt a long slash, sewed together; an irregularity at the back of his jaw, and farther back, a bandage covering the arrow's exit wound. He felt the rest of his face, tracing out the area of numbness, which encompassed most of its right side.

Ronar parted his lips and spoke slow, slurred words without moving his jaw.

"Don't worry. In my life I have never gotten by on beauty. I am sorry you were dragged back into all this. Why am I still alive?"

"You'd best ask the Elf lord, Aelvish, that question. Now please, do not speak."

As if on cue, the door opened, and in walked Aelvish Cres Leghe, immensely tall, dressed in a splendor of blue and gold. His beautiful face was grave and pale.

Ronar summoned his sword. To his surprise, a burst of heat and light from his chest burned his flesh and ignited the thin shirt he wore. It came from Natulakh's pendant; the ring had been removed from his finger. Nevertheless the sword appeared with its usual din, but Ronar was too weak to hold it up. It slipped, and would have fallen upon him and injured him, except that Aelvish darted forward and caught the blade, the cold iron of which seared his hands. The Elf dropped the weapon onto the floor mat and clutched his hands together. Meanwhile Emogen seized a pitcher of water and dashed its contents onto Ronar's chest.

Aelvish said, "Please, Ronar, make no more noise, and offer no further attack. I am not your enemy. I see you doubt me, as well you might. I tell you I had no choice but to fire those arrows, or those other Elves, most of whom were of the household of Cotavion, would have slain us both. I made the only head shot I could that would not be immediately fatal. It did not go exactly as I wished, because of your efforts to evade it. But only that sort of attack would have satisfied the Queen's minions.

"I will try to anticipate your questions, to spare you the effort of speech. I have brought you to my ancestral garth near the old western border of Faerie. I do not approve of Seren's plan to subjugate the world. You see, I am mortal-born. Most of us who were born of ordinary men and women do not like to recall the days before they felt the call of Faerie, but I feel no shame in it. In fact, I was born on Earth. I passed through a Bronze Portal, like you. I was one of the first on Colibdis to become fey. I was a founder of our version of Faerie."

"Then—Namirnakh—was wrong. There are more than —three—Earthmen here."

Aelvish raised his eyebrows. "Namirnakh? I know little of him, but I wish no ill on mortal men or their children. What Seren does is the product of her unique darkness of heart. Do you know she is only the fourth ruler Faerie has ever had? Her father ruled for hundreds of turns. He could be cruel, as any of us are wont to be, but he was content with the way things were. Then his brother and son slew him and usurped his throne. Their reign was brief. When those terrible Stones fell from the sky, and Seren used them to overthrow her brother and uncle, I was disquieted. Those Stones are not of Faerie, nor of this world in general. Her rule is essentially un-Elvish in character. We are creatures of twilight, hewing neither to darkness nor to light, but she has given herself wholly to darkness, just as Cal-Cotavion gave himself to the light. He is gone, but she remains. She is our Queen, and most Elves remain faithful to her. Those who waver are easily daunted by her power. None can stand against her. If anyone can, I was hoping it would be you and the Sorcerer. But now I see you cannot. I should slay you, to recover the good will of Seren, and thus persist in my immortal life. Yet I do not wish to kill you. There is something faintly Elvish about you, for all your mortality."

"Ah ha," breathed Emogen softly.

Ronar parted his lips. Emogen spoke hurriedly, interrupting him. "Ronar wishes to know where Imhotep is, and also how Seren is accomplishing this expansion of her realm."

"As to the second, she has in her retinue some great sorceress who is working the magic. As to the first, I am told that my old friend the Gatekeeper has fled from Seren. I hope he will not come here, as that would only draw unwanted attention to myself. As for you, Ronar, since that Greek goddess saw fit to deliver this healing woman, many suspect you are still alive. I must encourage this uncertainty, or I will be thrown down as a traitor."

Emogen approached Aelvish and examined his hands. "I wish I could salve these burns with my magic, Lord Elf."

"So do I. I know not to handle that weapon again. I leave you now. Please remain inconspicuous. I will send a trusted servant to attend to your needs."

When they were alone, Ronar looked at Emogen and tapped the band of pale skin on his left ring finger.

"I removed your ring to prevent just such a thing as happened when the Elf entered. If I had realized the significance of that pendant, I would have taken it as well. I will return your ring if you promise to be good with it."

Ronar nodded.

A few moments later there came a knock at the door. It opened to admit a peculiar figure, the size of a child, with thin, loose-jointed limbs, a big head, large flared ears, and big bright eyes. Its skin was somewhat mottled and blotchy.

It wore a neat little costume of red and yellow. It grinned at them and bowed.

"I am Skiflick. I have been assigned to look after you. What may I bring you? Food? Ale? More water? Fresh chamber pots?"

"All of those, thank you," said Emogen. "And some clean, dry cloths. And blankets. And dry clothing for Lord Ronar."

Skiflick bowed again and gathered up the used chamber pot. He gave Ronar a wry look. "It's not every day I get to serve such a hero of renown, especially one who looks so noble in defeat." He chuckled and scampered out of the room.

Emogen sniffed. "Impudent goblin."

Goblin? That was the first time Ronar had seen such a creature.

When Skiflick had returned and then left them with food and drink, Emogen sat on Ronar's bed and held his hands. He looked into her eyes, hoping she could see the gratitude which was in them, but which he could not verbally express. He still feared greatly for her safety, and harbored a sick certainty that he would yet prove to be the agent of her destruction.

She smiled at him. "I am going to feed you, and then I want you to rest. Your healing will be sped by it." She chopped meat into very small morsels, and mixed these with porridge, watering it down to a consistency which he could take without chewing. Then she cast a spell over the mixture. She tried a spoonful, looked at it in dissatisfaction, lit candles, and cast another spell. And then another. Ronar, who was barely able to stay awake, could not follow the details, but heard her chanting, and imploring whatever gods she followed for assistance.

Then she made him sit up and spooned the food into his barely opened mouth. He noticed she looked drained, and was sweaty, though the room was cool.

Ronar wished he could speak to her, but found he lacked the strength even to remain awake.

He awoke to find Emogen asleep beside him with her head on his chest. He also found the goblin Skiflick standing nearby, looking at them impatiently.

"It's tough to communicate with you mortals when either or both of you is likely to fall unconscious at any time."

"What do you want?" Ronar was relieved to find that speaking was easier and less painful.

"My Lord Aelvish warns you to expect visitors. And he bids you prepare to flee, if you would live."

The goblin retired.

Emogen sat up, blinking. Ronar gingerly removed himself from the bed, conscious of the stiffness and pain which still afflicted him. With his head spinning, he started looking around for his clothing and armor.

"What are you doing?" asked Emogen.

"Getting ready to leave."

"You are still weak. You cannot travel, let alone fight."

"It sounds as though we must both travel, or become guests of Seren."

The door opened again. There stood Astil-Cotavion.

This Elf had changed considerably since Ronar had seen him last. His fine clothing was weathered and stained.

His hair was in disarray, and his face was dirty, haggard, and haunted.

Ronar took one look at him and strode toward him as quickly as he could, approaching with his left hand extended. Astil flinched and drew back a little, but then stood his ground, awaiting whatever was coming to him.

Ronar gripped the Elf's cool hand and looked into his silvery eyes.

"Astil, don't be afraid. I understand your dilemma. I realize you have done the best by us that you could. You have shown us more consideration and loyalty than we are owed by any person of Faerie. Welcome."

Astil stared into Ronar's face in amazement. "I wish you were the ruler of Faerie, instead of my aunt. I have always been taught that mortals are dirty creatures grubbing for ways to extend their brief and brutish lives. No doubt there is much truth to that, but there are also exceptions. It must be so, or men would have no culture at all, but would huddle alone in caves, fearing any shadow. In you and my other comrades of our journey into Darteharn, I have found such exceptions."

"What are you doing here? And where is Sha Totek?"

"I have fled in advance of Seren and her entire host. I am no longer welcome in her court. Sha Totek also comes. Oh yes, he comes. He moves more slowly than I, but he moves like wind through a field of grain, baffling and brushing aside all who get in his way. No mortal has ever moved through Faerie with such impunity. Yet even he flees from Seren. I expect he will arrive here within hours, with Seren not far behind."

Ronar looked at Emogen. "We will await Sha Totek, and then see what is to be done."

Once again the door was flung open. There loomed Aelvish Cres Leghe, backed by half a dozen heavily armed Elvish warriors. He stood there frowning at them, which struck Ronar as being similar to being frowned at by a sunrise.

"It seems the secret of your presence is revealed. You must all leave. You as well, Astil. If you do not all go at once, I will be forced to have you killed."

"But Astil is one of your own!" objected Emogen.

"Yes, he is. But you must understand. Among immortal Elves, each of us is to himself like an eternal kingdom, to be preserved at almost any cost. We have little sense of community and commonality as there is among mortals, where one short-lived generation must succeed another. Below our devotion to ourselves, the next level of Elvish loyalty is to our house or clan. Astil is not of my clan. You must go. I have already extended unprecedented consideration toward you. I will have trouble enough extricating myself from Seren's wrath. I do not wish to be wasted by those Stones and spend my immortal life in despair, or killed outright by the red ring."

"Sha Totek will seek us here," said Ronar.

"He can seek you elsewhere just as well. Go."

Ronar nodded. "My friends, gather your things and follow me out the door."

A moment later they followed the Elf Lord through the lower corridors of his keep, climbing stairs at times, with each level proving more airy and splendid than the one below. Ronar was little able to appreciate the delicate, restrained beauty of the Elvish architecture, because it was all he could do to walk in a straight line without visibly trembling. His aching jaw nearly immobile, he grimly regarded the back of Aelvish's head, remembering the star-arrows which had lately pierced him.

They entered a final great hall where the light of the merged sun cast shafts of light through high narrow windows glazed with colored panes arranged in floral designs. These beams struck the gleaming floor, which was composed of polished slabs and tiles of white quartz, lapis lazuli, and malachite, bouncing from there high into the vaulted ceiling, where they shimmered like auroras.

Ronar's party proceeded though this prismatic space, and then exited through a tall silver door. Only then did Ronar see and appreciate the grandeur of the place. It was a true faerie palace, tall with slender spires, its dusk-colored walls glowing softly in the sunlight. It was the most fancifully beautiful structure Ronar had ever seen, though he was given little time to admire it.

Aelvish urged them farther into the courtyard, where three horses awaited them. One was Astil's Moonmist.

"Here are the steeds you are to steal in your escape," said Aelvish. "We have asked them to bear you, and they have agreed, but at some point they may abandon you."

One was a golden mare with eyes of green crystal. The other was a great twilight-grey stallion with a tail and mane of white and eyes like ice. Ronar and Emogen had no trouble deciding which ones they should mount.

"Go," said Aelvish.

Astil led the way toward the great gate of silver and bronze. The battlements were fully manned with Elf archers. The three swept through the gate and westward over a rolling vale rich with trees, water, and flowers.

A terrifying shriek arose from the castle behind them. A hundred star-arrows sliced into the ground mere feet behind them, the fierce blue light of their points showing through the soil as if it were murky glass.

"They're trying to kill us!" cried Emogen.

"No," answered Astil. "If they were, we would all surely be dead. It is a gesture to show they tried to stop our escape."

They rode on. Ronar turned in his saddle to look behind them, though doing so made him dizzy. The castle had dwindled to a cluster of spikes. A peculiar glimmer showed just beyond the eastern horizon, a softly-colored nimbus that flickered like the distant lightning of a hot summer night.

Astil looked back too. "That is Seren's host. Our lead is slight. We will be lucky to escape."

Ronar squinted into the distance with his Faerie-enhanced sight. "What is that darker blur? That small hurtling shape?"

"I think that must be Sha Totek."

Ronar watched for a moment longer. "I agree. But he is heading for the castle." He raised his left fist and sent aloft a flare of scarlet light from his ring. The black shape immediately swerved and rushed toward them. They paused to await him.

In what seemed like mere moments, Sha Totek sat before them on a great black Elf-horse that gleamed like liquid midnight. The Sorcerer had changed. His clothing was in tatters, and his brown body gleamed with sweat. His dark eyes blazed with a fey and reckless light. He seemed febrile and somehow exalted, though it was obvious he had undergone much travail. He stared at them with a disconcerting grin.

"Well! Here we are, gathered again, that same unlikely foursome once bound for Darteharn. More or less. Ronar, you look like hell. I have seen purple cabbages with better color and more symmetry than your face. Now we flee. We can do nothing against Seren and her horde. We must flee, and hope to win to my Tower before we all change forever. The world is lost. Seren's scheme cannot be defeated. Ride!"

And he streaked off toward the west, forcing Ronar and the others to follow.

Ronar frowned. Sha Totek's words seemed out of character. He urged his horse to catch up to the Sorcerer's, which it did only with difficulty, so he could call out to him in English through the wind of their passage.

"It's Seren, isn't it? She used those Stones of hers on you, didn't she?"

"Yes, of course she did! But what of that? The Stone of Despair might as well be called the Stone of Revelation. The four of them together are a power surpassing anything I have encountered since Hamadan left this world. And her damned little Elf witch is also very formidable. Yes, I said an Elf witch. I would prefer to be dealing with a sand witch. To think I once actually encouraged that girl."

"I don't understand. If Faerie does grow to encompass the world, would that be so terrible? We would all become immortal. I myself do not desire immortality, but others might. And with the wave nature of light abolished, I'd be able to build telescopes limited only by their light grasp, not their resolution! The possibilities—"

"Telescopes, telescopes, telescopes!" snapped Sha Totek. "Is that all you ever think about? If I hear one more word about how wonderful it is to study IC 342 from

Colibdis, I'll summon clouds to cover Thunderbird for a full turn. Evidently you have learned little of Faerie. When mortals venture into this zone of peculiar magic, and are immersed in it, they can react in two ways. They can languish and die, too attached to their mortal nature to adapt. This is most common. I see signs of this in Emogen already. She is failing. Or they can change, becoming a creature of Faerie. But they do not all become Elves! Those who are haughty and who deem themselves wise will become Elves. No doubt you would make a most excellent Elf Lord. Those who are small and petty become Goblins. Those who are small and silly become Pixies. Those who are steeped in evil become Trolls. And so forth. Such changes can overtake mortals wherever they are, but in Faerie they are inevitable, that or death. Now do you begin to see?"

"Yes."

"And it gets worse. When we die, and our mortal lives are over, our souls depart to whatever fate awaits them. It is no different when our mortal lives end so we may become Faeries! Yes, they are all soulless creatures. Why do you think they are so amoral? Even our friend here, the Princeling, has not truly reformed. He tries to imitate you because he admires your strength and resolve, but his efforts come strictly from his mind, not from his heart."

"Cal-Cotavion was not amoral," objected Ronar.

"Wasn't he? I know little of his career after he left Colibdis. Who knows how he truly struggled with those Stones he carried? I knew him, a little. Did you?"

"No. I have only heard stories. But no matter. You say your Tower can protect us against all this?"

"Yes."

"Then we will go there and decide what to do next."

"There is nothing to do. As long as magic exists on Colibdis, this spell cannot be stopped."

"We shall see."

As they drew closer to the site of the Tower, Ronar's keen sight made out something strange. "I see a line, rising from where the Tower should stand and extending, it seems, to infinity. I remember seeing something like that once before."

Sha Totek squinted ahead and cursed. "The boundary of Faerie must already have engulfed the Tower. I empowered a djinn to erect a mirror cylinder to protect the Tower if this happened. Djinns are alarmingly literal in their interpretation of instructions. By the time I could convince it to bring down the spell to admit us, we would surely be caught by our pursuers and destroyed."

"Then we must go elsewhere."

"Why? Wherever we go, we must inevitably be overtaken by Faerie."

"We must go as fast as we can, to the most distant place we can reach, gain time, and there make our plans."

Sha Totek gave a bitter laugh. "Plans? Plans for our new lives as soulless vassals of Seren, or as her victims? I tell you, there's nothing we can do."

"I don't believe that! That's the Stones talking through you. There must be something we can do, and we will find it. Who else in this world is fit to take on this kind of challenge, if not us? Now tell me, what is the most remote land on Colibdis?"

"You know that as well as I do. Ka'ahkin Island. On the far side of the world."

"Yes. Your daughter will not be happy to see us again."

"You also know how long it takes to sail there! We can never get there in advance of Faerie."

"I think I can get us there faster."

Now that they were no longer discussing their companions, they had reverted to speaking in Eranian. Emogen, riding beside them, said "How can you do that?"

"Do you remember the story I told you? About how the wraiths of Ashelak captured my ship?"

"Yes."

"I still have that ship."

"You do?" asked she and Sha Totek simultaneously. "But how can that help?" added Emogen.

"It is such a ship as has rarely been seen on this world."

"I can't believe you still have that thing," said Sha Totek. "Where is it?"

"In Thunderbird. There we must go."

"Of course. Let us bend our path toward the southwest. I still say this is futile, but it should at least prove to be a colorful, amusing form of futility."

They rode with the single sun declining before them. They had no need to look back to learn the progress of the pursuit, for the bells and jangling metal of the Elven host grew clearer in their hearing by the hour.

At last Ronar began to witness the separation of the suns. Before his eyes, the Earthlike sun split into two, which moved apart and assumed the disparate characteristics of Photos and Kudu. How the people of Faerie arranged such an illusion, if such it was, and why they did it, were beyond his thought. At the same time the air seemed to grow thinner, and the dome of the sky deepened to the indigo typical of Colibdis. Also Ronar's eyesight dimmed, losing the Elvish clarity he had so briefly enjoyed. He sighed.

The horses began to slow, to stumble, to show signs of fatigue.

"We have overtaken the limits of Faerie," said Astil in a dispirited tone. "The horses are now more like mortal beasts in character. As am I."

"But the Faerie frontier is still advancing," said Sha Totek. "We must not stop, or it will catch us again, if not Seren and her host."

"I do not think she will pursue us beyond the border," said Astil. "She would lose some of her advantage over us by doing so. She will see no need. She need only wait for all mortal lands to be engulfed."

"Well, I for one am glad to be out of Faerie!"

They all looked at Emogen, who appeared flushed.

"I don't think that place suited me at all. I thought I was going to fade away. I feel so much better now. Let's ride on!"

And so they did, though their progress was slowed to little better than what ordinary horses could manage. They could no longer see the minds of their mounts, and had to trust them to follow Moonmist, whose rapport with Astil seemed undiminished.

Scarcely daring to rest, they rode through night and day, over the nondescript grasslands of southern Eranior. Ronar's strength was sorely tried. He was reduced to permitting Sha Totek and Emogen to use their magic to keep him in the saddle. He was not used to being the weakest member of any party. It was an affliction to his ego. Also difficult to bear was the inescapable thought that he was running away, fleeing from an enemy who he had no idea how to defeat.

By the time they reached the River Tal they were all reeling in the saddle. At the crossing the old ferry had been replaced by a wooden bridge, because of the increased traffic between Thunderbird and Eranior since the advent of Ronar. A small village had grown up at the site.

They arrived just after sunset. The village boasted a pair of inns, which looked tempting, but again they dared not stop. They rode up to the guard post at the foot of the bridge, where soldiers of Eranior interviewed those who would cross into their land. At the sight of them, Ronar's heart sank. Somehow he knew this could not go well.

Sha Totek spared him the need to make introductions. "Stand aside there! It is I, Imhotep of the Two Lands, Gatekeeper of Colibdis. With me are Prince Astil of Faerie; the witch Emogen, who is a friend of Eranior; and Leonard Ronar, the very King of your land."

At this Ronar winced. He had not thought to correct Sha Totek on this matter.

"Let us pass; we ride on business most urgent."

The guards, six in number, approached slowly, their faces doubtful. "Ronar the King?" asked their leader. "Why do you ride from the land in such haste?"

Because I'm running away, thought Ronar. Instead he said, "The forces of Faerie are moving against Eranior and the entire world. Soon this place will be a part of Faerie. We are riding in search of an answer to this attack. You men must stand fast. Endure whatever comes for as long as you can, and try to protect the people."

The man frowned. "I do not understand. If Eranior is under threat, why doesn't her King lead her armies into battle? Where is the Sword of Bran? Hasn't Eranior suffered enough indignities already, without her King rushing away from war?"

Ronar lowered his head in weariness and shame.

"Some battles cannot be won with swords and axes, no matter how venerable they may be," snapped Sha Totek. "This is one such. Some battles may not be won at all. Look at your King. He was wounded near to death by Elvish weapons. He half turned into an Elf himself. Now he struggles to regain his strength and to reclaim his mortality. He could throw his life away by flinging himself against the host of Faerie, or he can search for a way to master it. He is good with a sword, but he is better at thinking. Which do you and your doughty bridge-wardens prefer?"

The guard assumed a truculent expression. "It is not for us to ordain the doings of the King. But still, it is unseemly."

"So it is," said Ronar. "But I see no other path I can take. This I promise. We will find a way, or we will all share the same fate. There are no more Portals. There is no way to flee the planet, even for us. This is all I can do for you."

The guard stared at him for several moments and then nodded grudgingly. He and his men stepped away from the foot of the bridge. "May all remaining gods guard you, and all of us."

Ronar and his party clattered out onto the bridge's wooden deck. The Tal here was broad but not terribly deep. The bridge was built on pilings of stone. Ronar recognized the work of Thunderbird engineers in its making. They stopped in the middle of the span and looked back. The blue glimmer of Faerie was visible on the horizon.

Again Ronar spoke in English. "I suspected I was becoming an Elf, but I did not know it."

"Oh yes, that was clear the moment I looked at you," answered Sha Totek. "It's why the witch's magic was limited in its ability to heal you. Well, that and the fact that she herself was dying. Mortal magic is of limited use against the Fey Folk. They drink up the raw force of the spell, but the effect, as often as not, washes over them."

"I sometimes do the same thing."

"No, that's different. With your twisted scientific mind, you are sometimes able to ignore magic entirely. Faeries don't ignore it, they subvert it."

Ronar stared a moment longer at that pretty, advancing shimmer. No matter what they did, he knew, many of the people of that village, and perhaps of the whole world, would soon be dead, or would walk around without souls. It was by far the greatest failure of his long life.

As they rode on, a numbness settled over Ronar. His gazed turned inward, so that be barely noticed as the land began to climb and furrow into the erosional forms of red sandstone which characterized much of Thunderbird. Somehow they all stayed in the saddle, despite days and nights of riding with little food and almost no rest. If they were gaining any ground on the advancing blue nemesis, it was very little.

At last they drew within sight of Two Suns City itself, resting peacefully among the mesas where stood the University and the observatory.

"Astil, stop," said Ronar, and the Elf obeyed. They all halted, and the others gathered around him.

"I cannot enter the city at this hour. I cannot explain to its people why I am abandoning them. These people have never been comfortable with magic. The coming of Faerie will be very hard on them. Let us get off the road and rest for a few hours. We surely have at least that much lead on the Faerie boundary. Then we will retrieve my ship."

"You keep a ship in this desert?" asked Emogen. "Where is the sea?"

"Far from here. But as I said, it is a most unusual ship."

They concealed themselves in a stand of cottonwood trees that grew along a nearby stream. Astil took the opportunity to bathe in a pool, while Emogen collapsed and was asleep within moments. Sha Totek sat on a log with a sour look on his face.

Ronar laid down and tried to sleep, but had little success.

Astil roused them at two in the morning. The stars overhead seemed dull and lifeless as Ronar led them along a side road toward Observatory Mesa and his home. The area was not entirely deserted, so Sha Totek cast a spell of stealth over them that reduced their passage to a dim, murky breeze in the eyes of any beholder.

Ronar felt as though he were dreaming as they entered the little settlement which was home to many of the observatory's staff. It was like a visit to a place where he'd once lived but had never expected to see again. He looked at the domes atop the nearby mesa, housing the greatest technological artifacts on this planet, made largely with his own hands over a period of years. How he had labored there! If he hadn't been exactly happy, he had often been content. Yet somehow, just now he couldn't think of a single thing he'd ever learned or discovered there that meant a damned thing. Oh, he'd discovered the Milky Way's multiple nuclei, and mapped its barred structure far better than any Earthly astronomer could ever do. He had charted the massive star-forming nebulae which set its far side aglow. He'd discovered many other galaxies, including one large, unsuspected member of the Local Group. Other than that, his results had been modest. Despite the excellence of the vantage offered by Colibdis, the observatory's early twentieth century technology had limited his cosmological efforts.

Oh, and he'd determined that the universe was open and would never collapse, a matter of academic interest only.

He looked up and saw the faint moonlet Scylla, the new name he'd chosen for the former Eye of Ahriman. Once he had thought to place an observatory there. He had planned to request the help of Possum Perturbare in building immense instruments in its airless, low-gravity environment. Yet ultimately he had not wished to live out his days looking down on the world from a sterile, remote bastion of high technology. It was easier and more pleasant to spend quiet evenings sitting on his veranda with Flora, drinking lemonade from his own grove. Maybe some more obsessive version of himself would have built that mighty observatory, and more besides. But not him.

They dismounted before his own comfortable house, with its wide veranda and inner courtyard. They entered and he looked around, surprised to see everything just as he had left it. It felt as though he'd departed many years before, and not mere moonturns. The place seemed unreal. Now the heavy chairs of wood and leather were occupied by an Elf, a Sorcerer, and a witch of Darteharn, and that too seemed unreal. He would never see this place again; this he knew with a sudden cold clarity.

From his desk he withdrew a small white device, and then he looked around for writing materials. The ink in his bottle was dry, so he entered the room which had been Flora's study and dressing room. Somehow the room still retained Flora's scent. Flora, whom he had outlived so cruelly. He sat down stiffly at her dressing table, lit a candle, and set himself to penning a note, using her lavender ink.

Dear Son,

He sat and stared at this salutation. Had he ever before addressed his boy in this manner? No, he had barely been smart enough to recognize the illegitimate child as his own. Now Hal was sixty four years old, almost ready for retirement, a venerable figure with his thinning white hair and drooping mustache.

By the time you read this, I will be far away. Terrible things are happening on Colibdis. The Kingdom of Faerie will soon overtake Thunderbird and all the world. As you read this, it has either already happened, or it will very soon. It will come as a blue shimmering wall. Many people will die, and many others will be changed. Cling to your humanity as long as you can. Sha Totek and I are not fleeing with any hope of saving ourselves, but with the hope of stopping this disaster before everyone is lost.

If we succeed at this, and if there is still a University, and if we do not meet again, then I bequeath to you my house, all my possessions, and the position of Chairman of the Department of Physics and Astronomy.

I'm sorry I cannot stay to help you and the people of Thunderbird face this disaster, but this is the only hope of victory I see, small as it is.

You are a fine man and a great asset to the University. Farewell.

Sincerely,
Leonard Ronar
Your father

He sealed this letter in an envelope, addressed it, affixed a postage stamp, and then sat staring at it. It was a very small, poor excuse for a parting gesture, he knew.

He looked up and was startled to see his own face in Flora's mirror. It seemed like the face of a monster: swollen, livid, and bruised on one side, filthy, unshaven, with matted hair and haunted eyes. He was wounded, he was old, and he was tired.

Tears flooded out of him. He wept as he had not wept in many years, his chest constricting as though his ribs would break.

He was surprised to find Emogen standing beside him, stroking his cheek.

"I think you are now fully mortal once again," she said softly. "Now I can heal your wounds, if not your heart."

An hour later, Ronar and Emogen emerged to find Sha Totek and Astil sitting in his shadowy living room, chatting as though being there was the most natural thing in the world. They'd found a little food in Ronar's pantry, dried fruit and crackers mostly, and these they crammed into their mouths as if it were a feast.

Ronar led them all outdoors, standing in the side yard within sight of Asterope's grave and her flower bed.

Ronar pointed toward the northeast, where the blue glow now stood halfway up the sky.

"My friends, we haven't much time. The horses will not be able to travel with us. Now is the time to release them."

"I will see to them," said Astil. "I will not go with you, I think."

Ronar did not like the sound of this seemingly innocuous statement. "Why not?"

"I see nothing I can accomplish in this distant land you speak of. If I stay here, I can help these people understand what is happening to them, and perhaps give them hope. They will see that being of Faerie is not so terrible."

Ronar approached the Elf slowly, staring into those silvery eyes.

"That would be a fine and worthy thing to do, Astil. But when Seren comes, if she follows you here, you must be careful. Do not assume you will never see us again. If you do see us, you will be better pleased with yourself if you have kept faith with us. I would have taken you with us, given you a chance to take part in reversing the evil your aunt has done, or at least die fighting for what's right. If you decline to do these things, and if you cannot truthfully tell me that you will protect the people of Thunderbird, then leave now. Go back to Seren or wherever you will. But do not let me discover you have taken any part in the domination of my people."

Astil stared at Ronar. "You are a powerful man, despite your age, but I am surely the quicker and surer of eye. You look much better since you spent that hour with Emogen. Yet I think I could kill you, even so."

Sha Totek laughed.

Ronar's hand darted out and gripped Astil's arm. The Elf looked down in surprise, and then back at Ronar, all defiance removed from his face.

"Maybe you're right, Astil," said Ronar. "But let us avoid that contest. I know you are inclined to do right, even against your personal interests, but I also know you are operating under a terrible handicap when it comes to ethics."

"What handicap is that?" demanded Astil. "You mean that nonsense about we of Faerie being bereft of souls?"

"It is not nonsense," muttered Sha Totek.

"No? Well, if not, it makes very little difference that we can see. You mortals experience little difficulty in doing evil or practicing betrayal. We Elves are perhaps more straightforward and predictable in our dealings with others than you are. If we are capricious, at least you can count on us to be so."

"Do you think we could insult each other's races on some other occasion?" asked Sha Totek nervously. "The edge of Faerie is looming near."

Ronar released the Elf. "He's right. We must leave. Astil, I thank you for your help, and I wish you well."

"And I you."

Astil turned away, vanishing into the night within two strides. Ronar looked after him, brooding.

"Er, Ronar?" prompted the Sorcerer.

"Right. I must drop this letter into the mailbox. Then come with me into the back yard, both of you."

They followed him to that pleasant space, with its trees, flowers, and birdbaths. Someone, probably Flora's relatives, had kept it all maintained during Ronar's absence.

"Flora would hate what I'm about to do," he said, fishing the little white box from his pocket. "Stand back."

"What is that thing?" asked Emogen.

"It's a machine, a thing of Earth. It controls another machine. Watch."

He manipulated the controls with great care. With no more sound than that of roots bursting and birdbaths tumbling, the ground began to bulge up, to crack and split. From the fissures poured a hot orange light. The earth and turf broke into slabs which slid off an emerging shape. Puffs of dust drifted off, revealing a hovering form, quiet except for a faint hum. Dirt slid from its sides, as though unable to adhere to the gleaming white perfection of its surface. It was sensuously curved, wasp-waisted, about twenty feet in length. One end had a transparent canopy which blended into the white hull. At the other end was a great lens which now emitted a dull red light.

With trembling fingers, Ronar pushed the hovering flyer away from the pit that had concealed it, then used the control to cause it to settle to the ground. He had forgotten how awesome these things really were.

Emogen slowly advanced and ran her fingers over its smooth white flank. "This is a machine? It is so perfect, it is like the ear bone of the Goddess. You command such a thing, and yet you claim to be no magician."

Ronar caused the canopy to retract. "It was made by a man called Possum Perturbare. On Earth, he was to machines what Sha Totek is to magic here on Colibdis, only more so. There is no magic in this thing. Now quickly, get in. There are only two seats. Emogen, you must squeeze in behind the seats."

Sha Totek waved his hand. "Nonsense. The girl can ride on my lap."

They scrambled into the cockpit, where Emogen did indeed seat herself atop the sorcerer. Ronar closed the canopy. At once the air within was replaced and cleaned by the mechanisms of the flyer. Ronar sat staring at the illuminated displays with their colorful graphics.

Emogen reached out toward the console.

"Emogen, don't touch those lights."

"But they're so pretty."

"Where were you planning to seat Astil?" asked Sha Totek. "On your own lap?"

"Be quiet. I have to remember how to operate these controls."

"What about that talking machine?"

"You mean Brainchild? He is not here. I had hoped the flyer would contain some small part of him, but it does not."

"Flyer?" squeaked Emogen.

"Ah yes," said Ronar. "Hold tight. And hope I can guide this thing in the right direction, or we'll fly right into Faerie, which is now upon us."

In truth, the flyer's controls were simple enough, more so than the light airplane Ronar had once piloted thirty five years before. He brought it to a hover a few feet above the ground, yawed to face away from the imminent blue glow of Faerie, and then pulled back on both control sticks, igniting the main propulsion lamp and initiating a climb, though not quickly enough to keep them from plowing through the top of a nearby tree. Emogen screamed as the acceleration pushed them back in their seats.

"Oof!" grunted Sha Totek. "My dear, you suddenly seem heavier."

"We're flying!" she squeaked.

"Yes, thus the name of this contraption. Ronar, let me see if I understand this. You've had this thing for all these years, buried in your back yard. You could have used it at any time, to travel anywhere in the world with speed and ease, yet you preferred to walk."

"There was nothing easy about recovering it from the wraiths of Ashelak. After that fiasco I decided it was more trouble than it was worth. And besides, what man wishes to become dependent on a machine, when his own strong legs can carry him about?"

Sha Totek laughed. "Most men, I daresay. Ronar, you are a magnificent idiot and a most peculiar person."

"I have grown soft enough as it is."

"How did you get this thing?" asked Emogen, whose face was applied to the canopy, staring at the ground receding far below.

"It was the last time I ever saw Earth. I passed through the Bronze Portal to inform the Earth people of my decision to destroy the Portal, to save Colibdis from the doom that was overtaking that world. At the Portal's Earth side, Possum Perturbare had stored a little equipment for emergencies, including this flyer. It's one of his older models, less advanced than the later designs. I do not understand its workings very well. I was educated in a far simpler age. I decided Perturbare would never need it again. I brought it with some difficulty through the Portal."

By now they were flying over the ocean, and still ascending.

"Er, Ronar, why must we fly so high?" asked Sha Totek, peering out from around Emogen's shoulders.

"I don't know the exact coordinates of Ka'ahkin offhand. The best way to find it is to go high enough to simply look for it. Don't worry, it won't take long."

"The world is round," said Emogen softly.

"Yes, my dear, did you think otherwise?" said Sha Totek.

"I did not know. It does not look very round from the surface. I have seen many wonderful things since I met the two of you."

"Sha Totek, you have some kind of language-learning magic, don't you?" asked Ronar.

"I do indeed."

"Can you use it on Emogen? Teach her a few words of Classic Mayan. English would also be useful. There are too many things I cannot easily express in her own dialect."

"Why, certainly. You don't object, do you, my dear?"

"No, as long as it is not necessary for you to leave your hand where it is to use the spell."

As it turned out, it was not necessary. The sorcerer murmured into her ear, using words that seemed to sizzle as they traveled, and sometimes to loop around her head like sparks from fireworks. Now and then Emogen emitted a little cry of astonishment. After twenty minutes of this, they both fell silent.

"Well?" asked Ronar, in English. "Emogen, do you understand me?"

"Why, I sure enough do! I savvy you pretty good, I reckon."

Ronar gave a surprised horselaugh at this. "Sha Totek, I know you taught her to speak like Annie Oakley just to annoy me."

"Heh, so I did. My, we seem to be having a grand old time for three people who are fleeing something like the end of the world."

That sobered them, Ronar most of all. Yet as he sat in that cockpit, surrounded by this magnificent expression of scientific and technological mastery, with the curve of the planet's edge growing ever more pronounced as they flew beyond the atmosphere, it was difficult to take seriously the prospect of a new form of magic overtaking this world, turning everyone in it into Elves or pixies or gnomes, or else into corpses.

From this side of the world, and this altitude, the Whirlpool, the Milky Way Galaxy, was visible with aching clarity, etched against the blackness like an engraving on a crystal sphere. How many hundreds of thousands of years would this flyer need to reach it, even if its strange energy source was inexhaustible?

Ronar looked over at this friends. At first he thought they were staring through the canopy with wordless wonder, but then he noticed they had simply fallen asleep. Ronar slowed the flyer. It wouldn't matter if they took an extra hour or two to reach their destination. They were all exhausted. He set the flyer's simple brain to holding a fixed course and altitude, then reclined his seat. He fell asleep at once, knowing he would be awakened by sunslight once they overtook the day.

Chapter Eighteen

Ka'ahkin

"Look. Look."

Emogen's soft voice turned out to be the thing that woke Ronar up, not the suns.

"Look, a god precedes us."

That caused Ronar's eyelids to open more suddenly than they might have otherwise. He peered through the canopy. They were approaching a sprawling, hazy landmass. Much closer, perhaps a thousand feet ahead, was a golden light containing a vaguely human form, pacing them. It bore huge wings of bronze, and as they drew nearer, each slow wingbeat was like a crack of distant thunder.

"Who could it be?" whispered the awestruck Emogen.

"Looks like Athene," said Sha Totek, yawning.

Ronar squinted and raised his viewer.

"It is indeed Athene. In all her glory."

Ronar stared ahead, his thoughts lost in the past. Athene. Asterope. *Asterope*.

"So, Athene," said Sha Totek. "Strange. Why has she popped up now?"

At these words, the goddess veered aside, swerving back, flashing past the flyer. Ronar had a glimpse of a stern face, and then she was gone.

"Hmph," said Sha Totek. "A fickle guide, as gods so often are."

"And yet, it's nice to know she's keeping an eye on us, isn't it?" said Emogen.

"Perhaps," said Ronar.

Now their attention was drawn to the great green island which was drawing near, though still far below. It was over three hundred miles across, almost entirely covered with jungle, most of it low-lying except for a few volcanoes and some gentle inland hills. Some of its cities were visible as pale scars even from this altitude.

"Where shall we go?" wondered Sha Totek. "To one of the cities? To visit my daughter?"

"Our goal here is simply to make plans for dealing with Seren," said Ronar. "I see no need to entangle ourselves with the locals. We might better seek out some quiet, isolated spot."

"I see. Do we have any food?"

"No."

"Water?"

"No."

"A place to stretch out without bugs and snakes and the like?"

"No."

"Then perhaps some local entanglements will be necessary after all, unless you want to spend more time hunting and foraging than planning and plotting. Oh, I don't crave those entanglements any more than you do. I grew tired of these xenophobic bloodletters long before their Portal finally crumbled."

"How long do you suppose we have, before we are overtaken by Faerie?" asked Emogen.

"I don't really know. A few days, I should think," said Ronar.

"And then that blue shimmer will appear on the horizon again," said Sha Totek.

"I'm not so sure. Faerie may well be propagating as an expanding sphere, not wrapping itself around the surface. It may rise up from beneath our feet, without warning."

"Isn't it cute when he talks that way?" said Sha Totek. "My thought is that we may make out better with my daughter then in any of the cities."

"Yes. I don't want to have to convince their priests that my heart belongs in my chest, not on their altar."

"You've been here before?" asked Emogen.

"Yes, long ago."

"How did you come to have a daughter here, Sha Totek?"

"Oh, in the usual way," said the Sorcerer in a studiedly offhanded manner. He changed the subject. "Now that we've reached a decision, may we land? Emogen, you are a pleasant burden, but sooner or later even your light frame must put my legs to sleep."

"What is your daughter's name?"

"She calls herself Ixtab."

"That's not a very pretty name."

"No, it's not. Not at all."

Ronar guided the flyer lower and sent it along the great island's eastern coast. The first time he'd come here he'd arrived and left by boat, so he was not familiar with the appearance of these lands from the air. But when Ixtab's coastal compound came into view, he recognized it readily enough. Unlike Sha Totek, she avoided solitude, surrounding herself with supplicants and followers who served her in many ways. They inhabited what amounted to a sizable town in the lands around her palace.

"Shall we make a dramatic entrance, and land at her doorstep?" asked Sha Totek. "Nothing we could do would be more impressive."

"Or more threatening, maybe," said Ronar. "No, I think we will approach her in a more humble manner."

To that end, he landed the flyer in an abandoned farm field on the outskirts of the settlement. The canopy retracted. They climbed out, a little awkwardly after their long ride, and stood in the bright, humid air, stretching and looking at the surrounding jungle, from which came the cries of many unseen animals and birds.

"Do you think it's safe to leave the flyer here?" asked Emogen.

"No," answered Ronar. "Nor is it safe to send it away, not as long as magicians with long magical eyes inhabit this world. It is sturdy, probably proof against any weapons of stone and bronze. I'll chance leaving it where it is for now."

The stone watchtowers of Ixtab's compound were visible beyond the trees. Ronar led the way to the jungle's edge, where a little poking around uncovered a neglected trail.

"Be careful," muttered Ronar. "These woods conceal many deadly creatures. Watch your step, and touch nothing. You have never seen such a place, Emogen."

"You needn't tell me that. I didn't know such places could exist." Her voice was also hushed in the heavy, buzzing closeness of the jungle.

They padded along the path, first Ronar, then Emogen, and finally Sha Totek. After a few hundred yards it widened into a partial clearing, where someone awaited them.

"Speaking of deadly creatures..." whispered Sha Totek.

She favored them with a small smile on her delicate face with its sleepy black eyes. Her hair was likewise black, her glossy skin a ruddy bronze in color. Her clothing was very brief, consisting mainly of a G-string and a short mantle made of feathers of purple, scarlet, and gold. In her right hand she carried an ornate golden dagger. Her left hand was covered by a black glove and a golden bracelet. A chain connected the bracelet to the collar of a huge black jaguar who stood beside her, regarding them with ruby eyes which shared its mistress's deceptive gentleness.

"So," said Ixtab, "a second visit from the two of you, despite the lack of any invitation. How am I to explain this?"

"It's simple enough, Emuishéré," said Sha Totek. "Put up with us for a little while, and you will soon be rid of us, and we will all be better off."

Her face clouded. "You know better than to call me by that name."

"It is the name I gave you. I can't bring myself to call you by the name of a goddess, especially one like Ixtab."

Her heavy-lidded gaze was steady and unblinking. "My mother gave me another name. I chose yet a third. I am the goddess Ixtab, as far as my people are concerned. You and your lackeys come fleeing the advance of the Blue Magic?"

"It's more of a tactical retreat than a flight. I'm surprised you know of it."

She laughed. "Always you underestimate me."

"I do not. I consider you one of the five most potent magicians in the world."

"Yes. But where do I stand in that ranking, and where do you? And what is wrong with that pale mouse you bring with you?"

Ronar looked aside at Emogen. He found her knees giving way, and her eyes rolled back in her head. He supported her; her hand found his arm and squeezed it hard.

"Ah, I see. The poor bleached creature attempts a spell. Perhaps I can assist her." She raised the golden dagger, which flashed in the suns. The jaguar pricked up its ears.

Ronar interposed himself, his ring flaring red. "Do not touch her."

Ixtab looked up at him for the first time—considerably up, for she wasn't very tall—and her eyes lost their sleepy aspect to flash at him in ire. "Ah, the Great Stone Face speaks! Looking rather the worse for the intervening years, I must say. Don't be afraid for your latest pet, O Slayer of Gods. I do not seek her blood. She will have grief enough merely from her association with you."

Emogen released Ronar and stood out from behind him. "I am not happy to speak out against my host, but I would not have you speak around me as if I were not here."

Ixtab raised her eyebrows and fixed Emogen with an imperious stare. "I am not your host. I am the mistress of this half of the world, and I am deciding how to deal with three unwanted intruders."

"If you'll take the advice of a bleached mouse, you'll listen to what they have to say, or you'll find yourself gobbled up by this blue magic. You might also try showing some respect to your own father!"

Ixtab laughed again. The jaguar gave a choking cough that might have been feline laughter.

"Perhaps, if time permits, I will explain to you my attitude toward the Toltec. For now, you will all come with me, and I will hear you."

They followed her and the cat through the forest, then through cultivated fields, where naked peasants with straight black hair tended beans and maize and other such crops. These stood in respectful silence as Ixtab passed by.

A stench assailed them. They came to another open area, where a row of corpses, in various stages of decomposition, swung from wooden racks, hung by the neck with brass bars tied to their feet. Ixtab ignored them, and likewise the next several they encountered.

Emogen bit her lip at the sight of them, turned still more pale, and wrung her hands. Finally she burst out, "You monster! Why have you executed all these people?"

The only reply from Ixtab was a dismissive wave of her hand.

"She did not hang them," muttered Sha Totek. "Ixtab is a goddess of suicide."

Emogen gasped. "You mean all these people killed themselves? Why?"

Ixtab answered without looking back. "Oh, for this thing or another. For the loss of a woman, or the sickness of a child, or the barrenness of a womb. Or perhaps because of excessive headaches."

Emogen stumbled forward a few steps. Ronar reached out to restrain her from approaching Ixtab too closely.

"But why? cried the witch. "Why would you permit this, encourage it even?"

Ixtab shrugged her glossy brown shoulders. "Why not? They would all die anyway, only slightly later. Why should they not end their lives as it pleases them, rather than waiting to be taken willy nilly?"

"But—those causes you named. With time, they might have been healed of these hurts."

"True. But once they are dead, all their woes are resolved, and it all becomes moot."

Emogen hung back, forcing Ronar and Sha Totek to slow. Ixtab drew a little ahead.

Emogen clutched Ronar's arm. Raising herself on tiptoes, she whispered in his ear.

"This woman is terrible. She is twisted inside, fey and fell. We cannot trust her."

Ronar nodded. He was already thinking that he and Sha Totek had not considered long enough before deciding to take their chances with Ixtab. He looked aside at the Sorcerer. His face was set, his eyes narrowed, fixed on the back of his daughter's head.

She led them up an avenue paved with blocks of limestone, toward the great mansion she inhabited, a tall, complex structure of terraces and tiers, colorfully painted, with numerous carved glyphs and figures. A steep staircase led up the lower flank, giving access to the first habitable level. Passing through a short shadowed corridor, they entered a courtyard, where their flyer lay on the flagstones, flanked by muscular guards wearing feathered headdresses and carrying bronze-tipped spears and axes.

Ixtab did not wait for their inquiries. She waved at the flyer and said, "It would not be wise to leave this thing of yours in the open, prey to whatever men, beasts, demons, or serpents that might come along."

"How did you bring it here?" asked Ronar.

"It flies, does it not? I told it to fly here."

Ronar and Sha Totek exchanged a glance.

"Come then. Explain to me why I should lift a finger to help either of you." She continued across the courtyard into the main part of the mansion, where they entered a spacious hall whose walls were adorned with carved and painted scenes of savagery. She took her place on an elevated throne, with the great cat sprawled beside her in negligent ease, leaving the other three to stand below her like supplicants. More of her impassive guards entered and took up positions beside her.

Sha Totek explained all they knew about the threat of Seren and Faerie, speaking with an asperity unusual for him.

"We do not come looking for help, beyond the simple courtesy of food and drink," he concluded. "We merely seek a place in which to draw our plans."

"And why should I care about any of this? The Blue Magic will come. It will either kill us or make us immortal. You have already seen that death is no great matter here, either for me or my people. As for me, I am already immortal, your gift to me, father."

"And would you also lose your soul?" flared up Emogen.

"My soul? It is long since I have noticed its presence. As long as my life continues, I think its loss would not be a great burden to me."

"Not even you can ignore the coming of Faerie, Ixtab Emuishéré," rang the voice of Sha Totek. "Nor can I. For us, magic is like water. We run our hands through it, swirl it about, shape it, cause it to flow. The magic of Faerie is different. It is like ice, frozen into a single form, difficult to shape, resistant to our will. Your powers will be greatly reduced. Your subjects, those who do not die, will be transformed, and gain in power. You will become a servant of Seren-Cotavion, the Faerie Queen, should she desire it. You will not be able to stand against the forces she controls. You may yourself be transformed, and not necessarily in a way which will please you. Consider all this before you, in your enmity, deny us what little we seek."

Ixtab's eyelids lowered to half cover her eyes. They glittered behind her dark lashes as she looked down at them in a long silence.

"I deny you nothing," she finally said. "Make your plans. When the Blue Magic comes, and your predictions come true, then I will enjoy the sight of failure on your faces, and I will cast you out. For you will fail. I said you were uninvited, but not unexpected. The highest form of magic in Ka'ahkin is the calculation of the future. For turns now have I known of your coming. For many turns more we have all known that the end of the present age of the world is upon us, now only days away, and not to be avoided. Think, plan, scheme, flail away. You will not succeed."

She gestured to someone behind them. "Now, lead these three to chambers. Feed them. I tire of looking at them."

An old woman collected them and led them away. Ronar glanced over his shoulder on their way out. Ixtab still sat on her throne, glowering at him. The jaguar appeared to be asleep.

Sha Totek whispered to him in English. "Ya know, partner, you might have spoken up for us a little back there."

"I saw no need. We are getting what we wanted. My words to her, when they come, will be chosen with care."

"Why does she hate you?" asked Emogen.

Ronar grimaced. He did not wish to answer this question directly. It was another source of shame which had never left him.

"When I was here before, she tried to turn me into her personal monster. She tried to make me the enforcer of her will, a murderous, mindless thing. She could not persuade me, or seduce me, or coerce me into this role. She tried to turn me into it, literally, using magic. She succeeded for a time. Under her influence I did terrible things. When I finally threw off her influence, I made sure she was punished for her presumption."

"And you still dared to come back?" Emogen was round-eyed.

She was answered by Sha Totek. "Ixtab knows she would have to kill both of us, if either. Otherwise, I would shatter her. That girl is hundreds of turns old, yet she is still just a brat to me."

They were deposited in a suite of rooms with natural light provided by high windows. The walls were marred by the usual scenes of violence and sacrifice, by far the most common artistic motif in Ixtab's palace.

She Totek scowled at them and raised his hands. *"Uluvakk Luprae!"* he cried. Colored rays streamed from his fingers, leaching all the color from the murals, leaving the walls stark white.

Ronar grinned. "That will annoy her."

The Sorcerer shrugged. "What of it? If she's right, nothing we do matters anyway. And I must admit, she is almost certainly right. These people who carve the future into their stone wheels are never wrong. If they say Seren will win, then that's how it will be."

They sat down around a round wooden table where a pitcher of water, some cups, and a bowl of fruit had been placed.

"But that's *not* what they predict, at least according to what we heard from Ixtab," said Ronar.

"Eh?"

"She said only that the present age of the world will end. She did not say how."

"That's true!" said Emogen.

"It may be," continued Ronar, leaning forward, "that if the world is to change, it will be a result of something *we* do, not Seren."

Sha Totek looked at him in appreciation. "As always, my friend, your overconfidence serves as an inspiration to all beholders."

The old woman re-entered with a few younger servants. She looked startled at the blank walls, then ordered dishes placed on the table: tortillas, plates of meat and fish, and a thick drink derived from maize.

Sha Totek fixed the old woman with his gaze. "Woman, bring us chocolate! Do not stint. Pretend you are providing for a great feast. Make sure it has plenty of honey and vanilla. It is the Toltec, the father of your mistress, who commands you!"

The servants bowed and departed, flustered. Sha Totek laughed. "Chocolate! At least I gain something from all this travel and upset. Now, Ronar, my friend, what scheme is fermenting beneath that shaggy brow?"

"It isn't far enough along to be called a scheme, but something gnaws at my thoughts. Something has already been said, something that provides a clue as to how to stop the advance of Faerie."

They spoke then of their surroundings, and of inconsequential things, until the servants returned, this time bearing a large golden pitcher and three goblets likewise of gold. With these placed on the table, the old woman filled them from the pitcher, pouring from a considerable height to encourage the foaming of the rich brown brew. Sha Totek dismissed them, after instructing them to leave the pitcher.

He lifted his goblet reverently. With eyes closed, he tilted it into his open mouth. The other two watched his throat bobbing as he consumed the entire goblet in one draught.

"Ahhhhhh," he sighed, sinking back against his chair.

"This drink must truly be divine," said Emogen. "I shall try it." She took a small sip, then worked it around her mouth with an expression of quizzical uncertainty. "It is bitter."

"Try some more, my dear," urged Sha Totek. "This potion is a beneficent inspiration to every woman I've ever known."

She swirled a bit more around in her mouth and swallowed. "Well, I shall at least finish this goblet."

Ronar sipped from his own goblet as Sha Totek poured himself another. The taste reminded him more of Earth than of his previous visit to Ka'ahkin. On Earth, of course, the problem facing them now would be fundamentally impossible. Without magic...

Ronar dropped his goblet. A cavernous feeling of emptiness expanded within him. The spilled chocolate flowed toward the feet of Sha Totek.

The eyes of his companions grew round. "What's wrong?" asked Sha Totek. "Has she poisoned us? If so, I'll…"

"No."

The hoarseness of that syllable brought a sudden stillness to the room.

"I know now what we must do."

There was a silence. Emogen stamped her foot to bring Ronar out of his daze.

"Sha Totek, you said it yourself. As long as magic exists on Colibdis, Faerie cannot be stopped."

"So?"

"We must find the source of magic, and stop it."

Sha Totek's brown skin acquired a bluish tone as he took this in. "But—even if we could do that—it would mean the end of every magical creature on Colibdis. And every god as well. It would be the end of Asterope."

"I know that."

"And it would be the end of every magician whose life is extended by magic. Ixtab would die."

"I know that too."

"*I* would die."

"I know."

They sat and looked at each other, stricken, for a few long moments. Sha Totek's cup of chocolate was forgotten.

Emogen forced herself to speak. "What—what makes you think magic has a source? It is everywhere around us. It is the way the world works."

"Not true, Emogen," said Ronar "As far as we know, magic is unique to Colibdis. It doesn't work on Earth, and never did. Colibdian magic is—a difference in the way space works here. I know that makes no sense to you, but I can't explain it any better without you having a strong knowledge of science, which is the way nature works on its own, without the influence of Elves, wizards, or gods. Even I don't understand it fully."

"So where do you suppose magic comes from?"

"I think I may know."

Ronar thought back to a time in his life he normally tried to forget: that period immediately following the loss of Asterope to Ahriman, when he'd flailed about in search of a way to rescue her.

"I once sat on the shoulder of Mount Olympos in Mersinea, watching as the Eye of Ahriman reflected some strange influence, which rose up from the sea, to the old Island of the Gods, called Larlaninulius. I was later able to calculate the location of the origin of this influence. I ignored this finding then, as I have since, because it was not then relevant to what I was trying to do. Now it is relevant. This site is likely to be the source of magic. Mersinean lore calls it Etheros. It lies maybe a thousand miles west of the mainland."

"So if we go there," said Sha Totek, "and you are right, and we can do something to do away with magic, then I must die."

Ronar looked aside at his very old friend. Superimposed over his stunned face was a vision of the dispersion as he lay dying and very much regretting the passage. Ronar remembered how much this death—this little, minor death of a person essentially unreal—had affected him.

Ronar extended his hand to grip that of the Sorcerer. "No. I would not tell you that you must die, even if I had that right, or that power. Nor would I force that on Athene, or Asterope. It may be that what I propose is itself more terrible than what Seren is doing. It may be too high a price to pay. No, you must weigh the two choices. This is your world, far more than it is mine. For thousands of years, you have decided what is best for Colibdis, long before I came along. You must decide which option is best. You must choose what we shall do."

Their eyes stayed locked together, communicating a great deal in the silence.

"And what about Ixtab?" whispered Emogen. "Do you suppose she will let us kill her too? Oh, why did we come to this terrible place?"

A fair question, thought Ronar. It seemed even more *apropos* when, a moment later, Ixtab herself came storming into the room, her flesh flushed with anger, her black eyes ablaze with bitter wrath.

"Fools!" she spat. "Do you think anything goes on in my own house which I do not know or hear? And what do I hear from you plotters? Not only do you come unwanted and uninvited, but you mean to kill me as a mere side effect of your latest mad scheme!"

Ronar himself took a step or two back. Rarely had he beheld such an excess of fury in any person.

He heard Sha Totek muttering in his ear. "Ronar. Ixtab is about to order you to knock me unconscious. You must obey her at once." Ronar was about to ask if he had heard correctly when he was distracted by Ixtab.

"I'll show you what I do to those who would destroy me, whether they be father, lover, or whore!" she shrieked. She raised her hands, which coruscated with flickers of darkness that hurt the eye and brain to behold. From her lips came dreadful words of power.

Then Sha Totek raised his voice, ringing out with all the surprising authority he sometimes summoned.

"Jericho et bahstan brand! Karmatic transference, ab genitor ad filia!" These words jarred Ronar's consciousness, clashing as they did with Ixtab's continuing incantation. Then a spray of blood flew over Ronar's shoulder, striking Ixtab on the face and chest.

Ronar whirled to see what had happened as Ixtab's savage words faltered and died. The Sorcerer swayed in confusion while Emogen looked on in horror. He had slashed open his own palm with a small knife, and now stood reeling.

Ronar turned back to Ixtab, who had quieted. Her dark eyes smoldered at him from beneath half-lowered lids.

"Ronar," she said. "Strike him down. Now."

Ronar stared at her, his mind paralyzed by confusion.

"Do it, *amigo*. Do it now."

Ronar shrugged, spun on his heel, and sent his fist crashing into Sha Totek's jaw. The Sorcerer staggered, and a tooth flew out of his mouth, but he remained standing.

"Shit!" cried Ixtab in English. "Hit him again!"

Ronar drew back and struck again. This time he heard the snap of a breaking jaw, and Sha Totek toppled. Emogen cowered back as through she expected to be next.

What just happened here? wondered Ronar. *Has Ixtab somehow enslaved me again?*

He turned again to Ixtab. The sudden change in her demeanor revealed the truth to a man whose acceptance of unlikely events had become second nature by now. "It's you, isn't it? You've somehow switched bodies with her."

"Yes. I've had this spell prepared for a long time, in case I should ever need to turn the tables on that little vixen." He paused, pulled out the front of the feather mantle that covered his slender shoulders, and looked down. "Nice."

Ronar rolled his eyes. "That's your own daughter you're ogling."

"Yes, thankfully. The spell is not too difficult when we're this closely related. Emogen, my dear. Ronar was rough on my poor body, and my own gashed hand was not too gently done. Can you please look after my body for me? I may want it again someday."

Emogen blinked, nodded and knelt beside the Sorcerer's former body.

"Now what?" asked Ronar.

"Now I am Ixtab, as far as anyone here knows. We must keep the real Ixtab asleep, lest anyone think Sha Totek's ravings about being the sorceress have any merit. Hypnos and Morpheus will see to that, I think. Then we must quickly decide what to do, and flee this place. You say you know where we must go?"

"More or less. It seems to me that if we get near this Etheros, then you and Emogen, with your sensitivity to magic, must surely be aware of it."

"Then let's go."

"First there's something I've been meaning to do."

Ronar drew from beneath his shirt the pendant of Natulakh, studying it for a moment. Then he used it to summon the Sword of Bran with its usual flash and din.

The sound drew a squad of guards who were covered with tattoos and armed with short spears. They glared at Ronar as he stood holding the sword, until "Ixtab" approached them with hands raised.

"That's all right, boys," he said in a bantering manner, in their own tongue. "Ronar here was just showing off a little."

Their stares moved to their mistress, and their eyes narrowed. "Ixtab" blinked, swallowed, and drew herself up. "Did you not hear me, dogs?" she demanded in a more stentorian tone. "Withdraw at once!"

They bowed their heads, turned, and trotted away.

"I must remember that my daughter is a bitch," muttered Sha Totek when they were out of earshot. "Ronar, what did you bring that thing out for?"

"Look at it." Ronar held out the cold blade, so that both women could study the crust of corrosion that covered it. "This weapon is pitiful. If we're to go into some great battle, and I have little doubt that we must, I will not go bearing this slab of rust. I will clean the blade as best as I can."

"But the moment you relinquish it, it will return as bad as ever."

"Then I will not relinquish it, until the battle is over. Surely I can keep my mind on it for as long as that."

Emogen was still working over Sha Totek's body. "Ixtab" stood watching as Ronar used the point of his knife to pry out the garnet from Natulakh's amulet. He placed the stone into its socket on the sword's grip, then used the hilt of his knife to hammer in the bezel of its setting.

Sha Totek frowned down at him. "You'll need real tools to do this job properly, if you must do it at all. I'll see what I can provide." He left, yelling out demands for sharpening stones, oil, and such tools as are used by jewelers and fine metalworkers.

Ronar was left to scowl over the pitted steel blade while Emogen muttered over her charge.

A small cry and a strangled sound caused Ronar to look aside. He stood frozen at the sight of Ixtab, in Sha Totek's body, lying with his hand wrapped around the slender throat of Emogen.

"My father's body is strong, and your whore has done her healing work well," she said. "Now heed me, Ronar. When my father returns, he will undo what he has done, and then you will submit yourselves to my justice. You will do this, unless you want this little slut to die."

Ronar stepped forward, sword in hand. "No, Emuishéré. Here is what will happen. If you do not release her at once, I will kill you where you lay. I will then kill your father, in your own body, on the chance that your miserable self might somehow creep back into it. I will then await the coming of the Blue Magic. I will submit to it and become a great Elf lord. Once my soul has gone, I shall be utterly remorseless. I will destroy your land, kill everyone in it, in case any brat or descendant of yours walks among them. I shall become a worse monster than even you ever made of me. Then I will tame the Faerie Queen, and rule this world with a harsh hand for many centuries to come. This is what will happen. Observe; I raise the blade. If you still hold Emogen when it reaches its apex, it will come down on your throat."

With a bitter cry, Ixtab flung Emogen away from her.

"You must care for her a great deal."

"She is worth three of me, and a dozen of you. Now you will lay there, silent and motionless, until your father returns."

Ronar endured her glare of hatred until Sha Totek returned, leading a few servants who carried the tools and supplies he wanted. Ixtab's dark eyes flickered at the sight of them, as she weighed whether she could alert them to the true situation, but the approaching point of the Cold Sword dissuaded her.

Sha Totek, observing the situation, immediately called again upon the gods of sleep to quiet his displaced daughter. He then dismissed the servants as Ronar laid down the sword and went to Emogen, who huddled in a corner, massaging her bruised throat while tears flowed down her face. She looked miserable and lost. "How terrible," she whispered.

Who was more terrible in her eyes, Ixtab or himself? Ronar hovered over her, uncertain of what to do. He was much better, he mused bitterly, at threatening people with death than offering them comfort. He had always been hesitant to intrude on the distress of others, out of some perverse conviction that they would be embarrassed by having it exposed or acknowledged.

It was only when Emogen turned her misty green eyes upon him that he sank down beside her, gathered her up, and sat awkwardly stroking her hair while she sniffled and coughed.

"I'm sorry, Emogen," he muttered. "Don't give up yet. I'll get you out of here soon, and I will yet see you restored to your home."

Ronar noticed Sha Totek as he sat frowning down at his sleeping daughter, who was clad in his own body.

"This is not an ideal situation," said the Sorcerer in his incongruously high voice. "I don't dare switch back with Emuishéré, not as long as she is so hostile to us and we're still in her own land. And I, I don't even know where to go to pee." He looked around, obviously disgruntled. His gaze suddenly locked onto something, and his eyes grew wide. "Ronar," he said in a tone of quiet amazement. "Look there."

Ronar looked, expecting to see some new monster or marvel. Instead, all he saw was his sword, lying where he had left it.

"So?" he asked in irritation.

"So, you say? Exercise that scientifically-trained brain of yours. Have you been concentrating on the sword for the last few minutes?"

Events seemed to slow for Ronar as he realized the significance of this. "No. In fact, it had totally left my mind. Yet there it lies."

The two men stared at the inert weapon. Even Emogen raised her head to blink at it.

Sha Totek said, "Stand up, Ronar, and use your ring to summon the sword."

"But it's already here."

The Sorcerer rolled his great, dark-rimmed eyes. "Just do it."

Ronar shrugged, detached himself from Emogen, and stood. He looked at the ring on his finger. It responded readily to his will. With twice the din as usual, the sword vanished and then appeared in his hand. He stared at it like a mooncalf.

Sha Totek hooted. "Now release it!"

Ronar bade the weapon go. Far more quietly, it left his hand and reappeared on the table where it had lain before.

The same guards as before came charging in. They were confronted by the unexpected sight of their mistress dancing a wild jig with a great smile on her face. Seeing them, she assumed a scowl and ordered, "One of you go to the smithy! Have them fire up the forge! I have work to do tonight!"

Off they went, their puzzlement only poorly concealed.

Sha Totek resumed his dance. "Oh, this is a good omen, it must be."

"What has happened?" asked Ronar, annoyed that he must ask.

"Don't you see? That garnet, the one stolen by Natulakh. You used it to summon the sword, and then you replaced it in the sword's grip! Brilliant! What then could the sword do? It could not return to the cold waters, not with the stone that had brought it here back in place! The result is, it no longer lives in the Bay! The magic has been reset! It now exists here, with us! Oh, why didn't I think of that!"

"But it is still heavily corroded."

"Not for long, my friend. Not for long. Come on, we'll go to the smithy. Bring the sword."

"What about Ixtab? We can't just leave her lying here, hoping she won't wake up again."

"True. Emogen, my dear. Do you have magic to keep her asleep?"

The witch nodded.

"See to it. She is a very powerful sorceress. Given half an hour to herself, there are few limits to the harm she could work against us. Come, Ronar."

The two of them left their rooms and entered a corridor. Sha Totek led the way, strutting along with a confident mien. "Just try to look like we know where we're going," he said through set teeth.

"Do you know where to find the smithy?"

"Not really. I plan to look for smoke."

They found their way outside, where the suns were near the horizon, casting a bloody light over the structures and towers of Ixtab's domain, with blue shadows in the crevices of their deeply carved ornamentation. A column of smoke did indeed mark the location of the forge, enabling the pair to march their way there without appearing too uncertain about their path. The dim, hot space within was filled with short, muscular smiths who awaited their mistress's commands.

"Leave, all of you!" cried "Sha Totek. "I have a mighty magic to wreak here tonight, one which would fry your eyes were you to look upon it. Let no one disturb me unless I call!"

In a moment they were left alone. Ronar looked around the shop with its crude forge and meager bronze tools.

"These people are not great metalworkers," confirmed Sha Totek. "They work only in copper, bronze, silver, and gold, and do not know steel. I will have to supplement these crude facilities with my magic. But first...hold the tip of the sword over this crucible."

The Sorcerer laid two fingers on the sword's tapered point. To Ronar's alarm, it crumbled and fell into the crucible as a corrupted powder.

"Move the blade forward as it disintegrates. Collect all of the powder, every crumb. And do not fear. You once saw Namirnakh use a similar spell to destroy this blade. Like him, I am letting some of my own age pass into it, or rather, in this case, some of Ixtab's. It must be done."

Working slowly and carefully, Sha Totek reduced the entire blade to a beaker of rust, even the concealed tang around which the grip and hilt were built. Ronar was left holding the latter, almost weightless now, it seemed.

Sha Totek used long tongs to place the crucible into the forge. "This tepid fire will never melt such metal. It's time for Staq Mavlen, an extra-dimensional demon of fire, to lend a breath. I hope he will be able to hear me with this silly high-pitched voice of mine."

Apparently the invocation was successful, for with a roar the fires of the forge turned to yellow-white. The beehive-like brick structure began to glow a dull red.

"That should do!" said Sha Totek in approval. "The steel will melt, and the impurities be driven off. In the meantime..." He took the hilt from Ronar and muttered references to the deceased wizard Gromer. A ghostly greenish outline of the blade appeared, extending weightlessly out from the guard. The hilt also shimmered green. "Now you behold the matrix itself, the form defined by Gromer to define and restore the shape and integrity of the weapon when summoned by the gem." The Sorcerer flipped it around, eying it critically. "I have learned a thing or two about swords since such ancient weapons as the Sword of Bran were forged. This one can be improved." He ran his fingers along the long phantom blade, squeezing it, caressing it into a more tapered shape, drawing out the fullers, refining the center ridge. "It will be a bit lighter now, to take into account the metal lost to the sea, and better balanced. But never fear, it will have lost none of its potency. Take it while I check on the steel."

Ronar took back the hilt, holding it in a gingerly manner, fascinated yet a little unnerved by the ghostly blade it now bore.

"Good, the steel is melted and clean. And it is still subject to the Spell of Encoded Matrices. Now comes the tricky part, Ronar, my friend. Place the sword here, on this anvil, like so. When I give the word, you must use your ring to summon it back to you. The molten steel will be called into the matrix. It will remain liquid until I can cool it somewhat. You must then release the sword so I can finish the work. Here, put on this blacksmith's glove. This will be a test of your fortitude, my friend. Are you ready?"

Ronar cocked an eyebrow at him.

Sha Totek chuckled, or rather giggled. "Of course, of course, you are always ready. I will not be able to tell you when to act, because I must be ready with a spell. I will gesture instead. We now begin. Hold it well away from you!

"Brekbannin Tharrae..." He nodded wildly at Ronar.

Ronar set his jaw and bent his will to the ring. This time the initial glare and heat did not abate. He found himself holding an incandescent vane whose radiance scorched his face. The hilt heated up rapidly, right through the thick felt glove.

"...adversus solem loquitor!"

A pale influence streamed from Sha Totek's feminine hands, bathing the sword, moderating its fierce heat. The blade solidified, though it still glowed orange-white.

"Now!" cried Sha Totek. Ronar gratefully released his mental grip on the sword. It reappeared on the anvil. The Sorcerer gave a gleeful cackle and lifted a hammer. "Sometimes there's just no substitute for that particular legion of demons and their powers."

Ronar removed the glove and plunged his hand into a bucket of water. For the next twenty minutes he watched as the Sorcerer hammered away at the blade while Ixtab's body streamed with sweat. After a while the displaced Sorcerer threw off the feather mantle, leaving him almost naked in the lurid glow of the forge. Wild-eyed, he continued to pound away with a great bronze hammer while chanting spells which sank into the hot metal like flakes of ice into hot water. Metal rang, smoke and vapor rose, words in strange tongues echoed from the rafters, and strange lights flickered over the cooling metal of the mighty sword. Ronar watched, mesmerized.

At last Sha Totek stopped, panting, his breasts heaving. Noticing Ronar's gaze, he said "Will you please stop staring? Didn't you see enough of this, the last time you were here?"

Ronar started. "Why, yes, I did, actually."

Sha Totek plunged the sword into the water, which hissed for a moment. He withdrew it, examined it carefully, and laughed. "Call it into your hand!"

Ronar did so. He marveled at the renewed blade, its surface a flawless mirror, yet engraved with delicate designs which could not possibly have been created with a hammer. The weapon felt weightless in his hand, lithe and agile, cool and capable.

"The Sword of Bran," he breathed.

"Oh, to hell with that. You know what?" said Sha Totek. "Namirnakh was right. Bran was a pig. He could be fair-minded at times, but he was also brutal, coarse, violent, and quick to suspicion. Only in the minds of those who never knew him has he acquired his noble legend. The Sword of Bran? Not any more. This is the Sword of Ronar."

And indeed, inscribed on the blade just above the guard, was the name **RONAR**.

Ronar found himself moved to stammering.

"I—thank you. I—had no idea you knew so much about the forging of weapons."

"You pick up a lot of skills when you live for five thousand years. I also know how to make candles, distill brandy, and crochet. Now let's get out of here. We've been here too long, and I don't trust the situation with Ixtab and Emogen."

Ronar was again forced to carry the exposed sword as they returned through the torch-lit darkness of Ixtab's courtyards, because he had no scabbard for it. Ixtab's many servants and followers regarded the pair with considerable suspicion, though none dared express it openly before their strange-acting mistress. Luckily, Sha Totek had had the good sense to clothe his daughter's body again before venturing out. She still looked uncharacteristically disheveled and tired.

As they were about to enter the main palace, they were confronted by a stern-looking middle aged woman who was backed up by a phalanx of heavily-armed guards. Attached to the woman's gauntlet by a golden chain was Ixtab's black jaguar.

She reached down and detached the chain from the cat's collar. The beast slunk forward. Its hackles raised as it approached "Ixtab". It growled deep in its throat, revealing two-inch fangs.

"What is this nonsense?" blustered Sha Totek. "Call back the cat!"

"Who are you?" asked the woman, her lids heavy with confirmed suspicions.

"I am your mistress and goddess! Now withdraw, all of you, before I—"

"What is the cat's name?" interrupted the woman.

"His name? Do not play games with me."

"*Her* name. What is *my* name?"

"Your name shall be 'Victim' unless you get out of our way."

She gave a slight smile and gestured behind her. "Bring them forth."

From the shadows of the entryway came Emogen, her head hanging in misery, plus the body of Sha Totek, borne on a litter. Still more guards, along with a few probable magicians, accompanied them.

"Do not harm her!" demanded Ronar. "And do not force me to harm this animal," he said of the jaguar, whose demeanor was becoming increasingly menacing.

The woman clapped her hands; the cat flowed back to her side. "No one has yet been harmed." She looked again at Sha Totek. "You are the Toltec, are you not? Somehow you have changed places with our mistress."

Sha Totek suddenly slapped his forehead. "Ix'iloom!"

She chuckled. "Yes. You wish now you had recognized me a few moments earlier, eh? The last time you two saw me, I was but Ixtab's youngest handmaiden. Now I am her chamberlain, and she is dear to me. Toltec, undo what you have done. Restore yourselves to your proper bodies."

Sha Totek shrugged. "You have seen through my ploy. I see no reason to deny you." He made a gesture, spat out a word.

Now in his own body, he leaped up from the litter, gathered up Emogen, and stood weaving bands of colored magic about them with his free hand. Ixtab sagged, senseless. Ronar grabbed her before she could fall to the paving stones.

"Happy now?" asked the Sorcerer.

"Why is she still unconscious?" demanded Ix'iloom.

"Her mind is still subject to a spell of sleep. I think it best if she remains that way until we are gone from here."

"I think otherwise."

"Ronar, if any member of my daughter's staff should make trouble for us, by all means feel free to slit her tender throat."

Ronar said nothing. He was quite unwilling to plunge his sword into an unconscious woman, even Ixtab, but her followers need not know that.

"Yes, why not?" asked Ix'iloom bitterly. "You created her for your own purposes; why not destroy her when it suits you, as well?"

Sha Totek was visibly sobered by this. Now Ronar was driven to speak. "We did not come here to destroy Ixtab, or anyone else. As far as we're concerned, she can run this place any way she pleases, or any way that you people will tolerate. We stopped here on our way to confront a threat to this entire world. It was a mistake. We were so caught up in the threat of the Blue Magic that we did not fully consider the likelihood of conflict here. Whatever happens from this moment on, there will be consequences for us, for Ka'ahkin, and for you all. If you stop us, they will only be worse. None of us relish what we are doing. We will all lose something that is dear to us. But it must be done."

Emogen suddenly lifted her head, peering out from behind her dangling, matted locks. Ronar was startled at the look in her eye. She muttered something in a ragged voice. To Ronar it sounded like she was inviting a bear to hold its feet in her lap, if that made any sense.

The effect was that Ixtab suddenly awoke. Finding herself clamped in Ronar's right arm, with his sword held in front of her, she struggled, twisting, spitting, trying to bite and claw.

Ronar tightened his grip. He looked down into her eyes, and said quietly, "No." She grew still, though Ronar was still forced to endure her hate-filled glare. "Emogen. Why did you awaken her?"

The witch's lip trembled. "I am not very happy with either of you right now. When Ixtab grabbed me earlier, she tried to place herself into my body, using magic like that which Sha Totek used on her. She didn't have time for it to work, but in that moment of contact, I saw much. I know now why she detests both of you, and I'm not sure she is wrong to do so."

"You know nothing!" snapped Sha Totek. "You know only what Emuishéré thinks she knows, what you saw through her eyes, and what she believes. Do you think you can see through her eyes and see nothing but truth?"

"And why should my perceptions be any less valid than yours?" snarled Ixtab. "No doubt you and your enforcer here consider yourselves blameless in all things!"

Ronar glanced at Sha Totek, in whose regret-filled eyes this statement was refuted. He looked down at the sweating captive in his arm.

"No, we don't. Not at all."

For a few moments, silence held a restraining hand on everyone present, as they all waited to hear what Ronar would say next. Many errors of his past had come back to haunt him, it seemed. Their ill-advised detour to Ka'ahkin had perhaps given him a final opportunity to put one of them right. Perhaps, he thought, doing so was even more important than whatever vague plan he had for defeating Seren.

He released Ixtab. Taken by surprise, the sorceress almost fell to the ground. She turned, looking back at him in suspicion. He lowered the blade. He would have released it entirely, but this was not the sword as summoned by the ring. This was the sword in its resting state.

"When I was here before, Emuishéré, I misunderstood you greatly. In fact I made little effort to understand you, taking you on face value only. I did not realize..."

With that she sprang at him with a snarl, slashing his face with a sweep of her nails. "We do not...speak of such...*things*...before...*them!*" she hissed, gesturing wildly at her servants and followers.

The sword in Ronar's hand seemed to quiver on its own. He raised his free hand to his face, feeling the blood flowing as he stared down at this little fury, whose behavior so disappointed him, as it also had in the past.

The jaguar snarled, surging against its chain, nearly pulling Ix'iloom off her feet.

"Ixtab, hold back that beast," he thundered. "Or I swear, I'll leave its head rolling on the floor."

Ixtab flung herself on the cat, weeping sudden tears.

Ronar shook his head. His failure to get through to Ixtab on any level left him saddened and distressed.

"We are leaving," announced Sha Totek. "Try to stop us if you must. You will find that we are still leaving. Come, my friends."

"My Lady Ixtab, I have failed you," said Ix'iloom. She pulled a bronze dagger from her girdle and plunged it into her belly. It was too low a stroke to be immediately fatal, so she gripped the bloody hilt in both hands and rooted around in her gut, seeking her own life, her face a ghastly mask of pain and despair. She sank to her knees with blood pumping from a terrible wound. It was up to one of the other servants to finish her off with a thrust to the breast.

Emogen screamed.

"Monsters!" raged Ronar. "You demented beasts!" He would have flung himself at them, as though killing them all would have solved anything, had not the Sorcerer held him back.

"Come on, Ronar. We can't hope to fathom their ways, or change them."

Ronar followed numbly, shaken and sickened.

As though reading his mind, Emogen touched his arm and whispered, "I do not think there is anything we could have said to comfort either of them."

They made their way toward the courtyard where the flyer rested. Ronar noticed that Sha Totek too looked stricken. At first he thought it was because of their encounter with his daughter, but then he thought not. The Sorcerer was walking blindly, almost stumbling, his face as pale as it could possibly be.

"What's wrong?" asked Ronar at last.

Sha Totek turned him a haunted gaze. "It was driven from my mind as we enjoyed my family reunion. But now that we are leaving, I cannot escape the thought that if we are successful, I am going to my death. That is a difficult concept to entertain."

Ronar cursed himself for overlooking something so obvious.

The Sorcerer continued. "Now, I don't mean to complain. I've lived far longer than any human being ever has. If saving the world means that I must die, so be it. But it's hard to imagine. I was one of the first people ever to visit this world. I have seen its every nation being formed, ushered in every tribe, every culture. I have lived in every part of the world which is inhabited by men, and in some which are no longer. When you blew up the final Portal, I knew my role in this world would change. But I did not think it would end so quickly."

Ronar set his jaw as they found the flier, unharmed, lit by torchlight in its courtyard beneath the stars. He had indeed a very grim feeling about this mission they were about to undertake. He opened the canopy and laid the sword behind the seats.

"I'm quite sure I can squeeze in back there too," said Emogen. She did so, and the two men took their places, both staring ahead as the canopy closed over them. The air was refreshed. The flier rose up in silence. The structures of Ixtab's settlement dwindled beneath them, until they appeared like elaborate toys lit by pinpoint orange lamps. Ronar applied power to the main propulsion beam, and they slid away from the island of Ka'ahkin.

Chapter Nineteen

Etheros

Sha Totek trembled as he contemplated the mystery which awaits all men.

Emogen seemed to notice this. Leaning forward, she said, "I know you do not like to speak about this, but please, tell me about your daughter in your own words."

Sha Totek's voice grew firmer as he spoke.

No, the topic of Ixtab was far from Sha Totek's favorite, thought Ronar, *but it certainly beats thinking about his imminent death.* Ronar scowled as he listened to the tale. He'd heard it before, of course. His expression was due to his profound dissatisfaction with the future as he now perceived it.

"I was lonely among those people. I considered their culture baroque and grotesque, even compared to the many others I had known. They never accepted me, because I was unlike them. I therefore made a decision based on weakness. I wanted a companion. None of the Maya pleased me, so it would have to be someone I raised myself. I could have found some orphan, but I supposed my own offspring would be better suited to the life I envisioned. So I chose a woman, I offered her ease and wealth, and through her I had a child, Emuishéré. The mother, whose name I do not remember, I kept around to feed the child and to raise her whenever I was distracted. Mainly it was under my guidance that she grew, steeped in magic, learning much and eagerly. My goal was to teach her the very same magic that has kept me alive so long, to spare me the necessity and the choice of doing it for her. I made no such arrangement for her mother. I left that up to Emuishéré, to learn to apply the magic to others, if that was her wish. But that magic is hard to learn. By the time she mastered the art, her mother was old, too old to be worth preserving, and so Emuishéré allowed her to die.

"That loss darkened Emuishéré's always moody spirit considerably. I barely noticed that woman's passing, because if I paid attention to the death of everyone I've ever known, I would have no time for anything but grief. But in this case it would have been better if I had paid it some heed. True, that was during the uprising of the Dark Pharaoh, and I was unusually distracted. But still.

"At last the Portal in Ka'ahkin crumbled, and none too soon for me. It was time to move on to the next empty land, to await the first people to straggle through that weird bronze box that had just appeared in their country. But Emuishéré did not wish to go. She was born and raised in Ka'ahkin and was thoroughly a part of its culture. She turned on me and vowed she would not be my assistant or my pet. She hated her Kemetish name, using only the Mayan name her mother had given her. So I left her behind to pursue my duty in other lands. Much later she embraced the name, and the role, of the goddess Ixtab, after tricking Ronar and myself into assisting her in this goal. I was disgusted that she would set herself up as a petty tyrant, even pass herself off as a goddess, and dismayed that I had been responsible for bringing about her grisly suicide cult. I washed my hands of her."

Silence prevailed in the flyer for a few moments.

"Those are the bare facts, as Ixtab knows them," said Emogen at last. "But in her mind, the emphasis is different. She loved her mother very much. She did not forgive you for permitting her death. Also, parts of your relationship with her you have not mentioned."

Sha Totek shrugged irritably. "As for that, I spent the first few hundred years of my life in Kemet and the royal courts of Ammon. That is the way such things are done there. But the ways of Ka'ahkin are different. I realized this soon enough."

"It's not...natural."

He snorted. "Nature encompasses more than you seem to realize. And as our friend Ronar will gladly explain, nothing we magicians do is in any way natural."

Ronar did not feel like explaining anything at the moment. His mind was fixed on the vague, unpredictable, and possibly hopeless task facing them all. He brooded on this as the flyer continued its journey across half the world, cruising high above the atmosphere.

Presently he heard the gentle, purring snore of Emogen. That poor woman could sleep anywhere, it seemed, when pushed beyond exhaustion. Sha Totek's wakeful face was still ashen and tense in the dim lighting of the cockpit.

"I'm the one who finally ruined your daughter," muttered Ronar. "You know that as well as I do."

Sha Totek turned to look at him. "Eh?"

"She was troubled before we ever met, no doubt. Yet only after I finished with her did she become so wicked."

Sha Totek regarded him with compassion. "The part you played in her life was indeed unfortunate, and I've long been sorry I asked you along on that venture and made that possible. But the romantic disappointment she suffered at your hands was no worse than many suffer in their lives, perhaps more than once. Her exaggerated response, and her inability to move past it, was her fault and lack, not yours. I won't tell you to be at peace with it, because I know that's impossible for you. But don't let it haunt you. None of us are saints in this matter." He turned away to resume his contemplation.

Ronar leaned back and observed the stars, their fire undimmed by the canopy. There they burned, unreachably distant, casting their light over their own remote domains, places where Ronar, Sha Totek, and Colibdis had never been heard of. Whatever happened here, he was comforted to consider, those stars and the many worlds they harbored would go untouched.

Except...there was the time Ahriman had sought to spread magic throughout space, and not for the first time either, according to Sha Totek. Ahriman was no more, but there was nothing to stop a similar creature from arising someday.

Ronar frowned. The sound of Emogen's slumber reminded him of the vow he had made to her. His jaw clenched. How much of a hurry were they in? His hands moved toward the controls, preparing to change course.

"Don't do it," murmured Sha Totek.

"Don't do what?" asked Ronar, his hands hovering over the console.

"Don't turn aside to deliver Emogen to safety. She would not wish it. She has grown quite fond of you, and would not be parted from you."

"Really? She has seemed less than pleased with me recently."

"She has been disappointed by us both, but her feelings remain. Also she is flattered and dazzled to find herself, a humble village witch, at the center of world events. How many times have you tried to remove her from these affairs already? Somehow she always turns up again. There must be some reason for that. Finally, where would you take her? Faerie has surely overrun all lands by now, save the one we just fled. There is no safety for her."

"No. I suppose not." Ronar glowered.

"So what are we aiming to do once we get to this island of Etheros?" muttered the Sorcerer.

"I don't know. I don't know what we'll find there, except for this. Under the influence of the Blue Magic, we'll have to cope with the threat of death or transformation, on top of anything else. Whatever we do, it had best be quick."

"Of course."

Dawn was visible far ahead as a band of atmosphere lit with peach, yellow, and blue. Directly ahead, yet still thousands of miles away, this band seemed to bulge up slightly. Ronar squinted at it, wary and puzzled.

"What's that?" whispered Sha Totek.

"I don't know," said Ronar again. "Let me try to figure out how to use these instruments." He fiddled with the displays, fumbling through an interface which, though very well designed, was painfully removed from anything he had learned in the first half of the Twentieth Century, and to which he'd had little exposure since.

Finally he found his way to the flyer's multiple exotic forms of radar.

"If I'm interpreting what I see on this display properly," he said, "it looks like two great rivers of air are converging on our destination, from two different directions. Powerful enough to force the upper layers of the atmosphere upward for miles. One stream is coming from behind us. This can't be natural."

"Magic," said Sha Totek.

"But for what purpose?"

"Company coming," replied the Sorcerer, uncharacteristically terse. "We'd better hurry."

"Yes, maybe so. I'll have to fly this thing a little more radically. This may be uncomfortable."

Ronar increased power to the main propulsion lamp at the rear of the flyer. He and Sha Totek were pushed back strongly into their seats. Poor Emogen, who Ronar had briefly forgotten, was rudely cast against the cockpit's rear bulkhead, awakening her.

"What's happening, are we falling?" she asked in fear.

"No, my dear," answered Sha Totek. "We are merely eager to reach our destination."

Muttering to himself, Ronar eased back on the acceleration, lest he stupidly batter Emogen to death before they even arrived.

A blue flicker; a sudden feeling of difference. Ronar's vision grew sharper. Emogen moaned; Sha Totek gave a sharp hiss.

"Welcome back to Faerie," said the Sorcerer. "We will see only a single sun rise today."

Now the island which Ronar had expected to find, Etheros, came into view on the horizon. It was of no great size, and in shape was a concave triangle, with three similar bays. Dawn broke suddenly, and the false sun which Sha Totek had predicted burst over the horizon.

"Do either of you sense anything unusual about that place?" asked Ronar.

"No, I don't," said Emogen, "except that I will be very happy to set foot there, no matter what dangers await. This thing we ride in is unnatural. It doesn't even smell like a thing that belongs in the world."

"What were you expecting, Ronar?" asked Sha Totek.

"I don't know. I thought that if the source of magic really lies there, it might be apparent to you."

Once again Ronar felt a sinking thrill of doubt about the logic of his plan. He was staking an awful lot on his theories and speculations.

And then, just as Ronar was trying to interpret the curved, concentric shadows which lay across Etheros, the flyer's displays went dark, and its propulsion lamps became inert. The flyer began to fall in a long arc, and then to tumble. Emogen screamed. Ronar slammed the large button which should produce an emergency re-initialization of the flyer's systems, but it had no effect. Ronar reviewed his options in a few instants of extended mental clarity and found there were none.

"What's happening?" bellowed Sha Totek, even though their predicament was not at all noisy.

Ronar gripped the arms of his seat, trying to keep his head from slamming into the canopy. "The flyer has lost power. Evidently its technology is incompatible with the Blue Magic. It's up to you to slow our descent, or we'll all die." Somehow, the knowledge that matters were out of his hands was a comfort at this moment.

"Oh, fine, once again you expect me to pull some specialized spell out of my ass at a moment's notice—"

"The Breast of Mor!" cried Emogen.

"What?" asked Sha Totek in confusion.

"A spell I know! Just be quiet and let me try it. But I need to see the water!"

Ronar reviewed what he knew about the flyer. Having a vague memory of a button labeled "Emergency Stabilizers", he scanned the console, found and punched it. It was another mechanical button, which lent him hope that it might still work.

With a roar of wind, the flyer steadied and slowed somewhat, nose pointed down, toward the ocean. Ronar looked back. White vanes had popped out of the flyer's rear pod, stabilizing the craft like the feathers on a badminton shuttlecock. Evidently their action was purely mechanical, or at least very simple.

Emogen did not comment on this, but stared with round eyes at the rapidly approaching surface of the sea, her mouth working in blatant terror.

"Emogen!" barked Ronar. She started, then began frantically calling on the water goddess Mor in her own language.

An instant before impact, with a great soft hiss the sea beneath them turned a creamy green-white. They hit the water. The impact threw them all forward, but not fatally; rather their speed was slowed more gradually, as if the water had become less dense, and was now a fine, insubstantial foam. Ronar stared into this for a while as the flyer drifted within it. Then the water solidified into green-black. The flyer surged toward the surface. Ronar gazed into the depths of the Colibdian ocean during their few moments within it. He shuddered. With all the amazing and terrifying things he'd encountered on the surface of this world, there was no telling what or who might dwell within its oceans.

The flyer broke the surface, pitching on the great waves raised by the unnatural wind flowing from the direction of Ka'ahkin. The light of the anomalous single sun glared through the canopy.

"My dear, that was quite a fine spell," yelled Sha Totek over the tumult. "Where did you learn it?"

"I—made it up myself! When I was a girl, some friends and I used to leap from a waterfall into the pool below. My spell made it easier, and Mor seemed to enjoy our play."

"Perhaps I might learn this spell."

"I think you'd have to be devoted to Mor for it to work. Are you?"

Ronar saved him from having to answer that by saying, "I don't know how long this thing will remain afloat. Water's entering through the openings for the stabilizers. We'd better try to get the canopy open."

"Try?" asked Sha Totek in concern.

"Well, there's no power." Was there a manual method of opening the canopy? It was hard to think as the flyer plunged and bucked on the great waves. Wait—it was possible to disengage the entire cockpit capsule as a separate unit! Now where was that control—

"Bah! I'll do more than 'try' to get us out of here," said Sha Totek.

"Wait…"

But it was too late. A word from the Sorcerer produced a sudden bang, and all light was extinguished. The turbulence seemed worse, as their seats were severed from their moorings. They tumbled about, colliding with each other, battering and bruising each other and themselves. A form Ronar recognized as Emogen came into his arms. He clung to her, hunched over her, trying to protect her. She was sobbing. Bits of what seemed to be the consoles and other equipment from the cockpit kept smacking into them.

"What did you do?" bellowed Ronar.

"Mirror bubble! I'll try to steady us—ride it out!"

"Make the bubble egg-shaped if you can! That should help."

"I'll try."

The contents of the bubble shifted, and the ride indeed became steadier. They sat clinging to each other in slightly reduced misery, unable to see a thing, ignorant of the situation outside. Ronar felt Emogen's trembling body, and would have berated himself for exposing her to this danger, but in truth he could think of no safe place for her in all the world.

There was a scraping sound. The bubble tilted and grew still, except for a jolt every few seconds.

"We must have washed up on shore," said Sha Totek.

"Get ready to drop your bubble. We don't know what we'll find outside, so be prepared to defend yourselves."

But beyond the painful sudden glare of sunlight, the wild surf, and the vast tide of wind, they confronted no obvious menace when the bubble was dispelled. They ran inland to escape the waves, and then Ronar turned and ran right back, sifting through the sheared-off debris of the cockpit equipment whenever the pounding breakers would allow.

"Ronar, what are you doing?" called Sha Totek as he stood supporting Emogen.

"The sword! I've got to find the sword!"

For a moment the Sorcerer looked puzzled, and then horrified. He helped Emogen to a seat on the peculiarly hard surface of this island, then waded out to assist Ronar.

They did not find the sword, The waves increased in size and ferocity, forcing them to retreat.

"It must not have been included in the bubble I conjured," said Sha Totek as he wrung water out of his sleeves. "It must now be at the bottom of the sea, along with the rest of your flyer."

Ronar unreeled a string of fiery curses.

"Be careful what you ask the gods to do," warned Sha Totek. "On this world, you never know when they might take you up on it."

And then he began to laugh.

"What's so funny?" demanded Ronar. "After our amazing fortune in getting that sword out of the sea, there it is, right back again! It will rust away!"

"No, no, my friend," grinned the Sorcerer. "After all the spells I laid on that sword, it will never rust again. The sea floor may be the safest place for it. It will still come to the call of the ring."

Ronar looked at the ring, and bent his thought upon it. The reborn sword appeared in his hand, as perfect in its own way as the flyer had been. He marveled at it anew.

"It's cold again."

"Yes, I suppose so. Nothing a tough *hombre* like you can't handle. Let's see if Emogen is all right."

As they stood with her, Ronar fully took in his surroundings for the first time. There was little to see, merely a great sweep of a hard surface like yellowish porcelain, featureless except for driftwood and other debris cast up by the waves. The surface slanted up a bit towards the interior.

On the nearby horizon was a row of black specks. Ronar squinted, then withdrew the viewer from his jacket, the last functional vestige of high technology on Colibdis, as far as he knew. He aimed it at those distant marks, leaning forward unconsciously to better make out the detail.

He grunted in surprise.

Sha Totek, hearing this, turned away from Emogen and also noticed these specks. "What are those?" he asked.

"They appear to be...apes."

"Apes?"

"Yes, statues of apes."

"What are apes?" whispered Emogen.

"Large, hairy, man-like beasts who live in the southern jungles," said Ronar.

"What are they doing?"

"Nothing. They are motionless, as statues usually are. I wonder what tricks they have?"

"Tricks? What tricks can statues have?"

Sha Totek chuckled. "My dear Emogen, when you've been doing this sort of thing for as long as Ronar and I have, you soon learn. I have rarely seen a menacing statue that didn't come to life at the most inopportune time."

"Yes," said Ronar. "They will come to life and attack us." He shrugged in resignation.

"How—how can you be sure?" asked Emogen, her teeth chattering.

"That's how it always goes in these situations," said Sha Totek offhandedly. He sighed. "Well then, here we are, a trio of adventurers: a mage, a healer, and a warrior, though a warrior without any armor. Tell me Ronar, how come you never wear armor?"

"I wore armor quite recently, for all the good it did me. But I'm a professor of astronomy, not a warrior," said Ronar gruffly. "I wouldn't even have the sword, if I couldn't carry it as a ring—"

It was only then that he noticed the smirk on Sha Totek's face and realized he was being teased. He also recognized the fear beneath the Sorcerer's attempt at humor. Without thinking he stepped forward, resting one hand on Sha Totek's shoulder, the other on Emogen's.

"A trio of mighty adventurers we are," he said.

"Or perhaps a quartet," said another voice. "With the addition of a hunter, if you will."

All three of them jumped at the sound, finding that a strange, ragged figure had crept up on them without their noticing. This was a pale form, clad in a dirty grey cloak, with haunted silver eyes peering out from the hood.

"Astil," said Ronar. "What are you doing here?"

"I have come to warn you. Seren is also aware of the importance of this island. She will not permit you to interfere with her. She comes with a great fleet, driven by a gale conjured by her chief sorceress. They will be here very soon."

"Then we'd best be seeing what's to be done on this island. Come on."

Sha Totek and Emogen looked at each other. Seeing that Ronar accepted Astil's presence without question, they shrugged and hurried along behind them. Their footsteps chimed on the peculiar ceramic-like surface of the island.

"Let us be as quick as can be," said Emogen. "I can feel the unwholesome influence of Faerie working on me already."

Ronar heard a moan from Astil; the Elf's light footsteps ceased. Ronar also halted, steeling himself.

"Ronar, all of you," said Astil. "Turn now and behold the power of Faerie."

Turn they did. The sea was covered with ships, delicate Faerie ships of silver and blue, with many-tiered decks, their sails bright gossamer flashing in the sun.

"That's an amazing navy for a land-locked country," said Ronar.

"The ships are not completely real," said Sha Totek. "They are magical constructs. It is impressive. I look forward to a re-match with their chief sorceress."

"She is there, as is Seren, and thousands of warriors," said Astil. "I fear we are too late."

Ronar was inclined to agree, but Sha Totek laughed, turned, and ran off toward the waiting line of ape statues.

"There's no help in that!" cried Emogen. "If they react as you say, we'll be trapped between the two armies!"

"Just wait there!" called Sha Totek over his shoulder. "I'm going to get their attention. Whatever you do, don't attack any of the apes!"

Ronar shrugged, knowing better than to second guess the Sorcerer. He turned back to the Faerie fleet, its ships now running ashore. As they did they unfolded like toys, their parts fluttering away and dispersing, leaving behind ranks of shining warriors.

Ronar's sharpened eyesight also detected a mote of shrouded darkness in their forefront: Seren-Cotavion.

A great clamor arose behind them. They wheeled to see Sha Totek running pell-mell before a swarm of the apes, which were evidently metallic constructs of some kind, shambling and loping behind him, with still more coming.

"Run!" yelled the Sorcerer as he passed. "But do not attack!"

Practically in the midst of the robot apes, if that's what they were, Ronar and his band ran toward the waiting Elves. The apes, noted Ronar, seemed to be somewhat crude. Their dull sheen indicated they were constructed of base metals.

As they approached the ranks of Elves, Sha Totek cried, "Forward, my magical minions! Release your wrath upon our Faerie foes!"

Some of the foremost Elves raised their bows. They released arrows whose tips ignited with blue fire when in motion. These hissed down among the apes, each hit reducing its target to a pile of inert debris.

The apes immediately ignored Sha Totek and charged the Elves.

"Now turn and run away!" yelled Sha Totek. "Those apes will keep them busy for a while." He laughed again.

Ronar shook his head in appreciation of Sha Totek's trickery and followed. They mounted a low rise, the great circular ridge on which the apes had been arrayed, and faced there a steeper descent to another level, which then again tilted gently upward.

"Slide down," said Ronar. They did so, putting the Elf army temporarily out of sight. "This island seems to be shaped as a series of annular concentric zones, like a Fresnel lens."

Sha Totek cocked his thumb at Ronar and said to the others, "He's prone to saying things like that every once in a while."

"And what are those?" asked Emogen, pointing.

Arrayed along the next inward ridge were more specks. With the help of his viewer, Ronar saw them as though they stood mere feet before him.

"More apes?" asked Astil, squinting.

"Not exactly," said Ronar. "These look more like some intermediate hominid form, australopithecines or some such."

"There he goes again," chuckled Sha Totek. "Some sort of ape-men? What an offensive notion."

Ronar almost launched into a discussion of evolutionary theory, but then realized they didn't have time, and in all likelihood never would. Instead he said, "These look like they're made of bronze."

"The last ones seemed rather weak," said Emogen. "They won't hold the Elves for long. We'd best be moving on."

As they trotted along. Sha Totek said, "Ronar, a few words about your sword as we go."

"Yes?"

"It's now also a shield."

"What?"

"A spell I added. If something bad comes your way, just wave the sword in front of yourself. Trust me."

Something about that concluding remark caused Ronar to pound to a halt, nearly causing a pileup of his followers.

"Trust you? When have you ever given me cause to do anything else? I don't know if it took you five thousand years to grow into the person you are, or if you started out this way, but you are the most trustworthy man I ever met, apart from my father. If you say my sword is now a shield, then by every god, it's a shield!"

Ronar, having surprised himself by giving out this statement, was now embarrassed by the gratitude glistening in the eyes of the Sorcerer.

"Well. How could I be anything other than trustworthy, when confronted by the Great Hero of Our Age?"

A notion which had been building in Ronar's mind suddenly crystallized into an edifice of resolve, a structure of flawless integrity, fit to stand against the onslaught of time itself. It was the first time in many years that Ronar had known such strength and clarity of purpose. Truly, it came now at a fitting moment.

There was no point in talking about it. He looked around, having been distracted by thoughts of how to achieve his goal. There was much he had to do before the end.

Emogen was looking at him very strangely. She gave a tentative smile and said "Though my spirit is warmed by such a display of friendship, hadn't we best be moving along?"

Astil looked around uneasily. "The wind is changing. The gale which propelled Seren's fleet has been dispelled. Now another wind dominates, this one coming from far out to sea, from regions unknown to Faerie."

"Ixtab," said Sha Totek. Astil looked at him in confusion. "My daughter. A long story. Come, before we have two vicious magical minxes breathing down our necks."

A small fluffy pale thing was blown before that wind, straight for Ronar. It smacked him on the chest, where it clung with sharp talons…a tiny owl. It climbed to a more secure perch on his shoulder, where it sat blinking before fluttering away again.

Sha Totek laughed. Astil look on in amazement.

"This is a sign," said Ronar. "A good sign. Now let's see what those bronze ape-men have to say to us." He jogged forward, with the others following. As they neared the small metallic figures he slowed to a walk and said, "We don't know how sophisticated these robots are, or what their purpose may be. As we approach, keep in mind our own purpose for being here. It may be acceptable to the powers behind this island, and keep us out of trouble."

"What is a 'robot'?" asked Emogen.

"A mechanical man."

"Machines? Not magical?"

"I suspect not."

"It's strange to think that mere machines could do things that seem so magical."

"This entire island is a machine, I believe," said Ronar. "An artificial device designed to reshape the space through which this planet drifts, to make magic possible. I'm sure of it."

"You said before that Earth is a world without magic, but it's hard to imagine such a thing. It seems to me that living in a place where the hearts, minds, and wills of the people cannot affect their surroundings must suffocate your souls. Who wants to live at the mercy of cold and illness and other such hardships?"

"Not us. That's why we build machines and make things to master those facts of nature as best we can."

"But who could have built such a thing here? The gods?"

"Oh no, no," said Sha Totek. "The gods are products of the magic of Colibdis, not its originators. Whatever power is responsible for this is beyond anything we know."

By now they could see the coppery bristles covering the brazen scalps of the lean little ape-men. Their eyes were closed, their postures relaxed. They were scrawny, unlovely things, not very inspiring as ancestors of men. If not for their being made of metal, they would have seemed fragile.

At the feet of each of them was a small pile of rocks.

"Uh oh," said Ronar.

The eyes of the bronze ape-men snapped open. The closest four reached down to pick up the rocks.

"Get behind me!" said Ronar. He called out the Cold Sword. The quartet of ape-men snatched up rocks and hurled them with inhuman force. Ronar swung the blade; it blurred strangely, leaving behind an afterimage like a veil of water. The rocks struck this and fell back. More rocks were thrown and Ronar swung again. He caught most, but one got through, only slowed, striking him painfully on the clavicle.

"I can shield us—" began Sha Totek.

"No! We must move through these things, not stand here safely while our enemies advance on us from behind. Forward!"

And Ronar moved forward, doing his best to catch the stones on the blurred trailing edge of the sword, which grew wider the faster he swung it. It seemed to Ronar that part of the blade's substance was actually lagging behind as it moved. Each impact on this shield was transmitted into Ronar's arms.

He heard quick footsteps behind him and shot back a glance. Astil was running away. Ronar grunted in displeasure, but he could do nothing about it now.

A moment later an arrow came whistling over his shoulder, its tip a flare of blue radiance. It sank into one of the robots, where the blue fire quickly burned out a ragged hole, halting the contrivance. Ronar reached their attackers and swung against one of them. To his amazement, the blade severed one of the robot's arms with that one stroke. A second blow sheared the thing in two at the waist.

A bolt from Sha Totek ruptured a third robot, while another of Astil's magic-burning arrows devastated the fourth.

Four more robots charged them, two from each side of the now broken circle. They dispatched these with similar tactics, then dashed through the gap, down the sudden slope, and into the open space beyond. No more robots followed them, giving them a moment to halt and catch their breath.

"My arrows grow more effective the farther they travel, in case you were wondering about my retreat," said Astil. "Of course, I have only so many of them."

"I suppose we must conclude that the builders of this place do not approve of us," said Emogen wryly as she examined their injuries.

"I think otherwise," said Ronar. "Do you think all those other robots were unaware of us? They could have swarmed over us. Instead we were faced by only enough of them to prove that we are serious about going on. The intentions of the ones who built this place remain unclear to me."

"What do you suppose that next batch will do?" asked Sha Totek, pointing inward to an arc of shining glints.

Ronar fumbled out his viewer with unpleasantly shaking hands and studied the next rank. "These look like men, armored and armed. They look like they are made of steel."

"Steel! Surely not," said Astil.

"I doubt that the builders suffered from any shortage of iron. It's really quite common throughout the universe. The good news is that each circle is considerably smaller than the last, and so there are fewer guardians. Come."

"Hmph," was Sha Totek's skeptical reply. "Fewer, yet stronger, and as you pointed out, more than enough to overwhelm us, should they wish to."

Ronar grimaced. The Sorcerer's words were inarguable, yet poorly timed for the sake of morale.

And so they advanced, full of fears and misgivings, with the insidious temptations of Faerie always pulling at them as well.

Ronar's eyes were locked on the gleaming guardians until a sudden shadow swept over them. He turned. What he beheld took him completely by surprise.

Hovering in the sky was an immense flying creature, a winged serpent whose ranks of feathers were in rich iridescent colors. It hung suspended on great slow beats of those wings, while its slender, sinuous body writhed and its sharp bird-like face peered at him.

Perched just before the wings was the small figure of Ixtab, staring down at them with an inscrutable expression. Behind were a few lesser flying beasts of similar kind, carrying various lackeys of Ixtab: no army, but merely attendants.

"Enough," growled Sha Totek. He held apart his hands; between them appeared a diffuse blackness, a thing difficult and distressing to look upon, pulsating as though alive.

But something clicked in Ronar's mind. Here, he thought, was a possible answer to one of his chief problems. It was a chance to limit the scope of the disaster that was swiftly approaching, at a cost to himself that was small enough.

With a feeling of wild recklessness he said, "No, Sha Totek. There's no need for you to kill your own daughter. I will handle her. You three move forward, and pass through those guardians if you can. I will be with you again as soon as possible."

The Sorcerer look at him narrowly, glanced again at Ixtab, and gave a curt nod. "Come, you two," he said to the others. "We will give these shiny men a taste of the true power of magic, in all its forms."

They departed. Ronar let the sword pass away, then raised his empty hand to Ixtab. She studied him with a guarded expression much like that of her father. Then she directed her fantastic mount to settle upon the ground. Ronar walked towards her, forcing himself to ignore the liquid eyes of the creature's head, which was fully ten feet long. Its body stretched for well over two hundred feet. No beast this size could possibly fly without the aid of magic, he suspected. He took note of its vestigial limbs as he paced along the bright-scaled body. He concluded it had once been one of the great birds native to Colibdis, such as the Teratorn, reshaped by magic into an awesome mount suitable for the great sorceress of Ka'ahkin.

Ixtab dismounted and stood beside the creature. Her small stature did not prevent her from exuding an aura of menace. She held a jeweled golden scepter, no doubt a wand of great power.

He found as he halted before her that his face was relaxing into a genuine smile. He was truly glad to see her at this moment.

Ixtab appeared taken aback by this, and confused. "What's this? Don't think a glimpse of your teeth will spare you from my wrath."

"Of course not. I am here to offer you a deal."

"Deal?" she mocked. "I need make no deal with you. You are already at my mercy."

"Perhaps, though you know how resistant I can be to your magic. But do you really think you can handle your father so easily? I think his patience with you is exhausted. He expects to die soon, and it has made him a little testy."

Ixtab looked uncertain. "What do you offer?"

"First tell me—between me and your father, who do you hate more?"

She considered this, then her face twisted in sudden spite. "You!" she hissed. "I hate you! My father may have abused and ignored me, but he never actually wished me ill. You, on the other hand...your sins against me are grievous."

Ronar nodded somberly. "Yes. They are equal to the sins you have committed over centuries, in your habit of using and discarding people. I have long been ashamed of my offenses against you, and sorry as well, though I know that means little to you. I did not understand your heart. I did not realize what you were offering me. Not that I would have accepted it if I had, but at least I would not have treated you so lightly. Now I'm offering you the chance to gain your final vengeance against me."

"How?"

"It depends on your skill and flexibility in magic. Your father always complains when I ask him to do something for which he is unprepared or unfamiliar. If you can better him in this one thing, if you can do what I ask, your vengeance will be complete, and you will deal your father a serious blow as well."

"What do you wish?"

Ronar told her. The gleam in her eyes told him his proposition was of great interest to her. She laughed. "Yes, that is most devious, and I will enjoy the outcome. The task is made easier because he once shared this magic with you already."

But then her expression darkened once again.

"If you do what you came here to do, I too will die."

Ronar nodded. "Yes, you will die. But there are worse things, Ixtab, than death. One is to spend centuries consumed by hatred, bitterness, and cruelty. You cling to your life without thinking, as does almost any living thing. The time has come to decide not whether we are to die, for die we must, all of us, but how we are to die. You can choose to ensure life for the majority of the people of this world. Or you can try to stop us. Either way, your death is assured. You have said that dying means little in your death cult. Prove it now. Delight in the measure of vengeance you will achieve, and let that be your final act, if that's the best one you can manage."

She looked at him for long moments, then her face relaxed into a smile. "Very well. You are most eloquent. Let us join your little band of adventurers. Behind me is an army of strange men, powerful enough to daunt even me, and with them goes some terror that I do not understand. I will be thinking on how to achieve what you wish me to do."

Ronar nodded. "Will you bring this mount of yours into battle?"

"What, and risk the result of a hundred turns of careful breeding and spellcraft? I think not. No, I will send her away with one of my people. The others will remain with me."

Typical, thought Ronar. She was more concerned about the well-being of her animals than she was of her devotees.

"Send all your people away," he demanded. "Unless they are stronger or smarter than they look, they can make no contribution to the coming battles, except to die."

"Yes, and what of that? Still, I will dismiss these inconsequential people if it will make you happy."

Ronar shrugged. Redeeming Ixtab was beyond him. The best he could do at this point was to manipulate her into assisting him in his plans.

Now deprived of her underlings, Ixtab started toward the kaleidoscopic whirl in the near distance where Sha Totek and his allies battled the steel guardians.

Ronar ran toward the battle, not content with Ixtab's languid pace, though it exposed his unguarded back to any treachery she might have in mind.

He guessed the meaning of the look in Sha Totek's eyes as he approached.

"No, she has not enslaved me again. She has allied herself with us for the time being."

"Yes, father," said Ixtab lazily as she arrived at last. "Fate has thrown us together again. I shall be what you always wished, your—what would you call it?—your *sidekick*. A sidekick to a sidekick, how amusing."

Ronar did not like hearing Sha Totek referred to as a sidekick, and evidently neither did he. Glowering in the midst of a field of metallic debris, the Sorcerer pointed to the gleaming figures approaching from both sides. "These metal men seem less disposed to ignoring us than the last batches. Fight now, trade barbs later."

"They are but men," said Ixtab with contempt. "Steel men, it is true, yet men nevertheless. This fight need not be a lengthy one. Let's see how they stand up to the Flailing Sickles of Ah Cun Can." She gave a wild laugh, then gargled out a rapid string of Mayan words, accompanied by chopping hand motions. Ghostly sickles began to whirl in the air around her. These flung themselves against the first of the steel guardians to approach her. To her obvious disappointment (and to Ronar's as well), the magical blades battered and dented the guardians, but did not dismember them. One of Astil's magic-burning arrows struck another, but glanced off, sputtering uselessly on the ground.

"You'll have to try harder than that, my dear daughter," said Sha Totek. "Astil, you really must…"

"Yes, I know, lodge my arrows in the seams of their armor, or in their mouths. It is not so easy to do." The Elf snatched up the wasted arrow, nocked it, drew, and released. This time the shaft sank into the silently shouting mouth of one of the guardians. Its head became wreathed in a nimbus of blue fire. The robot halted and stood swaying. A look of wonder fleeted over its face as its head dissolved in the flames, leading Ronar to wonder just how automatic these automata really were.

But now he had no more time for musing. He called out the Cold Sword, swinging it tentatively, almost as an experiment. It rang off the guardian's metallic hide, and a long splinter of the blade broke off and flew away.

He was playing this game according to the island's rules, Ronar realized, and they didn't have time for that.

"All of you, quit fooling around with these things!" he yelled as he tried to evade the weapons of the one that was attacking him. "Back off until they lose interest in us! I don't think it will take long."

"You call this fooling around?" cried Sha Totek as he fled a string of guardians who had evidently been battering him despite the crackle of green magic emanating from his hands.

"Seren and her army are back there!" panted Emogen as she trotted by. "Which is worse?"

"Just retreat!"

Sure enough, the metal men soon stopped their pursuit and returned to re-form their circle, minus a considerable gap to account for those which had been destroyed.

"Their behavior is absurd!" sputtered Ixtab. "Surely those that remain can see us standing here."

"Absurd, yes, but useful," said Ronar. "All of you, follow me, single file, straight through the middle of that gap. Look neither right nor left. Brandish no weapon. Offer no threat. Don't aggravate them." He permitted his sword to fade and mend itself.

Using this stratagem they penetrated the ring of defenders without any incident other than the hairs raising on the back of their necks.

"What's next?" asked Emogen through chattering teeth.

Ronar looked ahead to the next circle, which was quite small, as they weren't far from the center of the island.

"I see about a dozen figures. They are made of some gleaming white substance. They are—only approximately human. They have huge black glassy eyes, like lenses beneath protective brows. Their contours and anatomy are subtly different from ours."

"What do you think they represent?" asked Sha Totek, squinting in their direction.

"A future stage in the development of Man. I suspect I once met a person of this kind, though I could not see his face. I do not think we will be able to force or trick our way past them. I hope it will not be necessary to try."

"I don't see what you are talking about," said Astil, peering from beneath a shading hand. "I see no obstacle. Let us go forward."

"What?" said Ronar.

"I—I don't know that I can go on," said Emogen, sagging white-faced onto the island's implacably smooth surface.

"And why should you try?" demanded Ixtab. "I was a fool to join you weaklings in this hopeless venture. Perhaps it's time for Ixtab to feel her own blade at last."

Ronar looked in confusion and alarm from one face to another. But it was the transformation which had overtaken Sha Totek that truly set him back.

He had never seen so black an expression on the face of the Sorcerer, who stared with heavy-lidded loathing upon his daughter. Then his wrathful gaze shifted to Ronar, striking him like malice given form.

"You! You seek to lure me to my destruction, or even to assist you in procuring it. I, Sha Totek, who has lived five times longer than all of you put together, and who is not to be trifled with. What do I care for the victory of the Blue

Magic? I will outlive it as I've outlived all else. And you, Emuishéré. You also plot against me, you ungrateful brat, who was little more to me than a pet. Do either of you dream you have ever seen the full extent of my magic? I have long held back from calling upon powers that would elevate me above any god, for reasons I now scorn as sentimental and weak. See now!"

With his eyes ablaze with insanity Sha Totek lifted his hands and spoke Words threatening to open Doors which could not then be closed. Behind them lurked Powers which could not be endured.

Ixtab gave a cry that was nothing more than a surrender to dread.

Calling forth the sword, Ronar flung himself on Sha Totek, penetrating the aura of anti-human wrongness that already surrounded him. Holding the blade to the Sorcerer's throat, Ronar twisted his head around, forcing him to look back the way they had come.

"Look there, Sha Totek! See those Lights. They speak through you now. They speak through you all. For the Elf who is easily led and misled, Illusion. For the healer, Death. For the goddess of suicide, Despair. And for you, Inner Darkness. Look!"

And indeed, arrayed along the next outer ring was the shimmering army of Faerie. In its forefront stood Seren-Cotavion, her cloak thrown back, the dire lights of her Stones shining, or casting shadow, in the case of the black pendant dangling from her neck.

But the revelation of the Stones was not enough to dispel their effects from their victims. Sha Totek snarled and twisted to stare at Ronar with his murderous gaze.

Ronar sighed, gave him a hard punch in the jaw, and stood up from the sagging figure, turning toward Seren and her army. He and his allies had taken too long to advance. Seren's forces could no longer be avoided. He carried a bitter memory of what those Elvish arrows could do to a person. He would have to bear the brunt of their attack himself.

He turned and yelled, "Go, all of you! Drag Sha Totek away from here! Get to the center; do whatever needs to be done! I'll hold them off."

But the others did not look as if they were up to making any kind of a retreat. They were defeated already, victims of those accursed Stones. Ronar snarled in rage and despair. He turned back toward Seren, confronting a constellation of blistering blue lights. He gave the sword a desperate swing, and managed to deflect the swarm of incoming arrows. The Elves released a denser cloud of arrows. Their blue flare dazzled him as he fended them off with another frantic swing. There would be no end to them. To stop their flight, he must close the distance between himself and the archers, and there discover whether they also carried magical blades before he was inevitably felled by their numbers.

With sword in hand he strode toward the dark figure of Seren and the brighter ranks of lesser Elves, which to his eyes were a mere blur behind her. Seren evidently felt his gaze, for her lights faltered and went dim. Ronar wondered whether his perfected sword could cleave through that thorny iron staff of hers. He would attempt to find out.

An arrow flew beneath his guard and sank into his left calf, barely missing the bone. Ronar gave a grunt of pain and rage and yanked the shaft out from the back before that blue flame could consume his leg. He cast the arrow back at the Elves, and it flickered weakly as it fell impotently to the surface of the island. He had burned his hand in handling the arrow. The foremost archers raised their bows. Ronar realized he had lost the sword. He could not summon it again before those arrows would pierce him.

A very tall figure appeared before him. It was the goddess Athene in full martial mode, bearing in one hand an immense spear, and in the other a shield upon which his gaze could not linger. She glanced over her shoulder at him, her face surprisingly delicate, her grey eyes flashing, her mouth bent in a small wry smile. Athene. Asterope. They were one.

Seren's army shrank with fear at the sight of this great power. And yet they were of Faerie, and their Queen was a great and intimidating power in her own right. Ronar felt pity for these Faery folk, pulled far beyond the borders of their land by the strange ambitions of this, surely the strangest ruler they had ever known.

Seren lifted her iron staff and pointed it toward Athene. At her command, a cloud of blue-flaring arrows howled toward the goddess. Most bounced harmlessly from her shield and armor. The rest pricked her, but Athene swept them away like mere nuisances.

An appalling din staggered Ronar, a sound like a world-sized bell under assault by the mallets of the Titans. Athene was clashing her mighty spear against her shield, resulting in a shattering blast that flung the foremost Elves off their feet.

The sight and sound of this terrible goddess as she routed the Elves without even casting her weapon filled Ronar with a sudden crashing sense of dread. Among all that tumult, the shadowy figure of Seren stood unmoved.

The weapons of the Elves might mean little to Athene, but Ronar wasn't sure she was strong enough to withstand the power of Seren and her Stones.

And there was still worse. With Asterope standing and battling mere feet in front of him, Ronar could no longer ignore the fate that awaited her, the dissolution that must come to her, the ultimate ending that could not be avoided.

Without thinking, he cried out, "Asterope! Asterope, get away! Run! Get as far away from here as you can!" Even as he said this, he knew the futility of his words. There was no place Asterope could go to escape her destruction.

Somehow Athene heard his cry over the thunder she was raising from her shield. Somehow her voice rang back to him as if it were falling from the sky.

"No, Professor. Go, do what you need to do. I will hold off these urchins."

"Then…you know?"

"Do I know what you must do? Yes, of course, How could I not? And I agree. It must be done. I know this, for I too am a guardian of this world, no less than you or the Sorcerer. Go and do it!"

"You will die!"

"So I will! So will many others. But what of it? My life has not been especially long, but it has been very rich, thanks largely to you. My girlhood in Thunderbird. My time as a young astronomer. And then, during my life as Athene, I moved freely across this planet, cast down much evil, and brought hope to many. Even my battle against Ahriman had its moments of triumph. I honor all these memories. Go, Professor, and be easy of mind. The fate that befell me so long ago was not your doing. Go. We will meet again, soon enough."

Ronar dimly realized that the clash of Athene's weapons had died away while she made this speech. All was quiet. Such Elves as were still on their feet wavered or stood inert. Ronar took note of the despair and dismay on those beautiful Elvish faces as this foreign goddess threatened to end their long lives.

Only Seren appeared to be fully in possession of herself, and she was advancing.

"Yes, Asterope, it must be done, whatever the cost," said Ronar. "But this, this woman who approaches us now, she is for me to face. You go. Help these friends of mine forward, into the heart of the island. I will follow."

The goddess turned and gave Ronar a long, level look. By now Seren was only a hundred feet away, advancing at an unhurried pace.

"You underestimate me, I think," said Athene. "But I will let you have your way in this. I will escort your friends. Follow, and don't be too long. We both have an appointment to keep."

She turned and ran back, and her passage was like a blast of wind that carried a hint of the scent of the small Mersinean girl Ronar had once known.

Seren continued her inexorable advance, her iron staff ringing with each slow step. Ronar limped forth to meet her. She halted and waited for him to close the final distance.

His hand lashed out, and the Cold Sword exploded into being with a flash and a ringing peal. The blade was already whistling through the air when it appeared. Seren thrust out her staff to deflect it. The great sword bit halfway through the iron shaft, and halted. Seren staggered back. Ronar yanked his weapon free.

"Stop this madness!" he thundered at her. She started. So peremptory was his command that she stood blinking. In the sudden silence nothing could be heard but the thin moan of wind over the face of Etheros.

Seren needed little time to recover her poise. Even at this precarious moment, Ronar could not be oblivious to her profound beauty, her face so perfectly made, even darkened at it was by the light of the Stones.

Seren studied him, then said, "I've been wishing to subtract the arrogance from your stubbornly ageless mortal face, Ronar. Now I shall." She reached up with her left hand, where pulsed the red stone of the Ring of Death.

Ronar laughed.

Consternation crossed her face, and she lowered the Stone. In genuine puzzlement she asked "You laugh at Death made into crystal?"

"Yes, I laugh at that and all your silly lights. They may fool others, but not me."

"What do you mean?"

"I know them for what they are. I have seen their opposites, and used one of them myself. Yes, I understand your shock. Maybe I'll explain the circumstances later, if time permits. The thing that matters is this. I have heard the story of the origin of those other Stones: Inner Light, Truth, Life, Adamance, plus the four you carry, their opposites. The mistake you make is to suppose that because they are opposites, your Stones are equal to those once carried by your cousin, Cal-Cotavion. Nothing could be less true. Take Life, for example. Death is not the opposite of Life. Death is not some force stalking the universe in opposition to Life. It is merely the absence of Life. It is nothing, in contrast to the Something of Life. The same is true of all your Stones. Illusion is merely the lack of Truth, not a thing unto itself. And so on. Your Stones are but a side effect of the creation of the set once held by your cousin, which are truly awesome things. Yours are but...a waste product. I will not be harmed by such trifles."

She stood staring at him for long moments, her mouth twitching.

"You are right, of course," she said at last. "You have seen a truth which no one else ever realized, not even Cal-Cotavion. My army and I cannot stand against your insight, the magic of the Sorcerer, and the power of a goddess combined. We shall withdraw."

Black rage, more intense than any Ronar had ever experienced before, inflamed his mind, dimming his senses, causing his thoughts to spin.

"Withdraw?" he snarled. "With all the mischief you have wrought, all the trouble and misery you've brought to the world, you think you'll be allowed to simply *withdraw?* You have wounded the world, perhaps beyond healing. Too often lately I've let villains like you walk away. You won't be another."

The Cold Sword moved in his hand. With two strokes he opened her belly and lopped off her exquisite head. He stood staring down as the silver-blue light congealed in her eyes. The Faerie army fled with pathetic shrieks of dismay. Ronar drew in several long, slow breaths as he watched Seren's blood flow around and over his feet. It was as red as any mortal's.

Releasing the sword, he bent to remove the Stones from her carcass: the circlet from her head, the other three from her body. He studied them as they lay in his hands—

contemptible trinkets, fraudulent imitations of real power. He flung them away in disgust.

Turning, he took note of his companions, just now rising and shaking off the effects of the false Stones. They had made no progress. Athene, now reduced in stature, looked at him in concern. His lip curled in contempt at their weakness. Their fearful glances darted between him and the corpse of Seren. Astil shambled over to his aunt, kneeling beside her, his hands fluttering above her, unwilling to touch the sprawling, decapitated thing.

"Why don't you keep her head for a souvenir, Astil?" snapped Ronar. "It might strengthen your claim to the Faerie throne, if you've got the spine to make one."

The Elf looked at him over his shoulder with an expression of ineffectual resentment that made Ronar laugh.

"Come on, all of you, get moving. Let's bring this hopeless farce to its conclusion. I'm sick of it all."

They stumbled further inland in the sickly yellow sunlight. Ronar knew he had little time to do whatever he hoped to achieve here. A taste of acid rose in his throat. His head pounded. His vision was fading, making everything seem unreal. His leg was badly wounded; his right hand burned. Faerie was dragging him down, he suspected. He would not, after all, become an Elf. He would merely die, unable to adapt to this new regime of being.

He stalked onward, trying to ignore the pain, seething with bitterness at being put into this position. Why must he always be the one to save this damned planet? Was no other competence to be found here? Sha Totek, the mighty Sorcerer—how had his vigilance missed the threat posed by Seren and Natulakh? Probably he'd been too busy with his arcane drugs and his multi-colored illusory sex partners to notice. The thought of shutting down the magic of Colibdis seemed suddenly appealing. He had always hated its chaos anyway. With one stroke he could restore sanity to this corner of the universe.

He never should have come here in the first place; he should have stayed on Earth! By now, with the help of the mighty scientific powers there, he could have made a telescope great enough to span the Solar System, rather than that creaking bronze contraption that was the best he could manage back in Thunderbird.

He fell back, permitting the others to draw a little ahead, which they seemed satisfied to do. His gaze lingered on Athene. A sick resentment darkened his thoughts. He thought back to all he had missed in life, all he had denied himself, for no reason that made sense to him now. He should always have taken what he wanted, without hesitation. No such opportunity would ever come his way again, of that he was certain. All such chances must pass away.

Well, Asterope's must, perhaps, but not his. His plans had changed.

Ixtab, that worst of all whores and bitches, was stumbling along just ahead, ludicrous in her costume of bright feathers.

"Ixtab."

She looked back at him with fearful eyes.

"I've changed my mind. Leave things as they are now. Do you understand?"

She nodded, returning to her hopeless trudge. She was already broken.

Emogen also looked back at him, but his glare caused her to avert her gaze. How insipid she was! Ronar could not believe he had ever been in any way attracted to her. No matter how many times he had tried to get rid of her, she had always turned up again to annoy him and to hold him back. He felt like raping her, to teach her a lesson, and to wipe out those sickening looks of doe-eyed worship she was always giving him. Didn't she know what kind of a monster he really was? Hadn't he already told her?

But it seemed he would not be able to carry out this plan, or any other. All strength left his legs. He collapsed onto the hot, hard surface of Etheros. His "friends" plodded on, taking no notice of his plight. He cried out to them, yelled, screamed, and raved, yet they ignored him, walking away, abandoning him, as he had always known they would in the end.

He lay there, helpless, cursing fate and all the gods he had ever known or destroyed. His failure, at the end, could not be more complete.

He wished to die, and yet he did not die. Someone, somewhere must pay for the indignity of his defeat. That single blazing thought was enough to stave off death.

He heard a faint rhythmic tapping, and then footsteps, growing louder. He raised his head and beheld an approaching figure, grey-cloaked, with the bearing of an Elf. Astil? No, this person was taller, and carried a staff. Seren? he wondered, though she of course was dead. Anyway, this staff was a mere stick of wood.

This was a male, clad in silver and white beneath his cloak. His appearance was unusual, even by Faerie standards. His face was sallow, severe, lacking the beauty which was the Elvish norm. His long silver hair was unkempt and not especially clean.

He carried Stones of blue, green, violet, and clear white.

"Cal-Cotavion," rasped Ronar.

The Elf nodded.

"But you are dead."

Cal-Cotavion shrugged. His voice was a thin whisper. "You are on Colibdis, under the influence of Faerie. I am dead, you say? That need not preclude all possibilities, not here."

"Why are you here?"

"Seren needs your help."

Ronar snorted. "She is beyond any help. I put her beyond its reach myself. I'm the one who needs help."

Cal-Cotavion lifted his hand to his throat. Glimmering there was the great smooth violet gem of Adamance in its silver setting.

"Do you remember this Stone? You have seen it before, touched it, used it to strengthen the faltering heroes of another world. Do you remember how it felt? You said then that you did not need its Light for yourself. A bold claim. Was it true?"

Ronar remembered the gem's cold weight in his hand. Its opposite was Despair. The opposite of Despair was not Hope, but Adamance, the refusal to yield, to surrender, even in the absence of Hope. That, thought Ronar, was a stronger thing, a nobler thing, and also a madder thing, than Hope itself. In some mysterious way, Despair and Adamance could coexist in a single heart, though Adamance, if present at all, must always be the stronger.

Adamance had always been the primary Light in Ronar's heart, where Despair had always been foreign.

Yet now, he knew them both.

"In addition to Adamance, you need Truth," said Cal-Cotavion. "These two, of all the Lights which have been made into Stones, are the ones that most define you. Yet many other pairs of Stones could also have been made. A Stone of Constancy would become you very well. There is no such Stone, but its Light can be found within your heart, as can Adamance and Truth. You must call upon them now. Seren needs your help. You must call upon them now. Throw off the shroud of illusion that Seren has cast over you. It is your only Hope, and hers. Rise. You are still needed."

Cal-Cotavion was gone.

Ronar closed his eyes. Sunlight filtered through his eyelids, red and orange and yellow.

Constancy. Adamance. Truth. Yes, these had always been the beacons of his soul. What had become of them now? What of Truth? What was believable about these last few minutes of his life? What terrible things had he done, thought, plotted, against himself and his friends?

He opened his eyes. Those hot glares, red and yellow and orange, continued to assault him. Through his blurred vision they were like a triad of destroying suns. He also perceived a deadly blackness, an offense to his thoughts and his senses.

He rolled over, pushing himself up onto hands and knees. He rose up off his hands, kneeling before those fiery glares. He stood. He took three steps, reached out, and took a delicate throat in his grip. He heard a cry of dread and disbelief.

"Stop this. Now," he said.

The Lights failed.

Clarity returned to Ronar's mind and senses. He saw what was real. Darkness departed his heart, though it left its shadow in his memory.

Hanging slack in his grip was the Faerie Queen, Seren-Cotavion, regarding him with awe and terror. She dropped her half-hewn staff, which clattered on the ground.

"You defied the Stones!" she whispered.

"Yes. I told you, I will not be beaten by such as these. I will not." He released her. "Nor will I again be goaded into doing something I know is wrong, tempting as it may be at the moment."

"And yet these Stones were strong enough to destroy my cousin," she said raggedly, putting her ring hand to her throat, where waited the orange Stone of Despair.

"You did not kill your cousin," said Ronar.

Now her hands fell limp, while incredulity stole over her face. "What are you saying? No one could survive—what I did to him."

"Possibly you put him beyond the reach of any salvation you can imagine. But the universe does not consist of Colibdis and nothing else, and magic is not its greatest power. Beyond Colibdis are many worlds, separated by mighty gulfs of space. Your cousin carried the Stones of Adamance and of Life, and was by all accounts very strong. He survived long enough to be saved by travelers, mariners riding a ship of space, visitors from the very world where the Stones where made, who had come in search of them."

"Yes. I knew them. At the time I thought they were... little lost pixies of some strange kind. I'm not sure I ever believed their stories."

"Ah, but they too were strong in their way. Together with Cal-Cotavion they could have wrested away your Stones and cast you from your throne, but Cal-Cotavion would not do it, for love of you. Instead he left to travel with them to Earth, leaving you to whatever fate you could devise for yourself."

Seren-Cotavion now looked much smaller. The Stones looked out of place, like costume jewelry on a little girl.

In a small voice she asked, "Is he then still alive?"

"No. I'm sorry to say he is not. I never knew your cousin in life, but I spoke to some who did, learning all I could of him, once I discovered he was a man of Colibdis. He was eventually killed by a creature who also came in search of the Stones. But you did not kill him. He survived for several more turns, learning and seeing things no Elf of Colibdis ever knew, growing in strength and wisdom, and shedding his Lights in the dark places of the galaxy. I was told that he harbored an intention to someday return to you, to surrender his Stones to you, and to make of you the Queen of Light he always wished you to be. I wish he had. I wish I had known him."

"I knew him," said another voice. Ronar turned to see a wary, bloody-lipped Sha Totek approaching. "As you know, little Seren, I kept an eye on Cal through that portrait of mine, trying to keep him on the right path, or to put him on one, I should say. There has long been a question I wished to ask you."

Almost against her will, Seren raised her eyes to meet his.

"Why did you take those Stones you bear? You were known as the Princess of Light. You were renowned for being as kind and generous and compassionate as it is possible for Elf-kind to be. Yet at the very end, when you and Cal-Cotavion hovered over those two opposite sets of Stones, your hand moved first, taking the negative Stones, leaving him no choice but to accept the others, to which he was poorly suited. He accepted his burden manfully enough, but still. Why did you so dim your own light?"

They could barely understand her reply, it was so faint and broken.

"To protect him."

Sha Totek nodded slowly. "Yes. To protect him from his own darkness, you sacrificed your light. In addition, you resisted the full corruption of these Stones for many turns. Seren-Cotavion, I salute you. If one must be ruled by an increasingly despotic evil queen, I would prefer that it be you."

"For those many turns I imagined I could wear these Stones, even use them, without falling too deeply under their influence. I see now that was only another illusion."

Seren stood trembling, shrinking from the Stones which so defaced her beauty. Ronar stood rooted in place, on the verge of going forward to comfort her, yet uncertain as to how that would be received. Again he cursed his inability to read the hearts of others.

Emogen labored under no such difficulty. She stepped up to Seren and took her hand, braving the baleful influence of the Stones, saying, "You could lay those jewels aside, you know. I'm sure your cousin would be happy to see that, wherever he is."

Seren looked into the eyes of this exceedingly mortal woman who presumed to touch and advise the Queen of Faerie.

A wild hope bloomed in Ronar's heart. Was it possible they could talk Seren down from her plan, making needless the drastic measures Ronar intended for her defeat?

"Without these Stones, I would never have become Queen," muttered Seren.

"Is that so very important?" smiled Emogen. "I am not a queen, and yet I am happy."

Astil came forward and knelt before Seren with his head lowered, trembling.

"Aunt, if you put down those Stones, you will retain my support in the Queenship at least, as poor a thing as that may be."

Seren smiled. "Yes, nephew, that is a poor thing indeed, yet maybe better than I deserve. You surprise me. I think you have actually grown somewhat since I gained the throne. I don't think the Astil I knew then could have done all you have done. Consorting with Ronar and his friends has done you good."

Seren bent down and recovered her staff. She eyed the cut that Ronar had put in it, almost in approval.

"I will consider your words, all of you. I cannot face a man who is able to resist and overcome the influence of the four Stones without doubting all that I have done and become. Greylock, thank you for the news you have brought me. It—it cleanses me, and eases my heart. I will at least order the expansion of Faerie undone."

"No!" This shrill cry came from a tiny figure who Ronar had barely noticed. It was that Elf-child, what was her name—Kortraine-Cotavion?

"No!" she yelled again, stamping her foot. "I *like* the spell. I like being able to go anywhere in the world and still feel at home. When I learned of the spell and told you what it could do, you thought it was a wonderful idea. You helped me to change your grandfather's mind. I haven't changed *my* mind, even if you have!"

"Do you mean to say," demanded Ronar, "that this infant is the Chief Sorceress of Faerie? The real mastermind behind this whole mad scheme?"

Sha Totek gave a strained laugh. "Ronar, clearly you don't realize how long it takes for Faerie children to mature. Kortraine is nearly as old as you, and she has put those turns to good use, or rather to ill. Still, I'm sure the child can be persuaded to be reasonable…"

"Oh no I can't!"

"Kortraine, obey," said Astil.

Seren tapped her thorny staff. The island trembled and reverberated.

"Kortraine."

"No! I won't fall down just because my stupid brother says so, or because you used to like our creepy cousin Cal! Here's another of my spells!"

With that she dwindled within her clothing. A moment later she shot out, now the size of a songbird, naked, borne aloft by humming jewel-colored wings. With a mad giggle she flitted high and away.

Athene raised her spear.

"No, do not presume to strike down my niece," said Seren. "I will seek her out and do whatever is needful to subdue her. Killing her would not undo her spell in any event. As for you, Greylock, go do what you must. Astil, come with me. Or remain with them, if that is your preference."

Astil stood, then bowed toward his aunt.

"I shall stay to see their mission completed."

Seren made a dismissive gesture, turned, and led her army away. They seemed to melt into the light of the single sun.

"Damn," said Ronar, thus deprived of a simple, painless solution to all their problems.

"Yes. Damn indeed," whispered Sha Totek.

"Ronar, your leg," said Emogen, looking at the singed hole in Ronar's pant leg and the blood that stained it. "And your hand. Let me soothe you."

Ronar could think of no reasonable objection to this, though he chafed at the loss of time, and her efforts should soon be pointless anyway. Nevertheless, he permitted Emogen to work her spells, and the pain subsided.

"There. I can tell by your fretting that you care more about going on than about being healed, so I have only eased you, and I will heal you in full when our task is complete."

"Thank you, Emogen. Come on then. Let's finish this." Ronar turned toward the center of the island.

"Leonard Ronar."

Ronar halted and looked back at Sha Totek, bemused by this unusual form of address.

"Before we proceed, Ronar, let me point out yet again what an astonishing character you are. Of all the people in the world, only you could have approached Seren-Cotavion, challenged her, somehow endured and then thrown off the power of all four Stones, and then disarmed her, simply because you came armed with exactly the right words to say to her. People talk about your mighty sword, and remark on your laconic personality, but the truth is, more often than not it's your flapping jaw that saves you. Quite often it also saves whoever it is you are speaking to."

Ronar waved his hand in dismissal. He looked from one face to another. They all shone back at him, full of admiration for his deed, unaware of how tainted it had been. They had seen him beaten down by those terrible Lights, and then they had seen him rise up, despite them. That was all. They had not seen what transpired within his mind as he lay there. They had not seen the depths to which he had fallen before making his recovery. It was not a matter he would ever reveal or discuss. Let Sha Totek's final memories of him be good ones, even if they were incomplete.

"I told you, I have seen through the illusory threat of her Stones," he muttered.

"Ah yes, an interesting theory, that. There's only one problem with it."

"What's that?"

"It's utter bullshit. You were plainly quite wrong about that. You think Death isn't a real thing, or any of the others? Life does not depart for no reason. No, there's more going on here than you have admitted, but keep your secrets if you wish. My mind is troubled enough already."

Ronar and Sha Totek shared a long look. Ronar nodded, turned, and started walking.

They passed Ixtab, who still huddled on the ground. Ronar extended his hand to her.

"Come, Ixtab."

She darted him a haunted look, then took his hand and arose in silence. She looked smaller than ever. She at least had no innate resistance to the Stones.

"Now stay back, all of you, while I address these creatures."

They had reached the next ring of guardians, where the tall white figures with shining black eyes awaited them.

"You know why we have come?" asked Ronar of the foremost of them.

It spoke in mellow, reassuring tones.

"We do, and we agree with the necessity of your action. You have proven yourselves to us. Go forward. We are the final guardians whom you will be able to see."

"Thank you."

And so they passed through the ring of gleaming humanoids and over their circular ridge, unmolested.

Emogen looked back in surprise. "How did you know those creatures would be so reasonable?"

"If I'm not mistaken, it's the nature of the beings they're modeled after to be reasonable. I can't say the same about men, or about any of our predecessors."

One final ring remained to be surmounted, this one only thirty feet across. It was guarded by nothing visible, yet they all looked around uneasily. Ronar had the distinct feeling of some nearby presence.

They stood atop the circle's rim and looked down. The center of the circle, and thus of the island, was a circular pit leading down into blackness, reachable via a spiral ramp which hugged the wall of the shaft.

"This is a very strange place," said Sha Totek. "A shortcut to the underworld, perhaps."

With Ronar in the lead they began their descent. Somehow the Olympian goddess had been accepted into their group as though she were merely another adventurer. The looming doom that faced them all had done much to level any differences in stature. Ixtab plodded along, her eyes downcast, uncharacteristically silent. Emogen walked beside Athene as though the two were old and comfortable friends.

Soon the sky was only a pale blue disk overhead. Their surroundings were dark and quiet. To Ronar it did not seem a threatening darkness, but rather a peaceful, contemplative one. There was no difficulty in seeing their way. Ronar summoned a red spark from his ring, while Athene, it seemed, could not help giving out a little radiance. It was a light that must soon be snuffed out.

Presently the shaft broadened greatly, and here were lights which they did not bring themselves.

Visible in all directions were faint threads of blue-violet light. These receded into considerable depths, overlapping each other, growing fainter with distance.

Ronar led his party away from the ramp. As they approached the lights they encountered the cool transparency in which they were embedded. Ronar ran his hand over this, a smooth curved surface. When examined with eyesight sharpened by the magic of Faerie, the closest filaments resolved into minute points and dashes, their colors ranging from blue to deepest purple.

"What are these lights?" whispered Astil.

"I don't know," said Ronar. "They may be somehow related to the generation of magic on Colibdis."

They walked around the circular platform. At two locations opposite each other they discovered gaps in the lights and their transparent matrix, forming two semi-cylinders, like a pipe cut along its length and set vertically. The gaps between the sections served as narrow corridors, enabling them to pad their way deeper into the lights, as far back as a hundred feet or more.

Blocked at last, they stood huddled together, looking into the mysterious pattern of faint lights.

"It's very beautiful," said Emogen. She too was whispering, as seemed only right in this place.

"I feel..." began Ixtab. "I feel as though we are somehow in the heart of the world."

Ronar shot her a glance. A remark from her which did not contain threats or bitterness?

"Let's move on," he said.

They returned to the ramp, and thus downward once again. Level after level was the same: darkness suffused with a dim web-work of lines, unmoving and unchanging.

They noted no differences until several hundred feet farther down. There half of the array of lights was as before, but the other section was only filled in at the top; the bottom was dark.

New lines were being drawn at the division. Ronar's party drew nearer, fascinated, to watch the slow crawl of the new filaments of light.

"I think this is some kind of writing."

This was Asterope the curious scientist speaking, not the doomed goddess Athene, thought Ronar.

"But who is doing the writing?" asked Sha Totek. "And what is being written?"

"No person is needed to record information, if machines are sufficiently advanced," said Ronar.

"Yes. I remember Brainchild, our unseen friend from turns past."

"Let us go deeper."

They had much deeper still to go. The very air grew thicker around them, approaching the density of the air of Earth.

Astil paused to peer into the depths.

"An ember glows down there."

They all lined up along the edge of the ramp, leaning over. Indeed, at some level below, its distance difficult to judge, burned a dim red point.

Silently they continued downward. The echoes of their footsteps gradually changed, indicating the approach of the end of the shaft. At last they reached it, permitting them to step out onto the deepest floor of this place of mystery.

At last they also reached the end of the glowing filaments in the half of the transparency that still contained them. At first they thought no new lines were being drawn there, but as they drew closer, they noted the very slow progress of what might well be the final thread.

In the very center of the floor stood a waist-high truncated cone, white, barely visible in the darkness. On its flat upper surface was a palm-sized glowing red disk, slightly raised.

"Does anyone understand the meaning of all this?" asked Astil with an edge of pique in his voice.

"I think I begin to," said Athene. "Knowledge seeps out of the air in this place."

Ronar was inclined to agree.

"And what is this thing?" continued Astil, reaching toward the red disk.

"No!" cried Ronar, but too late. Astil had pressed the button.

Chapter Twenty

The Sons of Man

We are the successors of Man. Someday we will arise to transcend the limitations of physical form, to master space, and indeed to look beyond the borders of our reality, into others, sometimes making our presence known there to varying degrees.

Ronar made no response to this calm inner voice, waiting to see what next would be revealed.

This universe bears two worlds inhabited by Man. The other is Earth, where his numbers are few, and dwindling, and will presently fall to nothing. On that world, Man himself invented the new and superior race which will supplant him. But we did not wish Man to vanish from the universe entirely. His is a crude, coarse animal species, of little worth for the most part, yet it does sometimes yield up exceptional examples of nobility and high aspiration. We recognize that the seeds of our own higher nature originated in him.

Therefore, because Man was destined to undo himself on his home world, we provided for him another. We searched the Milky Way for a suitable planet, finding the one upon which you stand, a rare clement world orbiting a binary star system. Wishing to spare it from any future discovery, we disrupted the gravitation of this system, causing Colibdis and the star Photos to be ejected from the galaxy. Eventually it reached this isolated patch of stars, where an encounter with the sun Kudu arrested its flight and led to the creation of a new binary system.

Here we installed a device, which you call Etheros, which bends space and warps the laws of nature to permit the operation of magic. The reason for this is to preserve Man in his present form. Magic, together with the peculiar shortage of iron on this world, prevents scientific technology from arising here. Here it is easier to invent magic than to learn the ways of nature. Here people who desire power seek out magic and magicians, rather than undertaking the centuries of labor needed to master the physical world. Thus the Human form and mind is preserved, except for trivial cases where it is altered by magic.

"And yet I myself have introduced a core of scientific thought to Colibdis," thought Ronar.

It will not survive as such. Without your guidance and will, within a few generations your observatory will degenerate into a shrine to your memory, and a place of veneration of the stars. We are sorry your efforts will come to so little.

Ronar too was sorry, and annoyed as well, verging on anger.

"If you are of the future," he thought, "how have you arranged all this, and how are you speaking to me now?"

We also transcend time.

"Of course."

As you've surmised, we provided Portals to permit the migration of many of Earth's most vital and original cultures here to Colibdis. Here they will thrive, in some form, for many years. Your friend the Sorcerer has served us very well in overseeing these Portals and preventing their misuse.

"Yet now your plans have gone awry, it seems, as indicated by our very presence on this island."

These events are included in our plans. We knew the introduction of such foreign, absolute powers as the Stones would create an anomaly which would have to be dealt with. Therefore, we also took part in creating another anomaly, yourself, to deal with the crisis, as you will shortly do.

"In what sense am I an anomaly?"

You are partly of another reality, a place where men of unusual stature sometimes arise in times of peril. We will say no more of that.

"So this entire island, and all its devices, are dedicated to the creation of magic?"

No. The recording devices surrounding you are separate. They make a record of the deeds, the words, and even the thoughts of all men. As we said, the history of Man on Earth is nearly complete, and so the medium of that device is nearly filled. Colibdis, however, has a long and peculiar history yet to come. These devices are in some sense redundant, for the universe itself does not forget anything that passes within it. But our devices also speak to a few people beyond our reality who are inclined to listen to them.

We leave you now. We are pleased to satisfy your curiosity to this extent. May it bring you some comfort in the trial which is to come. You already know what you must do. Goodbye. Farewell.

The voice in Ronar's mind fell silent. His awareness of the world and of the silent machines around him returned.

A blessed peace descended upon him. To be made privy to these insights, to these truths, was a gift for which he was profoundly grateful. Because he was human, he knew this sense of exaltation would not last long. But then, it did not need to.

"Did you all get that?" he asked in a husky whisper.

"Yes," said Sha Totek. "I got something, anyway." The others nodded, wide-eyed.

"It looks as though our race will amount to something after all. There have been times when I've wondered," said Athene.

"It's very strange. When you told me, Ronar, to expect a machine that creates magic, I imagined a machine similar to your great telescopes, with their oily gears and metallic groans. I never expected anything this...peaceful," said Sha Totek.

"These machines function in ways similar to the universe itself. The universe does not clank or groan as it goes about its tasks. At some point, the line between the workings of the universe and the deeds of thinking creatures blurs to nothing."

Lost in wonder, Sha Totek drifted away to examine his surroundings.

"I suppose now there is nothing to keep us from completing our task," whispered Ixtab in a lifeless tone.

Ronar looked in her direction with difficulty.

"Yes. Are you ready?"

"I am. Give me a moment."

She began to mutter softly to herself, using the language of Ka'ahkin. Ronar understood little of it, though he heard her invoke the names of Ronar and Imhotep.

As she proceeded here eyes grew wide and her expression pained. "Something's wrong. It's not working!" she hissed.

Ronar's mind raced, trying to guess what might be defeating her spell. Something occurred to him.

"Sekani. His real name is Sekani, not Imhotep."

For an instant her face bore a look so pitiful that Ronar was almost moved to take her into his arms to comfort her. Her own father had never even told her his real name.

Ronar blinked in surprise as it occurred to him that he was no longer certain he knew his own father's real name. Probably it was written somewhere in these curving walls surrounding him, if he knew how to read it.

Ixtab gathered herself and repeated her spell, this time using the correct name.

Ronar felt a weird stirring within him, a change which was difficult to describe.

And so it was done. There would be no turning back for him now.

Not that there had ever been.

Apparently Sha Totek felt something as well. "What's going on here?" he asked suspiciously.

"Nothing which need concern you, my friend. Come, let us complete our task in the light of day." He pressed the red button atop the pedestal. The floor upon which they stood began to rise, bringing the pedestal with it.

"What's this?" asked Astil. "When I did that, it served only to open our minds to those silent voices."

"It's a very sophisticated control," said Ronar. "It does whatever you need it to do, within the limitations of the machine. It was intended for human use, for our use, should some emergency ever require that magic be abated."

With little more sensation of motion than the popping of their ears the platform ascended rapidly, bringing them closer to open air and to many endings. Ronar felt numb. He knew indeed what needed to be done, and he intended to do it, but surely the full ramifications of his acts had not yet entered his consciousness. Just as well, perhaps.

The platform drew level with the surface of Etheros and came to a smooth halt.

"The next time that button is pushed, it will cancel magic on Colibdis and undo the Blue Magic of Faerie," said Ronar. "It will mean the end of some of us. It's time to say our goodbyes."

Yet nobody moved or spoke.

Ronar looked at Athene, who gazed back calmly.

"Athene. Before the button is pushed, please do something for me. I wish to see you once more as you were, as Asterope. Can you do that for me?"

She complied with a smile, dwindling to a semblance of her old human form, small and delicate. Ronar approached her and grasped her bare shoulders. She felt cool, too smooth, somehow unreal. He found it difficult to speak further, but he knew he must.

"No, Asterope. This is only a shade of your old form, a veneer. You can do better. Make your limbs warm. Send blood flowing through them. Feel the sunlight on your face. Make yourself truly as you were, once more, for me."

With a tender expression Asterope did as he asked, growing somehow more substantial before his eyes, settling more firmly under the influence of gravity, her hair subject to the random motions of the breeze. He stepped forward and embraced her, satisfied now with the feel of her body, conscious of the beating of her heart. He held her longer than was needed to determine this, loathe to pull himself away, thinking back to all he had lost, both to the actions of the malignant gods and to his own foolishness. He was about to lose it all again, this time forever.

Asterope.

He withdrew from her a little, still holding her hand.

Ronar glanced at Ixtab. She stood pale and shaking, terrified. Suddenly Ronar pitied her. His free arm went around her shoulders and rested there.

"Ixtab. Thank you for making this possible. Otherwise...I could not have endured what is to come. Don't be afraid for yourself. Your pains and trials are almost at an end."

She looked at him with her dark, liquid eyes. She lowered her eyelids and drew a deep breath.

Sha Totek cleared his throat. His trembling hand reached toward the button. "There's no point in drawing this out. Goodbye, my friends! I—words fail me. I have only moments to address the faults and failures of many lifetimes. I didn't think I'd face death like such a weakling. I must—"

Ronar could not bear to listen to this for a moment longer. He released his hold on Asterope and Ixtab, reached out and slapped the button.

The single sun split and separated into the familiar suns of Colibdis. The sky darkened to Colibdian indigo.

A gigantic silence settled over the world, broken only by a gasp from Emogen.

Sha Totek the Sorcerer looked down at his hands, still warm in the light of the two suns. Oddly enough, he was still alive.

Asterope, or Athene, was gone, gone so thoroughly that it was almost as though she had never existed.

Astil looked around with that supercilious befuddlement which had become almost endearing.

In Ronar's place lay an ancient mummy, of great size, with a broad chest, weathered clothing, and a proud, stern face still visible over the skull.

Sha Totek's mouth fell open. Suddenly he understood much.

"There, but for the grace of Ronar, go I," he whispered. He stood reeling. He had always understood that Ronar was mortal, but now, the sudden reality of a world without him was beyond comprehension.

Lying nearby was a withered, rapidly aging form dressed in bright feathers. Sha Totek knelt by her side. Somehow life still flickered in those shriveling, yellowing eyes, but it was waning fast. He would have taken her hand, but he was afraid of crushing it.

"So, Emuishéré. You schemed with Ronar to arrange this. You transferred my immortality, and my very age, to him, and his mortality to me. By rendering me mortal, you saved my life."

Her reply came as the driest, faintest whisper. "Yes. It was his idea."

"And why didn't you use that same magic to save yourself? Emogen is here. You could have taken her life for your own."

"I had intended that. But Emogen is happy and loving. I don't understand how she can be that way in a world such as this. The world is better off with her in it than with me. The Light of Despair ruined me. It made me face too much. I wish only to die. Goodbye, father. I—"

"Daughter, I forgive you. Forgive me, for failing you."

She spoke no more.

She looked so old, so terribly old. She had lived far beyond her time, and she had not profited by it. Could this wisdom have been in Ronar's mind as he plotted his own death?

He looked toward the noble ruin of Leonard Ronar.

"He saved me, his best friend. Perhaps he even saved Seren-Cotavion herself. He saved everyone who could be saved, except himself. I believe he saw no future for himself without the spirit of his Asterope still manifest in the world."

"He was a very great man," said Emogen, "but I have no tears for him. He lived as he wished and he died as he wished. Having lived a life any man might envy, he died as he chose to die, in his own time, cleanly, doing what was needful. I do not mourn for him. I cherish his memory in my heart."

Sha Totek stood up with difficulty, feeling very old himself. His tears wet the withered flesh of his daughter's corpse, but they were intended as much for Ronar as for her. He was quite sure that Ronar's life had not gone just as he would have liked, but he wouldn't ruin Emogen's mood by saying so.

When he was able to speak again he said, "Every spell ever wrought has been undone. The air is still. The gods have perished like soap bubbles. This world now has the feel of Earth, where men live their lives confined and doomed by the cruel laws of nature. Possibility itself has been stifled. Astil-Cotavion, how are you faring?"

Astil stood blinking.

"I think I am mortal! My senses are dimmed. I feel tired. I hope I shan't have to remain this way for long." Noticing the looks the others were giving him, he hastily added, "And Ronar was certainly a very great man!"

Sha Totek laughed, and then sighed. After some hesitation he pressed the red disk, causing the magic of Colibdis to be renewed. Once more the spells in Sha Totek's mind had meaning.

"It's a shame," said Sha Totek. "All those fancy new enchantments I put on that blade, and the man...the man barely had a chance to use them."

He crouched beside Ronar, and, with great care, removed the garnet ring from his finger. He stood and bent his will to the ring, but it did nothing more than sparkle in the suns.

The three of them took up the remains of the fallen and made their way back to the shore, unhampered and unnoticed by the rings of guardians, who seemed to have somehow replenished their depleted numbers. Reaching the water, they saw the masts of Seren's fleet in retreat, bound for what shore they could not say. A few boats had been left behind. They commandeered one and sailed away.

Sha Totek considered returning his daughter's body to Ka'ahkin, but ultimately he could not face or permit the bloodletting which would result. Better for Ixtab simply to vanish from that island of fools, her fate forever unknown to them. No doubt her cult would go on without her. In its memory she would remain a goddess, as she would have wished.

They made their way to Two Suns City, where Ronar was interred on the grounds of his observatory in a simple structure of granite. The entire state of Thunderbird went into mourning. No one there could remember a day when Ronar had not been its most prominent citizen and greatest hero. The elderly Professor Holder presided at his memorial, and his grief was painful for the Sorcerer to witness.

Out of respect for Ronar, Sha Totek allowed himself to age for a turn or two before making himself immortal once again. Wearing Ronar's ring on his own finger, he was able, with difficulty, to reestablish the magical link between the garnet in the ring and the Cold Sword which lay on the bottom the sea. He kept the ring against the day, however unlikely, when another hero might arise who was worthy to wield the Cold Sword of Ronar.

He began a phase of wandering. In Eranior he returned the Royal Torc and told the tale of what had befallen their King.

In the great cities of the world he raised statues of Ronar. Though Ronar never came to be worshipped as a god, those monuments had a notable effect on all who beheld them. All who saw them came away with their resolve strengthened, their intentions focused, and their goals clarified. They were reminders of the strength and dignity which was the potential of men.

With this task completed, the Sorcerer caused his Tower to erupt before the royal city of Ammon. There, under the name Imhotep, he overthrew the corrupt reign of the Pharaoh there, replacing him, and magnifying the power of

Ammon to replace the waning might of Eranior, which by then had all but merged with a more placid Darteharn.

One day a lone female figure, hooded and cloaked, arrived on foot to request an audience with the Pharaoh Imhotep. She gave into his hands a strange silvery box that contained the four Stones. She then retreated into the desert and was not seen again.

Imhotep took this box and sealed it with great spells. He then invoked the spell of Morluminar, summoning that boundless zone of otherness and nothingness for the first time in many turns. In went the box, and then he undid the spell. The box and its contents were thus removed from the universe, which was a great relief to Imhotep's mind and heart.

To Amulree Imhotep then travelled, seeking for Emogen, who was again living in her old village. After some gentle persuasion he brought her back to Ammon, raising her as Queen. Together they had a son, Teremun, whom they raised with great care, teaching him all they knew of life, love, and magic.

Long after, when that boy, now a man, stood tall and clear-eyed, holding in his hands great powers of sorcery and healing, and bearing upon his finger a ring of red garnet, Imhotep released his own immortality, permitting his very long life to end at last.

"If death was good enough for Ronar, it's good enough for me," he said.

As he lay dying, Imhotep spoke one last time. "My eyes have been opened. This universe, all universes, are flawed, but they will be set to rights. A wanderer will come, marching backwards through Time. He will come bearing Lights, and no dark thing will escape him. He will stand with every being in his hour of need. With infinite patience he will undo every wrong and heal every hurt. Hamadan, I called him, long ago. Little did I know. Oh, what a blessing to be granted this vision. This is the work of a power too great for me to perceive. Farewell."

FAREWELL.